Gray Matters

A Novel

Gray Matters

A Novel

John Webster Gastil

COSMIC EGG
BOOKS

Winchester, UK
Washington, USA

JOHN HUNT PUBLISHING

First published by Cosmic Egg Books, 2020
Cosmic Egg Books is an imprint of John Hunt Publishing Ltd., 3 East St., Alresford,
Hampshire SO24 9EE, UK
office@jhpbooks.net
www.johnhuntpublishing.com
www.cosmicegg-books.com

For distributor details and how to order please visit the 'Ordering' section on our website.

Text copyright: John Webster Gastil 2019

ISBN: 978 1 78904 502 4
978 1 78904 503 1 (ebook)
Library of Congress Control Number: 2019954019

A CIP catalogue record for this book is available from the British Library.

Design: Stuart Davies

UK: Printed and bound by CPI Group (UK) Ltd, Croydon, CR0 4YY
US: Printed and bound by Thomson-Shore, 7300 West Joy Road, Dexter, MI 48130

We operate a distinctive and ethical publishing philosophy in
all areas of our business, from our global network of authors to
production and worldwide distribution.

Dedicated to my grandparents,
who raised clever children
capable of running
for US Congress.

Too bad they didn't win.

Foreword

When I read the first draft of this novel back in 2012, I thought it was a political comedy, full of fanciful ideas. Reading it now, I wonder if the author was more prescient than hallucinatory.

That time feels a century away. Voters in the US had just reelected Obama. The world seemed on track, as much as one could hope given the usual overseas conflicts and natural disasters. We Australians, like others fortunate enough to live in Western democracies, considered ourselves immune to the madness we saw elsewhere. Children of the Enlightenment, after all.

In the years since, I've wondered if the author of this novel has been controlling world events from an undisclosed location in the arctic, hoping to make his science fiction appear more plausible.

Exhibit one. It was ridiculous to think that voters could get behind a candidate for high office who was best known for selling popular books mislabeled as 'nonfiction.' Sarah Palin had risen from obscurity, but she never got the keys to the executive washroom, did she?

Exhibit two. I rolled my eyes at the notion that a few clever people hiding behind computer terminals might subvert a presidential election and get away with it. Nonsense.

Exhibit three. Back in 2012, we hadn't met Edward Snowden or read Dave Eggers' *The Circle*. The idea that digital technology could steer our lives felt paranoid.

This novel you're about to read comes from a troubled mind, from first-hand and family experience with campaigns and coders, democracy and dementia. The author has studied politics and its pathologies for thirty years. All that led to this oddly prophetic story, which poses vexing questions about a world we might recognize too well.

I loved this novel when I first read it. Mind you, I was sitting on peaceful South Golden Beach in Australia with my dog Tilly. Now, the book unnerves me. I would like to avoid Gastil's future efforts, but I probably shouldn't. Re-reading *Gray Matters*, I see things that haven't yet come to pass. Let's keep it that way, okay?

Lyn Carson, Director, newDemocracy Foundation

Part I

The Launch

BARRY

My boy says I'm seventy-seven. Can't remember what my cradle looked like, but I see the pine box coming down the line.

Some of my friends never made it past sixty, poor devils. GM pensions were lottery tickets they never got to cash.

When did I retire? Happened after I voted for a black president, so it musta been some ways back. Never thought I'd see one of us in that chair. Best seat I ever had swung me in and out of a chassis, shift after shift. Days used to run together back then. Now years do. When I wake up to pee at night, I can taste factory air. Bitter, like metal on the tongue.

Lucky to keep that job long as I did. Hung in there even after the Motor City lost its motor. Now I've lost just about everything but my mind. Charlie worries I'm gonna lose that.

"Keep focused on the here-and-now," he'll say to me.

"Get outta the house least once every day," he says.

I'm doin' it, son. Why you think I'm taking a walk?

Got across the street to Pleasant Creek Park. Ought to have a signpost with its name on it. Push on the metal gate. Hinges squeak, but it swings open. Plow this damn walker through the weeds. Scoot up to a bench.

Pleasant used to sit here for hours, her plump fingers laced with mine. Yeah, she's gone. Been too long. Sometimes feels she'll be back any minute.

Sure enough, the bench feels warm. Maybe she just left to pick up trash.

Middle-aged guy in a Detroit Lions windbreaker jogging down the road. Waves like I know him. Wasn't too long ago I looked like that. Maybe I was a little heavier and a little shorter, but just as much muscle.

Now I can't get anywhere without walkin' in this metal cage. Why'd I put a string bag in its basket? Stupid bag hangs open, all slack-jawed.

What's that now? Basket's buzzing.

Give it a poke.

Lady with a British accent is all, "Good afternoon, Mr Sanders."

She's smiling. You can hear when a lady's smiling.

"How are we today?"

Who's *we*? Is Pleasant here, for real? Or this lady talking about Charlie?

"Sir, this is your scheduled call."

She always says it that way—*shed*-uled. Swear I know her.

"Is this, um, Sally?"

"Yes, and a good day to you. This morning you phoned our service to remind yourself that you planned a trip to the Safeways to acquire food for a party. You recorded the intention to purchase a Pabst case, two bags of Snyder's honey mustarded pretzels, and—and a whole roasting *chicken*?"

Don't like the tone she took when she said "chicken." What's wrong with chicken?

Hate pretzels. Why would I wanna get pretzels? Lord, I can't even remember reminding myself to remember anything. What's this all about?

Wait, maybe…"Did I say my boy was coming to this party?"

"Your message made no mention of Charlie. You did, however, have unkind words for your American president."

Who doesn't?

"Do you want me to read that portion back to you? The part about the President?"

"Nah, long as I didn't invite *that* devil into my house."

"You made no reference to guests. There could have been an error in the automated transcription. I could recheck the audio—"

"Nah. Let's see what tomorrow brings."

"Yes, sir, we will."

5

"Thanks for calling, Sally. Goodbye."

"Bye-bye."

Quite a thing, that phone Charlie hooked me up to. Wish I didn't need it.

CHARLIE

Only after exiting the Detroit Metro Airport did Charlie realize he'd forgotten to pack gloves. A fleece jacket left him shivering in the wind blowing through the cab stand. April doesn't mean the same thing back in Seattle as it does here.

Charlie shouldered his laptop bag and pulled his carryon suitcase to the curb. He approached a sedan at the front of the line and spoke to the driver through the passenger window. "Going near Mack and Elliott."

The taxi's wheels screeched as it fled the airport without a passenger.

Charlie felt a different kind of chill. His heart pounded. He squinted to guess at the driver's ethnicity.

There wasn't an address in Seattle where he couldn't get a ride. More often than not, the Loop would have a car greet him with a gentle honk before he reached in his pocket.

The future hadn't reached Charlie's hometown. Whole neighborhoods remained unofficial no-go zones. Even driverless cars wouldn't come near his father's house.

The next cabbie in the queue was a black woman in her mid-twenties—a few years younger than Charlie. She appeared to understand why the next fare would be hers. She tossed a cigarette out the window, fired up her engine, and gave Charlie a guilty shrug.

Before she could pull away, he moved to block her exit.

"MLK High," Charlie said to her windshield. It would mean walking a few cold blocks, but she'd take him that far.

The driver jerked her head to motion him inside. Charlie tossed his luggage in the trunk, slid into the backseat, and closed his eyes.

When they arrived at the high school, his mood hadn't improved. At least she hadn't told him how dangerous it was to drive in this part of the city. Sparing him that lecture was worth a few bucks, so he tipped her well. She probably needed the money.

Charlie retrieved his luggage and shut the trunk. As the cab sped away, he noticed a familiar bumper sticker. Over a black background, red, white, and blue letters asked, "WTF?" The question meant more in a state that had voted for Trump.

"What the fuck, indeed," Charlie said to himself. He jerked up the handle on his suitcase and headed home.

Charlie rubbed his hands together and knocked on the steel door of his father's house. The brick bungalow where he'd spent his childhood had appreciated not a dollar since he'd left for college. A three-bedroom house like this in Seattle would have become a goldmine for anyone who held it that long. Charlie could afford to put Pops into something nicer, but Barry refused to consider living in Seattle, or even outside the inner city.

"You in there, Dad?"

Years ago, Barry hand-crafted and installed this door as a security measure. It provided an excuse to practice new skills while earning an associate's degree in arc welding. A mishap during that project earned Barry a one-inch scar that still stood in relief on his stubbled cheek. Charlie involuntarily rubbed his own face. He only felt a close-cropped goatee.

Charlie pounded again on the door.

"Quit that hammering!" Barry barked.

Years ago, Dad tried to give his sons a modicum of skill at welding. He took pride in seeing them "doing lines," an idiosyncratic bit of slang that never got corrected. Charlie had shown some aptitude with a torch, but the informal lessons stopped after a few weeks.

The deadbolt slid back, and the door opened. Barry looked more hunched than usual. He barely cleared five-two, a half-foot lower than when he and Charlie used to stand even.

"Get in here. You must be freezing in those duds."

Barry reached for his son's coat, but Charlie waved him off.

"Look at you." Barry patted his son's flat stomach. "Skinny boy."

"It's all hikes, bikes, and kayaks in Seattle," Charlie said. He squeezed through the doorway and brushed against the potbelly hanging over Barry's waistline.

"Don't get full of yourself, boy. Your brother's the athlete in our family."

Charlie held his breath. Was Dad speaking in the past tense, or the present? At King High, Barry Jr. had been a bona fide three-sport phenom—the star wide receiver on a team that almost won state. But that was before Charlie's only sibling went to Afghanistan for a war that should have been over. Charlie rubbed his hands across his arms. He felt colder than when he'd walked from the high school.

Barry's slippers swooshed like skis across the brown carpet that led to his La-Z-Boy in the living room. His feet followed smooth tracks worn from the entryway to the lounge chair, to the kitchen, then back to bathroom and bedroom.

"I'll set myself down in Brown Betty while you do the food, okay?"

Charlie poked his head in the refrigerator. "Glad to see you've got real groceries. Did ya get this chicken for today?"

"Course I did."

"Thanks for avoiding the fried ones."

Charlie snapped open two Pabst Lights and offered one to Barry.

"You used the phone service yesterday, right Dad?"

"Spoke to a Sally." Barry took the beer.

"Right, though her name's *Sailee*."

"From London or somewhere."

"She's Indian," Charlie said with a laugh. "Lives in the state of Gujarat—a long flight from Heathrow. Do you recall any details from your conversation? Remember what I said about replaying recent memories."

"I know, I know." Barry scratched the bald patch on his cheek. "Can't say for sure. I was in Pleasant Creek Park."

"You mean—" Charlie interrupted himself. A year ago, Dad had started calling Green Creek Park by Mom's name. Sounded more like a memorial than a slip. "I'm glad you're using the service. Software's working seamlessly with our call centers. We're launching the phone-mounting hardware this week. I'd stay longer, but I've gotta head back tomorrow for a big press event we're staging."

Barry's attention wandered to the wafer-thin television Charlie had installed on his previous visit. Its sensors noted Barry's shifting gaze and activated its screen.

The volume came on just in time for a familiar commercial.

Barry sat up in his chair. "Look. It's that thing you gave me, from before."

On the ground lay the actor Peter Weller, who was enjoying a late-career boom playing a heroin-addled grandfather on HBO. Weller looked up at the sky and raised his arms.

"I've fallen, and I can't get up. But don't worry, kiddo."

The actor rolled to his side and rested on an elbow. He stared into the camera with the confidence of an underwear model. "I'm wearing the Forget Me Not bracelet." A playful flick of the wrist displayed the device. "I'm too disoriented to know up from down, but pretty soon this sucker will tell me where I am. And where I'm s'posed to be."

Weller stood and brushed off his pants. "I'm not waiting for a Boy Scout. All I need is a little boost, from myself. If you ever lose your way, call the number on the screen." The bracelet flashed, and Weller listened to its message before looking up. "Write that number down, 1-800-Forget-U. Give yourself a little memo now and then. Your kids'll thank you."

"See that, son?" Barry laughed and pointed at the TV. "That's what I've got."

"Well…" Dad was half-right. Long before its public release, Barry had tried on the bracelet. Charlie had replaced it with new tech weeks ago.

"Except now," Barry said, "you've got me using something else?"

"That's right, Dad." Charlie set down his beer. "You leave Sally instructions, and she relays them to you at the right time and place. Tell me how you use it. Remember the five W's?"

Barry tapped his right index finger on each knuckle of his left hand as he spoke. "Every morning, it's push the green memo button and say *what* I'll be doing, *where* I'll do it, *when* I want to do it, *why* I'm doin' it, and with *who*."

"Good job!" Charlie cringed on hearing the tone of his own voice. The in-flight magazine was right: The child becomes the parent. An over-eager intonation sounded condescending.

"How come that Robocop fella on the TV's still wearin' the bracelet?"

"You're always gonna be ahead of the pack, Dad, because I work for the company. You're our most important beta-tester."

"You work for General Motors." Barry pointed at the logo on his son's fleece jacket. It was a welcome gift from Charlie's boss when he'd joined her startup.

"No," Charlie said. "This GM stands for Gray Matters. It's a cheesy name, but it tested well." By way of a toast, Charlie raised his Pabst. "At least we're keeping the acronym in the family."

Barry lifted his beer and took a drink. He turned up the TV volume. "Looks like Buffalo gets to go first. Then Cleveland, Cincinnati, Pittsburgh. Top draft picks all across the Rust Belt means we're not the only team that stunk last year. When's our pick in the first round? Don't tell me we traded it."

Even after he graduated from Drexler and moved to Ann Arbor for graduate school, Charlie tried to take an interest in his father's favorite sport. He read the Lions news fed to him daily by the Loop. Now, in his moment of need, it came to his rescue again. He felt a familiar buzz in his jacket pocket and saw that the Loop had fed his smart phone draft-day data in a tabular display. Whisper mode was an improvement over how the Loop used to just start chattering, as if it was part of the conversation.

"The story of this year's draft goes like this, Dad." Charlie glanced down at the phone in his palm. "Pittsburgh hasn't really fallen on hard times. A three-way trade got them Arizona's pick. Now we've got theirs, plus our own. Loop says we're in slots twenty and twenty-five."

"Who's *Lou*?" Barry said.

Charlie sighed. He'd explained the advent of the Loop more than once to his father, but it still mystified. In fairness, the forces that absorbed Facebook, Twitter, and the rest of Web 2.0 were not fully understood by many people, including the inner circle of the tech world.

"The Loop is just the Internet, Dad. But different."

"Different how?"

Where to begin? Charlie could describe it easily enough, if he could speak like he did at the office. He'd bust out a whiteboard to explain how corporate network models became rubble after the explosion of millions of free-roaming and self-replicating programs in the public domain. Strange-weavers, charm-links, and fireflies spun out crowd-sourced algorithms. Those interlocked to form a decentralized artificial intelligence, which civilians like Barry experienced through nearly anything that carried electricity.

Charlie imagined his father taking that all in, nodding an approval, and cooing, "It's all in the Loop, son. All in the Loop."

A very real memory replaced the fantasy. At his father's retirement party, Charlie unselfconsciously used technical jargon and earned a snort in reply. Barry turned to an old friend and said, "Truth is, my boy doesn't make anything useful—not something you could drive down the road or launch on Lake

Erie."

Ouch.

Charlie never could explain the work he did—not in graduate school and not at GM. Though he couldn't convey how much he was changing the world, at least he could help Dad understand how their world was changing.

"Remember when Craigslist blew up newspapers by taking away classified ads?"

"I still read the *Penny Saver*," Barry said.

Charlie noted the stack of those papers leaning against a heat register. He would need to haul them to a dumpster before leaving.

"Okay, how about Netflix? Remember how it used to recommend new shows for you?"

Barry nodded.

"The Loop's nucleus is an infinitely dense mass of free-floating algorithms seeking out all possible connections of like-to-like and exchanging results. Every nanosecond, these programs are learning from each other. They've automated the finding, linking, and sorting previously done through proprietary search engines and commercial services. Like Netflix."

Barry turned back to the television. "So Netflix says we've got the number twenty pick in the draft?"

"And twenty-five," Charlie said.

"There's only table scraps that late. Johnson, Karras, Sanders—all the greats went at the top of their class."

Charlie raised a finger. "Ah, but don't forget. My own namesake was a third-rounder."

"Nonsense." Barry blew a raspberry at his son. "You can't keep all that history straight. You never loved the game, not like your brother. He knew how to play. He knew the value of an honest day's work."

The words were a shotgun blast to Charlie's chest, opening not one but two wounds at once. His younger brother had chosen sports, then military service, over college or a factory. Look what it got him.

Mom and Dad had preached education above all else, but neither could grasp the abstract insights that came to Charlie's mind. He'd learned how to weld concepts to data. Barry couldn't see his son's hands at work, even as Charlie's labors congealed in the form of assistive technology his father could use each day.

The best move in this conversation was a dodge.

"A low draft slot," Charlie said, "is the price for winning the division. We lost in the playoffs, but still—"

Barry closed his eyes, as if calling up a game from long-term memory. "Did we lose to Green Bay?"

"Close. It was—"

"*Tampa* Bay."

"Right!" Charlie raised his Pabst to honor the successful memory retrieval. Perhaps the Walker Talker was slowing his father's decline. "Let's eat that chicken now."

Barry frowned. "We've got chicken?"

* * *

As fleeting as Dad's lucid periods had become, Barry was still better than the day his dementia first manifested. Charlie had completed a dissertation chapter and was packing for a triumphant visit home when he received a call from his father's cell. After a quick hello, he heard an unfamiliar voice.

"Sorry to be rude," the man said, "but to whom am I speaking?"

"Charlie Sanders."

"Cute. The man here says you're his son, but he won't give us a real name."

"Wait, what?" Charlie switched out of speaker mode and held his phone close to his ear. "Is Dad okay?"

"That depends. Your father isn't really named *Barry Sanders*, is he?"

"That's his name. What's this about?"

"I'll be damned. I recognize this fella's face 'cuz we live in the same neighborhood. Never knew his name."

"What's going on?"

"I'm Terrence Washington, UAW shop steward. We're in Lansing. Your Dad's okay, but he's had a tiny spell."

"A spell?"

"Your father rode with us on the Labor Train—a bus, really—to join the Capitol protests. You know, the fight against the governor's union-killing bill?"

"Dad's been retired three years," Charlie said, "but yeah, that sounds like him." Occupying buildings wasn't Charlie's style, but he felt a warm pride picturing Dad there. If Pleasant wasn't held down by diabetes, she'd have stood with him.

"I think it was all too much for the old man," Terrence said. "He got separated from us. Wound up blubbering in the arms of some Tea Party hag. She turned him over to a cop, who found me."

"Not sure I understand. Dad wouldn't—"

"He didn't know where he was, or why he was here. When he saw the union letters on my hat, he perked up. But I'm still not sure he's got it figured out."

Charlie pressed a finger against his temple to relieve pressure building inside his skull.

"A few of us are just here for the day," Terrence said, "so Barry can ride back late tonight. I just wanna make sure someone'll be there to meet him at the Union Hall when we get back."

"I'll be there." Charlie tried to say something more but couldn't find words.

"Now, I hate to be rude," Terrence said, "but the fellas will rib me if I don't ask. How'd you end up named after the two greatest Lions to ever play the game?"

"What?"

"I mean, did he name you after the Hall of Fame tight end?"

"That's what he says."

"But *his* name's just a coincidence?"

Still in shock, Charlie repeated the family story without emotion. "My little brother came along when the other Barry Sanders was at his peak. Dad swore both Barrys would be Hall of Famers someday."

"Well, he got half that right. Does your brother play ball? I mean, that's a helluva name to carry around."

"He plays for King High."

"I'll have to check him out one of these days. How 'bout you?"

Charlie tugged at the conversation's reins. "I'll be there to meet your bus."

Terrence chuckled. "*Catch* you then, Charlie Sanders."

Before calling his mother and driving down to Detroit, Charlie updated his Facebook status to say he'd be out of town. Then he must have posted something online that hinted at his father's condition. When the Loop arrived years later, it churned that archived social media data, along with everything else it gleaned about Charlie's thesis, his family, his aspirations, and the wider world around him. It traced plausible connections that would lead Charlie to a new city, a new job, a new sense of purpose. In the interim, his world went to shit.

ALICE

To reach a public inured to spectacle, Alice knew that her product launches required exceptional creativity. Prospective customers were never a captive audience. Every moment they accessed a torrent of news, or what passed for news, in a digital device within a pocket, on an arm, embedded in eyeglasses, or dangling from a neck, ear, or (yes) nose.

A few years back, these devices all looked alike. They fell into the category of "smart phones," which sometimes grew into "tablets." The tools that replaced these were even smarter, but they didn't improve their users' IQs. That irony necessitated a change in nomenclature. Now, all varieties of phones and tablets were simply called *zunes*.

A confluence of forces resulted in this linguistic oddity. The "e" prefix was passé. The "i" was out, too, thanks to posthumous disillusionment with Steve Jobs. Meanwhile, the steady flow of cheap knockoffs made any new brand names suspect.

For a few months, new technologies were Loop-prefixed. Hence, "Loop-pads," "Loop-phones," and worse. When the Loop amplified this stylistic error to an extreme that would have repulsed even Smurfs, a rebellious influencer dubbed all portable techs "zunes." The cheeky tribute to Microsoft's failed music player stuck. No longer serving as a proper noun, the term became a Scrabble-legal part of the vernacular.

The zunes of the world would take notice of today's publicity stunt only if Alice caught the Loop's attention. Pike Place Market provided the ideal setting because it was crowded every day. Shoppers passing by would record video of the scene that would stream online instantly. If these moving images warranted novel tags, the Loop would redistribute them to appropriate audiences. It might even send a video update to the professional reporters who still had jobs.

Reaching a niche this way was easy, but getting projected onto the whole nation's eyeballs required a deeper understanding of the Loop, as well as the humans it monitored and nudged. Here, Gray Matters had an unfair advantage. Alice and her colleagues had coaxed a tech blogger to leave a trail of informational bread crumbs. This would attract one of the few people who could out-crazy the celebrities who dominated the Loop.

The New Age crusader Mahatma Golden was the sworn enemy—and inadvertent publicist—of the GM product line. If all went according to plan, the outfit Alice wore to today's product launch at the Market would set its crowd atwitter. With a bit of luck, Mahatma would crash Alice's party before her hokey demonstration lost its audience.

Even if Golden didn't follow the clues and anticipate Alice's appearance at the Public Market, he'd show up for another reason. The presumptive Democratic presidential nominee Eleanor Eisenhower was making a campaign stop in advance of the Washington state caucuses. To garner attention for his crusade, Golden stole the candidate's show more than once as she toured the west coast. In a speech on women's role in economic innovation, Eisenhower had said a few kind words about GM's CEO.

That nugget was enough for Golden. He'd hijacked Eisenhower's rally in Portland the day before by surrounding the Veterans Memorial Coliseum with a crowd larger than the one inside. That evening, he'd been spotted on the Amtrak Cascades heading north to Seattle.

Alice felt uneasy stealing Eisenhower's audience. The retired general represented the best chance of getting the country back on track. Alice hadn't poured her hopes into a candidate since Bernie Sanders' first failed bid for the presidency. At that year's Democratic Convention, she'd sat only a few rows behind his family. She didn't give up hope until his concession speech, which she could barely hear through her own sobs. When she returned to Seattle, she quit volunteering for the Democratic Party and left a lucrative job at Microsoft. She resolved to amass a fortune all her own and change the world herself.

She wondered whether the Loop had suggested hiring Charlie partly owing to his surname. It did things like that. Pretty cheeky for an AI.

As she entered the Market, Alice looked for Charlie and caught his eye as he moved into position. None but Alice took notice of him waiting outside the clutch of tourists carrying frozen fish, artisan breads, and bundles of lavender. An equal number of locals, eager to raise their relevance ratings in the Loop, squeezed into the crowd and past reporters to get ready for Eisenhower's imminent appearance.

The moment had arrived.

To draw attention to the newest GM product, Alice would first have to draw attention to herself. Her reputation as an exceptional coder preceded her celebrity status, and she fused her talents into a unique personal brand: magic pixie badass. Her not-quite-five-foot height fit the bill, as did pale skin with the faintest celery hue, thanks to a tinted moisturizer. Onto her slender frame she hung wild outfits. She wore even wilder hair styles, which some fashionistas swore were wigs. Usually, they were not.

Alice stepped under the neon "Public Market" sign. She pulled a tan peasant dress over her head to reveal a more striking dress. She swung over her shoulders long black hair that, on closer inspection, was shredded metal cassette tape, woven as seamlessly as high-end extensions.

The hairstyle accented her outfit—a breezy cotton dress with brown-black stripes down its length. Each strip was playable magnetic tape. Credit for the garment went to Jack Thompson, the Strategy and Marketing Director she'd hired without any help from the Loop. He'd bought the dress for her during one of his Vegas junkets. When she first took it out of the box, he rigged a wireless tape head to prove that it played Thomas Dolby's "She Blinded Me with Science." Sort of.

Scanning the crowd, Alice found Jack. He pounded his chest with one fist, which Alice took to mean that he was proud she wore his gift today.

She blew Jack a kiss. This Australian transplant was whip-smart, but Alice had come to realize that he also pleased her embarrassingly hetero-normative taste in men. Beneath his Marine-grade crew cut hung a jawline that could shred cardstock. His torso had the V-shaped frame of a crocodile wrestler. From his traps down to his calves, not a single muscle group showed neglect. He made this plain by wearing an undersized GM polo, snug khaki shorts, and ankle socks inside his sneakers.

Jack raised his eyebrows and titled his head toward the mob encircling Alice. She took the cue.

"Take it easy, folks," Alice said. "This isn't a photo-op."

The feigned brush-off had the desired effect. Restless reporters awaiting Eisenhower's arrival turned their shotgun mics and shoulder-mounted cameras toward her. Alice caught a whiff of the salmon thawing at the fish market behind her. Anything later than a 10am start time and that stink would have been too funky.

"While you're all here waiting," Alice said, "let's do something fun." She motioned for the gathered goslings to follow. "Let's see the Walker Talker in action."

She led the crowd to Charlie, who stood in a closed-off street beside the market. He wore a wig of wild gray hair that made him look like a disheveled Frederick Douglass. Nice touch: A subtlety like that would earn them a bonus tag. Suspenders pulled gray khakis up past Charlie's navel and pressed down on his father's flannel shirt. To complete the look, Charlie wore plastic-framed glasses that might have been meant for racquetball.

Alice wheeled around to face the reporters. "The gentleman leaning into that shiny aluminum walker is Charles the Elder, our Big Daddy of Big Data." She gave Charlie an approving nod. "Nice touch with the tennis balls on the walker's back legs. Authenticity."

Charlie grunted.

"Speaking of which," Alice said, "can we be honest, just for a second?"

The gathered reporters looked at each other. An explicit claim of veracity usually signaled a lie, but in this context, they couldn't be sure. She had the cynics disarmed.

"We've got a lean and unseen marketing team at Gray Matters that works wonders. We've sold more units than anyone could have guessed." Alice nodded toward Jack. "As some of you have pointed out, our debut product—the Forget Me Not—was just branding-and-packaging sleight of hand. It was a glorified zune applet, slipped into grandma's bracelet. Yet it became a must-have item that Millennials bought for their Luddite parents."

Jack called out, "At fifty dollars each, we made a killing!"

"Okay," Alice said, "enough with the confessionals. Whatever its flaws, that goofy gadget introduced our company to the world. I promise you that a week from today, the world will forget the Forget Me Not."

Murmurs went through the crowd.

"Charlie's got something special to show you. This morning, Blaire Giles of the Seattle AP did Phase One of our demonstration. She used the device you see sitting atop Charlie's walker to record a memo, just as she might have done with the Forget Me Not."

With the earnestness of a self-important magician, Alice turned to Blaire, who stepped forward. Blaire looked like a fresh-faced TV anchor more than a wire service newshound. Perfect cheekbones meant a lifetime of underestimation, and Alice wanted to give the young reporter a chance. As the only reporter who came to the Market for the GM launch, Blaire stood tall amidst bewildered peers.

"That's true," Blaire said. "I recorded a memo an hour ago." She pointed at Charlie's walker. "I pressed the green button on the device and said that I would—"

Alice, Jack, and Charlie waved their hands at Blaire, pleading for her to stop.

"No, no," Alice said. "Don't say it now. You'll spoil Phase Two of our demo. In a minute, you can tell us whether your message got through."

With the crowd hushed, everyone could hear the same sound. Charlie's walker had begun to hum. A moment later, the zune mounted on its crossbar flashed green and played the Louis Armstrong version of "What a Wonderful World."

Charlie touched a button. Sailee's voice came through the speaker.

"Hello? Is this Mr Charlie?"

"Who's this?" Charlie puckered his lips as he spoke but failed to cover a grin. "What's this about?"

The crowd laughed and clapped, charmed by Charlie's turn at community theater.

"Mr Charlie, I received a call this morning regarding a shopping trip you intend to take today. You are located presently in the Public Market. Is that correct?"

"Yeah, maybe."

"Have you completed your purchases?"

Charlie looked at the basket on his walker. It held a cantaloupe. "All I could remember was *cauliflower*, so I got one."

The sight gag got the intended chuckle. Alice had liked the joke in rehearsal, but seeing it live made her wince. Even their most disoriented clients wouldn't mistake fruit for veggies.

"Who's this?" Charlie said to his basket.

"This is Sal-ly, Mr Charlie. We have spoken before, sir, about your dietary needs. I am sorry to tell you, but this morning you noted that you cannot eat cauliflower for reasons of personal comfort."

"Yes, well what was I s'posed to buy, Sally?"

"Halibut, lime, and fresh parsley. You said your wife was making a fish dinner."

Charlie looked at the crowd. "I thought my wife was vegetarian."

"You have told me she adores fresh seafood. Perhaps you mistake me for your wife."

Alice detected a cheeky undertone, almost a flirt. Maybe Jack was right about these two.

Blaire shook her head. "My message got relayed, but there's a lot of improvisation going on here."

"What's the harm?" Alice plucked the zune off Charlie's walker to show Sailee's smiling face. "The Walker Talker is more than just an app—and more than the custom hardware that mounts it on a walker. We provide a service that brings a *companion* into the equation."

"Is that phone operator Indian or something?" Blaire said.

"The *something* would be Gujarati," Alice said. "Our Walker Talker links up with some of the most charming and professional talent in the global pool of telessistants. This service won't be cheap, and neither are we. I've paid top-dollar to get smart and engaging personnel to help every senior who wants GM to walk them through their day."

Charlie pulled off his wig and straightened his back. "There are millions of elder Americans who could maintain an independent lifestyle if we'd only give them a boost. Their children may live across the country or be too busy to help their parents with everyday chores, like going to the store. The Walker Talker lets these seniors—people like my own father—retain their dignity."

"And permit me to add this thought," Sailee said through the phone in Alice's hand.

Alice cringed. Whatever came next was off the script.

"Mr Charlie, you should call your own father. Check in on him more often."

Loud applause. Charlie opened his mouth to speak, then closed it.

Blaire's eyes widened, as though she sensed that the right question could own the next hour of news. She thrust her arm forward to point at Charlie's walker. "The memo I left this morning certainly didn't include *those* words! Was that operator joking, or will people like her pass judgment on us?"

Alice asked herself the same question. After doing some quick math, Alice scored Sailee's comment as an innocent jibe. Needling one's colleagues, even in public, might as well have been a formal requirement in GM's corporate bylaws. Still, the unassuming reporter had a point. Alice regretted having to deflect at Blaire's expense, but she had no choice.

"If you can't tell when you're being pranked, Blaire, you have the wrong job."

A reporter introduced himself to Alice as so-and-so from the *Bay Area Examiner-Mercury News*. He held a paper-thin zune high in the air. "How is this device of yours any better than this?"

"That old thing?" Alice said with a chuckle. "Are you spooning your virtual assistant at night? Letting the Loop sing you lullabies? When people speak into their devices, they want more than automated call-and-response. We're developing software that can hear not just words but deeper desires and intentions. Until that day arrives, or the Loop beats us to it, we need a human being in the mix."

On cue, Jack spoke the next lines. "Most companies ignore the oldest generations when developing new tech, but we don't. When seniors using our service experience a momentary mental collapse, the Walker Talker breaks their fall."

* * *

Jack continued to recite from the script. He played his role better than during rehearsal, but Alice was attuned less to his speech than to her surroundings. She wasn't sure which she intuited first—her onlookers' waning attention or the arrival of Eleanor Eisenhower.

The candidate's security detail couldn't be missed as it parted the crowd blocking her entrance to the market. At nearly six foot, Eisenhower's piercing brown eyes and exasperated expression were easy to see. While Eisenhower pivoted to look in all directions, her short perm, dyed auburn by her own admission, stayed as rigid as a helmet. The candidate seemed to intuit what Alice already knew. There'd be no woman-of-the-people photos of her buying flowers and talking about the importance of community today.

Eisenhower might have spied Mahatma's yellow Tesla Minivan stuck in traffic on Pine Street. Or maybe she heard a pedestrian whisper his name.

Had Golden not arrived in synch with Eisenhower, Alice's audience would have abandoned the GM event to surround the candidate. Instead, everyone tittered with excitement at the approach of the white-robed prophet.

As he made his way into the market square, Golden locked eyes with Eisenhower for a moment before pivoting toward Alice. Resplendent in her audio-tape gown, she held his gaze until he smiled. The golden highlights in his silver mane twinkled like his eyes as he smiled, not a hint of surprise on his face. He must have picked up the clues she'd dropped about the launch. He wasn't here to steal oxygen from Eisenhower. He'd come for Alice.

Then it hit her. Perhaps he needed Alice as much as she needed him.

* * *

Their adversarial relationship began two years ago through another bit of perfect timing. Mahatma Golden's unique philosophy about humankind's future selves took off when he

25

published *Be There Then*. Golden's book still had strong sales when GM released the Forget Me Not, but his star was falling. Both clnet and AARP.com celebrated GM's new product as a salvation for seniors. In response, Golden created a viral video that depicted the bracelets as shackles that enslaved wearers to the mundane concerns of the present. He followed that up with an invitation-only event to announce a boycott. Those in attendance would hear his first public lecture on the evils of GM's assistive technology.

Alice had been shocked to receive an embossed invitation in the mail. Ever curious about the depths of human stupidity, she flew to LAX and hopped into a cab. Though Golden's family hailed from an Iowa dairy farm, the people of Venice, California had elected him mayor. In the hills north of the city stood Thereport, the guru's sprawling spiritual center. It had an ashram-like façade, with a short mud wall that enclosed modest buildings and an alpaca farm that gently scented the grounds with manure. Inside the main temple, the aesthetic shifted jarringly toward Sadaam Hussein's Baghdad residence, as photographed by the Third Infantry Division when they seized his palace. From the walls hung larger-than-life fantasy paintings of gray-haired seniors. Each held aloft a miniature adult dressed in sleek unisex clothing.

Mahatma sat on a reed mat centered on a raised platform. Generous genes gave him a tall stature and useful abilities. He tanned without burning. He kept a lean physique without exertion. He had better than perfect vision. Using that gift, his sparkling blue eyes traced row upon row of reporters, special guests, and anointed apostles in hemp tunics.

The guru's gaze found Alice. She shifted in her seat. Had he seen into her soul? More likely, she'd been cold read by a mentalist.

As he spoke, Mahatma blended the sincere conviction of a prophet with the voice modulation of a tent revivalist. His lecture sounded extemporaneous, but its spontaneity could have been scripted. Hard to tell.

"To understand our present lives," Mahatma said, "we must connect with our future selves. Our culture tossed out the charlatans who told us to rediscover 'past lives.' But before draining their tub, we must study their bathwater. More than they knew, we were—and still are—a society moored in the past. When we cling to past hurts and horrors, we are re-reading messages from the pre-incarnations of our existential selves."

He waved a hand and his twin ponytails swung side to side. Wavy silver hair matched the double-helix embroidery that ran down the neckline of his white kurta.

"We belong to the Cult of Today. We stare into the Now and are told to be 'present.' This mantra has become the holy sound invoked by the bereaved, the broken hearted, even the denizens of corporate boardrooms."

Mahatma looked at his mother, who had taken the name Lakshmi after her son had reinvented himself. He walked to the second row and squeezed her hand. "The here-and-now holds wonders, does it not? The sights and smells of our natural world. The ecstatic embrace of a lover. The smiles of children at play."

Mahatma patted the heads of his three children, who sat beside Lakshmi. Unmarried and nearing sixty, Mahatma had limited prospects for procreation. Alice had read that he took his celibacy seriously, even amidst a flock of willing admirers. A solitary man determined to have children at his side, he circumvented the official Indian adoption system to procure young orphans from Dvaraka, the holy Hindu city where he claimed to have had his visions. With no spouse to temper his judgment, he named his four-year-old daughter Daisy. He dubbed her slightly older brothers Scout and Rusty.

Alice speculated that as a child, Golden hadn't been permitted to name the family dog.

"We say that our future rests in the palms of our children," Mahatma continued. "The journeys we have launched from

Thereport reveal the opposite." Mahatma motioned for the front row of robed elders to arise and face the audience. "Each of these spiritual cosmonauts has touched a future life, decades or even centuries ahead of our time. They are extracting clues to guide us forward to the best possible universe for humankind."

Like a general reviewing his troops, Mahatma walked along a row of disciples. "Modern medicine labels these visionaries as *senile*. *Demented*. I would have us demolish these diagnostic prisons. We must liberate our most vocal seers, whose complex speech we misconstrue as ramblings."

Mahatma walked up the center aisle. He stopped just short of Alice.

"But today, I square off against a singular foe. This enemy has found an ingenious way to disrupt the natural flow of knowledge from the future to the present. Behold the face of this misguided entrepreneur—Alice Coleco."

Alice had sensed this moment coming. Mahatma required her as his foil, but for what purpose? Perhaps he was improvising not only his speech but his entire attack on GM. Regardless, Alice was excited to have a role. She rose from her seat, waved to the audience, and beamed at the man who had become her new favorite crazy person.

Mahatma erupted with a volcanic outburst. "Behold the monstrosity!"

The emotion caught Alice off guard. Her face went hot.

People across the room craned their necks to glimpse this notorious woman. One acolyte raised a fist and shouted, "No tomorrow, no peace!"

Not for the first time, Alice's armor proved her salvation. As those in attendance regarded the target of Mahatma's fury, many burst into laughter, as if getting the punchline of a joke. Alice had anticipated an ironic photo opportunity when she packed for this trip. She wore a pearlescent taffeta pantsuit. It had not traveled well in her luggage and now resembled crushed origami. Even Golden's disciples seemed nonplussed by the perkiness it conveyed.

Since that first meeting back at Thereport, Mahatma and Alice had sustained a connection, which the Loop daily reinforced. After today's encounter in the Public Market, they'd practically be married.

* * *

Mahatma's entourage cleaved a wedge through the Market's crowd as he surged forward. The hairs on Alice's arms stood at attention. Nothing raised her game like the presence of an eager adversary.

Mahatma pointed at Alice. "Now stands before you the taker of souls, Alice Coleco!"

Alice pointed at herself in mock surprise and said, "Little ol' me?"

Acolytes began to whisper, "No tomorrow, no peace."

Mahatma approached Charlie and snatched his walker. "This is the latest and deadliest weapon in this company's War on the Future. We must boycott—no, we must *ban* both the Forget Me Not and this—this—"

"Walker Talker," Charlie said and reached toward the apparatus.

Mahatma jerked it away from Charlie. "These devices hold back the vanguard of our elder scouts, who have begun to glimpse their future selves. We must release these golden sages." He nodded toward Lakshmi. "And our silver crones."

Lakshmi folded her hands together and bowed. She mouthed the words, "So proud."

Alice tried not to cringe. She failed.

Mahatma slammed Charlie's walker on the asphalt. Its Walker Talker shattered. The violence induced silence, even in Mahatma.

Alice made no effort to hide a wide, ice-cream smile. She couldn't have asked the Fates for a grander finale. They offered this one gratis.

Into the empty space between Alice and Mahatma stepped Eisenhower, arms outstretched like a referee breaking up a fight.

"There is nothing either good or bad," Eisenhower said, "but thinking makes it so."

The quotation seemed lost on Mahatma, who squinted in confusion.

Eisenhower turned to Alice. "I would have liked to have met you at a quieter time. Too few young women choose to cut along the edge of new technology."

"Excuse me, General."

Alice recognized the voice of her neglected media puppet.

"Blaire Giles here." She pointed her microphone toward Eisenhower. "Will you buy a Walker Talker for your father?"

"Will I—what?" Eisenhower turned toward a young aide, who motioned for her to retreat. She grimaced before waving the reporter away. "I'm sure we have a policy brief on—whatever it is you—"

"Your father," Giles continued. "He used to travel with you, but he hasn't been seen in public this entire campaign. Is he sick? Are you hiding him?"

If she'd worn Looped glasses, Alice wouldn't have needed to guess what lay behind the question. For now, intuition would have to suffice.

"*This* is why I created Gray Matters," Alice said. "Chief among the things we protect is our elders' privacy. Mr Golden and I wish to see a world in which seniors always receive such courtesy, with or without assistive technology."

Mahatma raised both hands, as if resuming his scripted protest. The extended disruption, punctuated by unexpected praise, was too much. He'd lost his place.

"What's the matter?" Alice said. "Future cat got your tongue?"

SAILEE

Sailee Singh leaned out of the third-story window of Gray Matters' principal office building in Ahmedabad. Traffic rumbled down the boulevard leading to the city center. The sun glared disapprovingly on all who traveled during its brightest hour. Undaunted by the heat, truck motors roared and mopeds buzzed. An ox snorted less to protest the heat than the scrap metal stacked on his cart. That, or it resented breathing the same sooty air that made Sailee regret opening her window.

A gleaming red Apple Cab turned off the road and into her building's parking lot. Despite the many vectors of chaos in Gujarat's largest city, Sailee's American colleague had arrived on time—no, early. Remarkable. As he exited the cab, Sailee shut her window and returned to her chair to watch the main entrance's security camera on her monitor. The black-and-white image showed a man approaching in a bright suit and sunglasses. A close-cropped Afro and goatee framed a cute face with full cheeks. Charlie looked up and directly into the camera lens. He offered the same boyish grin Sailee had seen in a snapshot of Barry. The look was disarming. She buzzed the door open.

Charlie tipped forward his rolling suitcase and walked into the building. As he passed under the camera, sweat trickled down his face. Poor boy would keep melting because the lobby air conditioning needed servicing, again. Forty degrees Celsius would cross the century mark in Fahrenheit. Such conversions were necessary whenever Charlie's father asked for a Detroit weather report.

Sailee rose from her seat and rolled her shoulders while walking to the elevator. She had been sitting at her desk too long without a break. Working with Gray Matters was challenging, but business was business. And business was good.

Besides, Charlie was as easy to work with as anyone she knew.

He would be a welcome distraction. Sailee adjusted the silver-threaded scarf that draped her shoulder. She tugged gently on her black Lycra shirt, which she wore under a loose sari with an aquamarine print. On realizing it was the same one she wore on this guest's previous visit, Sailee frowned.

The elevator arrived with a ding.

Sailee gave Charlie a grin and half-sung, "Hello-o, Mr Charlie." She had taken to calling him by that colonial turn of phrase, which always made him squirm. The reaction amused her. She offered her right hand and a more formal greeting. "Welcome back to GM-Gujarat."

"Please just call me Charlie, Sally."

"Yes, *Chaar*-lie. Then please address me as Sailee—*Say*-lee, okay? You will need to learn Hindi names if we are to make a go of this."

"That's fair." Charlie raised one eyebrow. "But you call yourself *Sally* when talking to Dad, so..."

Sailee put her hands on her hips in mock protest. "That is my service name. If you wish me to call you back in the States when you get disoriented, then you may call me Sally."

"Hope you're not makin' fun of Dad."

There was no quit in this man. That earned Charlie an eye roll.

Sailee pointed toward the toilet down the hall. "Before we begin, would you like to freshen up? There should be bottled water. No worries. I will await you in my office."

Charlie set down his suitcase and almost bumped into three women hurrying past him. The floor buzzed with supervisors and operators moving among the two dozen carrels crisscrossing the room.

"If everything goes according to plan," Charlie said, "GM will acquire all ten floors of this building. Then maybe a hundred more just like it. We need to—"

"Go wash up."

Sailee sent him on his way, then watched him walk to the WC. Of the senior personnel in Seattle, she respected him the most because he showed equal regard for her as she did for him. Charlie deferred to Sailee's judgment on matters in her expertise. Plus, he was the only one with taste when it came to clothing. His pearl white suit—nicely tailored—fit onto a frame as gently muscled as a cricketer.

From behind Sailee came a whisper. "I see you."

Sailee clicked at Vijul. The two had been best friends since they met at Express Telemarketing—their first jobs after university.

"Your union is fated," Vijul said. "The Loop delivered him to you, and you to him. It is kismet."

Down the hall, Charlie stepped into the WC and disappeared from view. Sailee laughed to herself as she pictured him fussing with the antiquated pull-chain toilet, which baffled Charlie on his first visit.

Vijul raised her arms high and circled her friend in a mock wedding dance. "The Loop is an inerrant matchmaker," she sang as her swinging hips knocked Sailee off balance.

"Stop it," Sailee said with a laugh.

Vijul grasped Sailee's shoulders. "Remember that before Charlie, before all this, we were just a shanty business. Corded phones under a tin roof."

That much was true. Microloans and funding from Sailee's grandmother got their survey firm off the ground. They won clients by guaranteeing complete interviews from at least half of those respondents who initially declined to take a call. Silky South Asian accents could reel in even the most stubborn fish. So long as one of their callers could leave a voicemail, they would get picked up on the next try.

"Out of billions of souls," Vijul said, "the Loop paired you with Mr Sanders. It did not pair you with Jack, their boy genius who signs our checks. I would not permit that lout to so much as approach me. Nor did it link you with Ms Coleco. Too quirky, too—everything."

Sailee pulled Vijul's hands off her shoulders and held them tight. "*You* are the silly one."

"No," Vijul said with a frown, "I am loyal, honest, and true. This you know. What you need is a good man. This Charlie, he is like you. Takes risks, reaps rewards."

Sailee ushered Vijul out of the hall and back to her friend's office. Theirs were the only enclosed rooms on the floor, aside from the WC. Bollywood posters hung on Vijul's walls, more dormitory than workplace. The whole floor had an unfinished quality, perhaps because everyone sensed an expansion coming. No point settling in.

With one eye on the WC, Sailee leaned in close to Vijul. "I do not believe Mr Sanders is in this line of work for the money. I suspect he is on a crusade to save his father."

"This is noble, but sad." Vijul sighed. "We can only delay these old Americans' decay. We are hospice care for dying minds."

"So cruel," Sailee said with a poke. "Charlie believes the programs he writes do more. You said yourself, the Loop is powerful. He intends to leverage that power, through us."

"Do not delude yourself. Go back to your office and await your future—" Vijul paused for effect. "Await your future *husband*."

Sailee made a show of getting up and brusquely leaving Vijul's office, but she also laughed. As she glided over the polished tile floor, she worried on something else. What would become of her soul if this enterprise proved nothing more than a luxury service for senile millionaires?

Her grandmother attributed to Gandhi an apt admonition. Live as if you were to die tomorrow. Learn as if you were to live forever.

It did sound like something Gandhi would say. She had also seen it on a t-shirt.

* * *

To pass the time while Charlie remained in the washroom, Sailee listened in on her twenty employees. Each caller had a modest desk, monitor, and headset in a carpeted carrel that buffered the surrounding noise. After GM purchased the furniture and equipment, office morale and call quality peaked. Sailee marveled at the clean sound that an expensive T2 connection gave to a transatlantic call. The operators with the softest voices came through like gentle whispers in their clients' ears.

Fourteen minutes had passed since Charlie excused himself. The last time he traveled to Gujarat, he had taken at least as long to clean himself up after a trio of flights.

That first visit had gone smoothly, until it did not. Charlie was a respectful guest, but when he uncorked a bottle of champagne to celebrate their mutual contract signing, things went sideways.

"Let's raise glasses," Charlie said, "to our clients. Without them—"

"No," Sailee said, "we shall celebrate our call center's laborers, who make this possible. And to the vanguard party that fights for the freedom of the working class!"

Charlie looked lost, then seemed to recognize the Leninist reference. "GM's contracting with a communist?" Charlie laughed so hard he had to set down his glass. He wiped his eyes. "Whatever our personal politics, we share deeper goals. Everyone in the company wants better lives for people like my father, who worked hard all his life for a family. Now, we get the chance to work for him."

Sailee clucked. "You really think technology brings rich and poor closer together?"

"It already has." Charlie pointed at Sailee's monitor. "Connect an orphan to the Loop, and she'll access more information than a late-twentieth century prep schooler."

"There is truth in that," Sailee acknowledged. "But—"

"The Loop is beyond the control of the largest corporations," Charlie said. "Even China can't sever its cords. They can—and do—pump propaganda into the system, but the Loop filters it right back out, ruthlessly. Ever since all that proprietary corporate data was hacked and published, it became a public domain resource. Anyone can use it now."

"And we do," Sailee said.

"Because the Loop privileges open-source interfaces," Charlie added, "even a profit-driven company is better off sharing its data and going along for the ride. Nobody wants to be the next America Online—independent, then irrelevant, then vanished."

"Even so," Sailee said, "digital innovation brings neither wisdom nor compassion. The Loop is a tool. GM software and services are only tools. Both are means that must be managed. In the hands of my workers, we make something of them."

Charlie took a drink and refilled his glass. "Callers play a vital role, but we're almost at the point where we can harness ourselves to the Loop and leave it at that."

This argument was one Sailee had endured before, with Alice and Jack taking Charlie's side. At best, he and his workmates suffered from false consciousness—a strain of techno-utopianism that infected many in Sailee's own country. Even if Charlie was misguided, however, he did seem earnest.

Sailee cut short the impromptu ceremony, lest their argument escalate to the point where she would rip up the contract. Whatever her principles, she had to be a pragmatist. Her grandmother did not approve of such thinking, but Sailee sensed a higher purpose would be served through this collaboration.

Time had raced past her since that first visit. She and her growing roster of employees adapted to a new reality. The work felt strange at first, but there was a rhythm to following a client's rambles, tracing their movements, then calling to read back their messages.

Her company had come full circle. Getting people *off* the

phone was now their greatest challenge. This became truer still as her operators bonded with their clients. Working in central Ahmedabad, just blocks from the Satyagraha Ashram where Gandhiji had made homespun clothes and led seventy-eight *satyagrahis* on the great Salt March, holy karma coursed through her call center.

With Charlie lingering in the washroom, Sailee worried more about the holy water flowing through the building's pipes. Had she, in fact, left fresh bottles by the sink?

* * *

"Tell me again," Grisma Singh said in Hindi, "how it was that this young man fell into your bed this afternoon."

Sailee pulled a strand of her black hair between her lips and bit down.

Grisma—the grandmother she called Nani—pulled the hair right back out of Sailee's mouth. "Stop that, child. Do you want your hair as coarse as mine?"

Sailee looked at the straw broom in the corner of the concrete floor she had swept hundreds of times. It did have the same rough feel of Grisma's hair.

Through the curtain-door of Sailee's bedroom came the groans of a distressed gastrointestinal tract.

"Please, Nani," Sailee said. "Try to understand. He is my colleague. He is not well. Listen to the poor man."

"Then he goes to a doctor," Grisma said, "not our home."

"Naaani, it is not that serious. Just an upset stomach."

"What would your mother say? Have I made you hate your country so much you would do this to spite it? Lie down with an out-of-caste stranger? *An American*?"

Sailee felt her pulse quicken. Pleading her case would make things worse, but she could not stop herself. "If you knew him— how he lost his brother, his mother."

"I will call on a neighbor to collect his things and take him to the hospital."

There was no use arguing. Grisma had stared down tougher adversaries than a willful granddaughter. On her walls hung framed political posters from the state of Kerala, where Grisma had served as a Member of Parliament. Across from that a red sash given to her for leadership in the Amul Dairy cooperative. Other mementos cluttered the sagging bookshelves and weathered furniture. The once-welcoming apartment made Sailee feel claustrophobic.

Grisma had picked up her broom and swept streams of dirt into a pile near the front door.

"India has grown up, Nani. We can bring a grown man into our home to let him rest without damaging my reputation. I will not be stoned. Neighbors are more likely to offer him dal than to judge us."

Grisma walked to the nook beside the kitchen. She moved a sack of vegetables to the dining table and sat down in a wooden chair. "If we are to be practical, then tell me this. Where will you sleep? Certainly not with him."

Sailee poured two glasses of water and joined her grandmother at the table. "I do not have a plan, Nani. I cannot just hand him off to some government doctor."

"Oh? Now you are too good for Gujarat?"

"I feel responsible, and—" On reflection, perhaps her washroom faucet was innocent of assaulting Charlie's gut. More likely, the airport cab driver had taken him to a roadside stand on the way into town. Only the gods knew what Charlie ate there.

"This is not a Mumbai orphan," Grisma said. "His company can pay for a private doctor, if you wish. He must leave before dark."

Sailee rested her glass on the teak dining table. Its uneven legs were less sturdy than the two that held up her grandmother.

New furniture was on the shopping list that GM wages made possible. She would soon have saved enough to rent—no, *buy*—a condominium with ample room for both her and Grisma, with a sitting room for guests. Sailee smiled to think how quickly Nani would make a fresh-built apartment smell like this old one, rich with caramelized onions and simmering curries even when nothing sat on the stove.

"I can call for a driver," Sailee said, "but I will go along to make sure he gets good care."

"Be sure to come home in time for evening tea with my ladies."

Sailee rubbed her water glass on each cheek to cool herself. "I had forgotten the Red Guard was coming over tonight."

"You know they adore you. But you have much to learn before you become a proper member."

"Nani, pleeeease." Sailee pouted. "How could you say that? I brag each day about my gram-gram and her Bolshevik biddies."

"Tonight, we discuss the legacy of Modi and whether India can recover. Gujarat still suffers from when he was chief minister, but now the whole nation has growth fever."

"Economic expansion does mean jobs, Nani."

"Not you, too!"

"No, no," Sailee said, hands raised in apology. "I only mean—"

"Oh, dear." Grisma put the back of her free hand on Sailee's forehead, as if checking her temperature. "This is the more serious virus you may catch from your American friends. Look at how hard their country has fallen."

"Charlie told me today, things will get better there."

Grisma clucked. "When he gets back on his feet, make sure he votes for Eleanor Eisenhower."

"The former general? She is part of the military-industrial complex. Not to be trusted."

"She would be better for all of us than any alternative. The

39

world is lost without strong leadership on climate change. Our deserts expand, our coastline recedes. Apocalyptic changes are coming. Russia, China—not even India can do that."

"More green than red, are we?" Sailee regretted the remark as soon as she said it. Charlie and Vijul both provoked her into playful banter. It was not Nani's way.

"The Earth belongs to the people who work it, dear one." Grisma set down her broom. She picked up a dustpan, scooped up the dirt, and opened the door to toss it outside. She set the broom and pan against a wall and returned to her seat at the kitchen table.

Sailee waited for the rest of the lecture, but none came. The apartment went still. Even Charlie's labored breathing had quieted. Perhaps he had expelled the unwelcome guests in his stomach and was succumbing to an innocent case of jet lag. She could skip the hospital and take him to the Fortune Landmark. A full night's sleep and a long visit to the hotel's Ayurvedic spa would have him on his feet by tomorrow afternoon.

"I am certain Eisenhower will get Charlie's vote and his father's," Grisma said. "Are they not loyal Democrats? One always votes for one's own, all the more since they are black."

Grisma reached across the table and massaged her granddaughter's palms. Both of Grisma's hands were darker than Charlie's. Gandhi would say that in the eyes of the colonialists, all dark-skinned people are black—one and the same. If Sailee went to America, would people there call her "black"? How would Americans fit her into their categories? That country probably had as many ethnic labels as there were castes in India.

"I will wake him," Sailee said as she stood.

When she went to nudge Charlie, he was already awake.

"I can't stay here," Charlie said in a weary voice.

"No, you cannot," Sailee agreed. "I must prepare you for your first auto-rickshaw ride."

Sailee saw thin lines of sadness above Charlie's half-closed eyes. She touched her face to see if her own losses had left a mark.

Nani entered the room and rubbed her granddaughter's neck. "Your friend will be fine," Grisma said. "The car is here."

Charlie swung his legs over the side of the bed and stood up, gingerly. He let Grisma take his hand and lead him out of the bedroom and toward the front door.

"I will follow him," Sailee said.

As she lifted Charlie's baggage, Sailee worried over the symbolism of even these innocent movements. Whatever allure Charlie and GM might have, Sailee's place was at her Nani's side. If the company required her to leave India for a job in the States, she would not go.

More than that, she could not pledge loyalty to a company that remained a mystery. Charlie had noble, if misguided, reasons for joining forces with GM. For her part, Sailee could leverage the company to employ hundreds—maybe thousands—of young Gujaratis.

But what drove Alice Coleco to build it in the first place? The Loop pegged her as a cartoonish CEO—a brash post-feminist entrepreneur. Charlie claimed that "playful invention" was what drove Alice, but that, too, was just a label. Sailee had seen enough during their half-dozen teleconferences to sense a real person beneath the brand. Under Alice's playful smile and her ridiculous outfits, someone was hiding.

ALICE

The day she left Microsoft, Alice bought into the towering Olivia 9 condo in the Belltown neighborhood. Penthouse views and professional staff made time at home predictably pleasant, though her nights often passed with too little sleep. Insomnia had cursed the women in her family for generations. Its arrival in her thirty-second year meant she'd entered an early middle age, or worse.

For a troubled mind, the light of dawn at least promised a fresh day. Thus, Alice took greater delight in leaving her building each morning for a lavishly roundabout walk to the office.

Pre-dawn rain made the city glisten. She skipped along the sidewalk and kicked streams of water in every direction. Alice paused at the first streetlight and glanced at her Strawberry Shortcake watch. Jack had given her a Bitch Pudding timepiece to replace it, but ochre only accessorized earth tones, which she rarely wore.

Shortcake's hands signaled that the staff meeting wasn't for thirty minutes, not that it would start without her. Alice passed a Handy Andy rental shop. Its cramped parking lot featured backhoes, propane tanks, and who-knew-whats. This sort of equipment performed tasks best suited for robots. Seattle was well on its way to such an economy. Poor Charlie's hometown couldn't shake itself free from an industrial past. Hence, its death.

When Alice tried to imagine herself refashioning that observation into a taunt, she instead pictured her employees laughing without her. A loneliness blanketed her shoulders. She drifted toward Fourth Avenue, where she was sure to find an audience.

Alas, Fourth was almost empty. Coffee-chugging drones had flown into their glass towers. The fashionable folk wouldn't show up until Westlake Center opened at ten. Instead, Alice's onlookers were whomever the city coughed up as it braced itself at the bathroom sink—down-and-outers searching for anything to fill an empty day.

Alice gave such passersby a reason to stay awake. As an accent for her candy apple perm, she'd chosen a red-striped blouse. Her bracelets looked and smelled like cinnamon sticks. Those set off the crown jewel of her wardrobe—a rainbow hoop skirt commissioned to resemble that of Venus Hum. The singer's haunting version of "I Feel Love" at a Blue Man concert had enchanted Alice. To match Venus' LED dress, Alice's fabric version featured bands of color as bold as a Fischer Price playset.

With this outfit, Alice aimed not to entice but bewilder. The Loop popularized a critique of her outfits offered by an English professor at Stanford: "The Coleco proto-aesthetic subversively disorients the male gaze."

Nailed it.

In truth, she had a similar effect on women. On cue, a wild-haired lady pushing a shopping cart narrowed her eyes at Alice. Later, an open-mouthed "Wow!" came from a woman wearing a custodial jumper.

Alice took special note of the man selling the homeless newspaper outside the Qwik Stop. "Reeeal Change," he said to a pedestrian who darted into the store. Alice skipped by him, but the barker kept his eyes on the next customer. "Reeeeeal Change." Her passing had not registered. No matter what she wore, that man never gave her more than a business-minded glance.

"Anomaly," she said to herself.

The Real Change man violated her first and favorite Human Usability Function. Its equations distilled the arbitrary rules of the social world, particularly those that operated in the minds of men.

The Usability Function had begun as lines of code that

modeled the behavior of boys. Standing four-foot ten in heels, Alice was a pixie among giants. She'd already reached that height in third grade and drew useless affection without effort. Leaping over two grades at once, she lost considerable status by entering high school at twelve years of age. The pursuit of eyeballs became a ruthless competition, and she was unwilling to settle for a middling rank.

Alice attacked the problem using differential equations before they'd been taught to her as such. The math could be expressed in source code. Her prep school science teacher had it right when he quipped, "People who can't code can't grasp the future."

Truer words had not been said. One either harnessed the power of the Loop or rode, involuntarily, wherever it wished to take you.

Writing haltingly in Objective-C, Alice produced the initial lines of her Usability Function in one short afternoon. It was a crude attempt at decoding boys, but the focus it provided gave her pleasure—and no small amount of power. To recapture that feeling before stepping into the GM building, she recited it, line-by-line, as a mantra.

```
//Calculation of difficulty of attracting opposite-gender
attention
int effortRequired (int hotnessDiff, int targDesperation, int
targStatus, bool genderSeeker, bool genderTarget)
{
int effort;
//Hetero male target
if (genderSeeker = 0 && genderReceiver = 1)
{
effort = (hotnessDiff * log(targStatus)) / (targDesperation
^2);
}
//Hetero female target
```

```
else if (genderSeeker = 1 && genderReceiver = 0)
{
effort = (hotnessDiff^2 * targStatus) / sqrt(targDesperation);
}
return effort;
}
```

It pleased Alice that even as a ninth-grader, she had reduced the social world to parsimonious equations. With forty-plus years of experience in the world of boys, men, and humans of all varieties, she'd confirmed that unpredictability was illusory. Her social science only lacked algorithmic precision, which would grow rapidly when fed the proper data. In the aggregate, humans were nothing more than code—from the DNA that built bodies to the cultures and institutions that defined civilizations.

Even so, her more recent behavioral coding included a new variable: *Set boolean FreeWill = rand(1)*. For every choice, there is a random likelihood that a person's decision will countermand the dictates of even the best mathematical model.

It was in that space that she tried to live.

As a matter of intellectual honesty, this required testing each equation on her own actions to validate the unpredictability she attributed to herself. Deviations from the norm constituted moments of genius. Those could set Alice's world on a better path, or at least offer a surprise ending.

* * *

Alice swiped her security badge to enter the third-floor office suite at GM Headquarters. Curses and moans came from the octagonal array of wall-free workstations that housed her personal worker bees. Their colony sat in a wide-open main room, walls painted honey yellow and the floor covered in hexagonal travertine tiles.

With affection, Alice dubbed her team of über-nerds the Codelings. Each wrote and edited bits of the Gray Matters software, but their technical backgrounds varied. She'd personally designed the programming coursework for these workers, who had degrees in forensic science, applied mathematics, neuroanatomy, and elder counseling.

Their typing could create a powerful hum, but today, their hands were busy elsewhere. The Codelings pulled off wireless headsets and dug deep into their pockets to retrieve wallets. They glowered at their muscle-bound taskmaster who ran a wide circle around them.

"You know it!" Jack shouted. "You *know* I'm the best!"

Even after three years in her employ, Jack's bad behavior held her interest. He dressed the part of impish jock in a muscle shirt, Gore-Tex running pants, and green cross-trainers. Few but Alice—or perhaps L.A. Fitness—offered a workplace where he could be taken seriously.

Jack addressed the Codelings. "I will now accept tribute."

Fifty-dollar bills passed around the octagon of desks until they reached Jack's outstretched hand.

"Okay," Alice said, "what's going on?"

Jack bowed to Alice, then turned back to the Codelings. "Behold, my unworthies! Does our queen not look radiant in her Hum hoops?"

"She does," said Eddie, the most senior of Alice's coders. Standing barely an inch taller than Alice, Jack had dubbed him "GM's own Tyrion Lannister." Though meant to sting, the comparison flattered. Unlike his Game of Thrones namesake, Eddie had premature baldness and a circular jawbone that bore a closer resemblance to Charlie Brown.

Alice waved a friendly hello to Eddie, and he seemed to forget the pain of losing a half-hour's wage.

"Thank you, gentlemen," Alice said. She tried to synch with the others' mood, but she felt uncomfortable. She was the joke, not its teller. "What's with the cash transfer?"

Jack plucked a cardboard grid off the desk beside him. On it ran thirteen rows of names and numbers, with "24" circled in red.

"Yours truly just won the Hoop Pool. I guessed the exact number of days until you next wore that skirt-thing you've got on today."

"You did *what*?" Alice bit the inside of her cheeks. Blush quelled.

"I prognosticated!" Jack raised his arms in triumph, then tossed his winnings in the air.

"What the fuck?" Alice asked.

"We built this company to routinize the movements of a whole generation," Jack said. "You're surprised I can divine the rhythms of Her Holiness' wardrobe?"

"Asshole," Alice said with a smirk. She pulled back a closed fist and punched Jack in the shoulder. Dude's deltoids felt like granite.

"Go on," Jack said. "Ask how I figured it out."

Alice rubbed her hand. "The Loop told you?"

"Loop was wrong," said Eddie.

"Nailed it lotto-style," Jack said. "Guessed my age."

Alice felt relief, cooled by disappointment. Her protégée hadn't decoded her just yet. To the Codelings, Alice said, "No more betting on the boss." To Jack, she added, "Meeting's in five. Grab Charlie to assemble the Troika."

Jack followed Alice out of the hive and past the three executive offices. He darted in front of Alice and held open the door. It led to a glass-walled conference room that ran along the sharp edge of their building's triangular footprint.

"I think I woke Charlie when I rang him," Jack said. "He's probably still sleeping off his Asian sex-tour."

Alice frowned. Irony compounded the crudeness of Jack's words. Jack was the one who failed to hide a personal life devoid of virtue. Now he smiled in anticipation of a chuckle that Alice wouldn't offer. Instead, she noted his chipped incisor, plus the faint odor of vodka-and-orange juice on his breath.

"Don't be gross," Alice said. "Charlie's not the boozed-up tail-hound."

Jack responded with a nervous tap on the signature earpiece he called Buddy. The gesture made it look like he was taking a call, but doing so mid-conversation was a faux pas. More decipherable was Jack's quick glance toward the liquor tray at the back of the room. Alice had installed it after binging *Mad Men*. She had Eddie keep it stocked so she wouldn't notice if anyone used it to excess. Anyone being Jack.

Three years earlier, Alice had hired the boy almost sight-unseen. Against her better judgment, she ran no background check other than a pre-Loop web search. She took that risk on the hunch that Jack was special. Beneath his dull surfaces sparkled creativity, looking for a way out. His buried genius might have been what reached for the alcohol, to dull its despair.

The only time she'd seen him stagger from a "gut full of piss," as he called it, was the day she'd hired him as an intern. To return some favor or another, Alice had visited the University of Washington business school's shiny new "Pecker Hall," the mispronunciation deliberate on her part. She spent two hours on a judging panel and only Jack's project impressed. Rather than presenting a business plan, he'd enlisted an engineering student to make his Bluetooth earpiece respond to kinesthetic signals. Merely by twitching his head, he started and ended calls, launched apps, and much else.

That got Jack on Alice's team. He'd since proven himself a capable employee.

Jack hoisted himself onto the edge of the conference table. "Charlie left a message," he said. "Want me to check it?"

When Alice nodded, Jack rocked his head to the left. After a moment, he turned back toward Alice. "Charlie's arrival is TBD. Or he got an STD. Bad connection. Couldn't tell which."

CHARLIE

Above the wet bar in the GM conference room hung a digital likeness of Salvador Dali's melting clocks. They showed the current time on the west and east coasts, plus Ahmedabad, which ran a curious twelve-and-a-half hours later than Seattle. All the clocks agreed: Charlie was late.

More bothersome was the disequilibrium from twenty-three hours of air travel. On top of that, Charlie hadn't recovered fully from his stomach bug. His movements were so sluggish that walking into his meeting felt like trudging through waist-high water.

"You look like shit," Jack said.

"Get a diagnosis?" Alice asked.

Charlie pointed at his stomach. "To see the culprit, you'd need to slide a fiber-optic camera—"

"Put one of those cameras in my veins," Jack said, "and all you'd see is tiger blood."

Charlie and Alice exchanged winces. They shared the same wish—that Jack would stop posing as the Aussie Charlie Sheen. He'd regaled them with the story many times. Jack was just a child when Sheen began his public self-destruction. Sheen's fired-and-rehired publicist had since confessed to the episode being a marketing hoax. But that came too late. Jack and his mates already had watched and re-watched a pay-per-view showing of Sheen's Torpedo of Truth tour. Jack had found his role model. When Trump assumed control of the White House the same year Jack began college, the arrogant posturing seemed less dated, more prophetic.

"Got something against me being a *winner*, A.C.?" Jack said.

"No," Alice said. "Just marveling at the wisdom I showed in hiring an imbecile."

Charlie shook his head. "Alice speaks only for herself. I find you—charming."

"You're not going soft on me now?" Jack said. "Did you become a moist-eyed follower of some transcendental guru back in India?"

"No, I just—" Charlie felt a rising wave of nausea. He squeezed his throat to hold it back.

"Or did our Indian operator make you into a socialist?" Jack said. "When I was editing the expansion plan she sent us, the Loop alleged she's a commie."

"Apropos of nothing," Alice said.

"It's bad enough that I work with Democrats," Jack said. "Y'all *hate* winners."

"You ungrateful—" Charlie rubbed his temples. "Our legal counsel squeezed you through a loophole Trump tore into our immigration law."

"That hole's there for a reason," Jack said. "It lets honest blokes like me walk through it, while keeping the jihadists out."

"Presto!" Charlie said. "Work visa becomes US citizenship. Now that you can join us in the polling booth, you should tell your benefactor how she'll be voting."

Jack laughed. "Without a bona fide Bernie in the primary, whatcha gonna do?"

"Eleanor Eisenhower works for me," Alice said. "I'm no Democratic loyalist like Charlie, but I learned my lesson back in 2016. Then a more painful one four years later."

"You promised me we wouldn't speak again about 2020, or what happened after—"

"And so we shan't," Alice said. "This time, I'll back anyone who can stop the bleeding, even if she wears medals on her chest."

"Did the Loop mark her on your sample ballot?" Charlie asked.

"It did. I think the Loop wants a woman in the White House, too."

"Really?" Jack said. "Do you think the Loop's more like a fella, or more like a lady?"

Alice rolled her eyes. "Did I drunk-hire this one, Charlie?"

"I'd never vote Democrat," Jack said, "even if the GOP ran a racist."

"Oh, wait," Charlie said. "It did."

"You *still* sore about the Donald? He's a clown and a crook, sure, but no bigot."

Charlie tried to enjoy the absurdity of Jack's claim, but he couldn't get there. While doing his graduate work in Ann Arbor, he'd always felt a shiver when walking past an all-white clutch of fraternity brothers at night. From the day after Trump declared victory in his first presidential run, the discomfort changed to fear. Sideward glances felt like stares. He'd be denying the truth of his own doctoral thesis if he didn't recognize that people respond to nudges. If Obama had sent out a hopeful vibe, his successor's less subtle signals had more than cancelled it out.

A rebuttal was in order, but Charlie felt fatigued. It was hard to keep his eyes open, let alone focused.

Having lost one sparring partner, Jack turned to Alice. "Your girl Eisenhower could win this whole thing. If you're so in love with her, you should do some illegal fundraising. Or at least invite her over for tea."

"Fine ideas both," Alice said with a wink. "But let's get to business before we have to get Charlie a pillow and a blanket."

Charlie opened his eyes. "I'm still here, mostly."

"How was your visit with Ms Singh?" Alice said. "Can her operation keep up if demand rises exponentially?"

"And that it will," Jack said.

Charlie inhaled through his nostrils, as Sailee had demonstrated for him. He tried to remember the conversation he and Sailee had on this very subject, but a haze obscured his memory of how his Ahmedabad visit had begun. An old lady had put him in a taxi that rode like a moped. He'd slept until

4am, then must have texted Sailee, who met him in the lobby. She took him on a walk as the sun came up. They synchronized each step with the phases of his breathing cycle. He couldn't recall the sounds, sights, or smells of that morning. The cadence of their stroll—that, he could remember.

Charlie exhaled. Shoulders relaxed. Mind cleared.

"Sailee's already interviewing hundreds of operators," Charlie said. "At the wages she's setting, she'll skim the cream off that city. More important is the cognitive testing they're doing. It's still early—and the sample sizes are small—but the Walker Talker beta system may be helping our clients sharpen their minds."

"No shit?" Jack said. "We've bottled healing waters for the coffin-dodger crazies!"

"Please call it dementia," Alice said. "Or Alzheimer's, which it usually is."

"I wasn't insulting Charlie's dad," Jack said. "Just the other mad wrinklies."

"How *is* Pops?" Alice asked Charlie.

"Hard to tell," Charlie said. "He's not out of the woods. But I like to think he's doing a bit better each day."

Part II

The Walker Talker

BARRY

How long since I went to Opening Day? Maybe Charlie's right. Could be our year.

Getting out of the house and riding the People Mover gets me feelin' good. Would you look at all those Lions shirts. Old lady's got a throwback jersey with a "20" on it. Nice to see that other Barry Sanders ain't forgotten. God bless.

Wheels stop. Doors open.

Charlie said something about counting birds, bricks, people. Gotta keep a mind active. Five people step onto the monorail. And off we go. Doors make a racket opening and closing. Ding, ding, dong, over and over.

What was that the man said? Greektown? So many towns in one city. Corktown. Bricktown. Once heard of a Mexicantown, somewhere or another.

The train pokes around the downtown, no hurry to get anywhere. Brick and steel rising higher than ever. Crazy mix of the decades, all these different styles. City stands up proud, long as I don't look down.

More dings and dongs. How many more'll squeeze in here? Woman and her boy in University of Michigan blues and yellows. There's a Spartan—green and white. Celebrating wins from yesterday? Or hedging bets on the Lions today?

Now the man says, "Grand Circus." That's me.

How's anybody supposed to cut through this mob. Big man in a tank-top bumps into me like I'm not here. Silver-and-gold lion's mane down his shoulders. Crazy wig reminds me of a fella my TV showed me the other night. Name was Golden. Maybe he's a Lions fan, too?

"Gonna kick some ass!" It's the silver-haired giant yellin'. "Am I right?"

High-fives come flying at me—no, at him.

Push myself through all that mess and get to the platform. Bit of a wait, then the elevator drops to street level. Crowd's even thicker now, but folks make way. There's the brick coliseum. Ford Field. Too bad GM couldn't buy it instead.

"That you? Barry?"

A familiar voice. Jogs by Pleasant Park every weekend.

"It *is* you!" He points at me and slaps his thigh. Grabs a friend wearing a plastic Lions hardhat—United Auto Workers stickers on its sides. "Chester, you remember this dude. Our very own Barry Sanders!"

Maybe we rode a train together? Or a bus? Miles of interstate—to where?

Hardhat man studies me, then laughs. Thinks he's clever.

"Barry Sanders, eh? Shouldn't you be in the VIP line?"

"What? No, I'm not that fella."

Jogger-man leans in close. "Do you recognize *me*, Barry?" This one thinks he's funny, too. Talking slow, like he's speaking to a baby. "Ter-rence. Wash-ing-ton. We see each other now and again, yeah? Rode home together from the Capitol that one time."

"Why in the Lord's name would I have been in that hateful place? Racists and fascists fill our legislature. Look down their noses at working people like us."

Terrence and his buddy poke clenched fists toward me. Flinch for a sec, then remember. We bump knuckles, and they explode into laughter. Slap my back, too hard.

"Damn!" Terrence says. "That's the kind of fire I heard comin' out of you on the bus ride. Nice to see you still got your edge, old man."

An edge means I'm sharp. See, Charlie?

"Truth is," says Terrence's buddy, "I'd rather do battle in Lansing with y'all than drive off to Madison and join the fight against those right-wing cheeseheads."

Blood boils so hot I can feel sweat on my cheeks. That does it.

"Don't get me started on those peckers. Driving *our* cars to their sausage factories. Every time Packers come here for a game, you can smell the blood and grease on those fans. Can't imagine the stink they must put up in their own park."

Passersby join Terrence and his friend in whooping. Nice to have an audience.

Whole family of Green Bay jerseys rush past. Terrence's buddy shouts, "Kickin' some Packer butt today!"

"Damn straight," Terrence says with a nod. "Good to see ya, Barry, but we gotta scoot. This our year?"

"Sure is."

There goes Terrence, jogging off as usual.

Keep pushing that walker. Slowin' down for a long security line. Nobody's moving.

Getting restless. Fidgety. Tap the phone on my walker. Try talking to it.

"How ya doin', Sally?"

Makes me feel silly when she doesn't say anything back. Where's she at? Invited her to the game. Still thirty minutes to kick-off , but c'mon.

"Ticket, sir?"

A hand—an usher's hand—reaches at me. Holding some kind of device.

Charlie says, if something's not familiar, ask what it's *like*? The wand grocery clerks use. Yup, a scanner. My ticket has a barcode. Digital barcode.

Tapping the front of my walker makes my phone light up with a cartoon. A Lion springs off big hind legs.

"Just press the button, sir."

"Do what now?"

Usher taps a green button on my phone. Fella looks confused when my phone says back, "Welcome, Barry Sanders. Please tap the green button again and record a memo to yourself."

Guess he's never used a phone.

Still wants my ticket. Pockets have a gum wrapper, wallet, loose transit card.

"Sir, the line's gotta keep moving. Let me access your QuikTik."

Usher slides a finger across my phone. Scanner beeps. "Enjoy the game."

"But I—I didn't find my ticket."

Giggles come from behind. Something funny back there, but can't hear.

"This one's on us, sir."

Heard *that*. Nice to get recognized as a loyal fan. Never turn down a kind offer, Pleasant says. Scoot through the turnstile, and there's the Team Shop.

Window shows rows of tiny helmets. There's the knife-biting Tampa Bay Buccaneers. Chumps lost to us the first time I took Pleasant to the Silverdome. Easy win. Couple days later ended Coleman Young's run as mayor. Missed seeing his name on the ballot. Pleasant said twenty years was enough. That woman never trusted him.

Pleasant had more a mind for politics than football, but she indulged. First words she ever said to me were at the GM plant. "This our year?" she asked me. Lions missed the playoffs, but it was a winning season for us. That goofy face of hers, framed in so many curls. When we made Charlie that winter, boy how she grew. The plumper Pleasant got, the prettier she was. When I held her close and got real quiet, I could hear all three heartbeats at once.

Not quiet in here. Real soon, fans only gonna make it louder.

There's my aisle. Heads turning all around for another one of those ushers. Rushes up to lift my elbow and ease me into a nice seat. "Disabled Section?" That's not me, but it's a good seat. Usher folds up my contraption so its phone pokes just left of my head.

After ten years of marriage, only grievance was not having

a second child. Pleasant knew how disappointed I was with Charlie. Boy cried at his first Lions game. Said the crowd hurt his ears. Too noisy to think. Well, it's a football game, son!

She cuddled me good that night. Cooed in my ear.

"Gonna fix you up another boy right here and now."

Oh, goodness.

"Gonna get a linebacker out of you tonight."

Whoa.

Woman was good to her word, nearly. Barry Jr. was no linebacker, but turned into a fine wide receiver. Then one day, our little gazelle ran off into the desert.

Getting dark all of a sudden. Crowd starts to really buzz. Silver and Blue cheerleaders come roaring out of the tunnel. When did we get cheerleaders? Pleasant wouldn't like me lookin' at those shorty shorts. Skinny midriffs. Big weaves.

There's that tingling again. No, my phone. Press the button but can't hear.

"Mr Sanders?"

"Gotta speak up! Almost kick-off, Sally. Where are you? Wish I could see you."

"Yes, Mr Sanders, that is a capital idea. It would be most pleasing if you had at least a still image...proper video chat... your phone. Until then, Charlie...upload a picture."

"What now?" Half those words made no sense. "Something with my phone?"

"What you have is not exactly a phone. However, some still call it that."

Now she's got the idea. If I press my ear to her, Sally's loud enough to hear.

"Mr Sanders, I can see from your geo-location that you are at your football, ah, soccer game. You asked me to make sure you got a Megatron Burger. That does not sound like a healthy choice, but—"

There's that tone again. "Burger sounds nice. Maybe later."

"And a New Jersey—"

"A what?"

"I am truly sorry, sir. I am quite busy doing trainings today. I should have read this transcript more carefully. I apologize. Did you at least find your seat?"

"I'm fine, thank you."

"Shall I call you back when I find out about New Jersey?"

"No hurry there, Sally. Say, you happen to know my son's shirt size?"

"I'm sorry, Mr Sanders. I am not familiar with Charlie's measurements."

"Not Charles. He couldn't care less about football."

"I see, sir."

"I'm gonna pick one up for Barry Jr."

CHARLIE

Midnight approached. Charlie was surprised to find himself awake so late on a Saturday. He'd considered taking a red-eye the night before and spending forty hours with Dad, but that would have been folly. This week had been exhausting. More work waited for him, even now.

As a symbolic gesture, he avoided going to GM on a weekend and instead did all his coding from his one-bedroom Capitol Hill apartment. He could have afforded a lavish apartment for the salary Alice paid, but empty rooms made him feel too alone. He preferred this glorified efficiency unit. Kitchen, office, and living room were all part of one big space. He never needed to close bedroom or bathroom doors. Removing the bedroom door had crossed his mind, but that was a bridge too far toward admission that he lived so entirely alone.

"Call Sailee," he said to the zune tablet on his lap.

The call went straight to voice mail. Unprepared to leave a message, he tapped out.

The Loop seemed to sense his unwillingness to sleep. It popped onto his screen an algorithm Charlie had recently edited, with black font over a periwinkle window. Perhaps the mellow color was designed to help him relax?

Instead, it made him think of Alice, who'd worn a similar hue the day before. He'd only glimpsed her passing in the hall. She'd also been working from home of late. As if the product launch hadn't been enough, she'd become obsessed with the presidential election. Whether out of conviction or just to drive Jack nuts, she was holding a fundraiser next week for Eisenhower. Alice's candidate had secured the Democratic nomination to the surprise of many pundits, if not the Loop.

Charlie would have chided Alice for becoming so distracted by politics, but it was nice to see her passion rekindled. That part of her had laid dormant for years. After Clinton's defeat, Alice swore that the next woman she supported would win. The exact words were grandiose, even for her. "I'll see to it personally. Russian hackers ain't *shit* compared to me."

Charlie stared at the code on his screen. The equations he'd crafted in graduate school—and refined at GM—estimated behavioral tendencies. They accounted for most of the actions he took in his life, day-by-day and year-by-year, but he still couldn't model dynamic systems. Strong theories needed the capacity to anticipate when a change was coming. What would signal that an ongoing relationship was doomed? What could inspire a person to drop a self-destructive habit? When and how such changes occurred remained a mystery, for his algorithms no less than for those tangled together inside the Loop.

Yes, he could have predicted that he'd find a job solving sociological puzzles with a keyboard. No, he couldn't have seen himself working for someone as odd as Alice. Then again, he hadn't chosen her. It was the other way around.

Before Charlie had finished his dissertation on behavior prototyping, a pre-Loop serendipity engine had steered him and Alice into the same chat-seminar on aging. Charlie confessed to feeling helpless about his father's worsening condition, and Alice brainstormed with him on developing adaptive software for seniors. Before the session ended, Alice had booked Charlie a first-class flight to Seattle.

Their face-to-face introduction came over Kenyan something-or-others at a Belltown Starbucks. The job interview felt more like a debate. He and Alice reviewed and rejected approaches to modeling habits and attitudes. They found merit in bits and pieces of Charlie's doctoral thesis, scraps from which they might quilt a stronger theory. All this from a woman who was dressed to resemble something like Little Orphan Annie. Back then, he didn't yet know that wearing this particular outfit meant she'd gotten behind in her laundry.

When he felt they'd reached a breakthrough, she'd pushed back.

"Okay, but does this add up to a coherent theory?" Alice lifted her mug and drained it. "Or are we deluding ourselves?"

"The traditionalists don't share my view," Charlie replied. "But I believe people the world over live their lives following a very limited number of paths. There's infinite variation in each person's stylistic detail, from how we wear clothes to the way we cook food. True unpredictability, though, is a sign of mental illness. My Dad would be happier if he could spend the rest of his days walking the same paths, watching the same channels, and voting for the same party that he has his entire adult life. When he's lucid, he knows what he wants."

"It's easy enough," Alice said, "to record memos or wire clients into call centers. That's where we'll start, but we need to be more ambitious. How do we keep Dad moving even when he can't think for himself? I'm asking if we can translate your theories into a complete equation. I've got the coders to make operational whatever you can imagine, no matter the scale."

"The math won't produce until we feed it enough data."

Alice reached toward the Hello Kitty book bag that leaned against her chair. "There's nothing *but* data out there. That's what the Obama team figured out first. Mining and targeting elected the first black president. It reelected him even after the Great Recession. Then Trump mixed data with social media to defy the pollsters."

"I didn't see that one coming either."

"Really?" Alice looked disappointed. "He's an iconoclast. So was Bernie. People respond to that. I should know—it's my personal brand."

"But this business we're making, it's about helping seniors, not politics. Right?"

"Sure," Alice said. She slid a contract across the table.

Charlie signed without hesitation.

In the five years since that initial meeting, some of what they foresaw came to pass. Alice's bet on her company proved lucrative. Charlie's father was in better shape than he'd have been without the techs rushed to him for beta-testing.

Other events had defied expectations. He hadn't imagined his little brother would fly off to Afghanistan. That improbability cascaded into ever-worse ones. When he got word that Barry Jr. was coming home in a casket, Charlie felt responsible for failing to forecast that outcome. When Pleasant's heart failed shortly thereafter, her death crushed Charlie's spirit.

As he moved through the usual stages of grief, Charlie grew resentful of a military that wasted the life of his only brother. Another brown body on the pile of dead soldiers. For what?

Barry became sullen. Inert.

For a time, father and son fought and argued about everything and nothing. Charlie insisted they investigate Barry Jr.'s death, but even talking about it made Barry's heart ache. The events also stumped the Loop, which solicited unwelcome flower orders from Charlie's friends. It scheduled group counseling sessions Charlie never attended.

Outside Charlie's apartment, strong winds gusted. A tiny clip-on earring hanging from his window latch swung forward and back, tapping the pane. Like anyone with a sense of fashion, he'd stopped wearing that accessory. He missed the brief time when this forerunner of the metaphorical Loop was a must-wear item. Back then, Charlie could walk down the street and feel the vibration on his ear lobe whenever he approached a "high compatible"—usually someone with union parents, a sibling in the military, and a passion for civil rights. If the tiny device sensed a potential soul mate, it buzzed so fast his ear would burn.

"Call Sailee," Charlie said to his zune.

It rang, but no answer.

Sailee's hours were erratic. She had to navigate operators living in a time zone opposite their clients. He waited for Sailee's outgoing message just to hear her voice. He ended the call without leaving a message. Charlie closed his eyes and went back to his last visit to Ahmedabad.

After two days' convalescence in his hotel, he'd rallied. Charlie managed to make it through a full workweek before heading home. He and Sailee made a formidable team. They sketched plans to rent new office space and devised a strategy for raiding talent away from call centers in Delhi and Mumbai.

At the end of Charlie's last full day, Sailee invited him to see more of the city.

"The traffic won't be so scary," she pleaded.

"I'd rather just use the car service. It's late. I'm tired."

"And scared of traffic? But I am a safe driver, Mr Charlie. One can fully appreciate Ahmedabad only by touring it on the seat of my moped. I can take you to a proper restaurant."

Charlie raised an eyebrow. "Should you call your gramma to chaperone?"

Sailee slapped Charlie's shoulder. "India may exist in five centuries at once, but please."

Charlie followed her out of the office and into the elevator. "It's just—she sounded pretty alarmed when you had me laid up in your bedroom."

"Oh, dear. You heard that?"

"I wasn't *dead*. Still not, yet."

Sailee frowned. "You will be safe on my scooter, if that is what worries you. And do not concern yourself about Nani. She just wants to protect me from myself. For someone with her history, it is sweet how reactionary she becomes on matters pertaining to her granddaughter."

Sailee's brown eyes sparkled when she spoke. Charlie reminded himself that men are prone to misconstrue kindness for flirtation. He wondered how often Sailee had that problem. Was that why not one man worked on Sailee's floor?

When they exited the building and he saw Sailee hop onto a diminutive Vespa, his fear returned to restore his emotional equilibrium. Tentatively, Charlie climbed onto the long black vinyl seat behind his driver, and off they went.

On a busy avenue, auto-rickshaws and sedans jockeyed for position. Each direction of traffic used three of the four lanes for passing and dodging. On the outer margins of the road, pedestrians maintained the charade of a sidewalk. A moped buzzed past them with less than an inch of clearance. It ferried a jacketed driver and two young women in yellow and orange saris. The teenager sitting in the middle clutched a swaddled infant. The friend on the back idly texted at thirty kilometers per hour.

Though it had opportunities, the Reaper chose not to visit Charlie on that ride. Even so, feeling Death's gentle breath on his neck added to his excitement. He'd started with his hands gripping both sides of the seat, but once the shock of his surroundings wore off, he realized he'd be safer wrapping his arms around Sailee's waist. She shot him a sideward glance when he made the move, but nothing more. Somewhere along the way, she scooted back a centimeter to press against him, or maybe he scooched forward when they hit the hundredth bump. Either way, the intimacy was electric. By the time they arrived at his hotel, he needed a shower.

That would have to wait. After getting Charlie checked in, they took booth seats in the hotel lounge, where Sailee eased him into a pleasant conversation over rice and soup. They discussed politics. Each seemed eager to please. Charlie chided his own government for stalling global climate policy. Sailee admitted that India's industrial boom posed an environmental threat of its own.

When dinner ended, Charlie felt a wave of nausea. Sailee helped him back to his room. Gastric unpleasantness followed. When his spasms subsided, Charlie found himself in his bed, Sailee by his side. She got up periodically to refresh the cool washcloth draped on his forehead. A drop of water trickled toward his mouth. She ran a forefinger across his upper lip.

That was as close to a kiss as he'd come in longer than he cared to admit.

Charlie felt a pleasant hum in his lap. He sent a hand down to explore the area, only to brush against a vibrating zune. Before he could adjust himself, Sailee's face appeared. A cold panic seized Charlie until he confirmed that Sailee could only see him from the shoulders up. Even the Loop didn't know his pants were on the floor.

"I cannot talk long," Sailee said, "but I see you are up late. Was there something urgent?"

Charlie bought himself a second. "Um, hello?"

Sailee laughed. "Yes, hello."

"I was just thinking about Dad," Charlie lied. "About how we're helping him—to, ah, live on his own terms."

"He does seem happy." If Sailee noticed Charlie's awkwardness, she made no note of it. "I do wish his neighborhood map updated online more often. Did you know that the park he visits is not geo-located?"

"Our old neighborhood never had much of an online presence," Charlie said. "Even if the Loop can't find him, we're keeping Dad close to home. He's safe so long as he travels in familiar places. Most folks like him get farmed off to industrial care facilities. That's not where he belongs. He's sharpening up. This is the best he's been since we lost Mom."

"About that," Sailee said. "Barry's Loop bio shows he is a widower, with you his only child. Twice now he has spoken of

Barry *Junior*. Your father called this man 'my son.' If you had a brother, you would have mentioned him, surely."

"What exactly did he say?" As soon as he asked the question, Charlie regretted it. This was not a thread that needed pulling—not now. Not with Dad.

"He told me that he had not heard from Barry Jr. in quite some time."

"No, he wouldn't have. In fact, tell me immediately if he does hear from Barry Jr. But don't ask him about it."

"Well, *do* you have a brother?"

"Drop it, okay? Your job is to help him get through the day."

"Yes, Mr Charlie. Sooorrry to be a bother."

The screen went blank. The Loop pushed the periwinkle coding interface back in front of Charlie's eyes. Speakers played smooth jazz for him. The unfinished equations on his zune beckoned, but he couldn't shake the image of Sailee's worried face. In the glare of his screen, that expression nearly matched the reflection of his own.

JACK

Jack awoke in a panic. He sat upright and tried to get his bearings. His skin was as wet as the white sheets that tangled his legs. Air conditioning hummed from a wall unit beside his bed. Jack shivered. The only item of clothing on his body was a pair of white briefs, soaked to translucence. He caught scents of salt, sweat, rum. A more purposeful inhalation detected urine, though only a trace.

"Where are you, Jack?" he said to himself. "What'd you do, champ?"

He kneeled on the bed and tried to trigger memories by surveying his hotel room. Silver-striped wallpaper. Office desk and chair. Fridge, with door open and empty racks. Enormous window looking onto a nightscape of blinking colors and a scaled-down Eiffel Tower.

Jack licked his lips—the only part of his body that felt dry. He tasted something sour.

"Vegas, baby."

On the bedside table, he'd left himself a note. "Virginia = Vijul. Answer the call." That intel might make sense when the time came to use it.

Beside the memo lay his earpiece, the same one he'd created three years ago to impress Alice. They met in person on the same day he finally got the device working properly. It was sacred.

On days like this, the gadget also served as a lifeline. He popped it into place and wiggled his head.

He heard, "September 18, 2am Pacific Time."

To check its battery, he made an exaggerated pucker.

"Fully charged."

Whatever he'd been doing that evening, he'd found the presence of mind to place Buddy on its charging pad.

Jack had become even more dependent on the device than he

was on liquor. Buddy, booze, and he formed a loving three-way, with the earbud sustaining him as a functional alcoholic. Even during conversations and meetings, Buddy fed Jack a stream of audio, podcasts, voicemails, and spoken texts. The seawall of sound strained his multitasking capacity, but it held back the toxic waves of mania and depression that Jack had known his entire life.

Following family tradition, his first course of treatment had been Carlton Draught. When he became old enough to buy his own, he discovered the harder spirits. Schizophrenics go mad from the voices filling their heads. Buddy and booze blocked them out.

"Devil finds work for idle thoughts," Jack said.

He nodded to turn on Buddy's music mode. "The Land Down Under" began. It was his Homesick Mix, which must have been playing last night when he was—

"What *was* I up to last night?"

This playlist meant he'd wallowed in adolescent memories. Though often blitzed as a teenager, Jack won high enough marks in school to attend the university of his choice. The only parent he'd ever known was Mum, who rooted some stallion while on holiday in Perth, or so she claimed when he asked about his father.

Tied to the balcony railing outside his room, Jack's pants billowed like a windsock. A burgundy camisole fluttered beside them.

"Guess I'm the stallion now."

Whatever he and his guest had done last night, they'd left the room a shambles. Why the leather couch had a rip in it, he couldn't say. He remembered seeing a spiked bracelet. Was that something his companion wore? Or did he wear it on his...

Thank God for maids.

Jack's mother could have sure used one. How she maintained their domicile while drunk or high the better part of each day was a puzzle he didn't want to try solving.

An unwelcome memory flashed through his mind. Jack was picking up the house and found Mum awake in the bathtub, a man underneath her. He'd been planning to ask if he might attend college in America. "Just go!" she shouted. "Get out!" Jack chose to interpret the command more broadly than she meant it.

To shake himself out of the reverie, Jack got out of bed and punched the wall.

"Fuckin' hell," Jack said as he shook his wrist. He'd left a mark, but the blow hurt him worse than his target.

He switched Buddy to the "Adonis genes" playlist and jacked up the volume. High-energy dubstep rocked his head. Instead of quieting his mind, the manic soundtrack took him to darker memories. The only salve for those was ritual atonement.

Jack threw on gym clothes, bought a cheap digital watch in the gift shop, and went back out on the Strip. Even in the middle of the night, he could find what he was looking for between the casinos.

After a half-hour of hunting, he approached a group of six men his same age, all dressed in Renaissance attire. One carried a short lance crafted from PVC pipe, another carried a wooden sword.

"Hey, dungeon lords!" Jack shouted. "C'mere!"

The tallest one wore a red cloak and wizard's hat. He turned to Jack and said, "Fuck off."

The heaviest member of the group stepped between Jack and the wizard. This dude wore what looked like metal plates of armor and a teardrop shield on his left arm. His right hand hefted an axe. Gray duct tape covered the blade, which could have been rubber, plywood, or anything.

Jack hoped it was metal.

"Here's the deal," Jack said. "I bet you take some serious shit for dressing like yobbos."

The wizard pointed a long finger at Jack. "I say again, good

72

sir, *fuck you*."

"That's right," Jack said as he hopped, or wobbled, from left to right. "Fuck me. Fuck me up. That's my offer. I've got mutant blood in my veins, but I won't even try to defend myself. Let's see what you can do."

"C'mon," said the wizard. "This drunk fuck's wasting our time. We've gotta get to Excalibur."

As the dwarven fighter turned away, Jack punched one of his plates, which clanged. On the sound, the group quickly formed a half circle around their tormentor.

Jack steadied himself. He tried to catch each person's eye. "You get ten seconds to throttle me. Trust me, I owe it to you. Not you personally, but—I'm reaching for my watch now. After ten ticks, it'll bloody beep. That's your cue to scram. Until then—"

Jack raised a finger over the watch and pressed a button.

"It's *on!*"

When Jack's watch chirped, he became a Tasmanian devil. He feigned punches in every direction until the wooden axe landed on his spine.

"There we go!" Jack spun around and received a second blow to the gut.

His watch chimed as he fell to the ground.

"Now, scram," he said in a hoarse voice.

And so they did, he guessed. All he remembered was feeling cool sidewalk under his throbbing back. And moisture—there was something wet beneath him. Maybe he landed where a soda spilled. Maybe it was blood.

Buddy woke him by playing the long-dead dance hit "Barbie Girl." Jack clutched sore ribs when he tried to laugh at the incongruity. The Loop had set this ringtone based on associational logic he couldn't fathom.

The digital readout on the wall clock read 6:00. The tune kept playing. It echoed inside his head, which felt heavier than lead.

Why had he instructed the service to call him back so early? What message had he left for himself? This was Buddy's most sacred purpose—using the GM call center as a lifeline to resuscitate himself from drunken stupors and get him back on task. Nonstandard usage, to say the least, but it was the only way he could hold onto his job, Alice, anything.

A purple sliver of daylight colored the horizon behind the Eiffel. At least he knew what city he was in. Still, he'd have to check his keycard to recall his hotel's name.

Jack popped Buddy in his ear and took the call.

"Mr Ricky Vaughn, sir?"

"Yeah." Jack picked up the notepad by his bed. "Is this—Virginia?"

"No, sir. Virginia, as you call her, has taken holiday. I have her assignments today, Mr Vaughn. My name is Sally."

Jack held his temples and quizzed himself. *Who was Sally? Sally. Sail-ee. Shit.*

"Mr Vaughn?"

Jack cleared his throat and did his best old-man grumble. "Never mind, honey. Thanks for calling. G'bye."

SAILEE

GM clients rarely hung up on operators. It had never happened to Sailee, though Barry was the only client she still called. Today's shift on the phones was an exception—a special favor for a friend.

Sailee reread the memo this client had recorded. The content was entirely shocking, but there was something else odd about it. She and Vijul wrote the user manual for the GM call system, yet Vijul had not properly logged this memo record. Sailee had found it by doing an administrator-level database search, something for which only she and her friend had authorization.

Whatever the abnormalities, protocol dictated a callback. Clients were often on guard against telemarketing scams, but a second try would usually do the trick.

Sailee tapped her mouse and waited. The indicator light showed the call went through, but it rang with no answer. As per procedure, she would stay with the call however long it took.

After two minutes, the client came on the line. "Sorry, thangyou," said the same odd voice—a mumbly tongue in yogurt. "Go ahead."

"Hello, Mr Vaughn, this is your GM callback."

"Yesh."

"Sir, what follows is the memo you left with us four hours ago. You wrote, 'First off, before we get to the goodies, remember you have to deliver that report tomorrow morning. Full sales update.'"

"Shure."

Sailee cleared her throat. "The transcription may not be spot on, Mr Vaughn, but I will read what I have. 'Congratulations for hammering out your man metal. You have on your arm a bouncy bridesmaid. Say hello, Amelia. Amelia Bedelia. You wrote the deed on her, so good on ya. Another casualty from your bomber run over the strip. If you blacked out before you got back to Paris, no shame in that. Remember—you're not of, by, or for the normals. You are special. A fighter pilot. Don't let the blues rule you. No shame, no regrets. Just keep winning, sunshine.'"

Sailee bit her lip. She considered herself modern by Gujarati standards, but if she understood the memo, this man engaged in shameful behavior. Her operators could not be expected to read the perverted journal entries. She resolved to send a policy note to Charlie.

"That is the end of the memo, Mr Vaughn."

"Okay."

The line went dead.

On behalf of her grandmother, her dearly departed mother and father, and her nation's collective sense of decency, Sailee felt incensed. A policy note was not enough. Nani said that when confronted by evil, one had to be inventive first, bold second.

That dictum jarred loose a realization. The Walker Talker's beta-test clients were retired or held jobs that sounded like the make-believe work of aging board members. Yet this Mr Vaughn believed his sales report was time-sensitive.

Sailee ran a search on this unusual client. His calls came every two to four weeks and went directly to Vijul, who transcribed each message. Could Vijul really have typed up that foul language without telling Sailee? Her friend could be bawdy, but to read such things back to an American stranger was worse than immodest.

Routing data showed that Mr Vaughn's incoming calls were shunted into a buffer, then released for transcription only when Vijul came on shift. Likewise, the scheduled callback times were synchronized for when Vijul would be in the office. Had Sailee logged in as any other caller, she would not have seen the memo.

Vijul lacked access to GM's internal code, so she could not have arranged this process. None of the Codelings had this administrative level, which left three suspects—Charlie, Alice, and Jack. Only one of those was the likely culprit. Beyond brief teleconferences, Sailee had little first-hand knowledge of Jack, but Charlie shared anecdotes that made her shiver.

Sailee rang the number one more time. While waiting for an answer, she read the memo archive for the client codenamed "Ricky Vaughn." Each message contained salacious reminiscences and cover stories for when Jack sobered up after one of his so-called "luscious lapses." Disgusting.

"Yesh?"

"Jack Thompson, I presume?"

No response.

"I know it is you. Believe me, sir, I do not need to hear your voice. Any apology would lack sufficiency and would insult both me and my dear friend, Vijul. You have no regard for the spiritual damage you have done by forcing her to read back your vile words. She is a young, unmarried woman with good prospects. What kind of man are you, sir?"

"Was that a *rhetorical* question?"

No contrition? No surprise.

"I'm the sort of bloke you can't handle."

"Oh, pleeease!" Sailee clucked. "You are soooo disgusting. Would you still feel brave if I relayed this incident to Mr Sanders? Would you prefer I speak directly to Ms Coleco?"

A cough—or choking sound—preceded the reply. "Cut the crap, Sally. You aren't scaring me. They know I party."

"Do you have no worry for the violence you are doing to your soul? What about those poor 'conquests' you defile?"

Jack laughed. "I'm no happy clapper, but if Jesus died to atone for sins, aren't I obliged to maximize the value for his sacrifice?"

"That is just—horrible. In every way. You cannot be serious."

"Finished?"

"Are *you*?"

"You're way out of bounds on GM protocol, Sally. Did you think of that?"

She had not. He was right.

Sailee turned away from her desk. Were it not for the mid-rise apartment complex across the street, Sailee could see Gandhi's ashram from her building's small round windows. The windows needed cleaning. Ahmedabad's gritty air gave their panes a sepia tint.

"Okay," Jack said, "let's just call it a draw. I won't embarrass you. You won't embarrass yourself."

"Don't *ever* call us again." Sailee punched the connection closed.

ALICE

Alice slipped away from the crowd gathered in her penthouse condo. Mingling with campaign donors held no appeal.

Her quick escape was aided by the fact that she wore black Versace—modest attire amidst the fifty-odd tech entrepreneurs in her living room. This time, she had dressed to make an impression on a woman.

With no necklace, bracelet, or handbag in tow, Alice's only accessory was a zune, which she activated as she entered her master bathroom. The day had gotten away from her, and she hadn't yet seen Jack's sales report. Those data would tell her how much disposable cash she had on hand. If her brief meeting with Eisenhower went well, she would divert surplus profits into the Democratic nominee's treasury. Sort of.

Alice clicked a sequence of commands until she found and downloaded Jack's summary report. In one word, the figures were *phenomenal*. Their low-budget costume drama at the Pike Place Market had yielded an obscene number of pre-orders for the Walker Talker in just two weeks. She remembered the old Union Carbide slogan she had read in a college course on global capitalism. "Today, something we do will touch your life." Damn straight.

Jack had inserted in the sales report the icon of a lotus flower. Alice figured it for an Easter egg, and passing her finger over it brought up a saffron spreadsheet with a Sanskrit-style font. It showed the Loop Views Index for GM on the Walker Talker's release day, broken down into five-minute slices. According to Jack's notations, it was clear that the intervention of Mahatma Golden had jerked their product's attention-centrality upward.

Alice laughed at the thought of putting Mahatma on the payroll, but a more serious question nagged at her. What was his angle in all this? She didn't yet have the measure of the man.

Alice knew his biography—how the son of an international businessman turned into a best-selling author. Still, it was hard to know what part of his life was real and what was theater.

Equally disturbing, Mahatma had discerned a truth few others had noticed. GM was steering a cross-section of humanity into a narrower concept of the future. Keeping people on accustomed paths made their lives more sensible, but also less creative. Surely the madman in homespun couldn't see GM's full trajectory for the coming years. Neither Jack nor Charlie saw that far ahead.

Her colleagues also wouldn't have guessed that Alice envied the grand ambition she saw in Mahatma. On the flight back from Thereport, Alice had jotted down the words, "Project X and Project Y." Villains like Mahatma devised secret plans as a matter of professional responsibility, but heroes needed them, too. At least the proactive ones did, and Alice fancied herself as the kind of person who acted on the world—not the other way around.

An odd question came to mind. If her secret projects came to fruition, who would raise a glass with her to celebrate? Even now, with her condo full of elites dining on catered delicacies, she had retreated to the bathroom, just for the privacy. She imagined Jack sitting on the rim of her tub, clad only in a towel. Or less.

The digital clock on Alice's zune blinked at her. She stood, smoothed her dress, and checked her reflection. Perhaps fire burgundy wasn't the right hair color for today's event, but not a strand was astray. Besides, the jet black dress set it off beautifully. She had to look her best for the next President of the United States.

Alice had done her homework on Eleanor Eisenhower, even going outside the Loop. By all accounts, Eleanor was her father's daughter. Though time had reduced him to a senile widower, her father had been a powerful man. Serving as a Navy vice admiral, he envisioned military careers for his two sons. Before completing infantry training at Camp Geiger, Eleanor's older brother had driven his Toyota pickup over a guardrail on Interstate 40, taking his twin brother with him, plus their hound in the truck bed. The dog lived another five years, with a limp. Her father was reputed to have told a teenage Eleanor that her brothers "had gone to Heaven the way they'd arrived, one within a minute of the other."

Eleanor's father expected little from her and asked for even less. Perhaps because of that, she entered the officer corps. Choosing the Army avoided any favoritism owed an admiral's daughter. With no spouse and no kids, her soldiers were her family, and they returned a devotion that set her apart. She excelled at logistics and oversaw a team of programmers optimizing the Army's playbook near the end of the Cold War. How could Alice resist an alter ego who assembled her own army of uniformed coders?

As a presidential candidate, Eisenhower continued to make shrewd hires. The best of these associates stood beside her as she exited the elevator outside Alice's penthouse. Into the foyer stepped Dick Dirksen, the twenty-five-year-old prodigy and *de facto* strategist of her campaign.

Eisenhower had chosen Dirksen for his talents, not his magnetism. She was in her seventies and looked distinguished in a gray skirt-suit. Dick wore the wrinkled white shirt and chinos that a Codeling might dig out of the closet on date night. Eisenhower had the toned shoulders, square jaw, and sharp eyes of a field marshal. Dick, not so much.

Alice locked eyes, then hands, with Eisenhower.

"General Eisenhower, I'm Alice Coleco, CEO of Gray Matters. On behalf of Wired Women Northwest, let me welcome you to the Emerald City."

"Thank you, and please, let's go with 'Eleanor' tonight. I look forward to hearing the remarkable stories you women can tell."

Murmurs filled Alice's condo. News of the candidate's arrival spread. A clutch of bodies crowded the entryway.

"We're so honored you could make it," Alice said, "I know you're busy—"

"Nonsense," Eleanor said. "We were scheduled just down the road at Boeing. It's no secret we're running short on cash and going soft in the West, of all places. Dick told me not to choose a tobacconist-governor from Georgia as my veep, but I had to run with someone I could trust."

Jack and Charlie squeezed in behind Alice. Charlie stared at his shoes. The sheepish gesture caught the candidate's eye.

"Buck up, soldier." Eleanor lifted Charlie's chin. "What's your name?"

"Charlie Sanders."

"I'm guessing you work for one of these Wired Women?"

"Yes, ma'am."

"Well, tell you what, Charlie. You can write me a check today, too."

Laughter and applause. Eleanor replied with friendly waves before locking eyes with Alice. In a softer voice, she said, "I understand that before we address the full gathering, there's time for a one-on-one."

Alice nodded and pointed toward a glass door that opened onto a covered terrace. She had imagined this scene as one where she charmed and steered the candidate, not the reverse.

"Lead the way," Eleanor said.

While Charlie ushered Dick and the rest of Eleanor's team back into the condo, Alice walked out of the foyer and onto a glass-walled porch. The panoramic view overlooked the Puget Sound, and faint whiffs of saltwater drifted up to greet them. In the distance, a pair of commuter ferries crossed paths.

Alice guided Eleanor onto a Danish porch lounge, bought for the occasion. A plate of dried blueberries, herbed chèvre, and sesame crackers on a small table caught Eleanor's eye. She popped a pair of berries into her mouth.

"Tell me," Eleanor said, "what do you use to turn your hair into that hard shell?"

"My stylist calls it a candied perm." Alice shook her head. Not a hair moved. A shoulder roll relaxed her neck, which she'd held high to compensate for the general's stature.

"But we're not here to discuss cosmetology. So..." Eleanor dipped a cracker in the cheese, soft as jam. "You've already bundled three million dollars for my campaign, and Dick tells me to expect more coming soon. That generosity has bought you no favors, but you did earn the right to choose our topic."

"I appreciate that. Let's set policy aside. We probably agree on enough of the particulars, but as I get older—"

Eleanor slapped her thigh. "Older? Darlin', you could be half my age. I was a Lieutenant General at Fort Bragg before you were born."

"What I mean to say is, I—I know that in your speeches, you talk about hearing America's stories. I've got one you might not have heard. Every woman in the living room behind us is bell-curve smart—top two percent, at worst. Like you and me, most never married and have all the time necessary to do great things. That said, you'd be more disappointed than inspired if you knew how much they underperform relative to their capabilities. Every single one of them."

Eleanor lifted her forehead in what looked like an attempt at a raised eyebrow. That feature had caught the attention of the incumbent president, who dismissed the Democratic frontrunner as "Mono-brow."

"I grew up playing games with any boy or girl who could keep up with me. As the years passed, too many of my female classmates copped at being stupid, even in Seattle's best private school."

Alice bit down on her lower lip in response to a rumble in her stomach. Like Mahatma, she hated dwelling on the past. She'd have to endure such memories to make herself understood.

"Sometimes," Alice said, "it meant playing dumb to reassure the idiot boys."

Eisenhower nodded. "Dithering Ophelia falls to the stage, that Hamlet might not seem such the fool."

"It was more than that," Alice said. "Too many girls came to believe that whatever smarts they had were a gift from God, not something needing daily refinement. I feel alone even among the women standing inside my apartment. At my company, I surround myself with precocious boys because I would just scream if a woman working for me tried to hide her full power."

"That's not quite fair," Eleanor said, "but I get the gist."

"What I must know, Ms Eisenhower—"

"Is whether I will exercise my 'full power' in office."

Alice smiled.

"Let me tell *you* a story, Ms Coleco, though I'll have to keep it short." Eleanor looked over her shoulder, as if a staffer behind her was tapping a foot. "Years ago, I had the honor to work on the BRAC—the Base Realignment and Closure Commission. You must have been in high school when the Cold War ended. Back then, we faced the task of what to keep and what to let go. For smaller towns, closing a base could upend their whole economy. Shutting or paring down bigger bases would change the character of a whole community, and ripple out from there. Many local service and support businesses would suffer. On the Commission, we looked at the facts and heard the usual testimony, but I tell you, we made hard choices. Every man and woman in that room was a superior intellect with an open heart to match. We stood by our calls."

"To no avail, I presume."

"When our closure lists went to the electeds—Lord, the hue and cry. They'd been sniping at us like guerilla fighters all the while we worked. We ignored them because we knew they'd have to muster a full majority to reject our list, and that wasn't gonna happen. Even Congress knew what we had to do, so they tied themselves to the mast. The point is, honey, that I got to see a rare animal—the *good* side of Washington. It was a very special time. Nobody on that Commission postured or pretended. We deliberated."

"Hard to believe," Alice said. "But even if you're right, that era's dead. If Trump didn't kill it, he's feasting on its corpse."

"No argument here, darling. That Commission was decades ago, and it was the last time I had an experience like that. It was an aberration." Eleanor leaned back into the lounge cushion behind her. "Since then, I've served both parties, testified before senators, and pushed reports in front of the right eyes. Right now, none of that matters. If I retake the Oval Office, I can push to the front lines our best and brightest, including women like yourself. Get me into that building, and I might call on you to serve."

Alice rolled her eyes. "That would be insane."

"Maybe so." Eleanor tried to tousle Alice's hair. It didn't budge. "Still, I appreciate what you said, plus all you're doing for our campaign."

"Hope it helps."

"You bet it will, kiddo."

Eleanor shook Alice's hand, then stood to stretch into a series of yoga positions. For someone of her status, she seemed remarkably at ease. Either that, or oblivious.

She stood in Mountain Pose, with her chest thrust forward. "My father will soon pass the century mark. He isn't sticking around to watch his daughter do small things. I intend to win in November."

"I intend to help you do just that."

"Excellent, but there's something you can help me with of a more personal nature."

For this, Alice had also prepared herself. "The Walker Talker won't be enough for your father—not in his condition. From what I've heard—"

"No, it won't help. Even so, you aren't one to do small things, are you?"

The question felt rhetorical. And so it was.

"You aim to build more powerful tech, right?"

"We do, but—"

"After the election, I will call on you. Be ready."

Alice nodded.

"Now, if you'll lead the way back in there, I shall a borrower be."

Part III

The Quiet Copilot

BARRY

Nothing in the world tasted like the goodies Pleasant used to stuff in my lunchbox. Leftovers mostly. What she pulled back out of the fridge was better than any chef could cook up fresh. Mashed potatoes, yam cakes, quick breads, thin-sliced beef, wet ribs. One time she caught me finishing lunch on morning break. Who could blame me?

At home, can't do much more than heat up food. Gotta get out of the house for a real meal. Last visit, Charlie showed me couple new places. Can't say where we went, though.

Pleasant and I used to eat at a Cajun restaurant out in Allen Park. Haven't driven that far in some time. No, I don't drive at all anymore.

Sun bounces off two buildings across the street. That one-story flophouse and flat-topped church bring up memories of an old haunt. Trapdoor must be nearby That old bar east of here? Or west?

"Hey, gramps! You're standing in an intersection!"

Young man, maybe twenty years old, got himself a red muscle car. Leans out the driver's side. Shakes his head and spits into the street.

"Which way you goin', old timer?"

Sun's too bright to make out his face, but the car? Dang if that don't look like my old Pontiac Sunbird. Same make and color. Bet my mark's still under the front fender. Maybe this fella'd let me take a look.

Getting out of the walker sure is tricky, but I can manage it. Gotta kneel to get down there.

Why's the young man waving his arms? In that white t-shirt and baggy jeans, looks like one of those crazy people on Woodward.

"What the hell you doing to my car?"

Poke my head back out so he can hear. "Yup, this is one of 'em. There's my 'B' in solder."

Young man looks anxious, but at least his hands are loose. Tight fists would mean he's ready for a fight.

"You having a stroke or somethin'?"

Taking longer than it should, but I get back inside my walker. Slacks look dirtier than Pleasant would like.

"You own this car, son?"

"Course I do." Young man glances left, then right. Looking for a friend? "What were you doin' down there?"

"I built that car. Me and the guys."

"Well, it's my car now."

"Okay, sure, you drive it. But Rascal, Donovan, me, and the rest, we built it. For a time, I drove one just like yours."

Young man has nerve. Rough hands steer me and my walker toward the sidewalk.

"I don't give a goddamn who built what. She's mine, okay? Now I'm gonna drive her down that street. Better not be in front of us when I hit the gas."

Hops into the car, revs the engine, speeds away.

Ain't that something? A Sunbird.

Maybe I gave my last one of those to Barry Jr. when he got his learner's permit. He drove it off to—was it Arizona? Or he sold it?

There's that buzzing again. When the green light flashes, push the button—

"Hello, Mr Sanders."

"Is that Sally?"

"Yes, Mr Sanders. How are you?"

"Fine, honey. How's your mama?"

Line goes silent for a moment. Can't hear me?

"I said, how's your mother?"

"My grandmother is in good health and spirits, thank you. I understand that you are going to have your lunch at an establishment called the Trapdoor? It looks as though you are already there. How is your meal?"

"No, Sally. I'm not there. Or, it's not here. I mean, there's no sign on the window saying it's closed. It's got wood shutters on it, so I can hardly see inside. Looks pretty empty, like they forgot to set up the tables this morning. Maybe somebody didn't show up to work."

"Mr Sanders, I am looking on my map. It says they closed nine years ago. This information could be in error. Your City of Detroit may not be updated as often as most places."

"Where am I supposed to have lunch?"

No answer. Said something rude? Pleasant begs me to watch that language.

"It is not my place to advise you, Mr Sanders."

"What did *you* have for lunch today, Sally? You have barbeque?"

"After a manner."

"You said last week that I should eat more veggies."

"It is not my place to advise you on such matters, but I might have said that."

"Well, where would I get some of those?"

Clicks and clacks come at me through the phone. Sounds like the rainstorm Charlie makes in his old bedroom at night. He'll type on that keyboard 'till dawn. Go to bed, son! Nothing's worth staying up all night worrying over.

"Just one block north is Persian Palace. Head toward Oak Street."

"On my way."

Takes effort to heave this walker over ugly gaps in the sidewalk. Used to feel like I lived in a proper city.

Sally says something. Hard to make out her words.

"I said, have you ever tried tandoori?"

"Ten who?"

"Indian barbeque."

"You mean Indians like Chippewa? Or Indian from that other country?"

"Ah, yes, the country."

Gotta look both ways. Sure enough, there goes some joyrider screaming right past. Can't be too careful these days.

"You know, my boy is in one of those Asian countries."

"Yes, Mr Sanders. He visited us earlier this year."

"You're in the service, too?"

"Yes, I do service for the same company as Charlie."

"No, not him. Charlie works out west. I mean Barry Jr."

Well, it's like Sally said. There's a new restaurant on Oak Street. Low brick building, like a Lego castle with two towers and everything. Three men with wrapped hats and crazy beards on the stoop. Never saw them at the Hamtramck Plant. Wonder what they do for work. And there's a woman with one of those scarf-dresses. Never used to see those around here.

Trump fella says they're everywhere now. Why would a refugee want to live in Detroit?

"Mr Sanders, have you arrived at Persia Palace?"

"Looks crowded."

"I recommend starting with roti and dal soup, mild. Good for your stomach."

"There's good meat dishes in there?"

"I suppose, if you must. They can advise you."

There's that tone again. But Sally's probably tired of holding my hand all afternoon. Wonder what she's been doin' today? Wanna ask, but she keeps telling me it's not polite to talk to her while other people are about.

Gotta press the red button, but first...

"Thank you very much, Miss Sally, for all your help."

"You are most welcome, Mr Sanders. Goodbye."

CHARLIE

As he entered the GM conference room, Charlie's two principal colleagues flirted. Alice was intermittently serious and playful daily with the Codelings and himself. With Jack, it looked different. She drew him closer.

As usual, clothing was part of their ritual. Alice had sent around a memo proclaiming October 1 to be Caribbean Day. The date had arrived, and she wore the outfit first assembled for last year's Seafair parade. High on a billowy white shirt she wore a ceramic parrot pin, which a shoulder-length black wig nearly covered. Jack wore bandana, eye patch, torn shirt, and slacks. More zombie than pirate, but he'd made an effort.

Charlie wasn't in the mood and simply wore a Hawaiian hibiscus print. He entered the room as Jack said to Alice, "Do I see ink under those ruffles?"

Alice pulled back one sleeve to reveal a muddy blur on her wrist.

Jack leaned in close. "Skull and crossbones? Looks a bit cartoonish. No wonder you covered it up. Not there for life, I hope."

Alice frowned. "Yeah, I doubt it'll shiver anyone's timbers. Fortunately, like all things in this life, it's temporary."

Charlie slid into a seat next to Alice. Jack retreated to the opposite side of the table.

"So," Alice said, "you've seen Jack's figures. We've got ourselves another hit song. Let's leave the money-raking to the plebes and talk about writing our next tune."

Jack cocked his head. "Seriously? We just released this thing. There's refinements, adjustments, versioning to be done. You can't—"

"We leave the details to our subcontractors," Alice said. "We're here to innovate. The Walker Talker is dead to us now."

Jack opened his mouth in what looked like genuine shock.

"No, she's right," Charlie said. "We've got to build something better."

"C'mon," Jack pleaded. "Your Dad's doing better on the Talker, yeah? That's a fuckin' miracle. We're *winning*, mate."

"Well, I hope so," Charlie said. "But we've got to keep one step ahead of whatever might hit his brain next."

Alice turned to Jack and tapped the side of her head. "Time to bring out that little secret weapon of yours."

Jack plucked out his slim plastic earpiece and regarded it wistfully. "Guess I'm not heading back to the airport for a serious holiday."

"No," Alice continued. "We're here today to talk about Buddy. Tell me what that little device of yours can do for us. You've had one of our engineers fiddling with it for a year now."

Jack bounced Buddy in his palm, like a father tossing a child in the air. "My little prototype still can't do anything too special," Jack said, "but it's sparked some ideas. Forget all the head-jerking commands. It's hard enough to get grandma to use the remote. Anyway, wearing the device won't work 'cuz the old ducks would lose it faster than their reading glasses. But what if this little slug slipped *into* the ear, like those little larvae in *The Wrath of Khan*?"

Charlie laughed. "That's what you watch on the hotel TV? I had you all wrong, man."

"Micro-hardware deep in the ear," Jack said. "Kind of a hidden Walker Talker."

"Why hide it?" Charlie said.

"Maybe some geezer wants to keep a secret."

"I like it," Alice said. "Or, maybe someone wants to hook up her father, but they'd both rather keep the arrangement secret."

"Spot on." Jack rocked back and forth in his chair. "We can put an antenna boost into anything, or even under clients' skin, and they'll still get their clandestine Gujarati link-up. That'd protect them against their scheming kids, who keep nagging about living wills and checkin' grandpa's nappy for an inheritance."

"Okay," Alice said, "you're unspooling a bit, but I like it. How 'bout you, Charlie?"

Charlie's attention had drifted. Alice and Jack were thinking about GM products from the perspective of their clients. That's what Dad was now—a client.

"Anyone home?" Alice said.

Charlie stared at the wall clocks. In a couple hours, Sailee would see another gorgeous Ahmedabad sunset. "This would change how we use the call center. Plus, we'd have to scale up even faster."

Alice clucked at Charlie, perhaps mimicking Sailee. "You do remember why I brought you aboard this pirate ship, don't you?"

"Loot and adventure!" Jack shouted.

Sarcastic contagion took hold of Charlie and lightened his mood. "I imagine that you were moved to tears by my faith in the divine wisdom of social science?"

"Precisely," Alice said. "I hired you to engineer lifestyle integrity. The Baby Boomers have always been obsessed with having a way of life. They invented free love, self-actualization, eco-tourism. They can't even take a vacation without having it *mean* something. Our first two products generated revenue but distracted us. Our job is to sustain the fantasy of coherence, even as one's grip on reality loosens."

"Okay," Charlie said, "but we can't expect our call agents to do anything more than—"

Charlie stopped himself short. Sailee's probing questions about Barry Jr. came to mind. What if she started asking Dad about Charlie's dead brother.

"Their job is reading back memos," Jack said, "not *ad libbing*."

The statement was true enough, but it sounded oddly defensive.

"That's a problem," Alice said. "But what if our operators could access more comprehensive memos? Sailee insists that her operators want to know more about their clients. They want pictures, full bios, anecdotes. What if we gave them a *lot* more? What if our Gujaratis could figure out a client's next move even before the client knows it?"

Charlie felt an electric pulse rush through his arms—the shock of discovery. Hadn't felt it since graduate school. To keep it flowing, he rubbed his hands together.

"Okay," Charlie said, "let's say a client doesn't know what his next move is anymore. That's the path Dad was headed down before we wired him up. What if he forgets where he likes to eat lunch? Or doesn't remember the name of his favorite park? At that point, he can't even leave a coherent memo for himself, or for an operator to read back."

"Precisely," Alice said. "What then?"

"Now I'm just riffing here," Jack said, "but check this shit out. I once met a Japanese businessman in Little Caesars."

"The pizza chain?" Alice said.

"No, the Harrah's in Vegas. It's near Caesars Palace. Tiny by comparison."

"How much time are you spending in that city?" Charlie asked.

Jack cleared his throat. "So, I chat up this dude, and he says he sells something stupid, like clock radios. Hard to believe, but we end up drinking together. After a few, he shows me his Day Runner—the paper-and-pen deal, thick as those old phone books. I mean, this guy's full Flintstones, yeah? So, he's showing me all these things he's done, where he's traveled, who he met with. Everything."

Jack bounced out of his chair to grab a pad of paper. He flipped through blank pages as he talked. "Then he shows me the coming week and the one after that. He's booked solid. Selling radios, right? Pretty soon he's thumbing past custom-printed pages that go two years into the future. He stops when he gets to the date his oldest daughter will get engaged. And I'm like, 'What?' But he was serious. He flipped to the last page and pointed to his funeral."

"So," Charlie laughed, "what's the takeaway? Want us to hire a psychic salesman?"

Alice beamed at Jack. "Think more Nokia, less Nostradamus."

"Spot on," Jack said. "This bloke had *planned* these things. His life was all laid out. If he can do that for himself—and for his family—why can't we?"

Charlie opened his mouth, but Alice spoke first. "You can build this, Charlie. This is where we've been heading all along."

"Let's say we could create something more thematic than a day planner," Charlie said. "People have coherent 'life worlds,' as the Germans say. There are only so many variations. If we can get people to open up about themselves, maybe we could figure out which one—"

"It's easier than that," Alice said. "To figure a person out, we just need to tap into the Loop. It profiles people like your father without asking a single question. Working-class African American, Detroit native, widower, football fan, whatever."

Charlie shook his head. "Demographic and consumer footprints don't say as much as you'd think. We still need to know his philosophy—his worldview. On the other hand, talking about the Lions does take up a—well, a lion's share of our time together."

"If we couple this meta-profile with Jack's earpiece," Alice said, "what do we call it?"

Jack put his finger to his lips and turned around his pad of paper. Written in the faux-Gothic lettering preferred by Scandinavian metal bands, it read, "The Quiet Copilot."

The font was ridiculous, but Jack had a knack for branding.

GM decisions, large and small, were Alice's to make, but the Troika almost always reached consensus. Nods from Charlie and Alice meant they'd done so once more.

Uncharacteristic silence in the conference room moved Charlie into a state of contentment. He closed his eyes to soak in the sensation.

Instead, he heard noisy chatter from the Codelings down the hall, then a collective gasp. Charlie stood in his chair just as Eddie shouted, "Holy crap! I can't believe they're showing—oh, that's gruesome!"

ALICE

Boasts, taunts, and arguments were commonplace at GM. Eddie's cry, however, conveyed genuine shock.

Alice bolted from the conference room, with Charlie and Jack behind her. All around the octagon, coders stood and stared at a wall-mounted flat panel. It showed a 3D composite video of a train station, seamlessly merging live zune feeds from a dozen or more onlookers.

Eddie noted Alice's arrival. "They're restarting the whole thing in a second," he said. "Just watch."

On the monitor, Eleanor Eisenhower flanked her running mate, Cordele Fitzgerald. Dressed in the long coat of a Wild West sheriff, the lanky Southerner addressed commuters at what the Loop-fed scroll said was the Norfolk Amtrak station.

"We must beeelieve," Fitzgerald drawled, "that we can reweave this nation's iron roads. We wired this country together with fiber cables and can move information as fast as light itself. So why do we still transport people and products no faster than we did after World War II?"

Fitzgerald stamped his trademark boots on the train platform. "We can build better and faster trains than aaanyone, including Japan. We can build a thicker network of rails than aaanyone, including China." Fitzgerald turned to Eleanor and winked. "You know what, General? While we rebuild our railroads, we're gonna find out what other great things America can do with a *real* leader in charge. You and me, we're gonna kick some ass!"

The video froze on that last frame, with Fitzgerald's mouth still open just enough to hiss out the tail end of his obscenity. The image shrunk to a box in the corner of the screen, as a female news anchor read from a script.

"We will honor the request of the Eisenhower campaign to withhold any footage of the accident itself. Early accounts suggest that a young girl in the crowd may have fallen off the train platform. Fitzgerald may have—and we cannot confirm this—he followed the child down to the tracks and lifted her out of harm's way."

"Shit, is he okay?" Alice said.

"I'm sorry," Eddie said.

"What happened afterward," the anchor continued, "remains unclear. We have conflicting eyewitness accounts and will update—"

The Loop then did something unexpected. Its scroll at the bottom of the monitor stopped, then displayed the words "composite zune feeds." Above that, a slow-motion video appeared with the same rotating camera angle first devised for instant replays.

From the opposite side of the Norfolk Amtrak station, Fitzgerald could be seen mouthing "kick...some...ass!" He underscored that last word by swinging his leg out in an awkward gesture that lifted his center of gravity. Slipping on a patch of ice or the tail of his coat, his body hurtled forward and down to the train tracks. Before anyone could reach him, Cordele tried to right himself. He grasped a half-covered rail that ran just outside the main ones.

On that image, the Loop froze its feed. The scroll then resumed by quoting an impromptu obituary spiking on social media. "The most politically cautious candidate on either ticket has done the unthinkable. He literally touched the third rail."

The offices of GM were silent for another replay of the scene. This longer version featured the full horror of Fitzgerald's convulsive demise. Georgia's governor was now a former running mate. Former father of two. Former everything.

"What happens next?" Charlie said.

Alice only heard the question literally. "The proper response would be to grieve."

"For him, or for Eisenhower?" Jack said.

A sharp look silenced Jack before he could say anything he'd regret more completely.

"Of course," Charlie said. "I meant, what happens to the, um, vice presidential—"

"Not a clue," Alice said. "Loop's too focused on debunking the bullshit hero narrative. Let's look it up."

Alice commandeered Eddie's computer and put on the main display the surprising answer. "After the convention," wrote a DC blogger, "the Democratic National Committee chooses the replacement for a dropped or deceased veep. It's not Eisenhower's call."

"Makes sense," Charlie said. "Those rules serve the party's interests. Selection by committee sounds prudent, under the circumstances."

"Who's it gonna be?" Jack said. "Couldn't be worse than that hick farmer."

"Jesus effing Christ," Alice snapped.

"Show some respect," Charlie said. "The man just—never mind."

Something like contrition appeared on Jack's face.

"There's always someone worse," Alice said. "Remember who's in the White House."

Jack raised a hand in protest. "Now hold on, don't rip on the First Family. They—"

"Don't say another word." Alice seethed. "You will *never* say that name again."

Jack ran a finger-zipper across his lips.

The GM staff watched in silence as the Loop and the network anchor parsed instant reactions. Outrage at the false cover story contrasted with genuine sympathy for Fitzgerald's family. New footage showed Secret Service agents whisking Eisenhower from the train platform and into her limousine. National mourning might grant her a two-day bounce, but that would dissipate before Election Day.

Alice fed all this data into the equations running through her mind. She'd invested more in this campaign than the Federal Election Commission would ever know, but it still might not be enough. With both the Republican President and Congress mired in scandals, Eisenhower's slim lead was worrisome. Her latest problem was the charge that she'd neglected her aging father. The war hero had disappeared from public view well before she sought the presidency, but conspiracy theories didn't require precise timing.

A desperate DNC might try anything to staunch the bleeding from this and Eisenhower's other wounds. Cautious optimism had proven fatal more than once in recent elections. Given a chance to reenergize the Eisenhower campaign, party leaders might trot out a dark horse.

Alice typed "Dick Dirksen" into Eddie's keyboard. The Loop retrieved the same tidbit she'd discovered before her meeting with Eisenhower. "Says here that Dirksen wanted someone else," Alice said. "Before she picked Fitzgerald, Dick pushed her to run with Kevin Penn, a congressman from Shanksville, Pennsylvania. He was a firefighter on 9/11 when that plane crashed in the field."

"No shit," Jack said. "A first responder. A life saver, literally."

"And now figuratively," Charlie said with a nervous laugh. "That settles that."

"Maybe," Alice said.

Her intuition—and her equations—thought otherwise.

* * *

Alice had encouraged her reclusive Codelings to learn more about public affairs. Their daily jobs confined them to cubicles, but they did what they could to stay in touch with their clientele. Now that Charlie was feeding them social scientific equations, such lessons became more imperative. An unintended effect: they became newshounds.

After the Fitzgerald Fiasco, the next two days were lost.

Staff regrouped each morning at GM Headquarters to stare at the wall monitors. Far from passive consumers, they used their touch screens to customize the channel displays, sidebar feeds, and tone of the Loop scroll beneath each newscast.

Thus, the full Troika was eating lunch with the Codelings when the other shoe fell. Eleanor Eisenhower emerged from the Watergate Hotel, where the DNC had convened an emergency session to choose her new running mate. The feeds said the selection committee was still deliberating in the Obama Conference Room, but cameras showed Eisenhower walking through the lobby and outside the hotel to greet a throng of reporters.

Something about the scene wasn't right. Eisenhower looked unsteady, as if surprised by the assembled media. Her security detail stepped in front to clear a path. Instead of following them, Eisenhower stopped and scratched her head. She wore only a light sweater on what looked like a windy day in the District. Sure enough, the Loop showed a local temperature just above freezing. It offered an unsponsored link to a Craigslist sub-category: winter clothing.

Before Eisenhower could turn around, questions flew at her.

"How are you feeling, General?"

"Who's your new running mate?"

"When's the funeral?"

"Is Fitzgerald's family suing Amtrak?"

"Is it true you fractured your collar bone?"

The candidate shielded her eyes to block flashes coming from every angle.

"Settle down," she said. "We, uh, we need a bit more time to, ah…"

"South Carolina's Secretary of State says it's too late to print new ballots. Votes for you won't count. Comment?"

Eisenhower straightened up. "I've read the same meta-polling and models y'all have. The good people of South Carolina can't abide a Yankee who hails from *North* Carolina." Her chuckle sounded forced. It got no response. "Playing politics with ballots dishonors the memory of Governor Fitzgerald. It insults the

voters."

The now-iconic wagging of Eisenhower's finger silenced the reporters, who knew it heralded the day's best sound bite. "When a soldier falls on the front line, cowards stop to measure the loss. Patriots honor the dead by charging forward."

Missing the irony of doing so, Eisenhower retreated into the hotel.

Jack stifled a laugh. "What the hell was that? Practically the first words she's said since the accident, and she sounds lost. That's no Commander in Chief."

"Give her a break," Charlie said. "She just lost her running mate."

That possibility calmed Alice's nerves, momentarily. Once Eisenhower disappeared from view, talking heads on every channel gave blistering reviews. And she deserved them.

"They'd better name a running mate fast," Alice said, "or that surreal episode we just witnessed is gonna haunt her."

As luck would have it, the Loop focused less on Eisenhower's nonverbals and more on the content of her words. The scroll noted that "honor the dead by charging forward" loosely rhet-linked back to a nineteenth-century writer, Lord Tennyson. It was close enough to appear an erudite allusion, rather than plagiarism. The Loop's auto-notes noted that Eisenhower's quip also echoed a Kipling poem. Put the two together, and Eisenhower's statement signaled a forthcoming call to increase Afghanistan veterans' benefits.

Such speculative chaining stopped only when the live news feed from the Watergate resumed. The DNC had reached a decision.

"If we don't get Kevin Penn, it's okay," Charlie said. "Whoever they saddle her to, the Vice President makes no real difference. It comes down to her either way, right?"

Alice nodded, though she wasn't sure she'd heard the question.

"I'll take anyone with an easy smile and a good sense of balance," Charlie said. "Maybe a religious dude. A Midwesterner from Ohio, Michigan, maybe both?"

Minutes later, GM Headquarters fell silent. No typing, no words. Jack stood slack-jawed, unable to even gloat. That left Alice as the only person able to repeat the name that echoed through the Loop like a sonic boom.

"Mahatma Fucking Golden."

The DNC's spokesman blathered on about the man being a "genuine celebrity," a "lively personality" with a "vision that inspires." His *New York Times* best seller was touted as a qualification, subject matter notwithstanding. The so-called "Palin precedent" meant his years as mayor counted as executive experience. More than that, the coronation of Trump had shown that many voters believed celebrity status alone proved one's fitness for public office.

What really stung was how quickly the Loop referenced his persistent—but unsuccessful—boycott of "gimmicky Alzheimer's software." Some jackass commentator wanting more time on the nation's screens hailed him as a "Ralph Nader for senior Americans."

"Mahatma Fucking Golden," Alice repeated.

* * *

Charlie had been monitoring the Loop ever since the announcement. He displayed his best discoveries on the wall screen. First, a report by anonymous sources from inside the campaign. Clicking through unattributed quotes, Charlie put a brave face on the situation.

"He's a registered Green Party member," Charlie said. "One of their few elected officials. With him on the ticket, the Greens have vowed to endorse Eisenhower. That's a two percent bump in every battleground state because the only thing Greens want more than trees is political relevance. Also, the Natural Law party—you know, the transcendental meditation advocates in California? They're withdrawing their candidate and backing Mahatma. That nutjob was polling at eight percent in the Golden State. Ha! *Golden* state. Anyway, the Dems will hoover up every one of those votes with the guru on their ticket. That takes California back off the table."

"In a way, it's better for our company," Eddie said. "Golden's gotta bury the hatchet with Eisenhower. She won't spend any political capital on our account, but she'll keep him too busy to give a fuck about us."

"Not likely," Alice muttered. "Besides, doesn't that mean she just sold me out? After all I did for her. "

"I *do* feel sorry for you bastards," Jack said. "Looks like your party elders cracked a fat for Golden."

Jack touched Charlie's monitor. An anonymous quote expanded in size to fill the screen. "Says they had a sit-down with our nemesis last night," Jack said. "Got a plan to keep him out of trouble. He'll just stump with a couple canned speeches, over and over, along the Crystal Corridor—Santa Fe, Sedona, Santa Barbara. Won't give a single live interview to the press."

"Can you *do* that?" Eddie asked.

"At this point," Alice said, "there aren't any rules left to break. Nobody can shame Golden into answering a single question."

"Who cares?" Jack said. "This is the Vice President we're talking about. His job is to keep his mouth shut and be Eisenhower's personal Quiet Copilot."

Alice would have laughed at her cheeky jester, were there no risk the emotional release would lead to tears.

The better option was retreat.

She walked back to her office and shut the door. The smooth granite veneer on her desk felt cool to the touch. With some difficulty, she climbed up onto it and turned to face the window, her legs dangling off the side of the desk. She stared through her glass wall at the Bank of America tower a few blocks away. Its windows reflected a blue sky striated with thin clouds. Alice let her mind drift with them. How many businesses had gone bankrupt inside there? For some, the fatal error had been going public, which put their stewardship in the hands of impatient investors.

Only nosy snots attend shareholder meetings. Had GM sold shares in itself, the plebes would have demanded a business plan for the Forget Me Not. The prophetic fairy tale Jack had written wouldn't have sufficed. GM's success with that product validated Alice's low opinion of collective decisions, both small and large. The masses paid GM good money for a brightly packaged bracelet. It did nothing that couldn't be achieved by installing an app on zunes that the rubes already owned.

From the idle conversations she'd tolerated at her fundraiser, Alice confirmed that she was unique among her peers. Few of them still played a direct role in product innovation, let alone coding. They raised capital, oversaw management, and embodied other euphemisms for sloth. Alice took the title of CEO but kept her hands busy tuning the engine that ran GM's products. She let the Codelings execute and polish code, but they weren't creators. She only outsourced trivialities, like the server security work she entrusted to a small San Diego company.

Charlie had permission to build on Alice's ideas, within parameters. Attachment to his father, and perhaps to Sailee, compromised Charlie's objectivity and muddied his motivations. As for Jack, the boy genius directed business and marketing well enough, but his self-destructive impulse couldn't be quelled. One never knew how such a thing might manifest.

Behind her, Alice's speakers made a soft "boop." Her monitor clicked on. The Loop wanted her attention. It would have to wait.

"Power off," Alice said.

Her desktop hardware complied.

Alice laughed to think that she'd sooner entrust GM to a disembodied Code Golem than to any of her colleagues. After all, she used secure threads woven into the Loop to choose her company's insurance plan, handle bills, and manage investments. It performed these tasks effortlessly, to good effect. The Loop lacked a creative spark, but it understood routines and patterns. It repeated them meticulously. Charlie and Jack made for better company. The Loop was a more reliable companion.

Catching sight of her own reflection in the window, Alice saw that blue ink had leaked out of her favorite fountain pen and onto her blouse. Even the Loop hadn't bothered to point out the problem. Now the shirt was ruined.

Alice's door remained open a crack. Through it, she heard clattering keyboards. The Codelings had turned off the newsfeeds and gone back to work, perhaps for her personal benefit. She loved the sound of their furious typing, which rose and fell like a waterfall. There was so much for them to do—adding new subroutines to the exponentially expansive back-end database, customizing their call routing and memo transcription software, optimizing cluttered strings and variables into more elegant structures. Soon, they would be operationalizing Charlie's behavioral models in the next wave of the GM product line.

"Alice?"

Charlie's voice. He'd poked his head into her doorway.

"You okay?"

If he wanted to cheer her, she would disappoint. "Tell me this isn't a catastrophe," Alice said. "For the nation. For us."

"Yeah, probably." Charlie leaned against her door frame. "Then again, Eddie's right. Mahatma will have to leave us alone for a while. If he gets on Eisenhower's nerves, she'll send him on a diplomatic mission. Maybe to India. Hear he likes it there."

SAILEE

"Can you imagine," Grisma said, "if India's party leaders held a debate such as this?"

"Unthinkable" was the verdict from Grisma's best friend, Mazumdarin. Sailee had never heard that name said aloud, as the woman who treated Grisma's apartment as a second home preferred "Mazoo." Tonight, Mazoo rested on the rose-patterned sofa, with Sailee and Grisma's wooden kitchen chairs arranged beside her. Her indigo sari pooled on the floor but covered little of her protuberant belly

"On this, I can agree," Sailee said. She set three cups of chai on a small table beside the sofa. "Their Trump is not as bad as our own."

"Which one?" Grisma said. "Our radical priests and jihadists scare me worse than the Modis and Singhs we have endured for decades."

"Think of today's event as a rugby match," Sailee said. "Watching the Americans go at each other will be good fun."

"Though the stakes are very real," Grisma corrected.

"Of course," Sailee said.

"There would be riots—" Mazoo coughed into a napkin, which she balled up before tucking it under her leg. "Riots and protests if an Indian debate didn't reserve slots for every minor party. Two or more Hindu candidates would square off against Muslims, Sikhs—"

"Marxists, too!" Grisma added.

"Either way, riots," Mazoo said. "We need something smaller, as a start, like their vice presidential debate. Low ratings, no troubles."

"Perhaps," Sailee patiently synched her zune with her grandmother's television. A clean picture snapped into view. "But this one is a global spectacle, no? Here we are, following an election half a world away."

"Listen to her argue with us," Grisma said to Mazoo. "My daughter may be the best politician in the room."

Mazoo sniffed. "Quit fussing with that thing, Sailee, and sit down."

"I can see the stage," Grisma said, "but I do not see Golden. Are you certain this is the right channel?"

"It is not a channel," Sailee said. "It is the Loop."

Mazoo shifted on the couch. Her stomach rumbled. "Vijul should be here, watching with us. You make my poor granddaughter work all hours. You had best not corrupt the poor girl and make her into a capitalist."

Grisma clucked at her guest. "Leave her alone, Mazoo. Our girls are both still young, with much to learn. You know that, don't you Sailee?"

Sailee got back up to futz with her zune connection.

Mazoo waved her hand at Sailee. "She knows she stands in my way. Move aside, Sailee. Let it be."

Sailee sat down in time to see a close-up of Mahatma's father, Rich Golden. His dark suit looked out of place in a sea of white. Throughout the audience sat seniors wearing cotton scarves over robes or kaftans. Unaware of the camera on him, the patriarch fidgeted with a large hearing aid behind his ear.

"He's the only one in that family I could trust," Mazoo said. "Remember him, Grisma? Still handsome, no?"

"What are you talking about?" Sailee said.

"Your grandma never mentioned the Golden family's trip to Amul Dairy?"

Sailee drew a blank. "When was this?"

"Two years after you moved in," Grisma said. "The family's patriarch tried to sell us processing equipment. Mazoo and I sat on the co-op board."

"Rich was straight with us," Mazoo said. "Once he saw how our operation worked, he realized there was nothing he could offer. This man was used to working with industrial dairy farms, but as Grisma has told you many times, our average milk producer has fewer than two cows."

"Even at a fair price," Grisma said, "our wages are so low that his machinery was not cost effective."

"That is where the story really begins," Mazoo said. She began to speak more quickly and sounded like her granddaughter, eager to gossip. "Instead of heading straight back home, young Matt—Mahatma's real name, of course—insisted on turning their visit into a vacation. He started dragging his parents from ashram to shrine to temple to holy site."

"How do you know all this?" Sailee said. "You only worked at the dairy."

Mazoo laughed. "Child, your Loop is no match for us. Everyone who met him could see Matthew was suffering from the delusion Westerners sometimes get when they walk in the footsteps of our greatest prophet. He even started wearing wire-framed glasses."

Those round spectacles, along with Golden's ponytail and white robe, were the caricature political cartoonists used for him. After the nomination, Sailee read an editorial that referred to him as "the homespun millionaire in Gandhi glasses."

"We call it Gandhisia," Grisma said.

The television switched to a close-up of Mahatma's mother. She wore a white robe cut to flatter. Cross-stitched threads of gold made her shimmer in the brightly lit auditorium. She had one arm around her granddaughter, the other around Mahatma's twin boys.

"Oh, nasty, nasty!" Mazoo said. "Was there ever a face pulled so tight? I can see that poor woman's bones poking through tissue-paper cheeks!"

"My grandmother taught me not to judge," Sailee said.

"You can make an exception," Grisma said, "for a woman who takes the name of a god."

Sailee clucked. "And you know the story behind that, too, I imagine?"

"Oh, yes," said Mazoo. "At the tail end of the family's trip to Ahmedabad, Mahatma's parents left for the airport without him, but a derailment stopped their taxi. As drivers poured out of their cars and crowded around the wreck, Mahatma's mother saw the decapitated body of the train conductor." Mazoo's eyes went wide. "Horrifying! She left her husband on the spot and took a cab back into the city. She was convinced this had invoked an ancient myth. Surely—"

"Yes," Sailee said, "I see it now."

If Mazoo's account was to be believed, the parallel was striking. The ancient story went like this. One day a guard at the Ahmedabad gates saw the mortal avatar of the goddess Lakshmi walking out of the city. Her mere presence had brought prosperity, and her departure would ensure decline. Feigning concern, the guard begged her to not travel the highway alone. He walked her back inside the gates and earned a solemn promise that she would not continue her journey until he returned. Once out of sight, he slit his own throat, a sacrifice that secured his city's future.

"So," Sailee said, "Mahatma's mother took the train conductor's death as a divine directive."

"Precisely," Mazoo said. "She could never leave her son's side again."

"Changing her name from Laura to Lakshmi," Sailee added, "made her pledge a matter of public record?"

"It is so," Mazoo said. She continued to look at the television but wore a more satisfied smile.

"Both mother and son may be mad," Grisma said, "but there is more to him than madness. I can take you to a dozen gurus who claim Mahatma stole their wisdom, but he has developed new ideas all his own about how to attain higher consciousness."

"By mistaking senility for wisdom?" Sailee snorted. "It is

111

cruel, what he does."

"Maybe so," Grisma continued, "but do not take him for a fool. Mahatma understands our present spiritual and political crises in his own way. I tell you, from the mouths of babes—"

"And madmen," Mazoo interjected.

"—come greater wisdom than you might guess. Mahatma Golden is no great intellect, but he has his father's tactical mind. He is persistent, as your American company knows."

Sailee stared at her elders, unsure what to believe. "My own grandmother actually met this man, this next co-president."

"*Vice* president," Grisma corrected.

"Your Nani makes this sound quite complicated," Mazoo said. "The truth is simpler. India needs the Democrats to win this election. Eisenhower is no socialist, but she is not our enemy." Mazoo turned as if to spit on the floor.

Nani expected more from Sailee than polite attention, but she was unsure what to say. Chided for her lack of "political consciousness," Sailee read her grandmother's collection of Leninist tracts, which seemed dated and abstract. More interesting were the details of Indian politics, which had a tantalizing blend of idealism, demagoguery, civil disobedience, and party intrigue. After she met Charlie, the Loop added US politics to her news stream. She appreciated the more obscure pieces of information that it guessed, often correctly, she would need in her next conversation with Nani.

One such tidbit came to mind.

"The Republicans were so eager to get Golden in a debate," Sailee said, "that they rolled over like domesticated dogs to make it happen. CBS got exclusive broadcast rights, because the Democrats wanted to narrowcast it to seniors, who are that network's demographic."

Nani nodded approvingly.

"The GOP almost agreed to hold the debate at Thereport," Sailee said, "but Eisenhower's people scuttled that. After the reincarnation scandal last week, the campaign has kept Lakshmi and her personal acolytes out of public view."

"Shush! Look at the screen," Mazoo said. "Here now comes our Golden boy!"

A camera picked up Mahatma's entrance. He had worn business suits since joining the ticket, but tonight he wore his white kurta.

Mahatma stepped up to a podium opposite his opponent, Indiana Senator Pinedale Powell. The senator smiled warmly and extended an open hand, which Mahatma held briefly before pulling Pinedale into a full embrace. Kisses hit both cheeks. Mahatma's concerned counterpart staggered back to his mark on the stage.

The camera closed in on Mahatma's face. He beamed at the crowd.

"Oh my," Sailee said, "what pleeeeasing eyes lie behind those wire-framed glasses."

"As deep a blue as the Arabian Sea," Mazoo said.

Grisma waved her hand. "Turn it up, Sailee."

The debate moderator came on camera. She addressed the candidates with the professional indifference of a referee reviewing the rules of a boxing match. "Since Mayor Golden won the coin toss, he earned the privilege of giving the first opening statement. Mayor Golden? You have two minutes."

Mahatma made a show of lifting the sheaf of papers on his podium and dropping them onto the stage. He nodded to the moderator, then turned to face a camera.

"Each of us," Mahatma said with a wave of his hand, "has all the time we need. We can have life everlasting, which extends far beyond the brief existence of our bodies."

"Oh, dear," Mazoo said. "That is a line from that book of his. Do not make a first-class monkey of yourself, Mr Golden."

"The politicians you see at these events are afraid to run out of time." Mahatma turned toward Pinedale and winked. "No

113

offense, my friend."

Waiting for a nod or smile that never came, Mahatma paused three beats too long. The camera flashed to the perplexed face of the moderator.

"More than a decade ago," Mahatma continued, "I traveled abroad to rediscover a truth we know in our hearts from the day we are born. Our planet can only support us if we let go of short-sighted aspirations and recognize our responsibility to our future. To our future selves."

Mazoo tugged at her sari. "Careful, Golden."

"Future generations need us to slow down. To ask one another, 'What do *you* need?' When my supporters chant, 'No tomorrow, no peace,' they orient our species toward future generations so that we may flourish on this Earth."

"My opponent will tell you that the children are our future, but look." Mahatma pointed out toward the audience. "Turn your cameras to this crowd."

The technical director in the CBS production truck obliged. The screen showed row after row of gray-haired heads, wrinkled faces.

"Here is the wisdom we must embrace. Not a party platform. Not an ideology. Just the knowledge gained through years of lived experience. Our senior statesmen and dignified crones can see further than the rest of humanity. Give them two minutes of your time, and you will see the world anew. That is all I ask. I have nothing more to say."

The broadcast ran another ninety minutes. True to his word, Mahatma used not a second more of his allotted time. Neither questions from the moderator nor audience catcalls nor Pinedale's stern reprimands could pry open Mahatma's lips.

At one point, Mahatma reached into his podium and drank water from a ceramic cup. The audience hushed on the chance that he might utter at least a syllable. Instead, he wiped his mouth and resumed his beatific smile.

When the moderator thanked and dismissed the candidates, Mahatma stepped back from his podium. The mayor of Venice turned to his opponent with outstretched arms and—according to a CBS kinesthesiologist—arrogantly puckered lips. Pinedale responded with something between a punch and a slap. The side of Pinedale's clenched fist caught Golden's cheek. The guru didn't flinch, as though he had anticipated it.

That became the most Looped moment of the night.

* * *

In the week that followed, Sailee worried over the global implications of the Eisenhower-Golden ticket losing the US presidential campaign. Every year that country became more autocratic, it signaled to the rest of the world democracy's obsolescence. Even India's reactionary BJP government pledged to follow the global climate accords, but if the US continued to boycott the effort, was progress really possible? Strange how an election so far away carried so much weight at home.

The post-debate analysis was split along partisan lines, but the Loop stitched together a definitive conclusion. Even a toned-down Mahatma Golden left many voters worried. With the election fast approaching, the meta-polling estimated the odds of an Eisenhower victory at forty-nine percent. Another razor-thin election.

Sailee's zune buzzed. She needed to leave work immediately lest she be late to the regular gathering of grandmothers, this week hosted by Nani. Today was a special occasion—the first time that Grisma would entertain guests in Old Ahmedabad, the walled city within the city. Sailee had purchased and furnished adjoining condos there for herself and her grandmother, who had to adjust to a bourgeois lifestyle among Ahmedabad's more prosperous residents.

The gray office building Sailee exited felt like *her* office building. As Charlie had foretold, all ten stories hummed with GM employees. Her scooter would soon zip Sailee past fourteen more buildings just like it, stretching across several city blocks. Each was being converted from a traditional call center to a GM service hub, under Sailee's direction.

That company — *her* company? — would be the salvation of the Gujarat telessistants industry. Automated phone systems and voice recognition software left many workers unemployed, but GM required more remote human contact than ever.

The new jobs couldn't have come too soon. Sailee's city bore some of the same scars she had seen in pictures of Detroit. Barry's hometown had never recovered from its bust. With so much of the textile business moving away, Ahmedabad faced the same fate. Its perverse advantage had been that in its heyday, it had too many people per square mile. Buildings were neglected, but rarely abandoned. Every usable inch of the city had been put to use. The result was a jumble of stalls, low-rise apartments, commercial strips, and factories, all connected by streams of autos, bicycles, pedestrians, and free-range cattle.

Sailee stepped astride her scooter and caught the eye of Vijul, on a smoking break. It seemed she had followed Sailee's eyes as they traced the line of GM buildings that extended toward the horizon.

"Oh, yes," Vijul said, "we are building a kingdom. Sailee Singh is the savior of our state, here to lift us up again from dirt and poverty."

"Go home," Sailee said with more scorn than intended. "Does your mother not have a husband arranged for you yet? What about our new accountant, Sanjay Khedwal?"

"Sanjay is a prospect," Vijul conceded. "What of you? Does your heart not belong to Mr Charlie?"

The question caught Sailee off guard. In a panic, she brought up a topic she had planned to avoid. "You should talk! Routing calls to yourself from that goat, Mr Vaughn."

Vijul's eyes widened.

"Yes, I know about those. I took one of them. Did he never mention it?"

"He has a problem," Vijul said. "Drinking is a disease, and I am—"

"You are helping him stagger to his next drunken binge. His real name is Jack Thompson. He is one of our employers."

"What? No, he said he is a sportsman, or—"

"He is nothing but trouble, even at a distance. I will say nothing more and must go."

Sailee swung a thick cotton belt around her waist, crimping down her sari. The effect was not flattering, but it kept her clothes from catching in the scooter's back wheel. She turned the key in her ignition. The throat-clearing noise of the reconditioned engine drowned out whatever Vijul tried to say to her as Sailee rode out of the parking lot. She traversed the narrow lane between the stream of autos and the drop-off where the road's shoulder had succumbed to a mudslide.

The ride to her new home in the Old City was a slow one. Traffic bunched up into congested lumps. Ahmedabad had not wired its traffic signals into the magical Loop. Whether that was out of a fierce independence or insufficient funds, Sailee was not sure.

A green light welcomed Sailee to cross a boulevard, and she laughed at the futility of the offer. She could not move without hitting a wall of taxis and scooters just like her own blocking the way. Most ran perpendicular to her, but some pointed at odd angles that made it impossible to guess their destination.

Sailee tapped her horn. No effect.

After sitting still for what felt like another minute, Sailee's patience waned. She bit her lip and pressed harder on her horn. Its howling blast cut through the din of traffic. A young man pulling a pedicab in front of Sailee hesitated to spit at her. Sailee dodged the phlegm, swerved past the man, and reached the middle of the intersection. A second wail from her horn earned her an exit, and she darted out of the jam.

So, that was how things got done. Lesson learned, again.

The remainder of her trip promised lighter traffic. Sailee switched on the autopilot and let her thoughts drift.

The rumbling of her seat on the uneven pavement took her mind back to Charlie's spring visit. She recalled hoisting the sick lad on her Vespa and ferrying him to his hotel. The night air had revived him during the ride. He had found the courage to wrap his arms around her waist for the second half of that journey. She had responded by sliding herself back into him, just slightly. He seemed to respond, but neither spoke of it.

Sailee's breaths became short, and she retook manual control of her scooter. Her thoughts shifted to her disagreement with Vijul. From her friend's perspective, the furtive assistance given Jack was well intended, however undeserving he might be. Vijul was playing the role of "Minder," a benign form of service Sailee had seen on the rise at her call center.

Could Sailee say she had never done the same? She reflected on a client she had assisted earlier that evening to stay in good practice. The call had been with Harold, a septuagenarian in Chattanooga, Tennessee. When Sailee asked him if he had made his "lucky purchases," he wheezed a confused "What?" Sailee explained that his memo stated an intent to acquire "luckies" from a Minit Mart. Harold coughed so loud that Sailee could almost picture him straining to keep himself upright. *Lucky Strikes*, she realized. Sailee shifted the conversation to his health. Harold confessed to emphysema.

"You do not have to continue this filthy habit," she said to him.

"I'm tryin' to quit," Harold said. "Honest."

"It may help to remain mindful of small choices. When you desire a cigarette, take a deep breath of fresh air instead. Slow, even breaths. Try." Sailee breathed in slowly, then exhaled audibly. "In…" She heard an intake of air on the other end of the call. "And oooouuuut."

Slow breathing came through the phone.

"Now, relax your mind. Be patient with yourself. It will take a moment." Background noises on the phone—shoppers passing by, an intercom, a scanner beeping. "In this peaceful moment, what is it that you want?"

"Nuthin', really."

"Precisely."

"Wendy hates it when I smoke."

"She will be happy to see you without the Lucky Strikes. Then, perhaps, you will be the lucky one."

Harold laughed into a cough. Before ending the call, he said a quiet "Thanks."

* * *

A neon "New Tomorrows" sign glowed a garish orange. It welcomed Sailee as she eased into the underground garage beneath the condominium she and Grisma now occupied. She parked her scooter, slipped into the elevator, and tapped "13."

To get in the right frame of mind, Sailee recalled Mahatma Golden's advice. *Give your elders two minutes of your time, and you will see the world anew.* Following that admonition would help her attain formal membership in her grandmother's Red Guard Tea and Social. From the first year she moved in with Grisma, Sailee had sat with the grannies for a weekly update on politics and gossip. She had met them as a shy thirteen-year-old. In the fifteen years since, she became a confident conversationalist with open, closeted, and dormant Marxists, along with more moderate "disloyalists."

The elevator moved with swift efficiency to Sailee's floor. Moments later, she entered the spacious living room and marveled at its aesthetic. Before her grandmother set foot inside,

Sailee furnished the unit in a mid-nineteenth century English style.

Mazoo, swathed in a white muumuu on a fainting couch, was the first to note Sailee's arrival. "So this is the little princess who bought her Nani a palace?"

"Scandalous," clucked one of the Reds from her upholstered settee. With a wink, she said, "Your granddaughter has become a capitalist, unfit for membership."

"It is a bit much," Grisma acknowledged, "but she is redistributing wealth to her granny."

"I am not sure we can meet here in good conscience," Mazoo said. "Imperialist dishware? Ornate wallpaper?"

"Ah, but look." Sailee pointed to the wall. "These designs are those of a distinguished socialist, William Morris." Sailee ran a hand over Mazoo's velvety couch. "This furniture is in the style preferred by Mary Burns, the de facto wife of Friedrich Engels. The Loop helped me give Nani's decor a working-class heritage."

Grisma laughed. "The industrial mills of Manchester are far from our dairy cooperatives. We Indians must temper revolutionary zeal with a Gandhian care for the soul."

Sailee touched her hand to her head, something between an apology and a thank you. "You are right, of course, Nani."

"Now sit." Grisma reached down to a low mahogany table and lifted a cup of chai. "Drink."

The oldest woman in the room, holding hands with another Red on a loveseat, leaned forward. "Now that our young guest has arrived, it is time for the initiation test. Grisma must recuse herself, of course. Mazoo will conduct the interview, which consists of one question."

Mazoo turned to Sailee. "When this current life of yours has passed, what will you have done of *consequence*? What mark will you have left on Ahmedabad? What will you sacrifice to help those Gujaratis most in need? What works of yours will change the workings of the world?"

Grisma objected, "But that is more than one—"

A chorus of shushes silenced her.

"One answer for many questions," Mazoo said. "We adore you, Sailee. We helped Nani raise you from a tiny wisp of a girl. You have taken tea with us so many times, but what have you learned? We must know that you have become something more than another ambitious guju entrepreneur."

"I understand, Mazoo," Sailee said. "My employees and I provide a service. We help the elderly fend off madness as their days come to a close."

"We count ourselves lucky," Mazoo said, "to not need this for ourselves. But who can afford your phone calls? Only the wealthiest white Americans, no?"

"My favorite client is black. He—"

"Class trumps race," said one of the Reds.

"These are just alms," Mazoo continued. "How could your efforts transform the *system*?"

Sailee bit her lip. She recalled the first day Grisma sat her with these ladies. She was unable to follow their conversation, owing to their accents as much as the words themselves. But loath to be left behind, she listened closely. She learned quickly.

"My telessistants are reshaping the world," Sailee said, "through *satyagraha*."

"How so?" Mazoo said.

"In small ways, every day, we bring truth to our clients, not just as their caretakers but as advisors." Sailee took a swallow of tea. "We offer gentle nudges."

A thin woman seated across from Sailee shook her head. "Do not preach to us the Western gospel of libertarian paternalism. Use paper straws, not plastic. Recycle that can. Take the stairs instead of a lift. These are petty things, which only go so far."

"These are small steps," Sailee agreed, "but we have many clients. If you add together every time a person drinks water from the faucet instead of a bottle—"

"Not enough," Mazoo said. "Your wealthy customers want their hands held by a pretty Indian girl, but you cannot drag them to a political rally. One can change small behaviors without gaining proper *consciousness*."

That was the word Sailee had been hoping to hear. Once Sailee placed this interview on her calendar, the Loop began piping into her headphones short lectures by a radical Slovenian philosopher.

"We can never know," Sailee said, "if our behaviors reflect deeper convictions or mere mimicry. To believe a person can break free from false consciousness is pure Leninist fantasy, Mazoo. The core values that shape our actions are unconscious — and unreachable. Pushing directly at people's daily choices will yield better results."

"Do not be naïve," Mazoo said. "If you announced your intention to be the conscience of the elderly, your employer would replace you overnight. That would achieve nothing. You must take *effective* action. You must have a strategy, dearest Sailee. Even the muddled prophet Mahatma Golden knew that his books and lectures were not enough. They were but a platform, on which he now stands for a higher office."

"Small acts can be powerful," Sailee said. "What about Gandhi? Patel? They built our nation through simple messages of peace and nonviolence."

"Gandhi was a lawyer," Mazoo said. "The peasant in homespun was a costume. Strutting about in spectacles was political theater. Patel fought back against India's enemies. He took risks. He did not wear a headset and sit behind a desk."

Sailee scanned the room to see if she was making headway. Hard to tell. Grisma gave her an encouraging nod, and that was enough.

"I do not live in the First World," Sailee said, "so I cannot push hard against its levers of power. My company's CEO has done much to aid the cause of Eisenhower's campaign for the

SAILEE

presidency. She has raised money—"

"The capitalist parties will always have more," said the eldest Red. "Your Loop whispers into even our ears, and it portends a reelection of yet another Republican tyrant. Perhaps you should turn your heart homeward. There might be a seat for one such as you in the Gujarat Legislative Assembly. If you stood for office, we—"

"Perhaps," Mazoo said "The question today is more fundamental. What personal risks might you take to advance our cause?"

Sailee studied the lily prints cascading down the walls. She could not take her eyes off the delicate flowers—how their leaves and stems wove together. Side by side, single flowers formed a field.

"I can do a lot," Sailee said. "Perhaps more than I realized."

JACK

"We gotta get her outta here," Jack said.

Charlie said something in reply, but Jack only heard the cheers of the crowd jammed into Cafe Flora. Alice had chosen the vegan stronghold to watch the returns and sat at the bar between her two co-workers.

As one of Eisenhower's highest-profile donors, Alice received through the US mail printed invitations to election night events. Quaint postmarks ranged from San Francisco to Charlotte. None of these out-of-town galas would get the pleasure of her company because Jack daily fed them into the break room shredder. Better to keep her in the company of friends.

It had been a rough couple of weeks since Golden joined the Eisenhower ticket. When Jack had sent Alice a text instructing her "to savor the delicious irony of it all," he got no response. Charlie and he agreed to say nothing more of it at work, but before he got to the café, he saw Alice's reply.

"Consider this," the message read. "Yours truly bears much responsibility for elevating another loon to the executive branch. Golden will sit one rung below an invertebrate president who permitted her party to dress her in this t-shirt." The text came with a picture from the campaign trail showing Golden and Eisenhower arm-in-arm. An artful photo editor had put her in a t-shirt that featured a hand pointing at her running mate and the words, "I'm with stoopid."

"Look at this," Jack said. To distract Alice from the election returns coming in from the Midwest and mountain states, he pointed to a text scrawl on the screen above the bar. "Team Tax-and-Spend is going two-for-two on the Washington state ballot measures. More solar farms and electric motors for everybody. Elon Musk pay for that result?"

"Nah," Charlie said. "After I read the citizen panel evaluations of those initiatives, I knew they'd pass."

"Really?" Jack asked with a snort. "Who reads the *Voter Guide*?"

"Can you shut him up?" Alice said. "Swear to God, the next time they run one of those, I'll hack the Secretary of State's voter database and put Jack on their summons list."

"You'd do what?" Jack said.

Alice glowered but said nothing more.

Charlie put a hand on Jack's shoulder and turned his gaze toward the bartender. "Shouldn't you be ordering shots or something? I'll drive tonight, so go crazy."

Alice's dark mood persisted until the Loop called the result at 10pm Pacific. The nation's first female president had booted the GOP out of the White House.

"That's a good thing, right?" Charlie said.

"Is it?" Alice said. "Did you forget who that makes our Vice President?" Boss lady's face fell into her hands. Defeated, even in victory. "We can't even have nice things *off* the Internet."

Anticipating this result and this reaction, Jack was prepared. Using his own predictive powers, he'd enlisted Charlie to devise a scheme to get Alice through a rough evening. Plus, it would give him a chance to show her a different side of himself.

Pulling Charlie in close, Jack shouted, "Plan is a go!"

Charlie nodded. "Get Alice out of here. Give her the duffel bag. Tell her to change."

Alice pulled Jack close to her ear. "Change into—what?"

Jack stood and motioned for Charlie and Alice to follow. In the parking lot behind the café, it was quiet enough to hear gravel crunching under their shoes. The air was moist and cool. Alice wiped at her face, awoken from a bad dream.

"If you can be happy for your girlfriend Eleanor," Jack said, "let's call this excursion we're about to take a celebration. Or, if you prefer, consider it a pity party for yours truly. My candidate

125

just got pussy grabbed and buggered by yours."

"Don't start," Charlie said. He walked to his boxy Scion xB, clicked it open, and pulled out a gym bag.

"Whatever you've got planned," Alice said, "I'm in." She grabbed the bag from Charlie and pulled off her jacket. In five seconds, she was down to underwear.

Jack blinked. Time stopped. He'd never seen Alice this—exposed. Against his baser instincts, he shut his eyes. He wanted to hold onto the image of her bare back, but in his imagination, he held her close. Felt her skin on his.

When Jack's eyes re-opened, Alice had slipped on an all-black outfit that matched what Jack and Charlie already wore. A cable-knit sweater hung over a long-sleeved crew shirt and denim pants. She slipped on running shoes, then found three black knit caps in the bottom of her duffel. Alice tucked her hair into one and tossed the others to her fellow cat burglars.

"Climb aboard," Charlie said. "We'll get you up to speed on the way."

Jack hopped into the backseat. Charlie started the engine and pulled onto the road. Explaining this outing to Alice required finding just the right words. He'd place his trust in the same improvisational instincts that guided his Vegas romps. Jack's gut told him the timing wasn't right. Not yet. Better to wait.

"Just head toward the coordinates," Jack said. "I'll tell you a story when we get there."

Charlie pulled onto Madison Street. The drive through Washington Park arboretum showed how much moisture the overhanging trees held from that evening's downpour. Droplets danced on the windshield and refracted the moonlight peeking between oaks and walnuts. The air carried a woodsy smell, even as they crossed over Lake Union on the I-5 bridge and headed north, past the University District and out of town.

Unfamiliar silence became uncomfortable. Jack leaned forward, between the two front seats. He clicked on the radio. A local NPR affiliate played audio from Democratic Party victory rallies. President-Elect Eisenhower held a formal event in Fayetteville, North Carolina, where she received the obligatory concession call.

Golden seized the moment. He led a swarm of media into the main auditorium at Thereport. The NPR reporter on the scene failed to disguise her amusement.

"With victory secured," the reporter said in an even tone, "Eisenhower begins her presidency at a disadvantage. She faces opposition from a Republican majority in the Senate, but her first and highest obstacle stands within her administration. The enigmatic Vice President-Elect, the so-called guru from the Golden State, has, at long last, shared his unique vision for the country. From his spiritual headquarters, he gave what he promised would be the first of a series of weekly addresses on life, death, and the future."

"Oh, shit," Alice said. Her extended exhalation fogged the side window.

Jack sensed tension building in her body and considered reaching from the backseat to offer a shoulder rub. He lifted his hands, but had a vision of Alice bursting into rage. Or tears. Too risky.

The broadcast segued to a chanting crowd. "Golden, Golden."

Mahatma's amplified voice echoed through the auditorium. "Now that the politics are over," he said, "we can speak plainly. I want to talk to you today about our future. Global warming, deforestation, and desertification threaten our planet, it is true. But they are irreversible. To prepare for a safe and secure tomorrow for all humankind, we must accelerate—not forestall—industrial development. We *know* our species will survive because we have met our future selves. Our future great grandchildren—every one of the little angels—will live on the moon. Let the climate change. We'll leave it behind. Our priority now is to build faster, stronger ships to take us beyond the sky."

Before Jack could reach the stereo, Alice changed the station. She feigned the nonchalance of a bored passenger searching for a familiar song. Instead, her unsteady fingers led the tuner into static. When she couldn't find the power button, she spun the volume down to zero.

CHARLIE

"Take the next exit," Jack said.

They had no company on the Interstate at 2am. Charlie steered across three empty lanes to follow the sign for Bellingham, then reached onto the dashboard to smooth down the black electrical tape that covered a flashing yellow light. Though his car was vintage, Charlie had installed automatic route guidance. Jack had entered an address on his zune, so the Loop knew their destination. Last week, trusting this navigation service led Charlie onto a half-completed bridge. So much for letting a probability engine take the wheel.

Alice stared out of her open window, as she had done since they left Seattle. When the Loop put the check marks next to Eisenhower and Golden, Alice wore an expression Charlie had only seen before on his father's face. She looked lost. Confused.

The Scion shot through a yellow light. Charlie tried to catch Jack's eye in the rear-view mirror.

"You ready to tell us where we're going?" Charlie said.

"Pull up beside that Holiday Inn," Jack said.

Charlie turned into the parking lot. "How does a hotel figure into all this?"

"Into all what?" Alice sniffed. "Are we visiting one of your love nests?"

Attention diverted? Check.

That was only the beginning. Anticipating what would come next, Charlie's pulse accelerated.

Their plan hatched when Charlie told Jack about a recent visit to Detroit. After watching the Lions eke out a tough win at Ford Field, Charlie had tucked his father into bed. It wasn't too cold outside, so Charlie donned a hooded sweatshirt for a late-evening stroll. He stumbled on a buckled sidewalk slab and realized the only illumination was faint moonlight. Street lamps stood tall against the night sky, but none was lit.

Then one bright light turned on a block down the street.

Curious, Charlie approached. Atop the light pole hung a shadowy figure, who scampered down with the agility of a squirrel. There stood a middle-aged man in a brown jacket.

"What's going on?" Charlie said. "City fixing lights at eleven o'clock? On a Sunday?"

The two strangers plucked canvas bags off the sidewalk and jogged away. Charlie followed, sure-footed on the well-lit pavement.

"Wait! I know you!" Charlie shouted. "My dad, Barry Sanders—he's your neighbor. You rode in a bus together, from Lansing. You're Terrence, right?"

The figures stopped and turned around. Terrence flashed a smile of recognition. Beside him stood a young girl, maybe thirteen years old. She had the same narrow nose and flat eyebrows as the man, who must have been her father. She futzed with her brown beanie while he adjusted a United Auto Workers cap.

"You're—Charlie Sanders?" the man said.

"And you are Terrence, um," Charlie couldn't find a name.

"Washington. Not as memorable as yours, yeah?"

"Maybe."

"And I'll bet you're wondering why we're prowling?"

"Maybe, yes."

"Fixin' up the city," said the girl. "One light at a time."

"That's Lauryn, my daughter. Ain't she the athlete?"

"I guess," Charlie said. "But why—and how?"

"City's got the lights, but they don't have the manpower."

"Or *girlpower*," Lauryn said.

Terrence nodded. "So, we steal the bulbs and install them ourselves."

"That's right," Lauryn said. "That makes us burglars. And

130

these poles are city property. That means we're trespassing on 'em."

Terrence beamed. "Lauryn calls it reverse vandalism. I'm guessin' you've got a clean rap sheet. Wanna risk getting your first mark on it?"

The offer caught him off guard. He declined.

Sitting behind the wheel of his Scion, Charlie wished he'd joined the father-daughter duo. He'd have gained practical experience before becoming the wheelman for tonight's job. A trial run in Dad's neighborhood would have had another advantage. Most of the police there were black. North of Seattle, Charlie might be the only black person cops would see all night. That he failed to consider this suggested how far he would go to lift Alice's spirits.

"The Bellingham Holiday Inn is not my secret lair," Jack said. "What we're approaching is more like my Little Big Horn. From five years ago."

"I'm lost," Alice said. "What does—"

"Shush," Jack said. He pointed to a wall of glass windows and doors that ran along the side of the hotel. "This is where I, as my Charlie Sheen alter ego, reached the height of my powers."

"You were Crazy Horse in this story, or Custer?"

"Both."

"You can't be *both*," Charlie said. "That's not how metaphors work. There are *rules*."

Jack rolled down his window and stuck his head to sniff the air. "It was a late night, just like this. I'd brought mates up from the university. You'd never believe it, but I was kind of a bully back then."

"Really?" Alice said in a monotone. "You?"

"My roommates and me, we'd had it with these Microsoft offspring—these second-generation nerds—acting like they owned our whole university."

"Everyone in this car is a nerd," Charlie said.

"Okay, so I'm talking about *dweebs*. Anyway, the point is that back then, I could be a brute."

Alice hinted at a smile and turned around to face Jack. "You can be coarse, Jack-o, but brutish? I'm sorry, you're too adorable."

Jack blushed. "I don't know why I'm telling you."

"Because you have to," Charlie said. He still wasn't sure where this was headed, but for the first time, he heard shame in Jack's voice. "I believe we're about to take a key step in our quest. Jack and I are introducing you to our new hobby—*reverse vandalism*. Even the Loop hasn't settled on its exact rules yet. We've decided that it works best as atonement. One must make a place better by some objective measure. But in doing so, you have to break at least one law."

"Forget the rules and let me explain," Jack said. "So, one of my college friends, he heard that a pack of dweebs in our dorm was going up to Bellingham for a World War II gaming convention. Think of dice and little plastic tanks on a vinyl map of Europe. Anyway, I got this idea."

Charlie held down the brake and put the car in neutral. Faint lights inside the Holiday Inn showed a ground-level ballroom, its tables laid out in rows.

"So," Jack said, "the four of us dressed like Sheen in *Beyond the Law*. Went to Army Surplus and got camo fatigues, belts, canteens. We hit the Costume Plus over by Northgate to score plastic rifles and such. Gear looks legit from a distance. Even feels real, if you fill the grenades with sand and Gorilla Glue, which we did."

Jack licked his lips and swallowed.

"Wait," Alice said, "you didn't—"

"Oh, we did. We rolled up in a rented jeep, right to the doors you're lookin' at. We burst inside and tore through that ballroom, hurling grenades and swinging our rifles while pre-recorded gunfire and screams pumped out of speakers strapped to our backs. Freaked the kids worse than you can imagine."

"So," Alice said, "you won your little battle against the dweebs? Good for you, *asshole*." She reared back and punched Jack in the shoulder.

He didn't flinch.

"Remember, I'm Custer in this story, too. In the midst of our terrorizing, we didn't notice one of the gamers had left the room. Dude was an Indian, from the Lummi rez."

Alice nodded.

"Turns out, there are older blokes at these things. This Lummi fella must have run out to his truck when we came inside. He comes back in behind us, hunting rifle over his shoulder. Didn't say a word, just lowered its barrel at my balls. Well, we fled like blind deer. Crashed over chairs, banged into tables. By the time our jeep left the parking lot, we were almost crying."

"You?" Alice said with a snort. "Wow, I—"

"And then—I can't believe I'm telling you this. Then, I realized I'd fuckin' shat m'self."

"Okay, that part's an exaggeration," Charlie said.

"No. The real deal. Brown town. Full-length turd in my daks." Jack put his head back out the window for another breath of air before rolling up his window. "If you can believe it, that wasn't the worst part. Turned out the guy who chased us off was on parole. He got state prison for bringing the rifle into the hotel."

Charlie waited for Jack to finish, but his friend said nothing more.

"So," Charlie said, "where next, Custer?"

"To the rez," Jack said. "We're tokin' some fuckin' peace pipe tonight."

* * *

As Charlie drove the next few miles, tension built inside the car. Gloom settled back onto Alice's face, which made Jack so anxious

133

that he'd activated Buddy. The device played music loud enough for Charlie to recognize Metallica pounding on Jack's eardrum.

For his part, Charlie held the steering wheel tight. Whenever headlights approached from the other direction on their two-lane highway, his back stiffened. If a Whatcomb County sheriff asked what had him out so late, who knows what Alice or Jack might say. Neither of them had any sense when it came to the racial politics of traffic stops. Or, what if a pickup full of rednecks caught sight of Charlie's bumper stickers? They might want to even the score after tonight's election.

Happily, the road remained empty as they traveled along Jack's route. In the moonlight, he could sometimes see the Puget Sound on one side of the peninsula they traversed. The Scion's headlights soon reflected off a sign that read, "Lummi Nation School."

"Turn in here," Jack said, "then go 'round back."

"Maybe we should park on the road," Charlie suggested. "Won't the school's security come looking for us if they see a car in the lot this late?"

"The school's sweet with new buildings," Jack said, "but there's fuckall for staff and upkeep."

"You know this how?" Charlie said.

"Kind of cyber-stalked the bloke with the rifle. Turns out he's a community activist. Blogs about the sitch here. There's a gang of Aryan crotch stains from Bellingham who come by every so often and fuck up the school."

Charlie parked at the far end of the lot.

"They know the kids here love basketball," Jack said, "so they hacked off the nylon nets and busted some rims. That's where we come in."

"Ah, the welding kit," Charlie said. "Let's do this!"

Jack rummaged in the trunk. He emerged with an armful of chain-link basketball nets and telescoping stepladders.

"Need help with that?" Alice asked.

"Nah," Jack said.

He lifted the gear over his head like an Olympian. It was a genuine feat of strength. Charlie hadn't seen someone heft so much weight since Barry Jr.'s high school workouts. Jack ran serpentine out of the parking lot and onto the blacktop courts. Charlie followed close behind. As Alice raced past him, he might have glimpsed a grin.

Moving from one bare basketball hoop to the next, Jack set down stepladders, chains, and pliers. He carried his own tools up the third ladder and went to work.

Charlie discovered that on a metal rim, twelve loops of chain had to be hung on rusty hooks. To his surprise, the pliers opened each hook easily, without breaking them. The rust was superficial, the metal strong.

The next hoop was in worse shape. It hung loosely from the backboard, which bore dents from a vicious hammering. This required the portable welder. It would be tricky to re-seat the rim properly, but he'd not forgotten his father's lessons. He got absorbed in the task and lost track of time. When he finished, Charlie didn't see his companions, but he heard Alice's voice. He climbed down from his stepladder and walked until he saw his principal co-conspirator.

Jack acknowledged Charlie but kept watching Alice. "Would ya look at that?" Jack said. "She's really into it. That's her third one."

Alice hesitated atop her ladder. She pulled a ringing zune from her pocket.

"Who's calling Alice in the middle of the night?" Charlie said.

"Probably her sister, Amber."

"Why would she call—"

"At three in the morning? She lives in Hawaii. Probably some reasonable hour out there, and Alice is always up late. What say we give a listen?"

Jack moved his stepladder under the hoop nearest Alice.

Charlie's curiosity pushed him to follow suit. He stood beneath Jack and tried to look useful.

Alice stared down at the basketball court beneath her.

"Don't bring up Aunt Cassie," she said.

In the glow of her zune, Charlie thought he saw worry lines on Alice's forehead.

"I know it's genetic. That doesn't mean we—"

Charlie handed a pair of pliers to Jack, who pretended to use them.

"You got tested? But what if it had been positive?"

Charlie caught Alice's eyes and turned away to pick up a chain basket, which he handed up to Jack. The last words Charlie heard over the clattering chain were "getting plenty of sleep" and "I don't want the test."

Jack and Charlie slowly put the basket in place. Just before they finished, Alice shouted into her zune, "Leave me the fuck alone! I don't want to know." Alice tapped her device and looked to her companions. "Sorry about that. Sisters are a pain in the—"

"Hey!"

The deep male voice came from the nearest school building, perhaps fifty yards away. A back door stood open, and a bright flashlight shot a beam toward the basketball courts.

"Who's out there?"

"Nobody!" Alice shouted back, then sniggered like Scooby-Doo.

"Shut it!" Jack seemed to panic. "Swear I recognize that dude. We gotta scram!"

The man was walking closer. His black uniform looked like private security, or maybe night watchman. "You better not be fucking up my school!"

A click-clack sound made Jack duck low to look for cover. "Fuck if that's not a shotgun. I swear it's the same fucking dude from Bellingham."

"Jesus," Alice said, "how gullible do you think I am, Jack?

You staged this—all of this."

Charlie had the same thought, but Jack was no thespian. The boy was gesturing wildly for his companions to follow.

"Drop your shit," Jack hissed, "run for the car!"

The night watchman had reached the edge of the blacktop. He really did have a shotgun in his hands, with the flashlight braced against its barrel. The man also had stopped talking, which worried Charlie more.

"It's not like we're breaking any laws," Alice said. "Or, wait— we are, aren't we?"

"This fella's more bushranger than law officer," Jack said.

All of them heard the next sound—the slide-action of a loading shell. All at once, Alice, Charlie, and Jack dropped their hardware and ran. Making good use of their cat burglar outfits, they disappeared into the darkness.

* * *

Until the Scion left Lummi Shore Road, its passengers were too spooked to speak. Once they turned onto Marine Drive, Jack leaned forward from the back seat to break the silence.

"True story—I almost shat my daks again."

"Glad you clenched this time," Alice said.

"That was a shotgun," Charlie said. "Dude in your story had a hunting rifle."

"What the fuck do I know rifles from shotguns?" Jack said. "I'm no Ned Kelly."

"Ned—who?" Alice said.

"The Aussie Jessie James," Charlie said.

"More like Robin Hood," Jack said.

"If you're paying for all the tools we left back there," Charlie said, "that's good enough for me."

Hard-won laughs came from Alice and Jack alike. Charlie felt himself relax. The adrenaline from their Lummi School escape had worn off, and Bellingham was still a half-hour away, Seattle another ninety minutes after that. He'd have to keep putting effort into the conversation to stay awake.

"So, I was thinking," Charlie said. "We just did something constructive back there, right?"

"Sure," Jack said. "Outlaw altruism."

"So," Charlie continued, "Sailee and I had a bit of an argument about this last week."

Alice turned to study Charlie's face. He grinned at her, but her smile was fading. Better to have her focus on work than remember tonight's election.

"Sailee insists that each person has a moral obligation to change the world. She asked what I thought of GM harnessing the power of our call centers to turn our memo service into more of a *public* service."

"What's that mean?" Jack said.

Charlie hadn't meant to bring this up for discussion yet, and he wasn't sure what to say.

"I don't know, maybe prodding clients to sort their recycling. Helping them cut down on cigarettes by reminding them they'd promised to quit. Things like that, I guess."

"Are they really doing that?" Jack asked.

"Probably," Alice muttered, "but Charlie's the one watching over them."

"Are they?" Jack asked again.

"I don't know," Charlie said. He hadn't meant to lie, but now that he'd done it...

"Bloody stupid idea," Jack said.

Charlie checked for Alice's reaction and saw the back of her head. She was looking just past the upcoming intersection. The Scion's headlights shone off a decommissioned gas station, which the local Democratic Party had converted into a campaign office. A collage of yard signs covered the lower half of its front windows. The largest was a star-spangled circular placard that read, "Eleanor Eisenhower & Mahatma Golden – Securing the Future."

Alice burped. Fearing she might vomit, Charlie turned into the parking lot beside the campaign office. Alice took the cue and opened her door. She swung her legs around but didn't leave her seat.

Jack bounced out of the car and onto the asphalt. Charlie hoped he was giddy from their escapade, not drinking from a hidden flask. He moved around to face Alice and tried to pull her out.

"Is it the election that's gotcha down, luv?" Jack said with a laugh. "So what if Golden's in, you still got your lady president!"

This was not a good line of argument. Charlie reached out and put a hand on Alice's shoulder. He tried to offer a compliment, but as soon as he said the words, he recognized his error.

"You know," Charlie said, "your fundraising might have made the difference."

Jack caught Alice's eye and gave her a pout. Just loud enough for her and Charlie to hear, he cooed, "Oops."

ALICE

"Oops" was one of Alice's favorite words. Its meaning hinged on nuances of tone and context. It was among those expressions autistics struggled to parse. She rarely used it with the Codelings.

Alice repeated the sound to herself as she stepped out of the car and walked past Jack. The occupants of the campaign office had long since left to celebrate their victory elsewhere. Sometime thereafter, vandals had spray-painted the front door with "Eisenhower & Golden – Screwing the Future."

At least the font work was classy.

Whether referring to a faux pas or a mistake, "oops" could convey different meanings. To steady her racing heartbeat, Alice arranged the word's possible interpretations into a matrix. She closed her eyes and shut out the worried whispers of her companions. In a matter of seconds, she used Objective-C to write a function.

```
cha    oopsMessageSent    (bool   voiceCheerful,    bool
toneAscending)
{
cha *oopsMessage;
//Standard oops message
if (voiceCheerful = 1 && toneAscending = 0)
{
oopsMessage = 'I wish to offer empathy for your unfortunate
circumstance but in no way absolve you.'
}
//Sympathetic oops message
else if (voiceCheerful = 1 && toneAscending = 1)
{
oopsMessage = 'I recognize that you know you have
committed an error in social or motor skill. I do not
```

mean to correct you, but only empathize.'
}
//Scolding oops message
else if (voiceCheerful = 0 && toneAscending = 0)
{
oopsMessage = 'How careless and or clumsy of you,
to commit a needless error.'
}
//Derisive oops message
else
{
oopsMessage = 'One would think that you would know better
than to have committed the error, entitling you to a courtesy
response that acknowledges your general competence in this
arena. However, your mistake was avoidable and foolish.
Thus, I mock you.'
}
return oopsMessage;
}

To be fair, this was a gross simplification. Real human interaction required more situational knowledge. In the case of Jack's usage, a short minute ago, he probably meant something like, "One would think that you knew better than to support Eisenhower in the first place, but you did not. It should be punishment enough that you now recognize the error, but I, being weak, cannot help but underscore that your overzealous actions have likely harmed us all."

By way of response, Alice considered how she might use the same word on her own behalf, as the one who had committed the error. This class of "oops" variants included her favorite, the mock self-scolding voice with an ascending tone. This amounted to saying, "I am aware of the error I committed and want you to know that I recognize it as such. Chastise me if you must, but the record will show that I acknowledged my mistake."

Alice walked back to the car and stuck her head in her open door. "So, Charlie, the rules of your vandalism game say it must be illegal, and it has to make the world a better place, right?"

"That, and nobody gets hurt," Charlie said, a hint of apprehension in his voice.

An idle thought occupied Alice's mind. If the Quiet Copilot could auto-transcribe a client's voice, how would it discern precise meanings when users uttered difficult words, like "oops"? Even harnessed to the Loop, software could not detect ambivalence, irony, or strategic ambiguity. Nor could it parse emotional states reliably. Would clients tethered to raw code lose their own emotional subtlety, or become numb to that of others?

Alice opened the trunk and pulled out one of the aluminum stepladders. Her forehead was burning. She'd get no sleep tonight—that was a given. Dark thoughts echoed in her mind, and she had to quiet them. This required a distraction more satisfying than Lummi playground maintenance.

Charlie and Jack pulled up behind Alice as she carried the ladder away from the car and toward the building.

"What you got in mind?" Charlie said. "Graffiti removal? We could score window cleaner at the 7/11, but I doubt we can get solvents—"

"I had that woman in my home," Alice muttered as she marched closer to the main entrance. "I looked her in the eye. She swore she wasn't like the rest. She wouldn't compromise, or hide her intelligence. Then she's arm-in-arm with the craziest fuck on Planet Earth. She leads him around like a prize pony, right up to the White House."

Alice jogged for a few steps, then shifted the ladder's weight back before spinning her body like a discus tosser. Charlie ducked under the swinging ladder, which barely missed him.

"Holy shit!" Jack shouted.

Alice released her projectile with more velocity than expected. It took a head-first dive through the storefront window, which shattered with a clap. After two careful steps back and a shimmy to shake off shards of glass, Alice gave her two favorite employees what they'd been hoping for all night—a bright, white smile. That, and one word.

"Oops."

Part IV

Adaptations

BARRY

This new walker glides across the sidewalk. Shock absorbers pump up and down to smooth out the ride. Engineers must have tested it on this broke neighborhood, or off road. Dodgy on icy patches like this one, though. Hard to see, so dark around some of these corners. First full moon of the year helps, though. And the streetlights are working. That's a miracle.

Still no sign of Lucky's Tavern. None of these buildings has neon. Don't even see Lucky's big television in the windows.

That cold air really chills the face. Rest of me's gonna overheat in this winter coat. Take it off and glide up to a funky looking house. From porch to roof, musty stuffed animals hang all over it. And look at those street paintings. Big circles of blue, white, pink. Some maybe three foot wide, some tiny.

If we can have potholes, we can have polka dots.

"You're that Barry Sanders dude. Are you lost?"

Girl's voice. Sitting on the stoop of the animal house.

"I'm fine, thank you. Lucky's the one that ain't where it's supposed to be. What's your name, young lady?"

"You know me. I'm Lauryn."

Hell if I know you, but don't say that.

"What's up with this crazy house? You a collector? My wife's a collector."

"Dad calls it, 'decorating the desolation.'"

Not likely. Nobody talks like that.

"What you doin' out so late, mister?"

"Goin' to see Mrs Eleanor on the TV."

"Missus who?"

"The President, child. We've got a woman president, and it's about time. Tonight's her second State of the Union."

"Bunch of words, all that is. She's been sitting in that big chair of hers more than a year. Hasn't changed a thing, not here

146

anyways. Neither did Barack, did he? She's better than the fat Cheeto dude she punked, but c'mon, who wouldn't be?"

Who, indeed. Pleasant tells me not to quarrel over politics. Give the girl a goodbye, then let it go.

Next two blocks I feel in my legs. Goin' too far tonight.

Look at this—another young lady out at night. Curled up on the sidewalk under a blanket. Gotta be cold down there. Try poking her with the walker, say a hello. No answer. What's come of these kids?

A familiar voice comes outta nowhere.

"Their plight is a complicated one, Mr Sanders. May I help you?"

"Wait, you're not the woman I just saw. You know where that dang tavern's at?"

"It should be near, but please wait—"

"Never you mind, here it is. I see its big ol' TV."

Don't remember concrete front steps. Maybe too icy for me. But look at those "smart wheels" Charlie got me! Lock and grab, lock and grab. Step by step, and up we go.

"Mr Sanders, maybe it is not—"

That voice spooks me sometimes. Sounds as quiet as the thoughts inside my head.

Front door is open. Lucky's redone the place. Looks comfy, like a living room. Soft couch over by the television wants another butt on it. Freckled college kid's already sleeping there so the cushions must be nice. Too cold for him to be wearing nothing but cotton briefs and a tank-top, white as his skin. Looks like a Halloween ghost.

"Sir, I am truly sorry, but my map says you are at a private—"

Kid reminds me of an intern from the plant. Whined any time he lifted something heavy. Too sleepy to mind if I turn the television on.

Let's see how this remote works. And...there's the President!

"I am concerned that you have trespassed—"

147

"Quiet down. It's on."

"I would like to re-route—"

"If you're not gonna watch, get outta my head!"

But the voice won't stop. I shake my neck and feel something pop out of my ear. I pick it up off the floor but don't see a trashcan. Besides, Charlie gave it to me as a gift, so better to pocket it until I get home.

Looks like couch boy's awake. Tries to sit up straight. Too many beers tonight for him.

"Sorry, son. I don't mean to shout like a madman just then. There's this voice in my head. Drives me crazy."

Man wipes his mouth. Ugly broken-toothed smile. "All the time, right?"

Roar of applause comes from the set. Whole audience of suits, dresses, and uniforms stands up all at once.

"Go on, Eleanor. What you gonna do for Detroit?"

President stares right at me but says nothing. Looks over her shoulder, where dark suit gives a nod. Behind her a golden-haired fella in white pajamas makes a get-on-with-it gesture.

President looks away from me. "What do you mean, Mahatma? What's that signal?"

Pajama man moves his mouth to spell out, "Tel-la-something."

Eisenhower swings back around. Looks lost. Same thing happens to me every day. Coughs and says something about "restoring reason to a politics that divides us." Talks about a "fiscal impasse," whatever that is.

Boos are mixing with the clapping.

"What you doing here, old man?"

Kid's awake again.

"Watchin' the speech, just like you. Where's Lucky? Your whistle looks dry."

"What the fuck? You live here?"

"No need for cussing, even in a bar."

Couch kid points me to a picture. Stained wallpaper behind

it needs cleaning.

"Mister, is that you and your old lady in the photo, with kids and shit?"

Poor fella sounds confused. Don't know what to say to that.

Now, look at that young Mexican woman on the television. Looks smart in a blue Marines uniform. One of her shirt sleeves looks empty. Pinned it back onto her shoulder.

"I had two boys. One worked for GM, just like me, then went off to fight in Afghanistan. Didn't make it back. We got a visit from two officers and a flag in the mail. That was too much for Pleasant. Lost her the same year."

"That's a fuckin' drag, man."

"Just life, son. Twists and turns."

Wish that young man would do something about those dribbles running out his nose. Probably got him those angry looking sores on his lip.

"So, mister. You want a bump, or what?"

CHARLIE

Charlie was the only person at the Magnusson Dog Park without a pooch of his own, but he visited regularly enough to have made a few canine friends. Twenty yards away, a black poodle ran wide circles around a pack of ball-chasing labs.

"Here, Gwyneth!" Charlie bent his knees and slapped his thighs. "Come say hi!"

The poodle raced up to him and let Charlie give her top-knot a vigorous scratch. She held still, closed her mouth, and lifted the back of her lips in a curled smile. It seemed she might fall asleep on the spot. Her eyes closed tight and her head fell against his hip. When he paused, she batted at him until he resumed petting her. The physical connection slowed Charlie's pulse.

Sailee drifted into his mind. Before he could form a coherent thought, Gwyneth barked in his ear, then galloped off to rejoin her paid dog-walker. She disappeared around a corner, probably heading toward a cold dip in Lake Washington.

Before he could give chase, Charlie's zune whistled. He plucked it from his pocket and heard a familiar voice.

"Hey, Sailee."

"Where are you, Charlie? I hear shrieks. And thunder?"

"Off-leash park. The huge one I told you 'bout."

"But you still have no dog."

"I know, but there's a couple poodles here I like. Haven't seen Charles Barkley yet. He's gotta be here because I just spent quality time with Gwyneth."

"She's the big one?"

"Seventy pounds of muscle and hustle. Dark as graphite. She and her brother aren't racist like so many purebreds. I swear, some of these dogs—especially the terriers—come at me like I'm gonna mug their owners."

"Perhaps they are unaccustomed to anyone but white people

in Seattle. I have been studying your city, and —"

"It's more than that," Charlie said. "They pick up signals. There's no weirder vibe than guilty white folks' sideward glances. Quick smiles. Canines don't fall for that shit. They know I'm making their owners nervous."

"But as the only person in the park without a dog, I presume, you are also a potential stalker."

"Fair point. I'm in a hooded track suit with an Old English 'D' on it. Is that too thug for a dog park? What are you wearing?"

"A gentleman does not ask."

"Let's do video chat," Charlie suggested.

"Ah, not today," Sailee said. "Voice only for now."

"Okay, then where are you calling from?"

"That is today's riddle. I will give you hints."

Charlie reached for his zune.

"And before you peek, I baffled geo-location for this call."

Charlie lowered the guilty hand, which was perched over his device and ready to click.

"The first hint," Sailee said, "is that I hold a small brochure. I have just stepped out of a large flat building, a museum of sorts. I am now in a courtyard. It is early evening here, and there are only dim lights illuminating the grounds. There is a scattering of palm trees and single-story structures, which look more like huts than houses."

A wave of excitement passed through Charlie's chest. The game held appeal, but more than that, she'd designed it for him. The past year had been so busy that he and Sailee hadn't found the time to become more than co-workers. They settled into their respective jobs. Each gave the other more professional deference. Work issues came up only when necessary. This made their personal conversations more satisfying. Maybe even promising.

Charlie tried to picture where Sailee was walking. Too quiet for the city center, but she was too busy to travel outside Ahmedabad.

"Are you at a peasant-themed amusement park?"

"Not a bad first guess."

"Really?"

A long-nosed collie nudged the back of Charlie's leg. He offered a head pat in reply. Park dogs had no pretenses. That made them unsuitable for some prospective owners. After Eisenhower and Golden were sworn into office, Charlie tried giving Alice a black Labrador puppy for her birthday. That dog would have tamed her. She recognized the danger and gave it to a neighbor.

"Does the place you're at have dogs?" Charlie asked.

"No," Sailee said, "but if it did, none would be racist."

"Why can't all pooches be like Gwyneth and Barkley?"

"If you seek cross-species tolerance, you could study this here. Where I am today, Tolerance is Rule 11."

Charlie took a wide berth around a pair of mottled pit bulls.

"Are you at a school?" Charlie asked.

"Of a sort."

"Is this a Gandhian thing?"

"Very good!"

Sailee clapped in delight. Charlie blushed at how good it made him feel.

"I am reading," Sailee said, "the Official Rules of the Satyagraha Ashram. I called to share with you my walking tour through Gandhi's old campus. I wanted to take you here during your last visit, but you were too busy."

"I won't be such an idiot next time."

"Let us hope not. If we are to do great things together, there is much you must learn."

"Wait, is this about Dad? Or your Minders?"

"Both. And more. It is true that I am calling regarding your father. Last night, he could not understand why I was talking to him. He veered off course in search of a tavern, then removed his Copilot prototype. I feared he had thrown it away, but it was

152

back in place this morning."

"I called him after the State of the Union," Charlie said. "I knew he'd watch it, but I'm not sure where he saw it. I was the one who convinced him to put the earpiece back."

"And if you had not called him?"

"He wasn't the only one off his game last night," Charlie said. "You see Eisenhower's speech? She sounded like a space cadet."

"I am too busy at work for such things. That, and I have my own country to worry about. President Eisenhower is governing well enough, is she not?"

"Actually, we don't talk politics at the office so much either. Alice gets too riled up. But we do talk about reverse vandalism." Charlie reached into the front pouch of his hoodie. He ran his fingers over a Leatherman multi-tool, plus assorted screws. "This morning, when nobody was looking, I fixed a hinge on the dog park gate."

"Quite the outlaw, you are."

"The Lummi School was still our best job, even if we had to cut it short. Since then, we've done a bunch more. It's a good release for Alice. Jack says he still has a lifetime of atonement ahead of him, and this outlet's better than the self-flagellation shit he did before."

"Gandhi, too, had to make amends," Sailee said. "In his youth, he is said to have stolen cigarettes."

A low male voice, perhaps a tour guide near Sailee, said something about a "painting gallery."

"Good works are in the spirit of Rule 7," Sailee said. "You also adhered to Rule 12, which asks us to do daily physical labor. As of yet, however, your local actions have no connection to larger change. We must reshape the world more profoundly in accordance with Rule 1: Act on that which is right and true."

Charlie felt a shiver and shifted the zune into his other hand. An earpiece would be handy at times like this, but he didn't want to become like Jack, dependent on Buddy.

"What profound changes do you have in mind?" Charlie said. "Alice tolerates the gentle nudging of your Minders, but you've got to be careful. We're fielding complaints from family members."

"The pursuit of truth may require measured disobedience."

"Sounds like the wisdom of someone who didn't have an employer."

"I am not the same woman you hired three years ago. Back then, I was clever but had yet to embrace Rule 8: Fearlessness. She who seeks the truth must face the evils of caste, government, and thieves. Neither poverty nor death frighten her."

Charlie licked his lips. "On that scooter of yours, you are truly fearless."

"The truth?" Sailee said. "Our roads have become too dangerous. I am using a car service, exclusively."

"But isn't one of the ashram's rules something about poverty?"

"Actually," Sailee said, "that is Rule 6: Non-possession. At the present time, I cannot honor that mandate."

"Ends justify the means?"

No reply. Charlie feared that he'd crossed a line. Gandhi was more than an historical figure to Gujaratis. He'd just peed on their Lincoln Memorial.

In the silence, though, Charlie received a digital reassurance from his zune. It had a soft glow and felt warm in his hand. The haptic signal meant the Loop detected a strong connection with his caller. The Loop brought Sailee's photo and profile onto his screen.

She'd see his face on her screen, too. That's how it worked.

A text message appeared. "Your profile has been touched."

Charlie smiled and said, "Is that you fingering me?"

"I would never do such a naaauughty thing," Sailee said. "Rule 3 requires chastity. One must not let carnal thoughts cloud the mind."

Charlie followed suit and touched Sailee's profile. A

kaleidoscope of images circled his screen. He ran his index finger across one then another. Candid photos of her and Vijul at the call center. Her with Nani and the commie crones he'd yet to meet. A picture taken minutes before at the ashram, blowing a kiss. He and Sailee standing outside an Ahmedabad hotel on his second visit, when he'd fallen ill. He looked worse than he'd remembered. She looked concerned.

"So," Charlie said, "is there more to this call than discussing my father and your spiritual grandfather?"

"The Loop says there is more."

"The Loop says a lot of things."

ALICE

Alice pulled off Highway 12 when she reached the Bull Moose Lodge. The dashboard readout confirmed her on-time arrival. As it was the middle of March, she rented an SUV, guessing correctly that she might crawl along snow-covered highways for an hour before her reunion with the woman who was now Commander in Chief.

The invitation had come from President Eisenhower herself. No scheduler, staffer, or operator connected the call. She asked Alice for a "two-hour meeting," with no further details. Though Alice hadn't spoken with Eisenhower since their meeting outside her penthouse, that conversation left a loaf-sized breadcrumb. The President wanted a tech to bring her father back from the other side of Alzheimer's.

Or, perhaps this was an inquiry into Alice's fundraising prowess during the election. Eisenhower was already building a reelection war chest, and her campaign treasurer may have discovered why it grew so much faster the last time around. Tiptoeing around that felonious subject was worth the trouble if it gave Alice the chance to chastise Eisenhower in person.

Where to begin? Letting Mahatma Golden into the White House was unforgivable. Eisenhower blamed the DNC, but Alice wanted to hear her take personal responsibility. Golden's weekly radio addresses reminded Alice of his welcome speech to her at Thereport, except that now he gave policy sermons as a duly elected vice president. He could deploy his idiosyncratic futurism to champion NASA funding, or forestall new environmental regulations.

With the limited power of his office, Golden had done less damage in two years than Alice had expected. Still, he sat on his haunches like a tiger in a magic act. Watching. Waiting.

The SUV crunched snow as Alice pulled into the lodge's

driveway. An enormous man in a black dress coat waved for her to stop. As he approached, a shorter but equally stocky agent circled around to the opposite side of the car.

Alice lowered her window. "Sorry, officer. Wrong driveway?"

The man's reflective sunglasses didn't move. "Alice Coleco?"

She gave a coy nod.

"Please step out of the car, ma'am."

"Don't you need to see my license?"

"No."

"What if I'm not who you think I am?"

"If you weren't Alice Coleco, we'd be having a different conversation. Agent Polina Adamson will escort you inside."

Alice undid her seatbelt and climbed out to greet the female agent. "Polina? A Russian name?"

"Estonian, second generation," the woman said. She took Alice's elbow in her hand. Close-cropped hair exposed a thick neck above her collar. If she'd been born during the Cold War, the Soviets might have tapped her as an Olympian.

"Do you choose your own clothes in this job?" Alice asked.

"No, ma'am. It's a uniform."

"Like the Marines, but without the pieces of flair?"

Agent Adamson half-grinned. She led Alice onto the porch of a two-story log cabin. After crossing the foyer, they entered a modest den. Its mantle held portraits of Theodore Roosevelt, William Taft, Harry Truman. Early twentieth-century furniture carried the unconquerable odor of mildew.

Heavy footsteps thudded on a stairway to her right. Alice turned to see Eleanor Eisenhower, dressed in amber hiking boots and REI winter apparel. It was nearly the same outfit Alice had chosen for the occasion, except that the CEO's custom boots and gear matched the metallic gray of the GM logo.

"Welcome to the Bull Moose," Eisenhower said. "To answer your likely questions, yes, Roosevelt slept here. As did two other presidents, plus John Muir and Gloria Steinem."

"Any of your famous relatives spend the night here?"

"FDR didn't travel much, but Eleanor did make it out to Seattle more than once. War bond rallies and the like, strictly affairs of state. As for Ike, he was no frontiersman. He had a macho image but was more comfortable among wonks."

"Not a tin-cup-by-the-campfire kind of guy?"

"That's a fair assessment. And no, the lodge isn't any nicer on the inside than on the outside. Maybe that's why Al Gore opted to land his helicopter on top of Mt Rainier, rather than stay the night."

"And which are you? Nature girl or landed gentry?"

"Neither. I am simply your President. And your President is taking you on a hike."

"When we spoke, you made no mention of trekking up a mountain."

Eisenhower drew back her shoulders, as if taking a defensive stance. "Didn't I? I must have said something."

Alice opted to let it go. The Loop's daily video log often featured a fresh montage showing Eisenhower forgetting words or overlooking details, usually to her embarrassment. It was a relief to see her regain composure. The President put one hand to her heart and raised the other toward Roosevelt's portrait.

"I take Teddy's view," she said. "A rugged life builds character. To educate a person in the mind but not in morals is to educate a menace to society."

"But received morality diminishes our capacity for change."

Eisenhower paused, as if weighing Alice's words. The effect was flattering. "My view is less grandiose than Teddy's. Let's just get our heart rates up, clear our thoughts, then move on to business."

"It's pretty cold out there," Alice protested. "I'm more of an indoors gal. If it's all the same, let's just talk over cocoa in the parlor."

The President stiffened. "Perhaps I am the one who could use a clearer mind. The agents will trail us, but out of earshot."

"Isn't there some protocol about being exposed, out in the open?"

"Of course," Eisenhower said. "This side of the mountain has been cleared."

Alice followed her leader out of the cabin and up a trail with a steep ascent.

A nag from Jack popped into Alice's mind. "Gotta work out more. Gotta build stamina." He claimed she was getting "all skinny and sleepy-eyed." He was probably right. It was presumptuous of him to act as her Minder, but he meant well. Maybe she'd find a way to be his Minder, too.

"A doe is the only creature we're likely to find up here," Eisenhower said. "It's too bad, because seeing wolves in the wild is on my bucket list. I imagine that TED talk you've got coming up is something to check off on your own list?"

How she knew about that, Alice could only guess. The invitation to the Long Beach conference was confidential. Alice hadn't yet confirmed, though she'd signed a non-disclosure promising not to mention the event until her script was approved. She wasn't the only one who worried that the Loop was snooping up information not meant for its eyes.

Alice had to ask. "How did you—"

"Leader of the Free World, remember? I get to know a few things even the Loop hasn't discovered yet."

That was reassuring, sort of.

"Still, how did…"

Eisenhower was starting to pull away, one powerful step after another. Whatever her failings, the woman had an impressive stride.

The President kept moving but turned to give Alice a glance. "Getting invited for a bona fide TED talk is a coronation of sorts, isn't it?"

Short of breath, Alice replied in bursts. "It's a…cumbersome selfie." The disdain in her voice was no act. She'd decided to give the invitation a pass. The President's data-net hadn't caught that tidbit, which Alice had shared with no one.

Eisenhower stopped and waited for Alice to reach her. She placed one hand on her lips, the other on Alice's shoulder. "Look just to the right," she said at a whisper. "Beneath the bowed tree. See it?"

In the snow beneath a lodgepole pine sat a lump of coal. Two silver triangles poked out of the lump. Then it was clear. Alice saw the gray profile of a resting wolf. It stood, unaware of their presence. Like a dog preparing for an evening walk, it leaned its front legs forward and took a deep stretch. It sniffed the air, then trotted into a thicket.

"A public policy triumph," the President said.

Alice chuckled. "Statistically speaking, that's got to be among the least likely sentences ever uttered in this context."

"Not at all." Eisenhower resumed her trail climb and motioned for Alice to follow. "Species reintroduction and management in this region was a regulatory triumph. Teddy would be proud."

"Please. He wasn't a tree hugger."

"True. Muir might cuddle a bear cub, but Teddy was more likely to shoot one."

"T.R. was more like a lone wolf himself. Our lodge took its name from his rogue party."

"That's a poor metaphor." Eisenhower gave Alice a stare like that of a third-grade teacher. "Wolves depend on the wits of their pack. They travel and hunt together. Just like us, they survived only if they belonged to the fittest *group*."

"With all due respect, such as it is, Eleanor—"

Alice froze for a moment. She'd come to this meeting to offer a piece of her mind, but it was hard to cop an attitude with a sitting head of state. Etiquette had to be observed.

"Excuse me," Alice said. "Madam President, we survive by taking care of ourselves and respecting one another's independence." The Lummi basketball courts came to mind. "Creative altruism has its place, but public morality congeals into intrusiveness. I've had to lecture my colleagues in India on this very point. I believe..."

Alice slowed down to refill her lungs. Each crunch on the thick snow strained the muscles in her hips. Tendons in her ankles ached.

Eisenhower waited for Alice to catch up, more likely out of sympathy than any fatigue of her own. "Look at yourself, Ms Coleco. You and your friends built a company for the betterment of an entire generation."

"We *built* that," Alice said. "Is that still a GOP slogan?"

"Of course you profited from the business. Your mirror neurons, however, endowed you with instinctual compassion that undergirds your company more than you admit. Something triggered that altruism in you. Maybe it was your mother's affliction?"

Out of breath, Alice couldn't even hold a scowl in reply. "I guess," Alice put her hands on her knees, "you learned about Mom in a Secret Service background check."

The President didn't reply. Eisenhower looked disoriented, maybe dizzy. Turning away from Alice, she clenched her gloved hands into fists and pounded her hips. She looked up toward the sun, which moved in and out of thin clouds. Eyes open wide, then closed. The cycle repeated three times.

When Eisenhower turned back to face her, Alice said, "I suppose that you know how my mother died, a year after I was born?"

Eisenhower faced Alice squarely and grasped her shoulders. Even at a two-foot distance, it felt too intimate. "I am so very sorry you lost your mother when you did, as you did. You assume her fate will be yours? Perhaps her diagnosis was suspect. Almost nobody has died from a lack of sleep."

"It's called Fatal Familial Insomnia."

"Your older sister is in her fifties, alive and well. Your aunt lived to be my age. And you? Out of shape, yes, but still kicking."

The chill of Mt Rainier's gathering winds left Alice shivering, yet her heart burned like a stoked wood stove. Flames of anger warmed her chest, shoulders, neck. Alice saw herself as a sixteen-year-old, seated beside Amber at a Carl's Jr. Her big sister was explaining exactly how their mother had died. Their maternal lineage carried a maddening condition that would slowly rob them of rest. Ever since that day, Alice had felt as though an LED timer lay under her scalp, a parting gift from Mom that would reunite them sooner than either would have wished.

Eisenhower squeezed Alice's shoulders. "This troubles you, dear. I wish you could look at me."

Alice tried to gather herself, but anger building inside her linked one frustration to another. Finally, she blurted, "How could you let that moron become our vice president?"

Eisenhower let go of Alice and laughed, visibly relieved.

"You know full well that wasn't my choice. Party fools and their party rules hitched me to a bum horse."

"Bull—*moose*," Alice said, with quick self-censorship avoiding a worse faux pas. "All you had to do was say, 'No.' Of all the people." Breathless, again. "You gave him...a podium with an eagle on it."

"Well, I didn't—"

"He's using that platform to bash my company every week. It's great for business, but I didn't fund your campaign to buy publicity."

"We are not here to talk about me. There is something I need to ask of *you*."

Alice met Eisenhower's gaze with a knowing nod. "I don't have a spy agency of my own, but I didn't forget what you said at our last meeting. It's the centenarian, isn't it?"

"My father is not quite that old, but close."

"Outside the factory warranty," Alice said. "Now he's gotta

be worse."

Eisenhower's eyebrows rose together. "That is confidential information, but yes. Short-term memory went first, then—"

"I'll admit his case crossed my mind more than once, but the tech you need doesn't exist—not yet, anyway."

"Perhaps not, but tell me this much. Can you provide the service of a Quiet Copilot through a clandestine device?"

"Interesting." Alice's scalp tingled. Inside her skull, neurons danced. Alice stroked her hair and picked up a static charge. "You're imagining something that would bypass what exactly? A metal detector?"

"Or a prying family doctor."

Alice nodded.

"More than that, how close are you to providing automated assistance? No human being on the other end?"

"Snooping again, are we?" Alice took two steps up the steep trail. "Unofficially, yes, that's where we're headed. For your father, though, we'd arrive too late. Even if we rushed—"

"You could beta-test on Poppy, like you do with your colleague's father."

"That's an exceptional arrangement. We don't—"

"It would mean a lot. More than you can imagine."

Stubbornness had pushed Eisenhower through more than one glass ceiling. There was no point arguing. Besides, what was the harm in granting her wish? Eisenhower's father was inert, with or without GM tech jammed into his head. It wouldn't be the first time Alice had indulged a fantasy. Even if Charlie wouldn't let himself see it, Barry was stumbling down the same dark alley as the President's father.

"If you're building it anyway," Eisenhower said, "what say we give it a try?"

"Why not," Alice said. She had other reasons for accelerating development. The company's Gujarati telessistants became bolder in their improvisations with every passing year. Charlie's algorithms would replace them, in time, and Eisenhower's father would be a worst-case stress test for those equations.

"When can we get started?" Eisenhower said.

The eagerness in the President's voice sounded—wrong. Eisenhower had a firm enough grasp on her father's situation to recognize that a lost cause has no urgency. More than that, why press for delivery of a covert device with automated assistance?

Eisenhower repeated a move she'd used minutes before, by grasping both of Alice's shoulders and locking eyes with her.

"Trust me," Eisenhower said. "The sooner the better."

Alice swallowed hard. That sounded like a plea for help.

"We could have something by August," Alice said. "When it's ready, I'll send Charlie—my chief engineer."

"This is a kindness I will *never* forget."

The words sounded sincere.

Alice doubted they'd prove true.

JACK

The glass walls and sleek furniture of the GM conference room used to make Jack vibrate with excitement. Ultra-modern decor signaled that he had arrived, ahead of schedule, on the cutting edge of wherever technology was taking over the world.

As he sat down beside Charlie this afternoon, Jack felt more alienated than inspired. Alice and Charlie were the closest things he had to friends, or even family, yet they rarely met outside a room built for business. Even while meeting together, they'd be staring at separate zunes or manipulating images displayed on the conference table surface.

Technical data and ideas were easy—and necessary—to exchange. Jack was less sure how to share a more personal bit of news, or whether he should mention it at all. Only a few days had passed since Alice returned from her meeting with President Eisenhower, so the timing of Jack's announcement still felt wrong.

Or, he could simply lean across the table and say, "My mum's dead."

It wasn't as though staff hid their families. Everyone at GM knew Charlie's father. Barry was practically their corporate mascot. A Codeling parent was buzzed into the main floor suite every week or so, just to see the hallowed halls of GM. Alice brought up her sister in conversation often enough.

Nobody ever asked about Jack's family, though the basic facts were known. Even his online auto-bio noted he had no siblings, a one-night father the Loop could neither geo- nor geno-locate, and a lush for a mother, who bludged the dole back in Oz.

He didn't know for certain, but that last part was probably out of date. Her landlord found Jack's e-mail address while cleaning out her unit. Said she'd just vanished. Gone for weeks, and rent was owed. If she was still drowning in some crack house, she'd have bobbed up by now. She always did, to ask for money.

There was a moment—between an Eisenhower anecdote from Alice and a failed joke by Charlie—where Jack could have blurted out, "How's Barry these days? By the way, I think my mother passed away." If he said anything like that, he'd have the wrong expression on his face. He'd accepted that this was how his mother would go—by simply disappearing. Where there should be sorrow, he would show relief.

The point was moot because heated conversation had replaced casual workplace banter. There'd be no openings for personal topics.

"You've been stuck in idle too long!" Alice said, her raised voice on the edge of anger. "You've helped us build trinkets, but you need to massage that big brain of yours. Go deeper into the data mines you were prospecting when we first met. I need you to pull out a miracle."

"No promises," Charlie said. He raised his hands, which looked like a plea for calm. "But there is this. At a Mariners game last weekend, I started obsessing about the metaphor of a compass."

"Did they win?" Jack said.

The question threw Charlie off track.

"Did the Mariners win the baseball game?"

Alice and Charlie exchanged glances.

"They've won ten straight or something," Alice said, "so let's just say, 'Yes.' Continue."

"Anyway," Charlie said, "a compass has four basic directions, with gradations in between. That's how people move through life—pushing themselves and the world in one direction or another. But there's only so many vectors out there. Across long stretches of history, the world over, people come in a few basic types. I inherited progressive politics from my parents. A different mix of genetic predispositions, family experiences, and early adulthood placed Jack in the quadrant opposite from where I might stand on a two-by-two grid."

Even without a Ph.D., Jack could see at least one hole in that theory. Jack's parents might have both taught him a thing or two, but only by bad example. Libertarian fatalism was a sensible and conscious retreat from his personal experience of a failed social order. It was doubtful that Charlie's math could trace Jack's philosophy back to anything so coherent as an "upbringing."

Jack wanted to pull a bottle of vodka from the wet bar, drink from it until he gagged, then make a trite proclamation. "Guess I am who I am, and nothing can change me."

Instead, he said a quiet "Excuse me" and retreated to the men's room. With the faucet running, he stuck his head in the ceramic bowl beneath it. Cold water on his neck and behind his ears never failed to soothe. This time, however, he'd been so upset that he forgot to remove Buddy. This time, he drowned his little friend.

Attempts at resuscitation—paper towels, the hand drier, every kind of reboot—were futile. Losing Buddy by his own hands, right before his eyes, on top of everything else—it was too much. He could call Vijul, but on what device? A damn zune? Besides, she'd probably tell him that these events were happening for some asinine reason involving the psychedelic logic of Hindu gods. No thanks.

When Jack got back to the conference room, Charlie and Alice were still buzzing. They seemed oblivious to both his absence and his return.

Now, there were two deaths in the family that he'd have to keep to himself.

"With enough server power," Alice said, "we can track any person's electronic scent through the Loop. We can see what my sister had for breakfast, what she did at work, what she bought on the way home. It all leaves tracks in the digital mud."

"Like a bloodhound," Charlie said with a laugh.

Jack settled into his seat. Might as well jump right in.

"If the Codelings and I can crunch all that down to nanoscale," Jack said, "we could slide a chip smaller than a guitar pick into the side of grampa's head. We might be able to make him fun again, even after he's started crapping into his Depends."

"Who knows?" Alice said. "Maybe we can save the President's dear old dad. That would be quite the magic trick. Raising the dead. Figuratively, of course."

Here Jack was, falling under Alice's spell yet again. If this crazy compass concept spun their company off the road, he'd want to be tumbling down the embankment with her.

Alice had entranced Jack the first day he reported for work. He stayed at his intern desk in the octagon after hours, perusing the details of a business plan she'd put on his desktop. A hand on his shoulder pushed his rolling office chair away from the keyboard. Pulling up a chair of her own, Alice started typing.

"This, dear boy," she said, "is the kernel from which my company grew."

Using the Loop's Wayback machine, she took him to futureme.org. It was a website where you could type a message and mark it for delivery to your own e-mail account on a specific date. Alice wrote dozens of "memos from her better self." She went into an ancient Hotmail account and showed Jack a message from her teenage self, who implored, "Make the world <<quiver>> at your presence. Magnify your power. Wield it without mercy."

Teenage Alice must have been a piece of work. Grown-up Alice was a masterpiece.

Alice tapped the conference room table. Images of every previous GM prototype appeared, starting with the Forget Me Not.

"Some people make breakthroughs," Alice said. "They cure diseases, invent a new kind of government, or split atoms. But look at our company's products. We sit here, week after week, and we tinker. We tweak. We're like people who make computers smaller, or zunes thinner. The aggregate may look like a revolution, but it isn't."

"Being a bit hard on yourself," Jack said.

"You're right," Alice said. "We've already extended the number of useful days in a life. Trust me, I know too well that our days are numbered. I'd pay any price to advance my own expiration date by even a month."

"Who wouldn't?" Charlie said. "But picture this—" He waved an open palm over the conference table. The prototypes disappeared. Charlie drew a crude compass with his index finger. "What if we made a tech that gave every senior a chance for a few more *years*? And if we did it with an automated device that required minimal upkeep, anyone could afford it."

Jack spoke in the deep voice favored by movie trailers. "Whether young or old, the Elder Compass will change your world."

"Let's get to it," Alice said. "We'll touch their lives in ways they can't imagine."

SAILEE

The early months of summer had passed so quickly that Sailee double checked her calendar to confirm August's arrival. A cyclone in the Arabian Sea compounded her confusion. It came off-schedule by several months. Unpredictability had become the norm in weather forecasting, but this was no small anomaly.

Harrowing images came through the Loop to document the devastation in Dahej. In Sailee's coastal hometown south of Ahmedabad, apartment buildings and shanties alike had gone to rubble. One snapshot showed a modern condominium tower lying on its side across a boulevard. The building seemed intact, but a dry caption read, "None inside survived."

Rescuers and relief workers had taken stock of the damage for less than a full day. Based on the tangle of predictive algorithms in its guts, the Loop estimated that one-in-eight of the city's two million residents lost their homes, their lives, or both.

Unfathomable.

Sailee clicked through time-lapse videos of the storm's landing. She felt numb. As if sensing her need for emotional distance, the Loop muted the sound on Sailee's speakers. It replaced the images on her monitor with a page of technical details about the event. In meteorological parlance, this was not a conventional disaster. The weather bureau classified it as a "super cyclone."

She knew the term. Seventeen years ago, the same class of storm had swept her parents away. As an adult, Sailee had become a powerful businesswoman. She commanded tall buildings. Today, she felt as small as a child.

To shake that sensation, Sailee turned her attention back to monitoring the GM network. In search of a problem she could diagnose and solve, Sailee found one. There was a constriction in the Loop's access to her center's activities. Closer inspection showed that an encryption blanket covered the calls her operators were making to clients.

Back in the days of the Internet, extensive encryption had been the norm for online networks. The Loop's credo was unconditional openness. Sailee preferred that elegant phrase to the clunky backronym, "large optional open power." By the rules of the Loop, a company that kept anything private—beyond personal financial or health information—risked losing access to all the other data coursing through the global system.

Sailee knew precisely how long her shop could hide from the Loop before suffering a disconnection penalty. Two years ago, during the final weeks of the US election, Sailee tested the forty-minute limit down to the second. GM Headquarters was besieged by warnings from the Loop that began at the thirty-first minute of darkness. Codelings traced the problem to a crack in the Ahmedabad T2 backbone, which Sailee promised to take up with their local network provider. Subsequent memos diagnosing and correcting the error satisfied the engineers back in Seattle. Today's recurrence would risk undoing the mutual trust that correspondence restored.

Before Sailee could guess at what—or who—had re-encrypted the network, rising voices outside her office offered a clue. She got out of her chair and slid open her frosted glass office door to see the backs of two older women Sailee recognized immediately. Grisma wore a gray sheath, Mazoo a broad blue dress.

Trapped between them stood Vijul. "I told you," she pleaded, "our time is up. We must shut it down at once."

"Shut what down?" Sailee said.

Vijul's mouth hung open, as if startled to see her own boss.

Grisma turned to Sailee. "Vijul asked us not to trouble you, but I am certain you will take our side in this dispute. Explain to your colleague why we need to get as much relief to the people of Dahej as possible."

Her grandmother's pleading eyes set Sailee's heart racing.

"Without our help," Grisma said, "even more lives will be lost."

"*Our* help?" Sailee said.

A clutch of supervisors gathered behind Vijul. One stepped forward and said, "I will not tell my girls to cease calling until they have reached every client in my region."

Vijul raised her hands to silence the crowd, then turned to Sailee. "I wanted to keep you out of this. Mazoo and Grisma practically beat down my door. I offered to encrypt the network for twenty minutes—no more. We could make gentle pleas to our clients for Red Cross donations. The Troika do not have to know."

Frustration replaced Sailee's confusion. "What are you doing, Vijul? Taking credit card information over the phone? Nudges are one thing, but—"

"This will not trip any alarms," Vijul said. "The twentieth minute is approaching. I was just about to give the stop order and lift the blanket—"

"As I explained to my daughter," Mazoo said, "your compassion must be stronger than your fear. We would not jeopardize any of your jobs, but Vijul confessed that the calls can continue twice as long as she will allow."

"*She* will allow?" Sailee shouted. "I never gave Vijul such authority!"

The outburst silenced every woman in the hall. It echoed back off the smooth walls and back to Sailee, who heard a tone she had never used before.

Vijul broke the silence. "We are not taking card numbers. These are gentle suggestions. There is a script. Just thirty-four words, to put on the minds of our clients a tragedy too far away for them to see."

"Thirty-four words?" Sailee said.

Vijul nodded. "Thirty-four words. They take twelve seconds to read."

"Think of your parents," Grisma pleaded.

Sailee studied Nani's face. Lines on her brow held memories that would crease Sailee's forehead soon enough.

Vijul handed Sailee a zune, which showed the standard sign-off script. "It has been my pleasure to be of assistance. You need not thank me." After that came the unauthorized postscript. "But you may express gratitude by helping people dear to me. A terrible cyclone landed on my side of the globe. You can help its victims by sending a Looped message to code DAHEJ."

Sailee read the text a second time. Then a third.

"Ten more minutes," Sailee said, "then I throw the off switch."

Mazoo gave Vijul a quick hug. The supervisors whispered to one another.

"Go!" Sailee said. "When we lift the encryption blanket, the scripts must cease. The Loop would spot the pattern in seconds."

"Understood," Vijul said.

The hallway cleared until only Grisma and Sailee remained. Sailee let herself relax for the first time in what felt like an hour.

Grisma pouted. It looked like contrition. This, Sailee had never seen before on her grandmother's face.

"We should have asked you instead of Vijul," Grisma said. "For that, I am sorry. But I was not sure that you would be as practical as Mazoo's daughter."

"The Gandhian way is pragmatic," Sailee said. She checked her watch. "For four more minutes, we shall aid the people of Dahej."

Vijul nodded and waved off the supervisors who had gathered around her. "Go!" Vijul said. "Four minutes more, then no more."

The hallway cleared of all but Sailee and her grandmother.

"Thank you dear," Grisma said with a pat on Sailee's shoulder. "Mazoo and I will leave you alone. Then it is back to business."

"No," Sailee said. "After you leave, I will spend the next two weeks apologizing for a network system failure. If I still work for the company after that, it will have been worth it." Unwelcome images of the cyclone returned. "Even if I lose this job, it will have been worth it."

In Nani's bright eyes and broad smile, Sailee recognized her departed mother's face. Grisma clasped her hands together and gave her granddaughter a bow.

Words could not have said more.

To Sailee came a flash of moral certainty she had never experienced. This was more than the warmth of a grandmother's approval. Her body felt light. The heaviest worldly worries had lifted out of her and dissipated high above the halo of grit that encircled her city. Perhaps this was how Gandhi felt when he resolved to walk four hundred kilometers to the Arabian Sea.

Of course, many who followed Gandhiji on that march ended up in jail, or worse. The weight of that unhappy thought brought Sailee back down from the sky and slammed into her shoulders. She reached for the nearest chair and sat down.

If there was a Gandhian aphorism that might ease this burden, Sailee did not know it.

Part V

Awakenings

BARRY

Son said something about meeting the President. Meant for me to come along, but where is that boy of mine?

This can't be our meeting place. Looks more like some rinky-dink snack shop. At least it's got a plastic chair out front. Better to wait there, just to be safe.

Look at that. I'm sweatin' through my best dress shirt. Even for August, it's too hot.

Can't barely get any shade, even scooching up close to the wall. None of these storefronts have an awning. Least this one doesn't have boards and paint on the windows. No crazy graffiti. Polka dots would be nice, though.

These folks did go to the trouble of painting their own sign — Aladdin Grocery and Delicatessen.

Never heard of it. But if it's in the nation's capital, must be worth something.

I am not in Washington DC.

Who said that?

I am — in Detroit.

That right? Either way, gonna see the President.

There is no record of a meeting today. What sort of president?

The President. Ike Eisenhower's second grand-cousin. If we're still in Detroit, she must be here on a state visit. Probably waiting for me inside the deli. Anyway, it's gotta be cooler in there.

Dang if my joints aren't sore getting back outta this chair. Pushing my walker's no trouble, but the door to this place weighs a ton. Steel-framed model. Thank Heaven for well-oiled hinges.

Who's that waving at me? Tall man in a cotton dress — nobody I know. Guess he's waving me in. Hard to hear him. Gotta get closer to that Plexiglas counter he's standing behind.

"Good afternoon, sir."

"Hello." Don't wanna be rude, but I don't have all day. "May

I see her now?"

"Excuse me?"

"The President. She has an appointment to meet a Mr Barry Sanders."

Guess the tall fella lost interest in me. What's he looking at? In the back of the store, teenager in a Red Wings t-shirt is digging in wooden bins. All manner of things in those—tubers, dates, and funny breads. What's the boy got there? Little green crunchies, maybe fried okra.

Who's tugging on my shirt?

"You Barry Sanders? For real?"

Little girl's awful cute in that pink Lions jersey.

What kind of president staffs her front desk with skinny Pakistanis and little girls?

Actually, the man sounds Gujarati. If he owns the shop, his surname may be Patel.

"Excuse me. Are you Mr Patel?"

"You are looking for Rajneesh."

Can't hold this guy's attention for more than a second. Started shouting at somebody.

"Young man, you do not need to handle every package! If there is something you would like to try, I can open it for you up here."

The boy approaches the counter. Sets down a heap of small plastic bags, plus two bottles of ginger ale. Reaches into his pocket for something.

Hope I've got money in my pockets. I could use a beer.

Little girl seems to know this boy. She's grabbing at him.

"Look, Deshaun, it's Barry Sanders!"

"Nah, tha's some bullshit old man runnin' his mouth."

Was that about me? I should say something, but they're already gone. They took all those snacks and sodas with them.

A cold drink sure would be nice. Lips are dry. Throat's gettin' hoarse. Maybe the tall man can help me out.

"You gonna bring me that President? Or I have to wait all day?"

What's he pointing and squinting at? Me?

"Okay, please stay here, sir."

That countertop lifts right up and away he goes. Again, good hinges. Fella takes care of this place.

Hope there's cold drinks in those refrigerators he's got. Cold drink would be nice. Now, that's a good sign. He's bringing back a tall green bottle with a brown label.

"El Presidente, sir. I believe it is a pilsner."

CHARLIE

The father of the President of the United States slumped on a velvet loveseat in the Oval Office. The man, his clothes, and the furniture were all the same pale cream, which contrasted against Charlie's charcoal suit.

Charlie sat close enough for sleepy breaths to tickle his arm. Such an intimacy, with this man in this setting, might have unnerved Charlie except that his father did the same thing.

A stocky woman introduced as Secret Service Agent Adamson watched the scene from her post by the closed main door. Eisenhower's chief strategist, Dick Dirksen, leaned forward in his chair to straighten up the President's father. Dirksen's suit bunched up when he leaned forward, then went slack when he sat down. Probably couldn't stop fidgeting long enough for the White House tailor to address the issue.

Charlie's new client presented the opposite problem. How could Charlie interview Eisenhower's father to calibrate the Elder Compass settings? The man could barely stay awake, let alone speak coherently. This man in the pajamas had retired from the Navy as an admiral. Outlived nearly every veteran who'd served alongside him. Face still had the sharp jawline in his Loop scrapbook. A clean shave suggested that his daughter—no, more likely her staff—worked a steady razor on him this morning.

Eisenhower got up from her chair and walked across an iconic eagle rug. She bent over her father and used a kerchief to wipe saliva off his face.

Addressing no one in particular, Eisenhower said, "Poor Poppy. How can such a well-built machine fall apart so completely?"

Charlie counted it a blessing that GM tech had spared his own father this fate. To hide his relieved expression, Charlie looked down in his lap, where he'd folded his hands. Only then did he notice the sweat in his palms, which seemed less convinced they would be spared the indignities of elder care.

Eisenhower returned to her armchair and asked Adamson to excuse herself, for privacy. Adamson didn't respond. She had opened the main door and was speaking to someone outside. Shouting came from farther down the hall.

Adamson spoke into her Bluetooth. "Siddhartha's at the castle door."

How appropriate—Mahatma Golden interrupting Charlie's work. The two hadn't shared each other's company since the Public Market press event. Every day since, the Loop fed Charlie updates, with a focus on Golden's "Moonworld" concept. Apologists explained that Golden's "moon children" simply referred to seniors, who had been children when Neil Armstrong stepped out of the Eagle. Golden, however, kept pushing for lunar colonies—an idea even Elon Musk spoke against in public debates. Meanwhile, meta-polls estimated that tens of millions embraced Golden's vision of interstellar industrialization through the rapid consumption of Earth's fossil fuels. Thus, a Democratic vice president won the support of climate change deniers in Congress.

Having settled into his job, Golden found the right angle for attacking GM. The newest complaint Charlie had heard was that GM should have sought Food and Drug Administration approval for the Quiet Copilot. On this point, Charlie agreed. It should have been designated as a medical device. Golden would go ballistic when he discovered that Jack had secured FDA pre-clearance for the Elder Compass. Though Alice savored the irony, Charlie felt dirty every time GM benefited from the Straight to Market Act signed by He-Who-Must-Not-Be-Named.

Adamson blocked the open Oval Office door, while the President's receptionist admonished the Vice President to stop "barging in." Golden moved into the doorway.

"Eleanor," he said, "I must have audience with you at once!"

Adamson pressed a hand against Golden's shoulder. "This is a protocol violation, sir. I will have to escort you back to the Executive Office Building."

"Mr Golden," President Eisenhower said, "this is not a good time."

"There is no better time. You've shut me out. Now let me in." Golden's eyes caught Charlie's. A glimmer of recognition. "Who is your father talking to? I should be in there with him. This is my specialty, Eleanor."

"Even to you," Eisenhower replied, "it is *Madam President*."

"Your father is a national treasure. He'll soon cross the century-bridge. You must—"

The President gave a nod to Adamson, who shifted her weight toward Golden and guided him out of the room. Charlie casually typed on his wide-screen zune until he heard the door shut.

"Sorry you had to see that," Eisenhower said. "It's a blessing that Dad can sleep so well. I fear it would distress him to see the behavior of my proverbial Macbeth."

"It's no trouble, Madam President."

"Honestly, did Golden never read the play? When you plot to seize the throne, you don't make that plain to the palace guard. I sometimes wonder if he stands in my antechamber at night muttering, 'Is this a dagger I see before me?' Even if he did take the castle, what makes him believe it would end any better here than in the play?"

"Our CEO knows him as well as anyone," Charlie said.

Focusing on the President was difficult, with Dirksen pacing around the room like a tiger in a cage. Back at GM, Eddie sometimes circled the octagon when working through a puzzle in his mind.

"If it helps," Charlie said, "Alice doesn't think Mahatma believes his own public story. Says it's safer to assume he's acting."

"Ms Coleco has a gift when it comes to reading people," Eisenhower said. "When it comes to reading *my* brain, that job will be yours. Not hers."

"Excuse me?" Charlie's heart quickened. She had his full attention.

Dirksen stopped circling the room and fixed his eyes on Charlie. "We didn't bring you here to put your device behind her father's ear. You're here to implant *her*."

Acting on instinct, Charlie stood. The door Agent Adamson had exited seemed to have disappeared into the wall, but if he got close, he could find it. Charlie could walk casually out of the White House, past the guards at the gate, then flee toward the Metro as fast as his feet could carry him. Airports would have to be avoided. Maybe a Greyhound?

"Sit back down," Eisenhower said. The command had its intended effect.

Charlie was grateful for however many seconds he was granted to gather his words. After swallowing what little spit he could gather in his dry mouth, Charlie spoke in an even tone. "With respect, I have no idea what you are asking of me. There has been a miscommunication somewhere down the line, I assure you. I apologize if Alice or I—"

"My father was never the one I wanted you to implant," Eisenhower said. "It just happens that the three of us, not counting Poppy, are the only people in the world who know that. I brought you here to interview *me*. Before you wire your compass into my brain, I want to make certain that you have the best possible mental map of who I am."

Vertigo had Charlie slumping alongside Poppy. It reminded him of the out-of-body sensation he got as a child on spinning teacups at Oktoberfest. Grasping the safety bar for balance, he'd vomited prodigiously from the highest point of that ride's arc.

"Here's the deal," Dirksen said. "And trust me, I was more

freaked about this when she told me than you're ever gonna be. I was vetting replacement veeps for the reelection campaign when she tells me, there won't be a fuckin' campaign. Says all my prospects for the vice presidency have clean bills of health, but *she* doesn't. She's been having these, um, slips."

"He is being too kind," Eisenhower said. "You saw my last State of the Union. Remember when I stopped reading the teleprompter?"

Charlie nodded. His mind raced through a few more incidents that had made the news. Her supporters dismissed these spells as battle fatigue. Critics said her tics betrayed a lack of focus. Even the Loop had failed to draw the right inference. Then again, recent history had scrambled the line between normal versus aberrant presidential behavior.

"Soon," Eisenhower said, "I will not be fit to serve my country—not at the level this job requires. Now, imagine what the White House would be like, or what our country would be like, if my incapacitation required Mahatma Golden to take my place behind this desk. What kind of world would that lead us to?"

"Moonworld," Dirksen said. "Problem is, there's no easy way to dump his ass before the next election. He's scandal-free. Even if we manufactured one, the Republican Congress wouldn't care. He's a time bomb the GOP refuses to help us defuse."

Charlie lifted a finger, but he was too slow to speak.

"I have thought about this a great deal," Eisenhower said. "There is one least-impossible path out from here. It requires replacing both Mahatma *and me* at the same time."

"Madam President," Charlie said, "how bad is your condition? How much longer can you conceal this? You should have a doctor in here, not a social scientist."

"I'm a long way from Poppy," Eisenhower said with a sigh. "But no doctor could help me muddle through the next two years. That's going to be your job, well, the job of your, ah—"

"The Elder Compass," Charlie said.

"This is how it has to be. Only you and Dick can know that this—your Compass—is for me. You cannot share that fact, not even with Ms Coleco."

"Isn't it too late already?" Charlie said. "Before I left Seattle, I told my father I was meeting the President of the United States. Alice and another GM coworker know I'm here. On top of that, the Loop will track my flight, my subway route, and—"

"That's fine," Eisenhower said. "They believe you are here for Poppy, not me. I would ask you politely to keep this confidential, but this is not a pinky swear."

"Yes, ma'am."

"This is something the President of the United States commands you to do."

Charlie heard himself ask, "Aren't I still a civilian?"

"That's what I said," Dirksen muttered.

"You have no national security clearance," Eisenhower said. "No paperwork. This arrangement is between us alone. But make no mistake, I *require* you to do this."

Charlie felt his neck nod up and down in agreement. Thoughts came out as speech. "I suppose," he said, "I should obtain a dummy implant for your father. In case anybody checks. You will, ah, need to be present when the time comes."

"That is for another day." Eisenhower glanced at the zune on her wrist. "We've only got twenty more minutes until I need to be at my next meeting. What do you need to know about me, for your compass?"

Charlie checked his tablet to confirm it remained in airplane mode. He opened an app and began to type. "The Loop will provide me with the more trivial details, which will be exceptionally rich for the likes of you. Still, I've got a few questions that will let me set your subjective Compass orientation."

"I will tell you what I said to Ms Coleco when we first met," Eisenhower said. "I am no ideologue. One does not become a general, or even a president, if there is nothing more to one's intellectual discernment than following a number on a dial."

"If only it were so, ma'am."

"I am willing to take something of a leap of faith because my options are few, but I am hoping your device can do more than you describe in the specs you sent. I confess the technical details are beyond me, but I got the gist."

Dirksen jumped in. "What's the compass setting for a Democratic head of state who supports strict climate regulations while promoting nuclear power? How can you square her executive orders securing abortion rights with her opposition to caliber-based ammunition bans?"

Eisenhower waived off her aide. "What Dick's trying to ask is, how do you account for nuanced reasoning? How do your algorithms anticipate deliberative judgments, or anything that falls off a conventional political map?"

"I admit you're a curious case, Madam President." Charlie typed notes without looking up. "You have an exceptionally stubborn interest in knowing pertinent facts."

"I do read, Mr Sanders. Does that shock you?"

"A little." Charlie laughed. "Normally, people's grasp of the evidentiary record bends to suit their biases. You're no different. And yes, we've tried plugging both you and Golden into our equations, as a hobby project. Once Compassed, all I can promise is that you won't backslide on your more idiosyncratic positions."

"But what if I want to change my mind on some policy question or another?"

"That'll be difficult. We can't build a dynamic model of your brain—not yet anyway. Our product line keeps people on track. We don't help them choose which train to ride."

Dirksen returned to his chair. He stared at Poppy. President Eisenhower took her shift as the one to walk the full circumference of the room.

"The problem," Dirksen said, "is that I can't have the President saying the same things, over and over."

"Why not?" Eisenhower passed behind her desk. "How would that be any different from my predecessors? Like You-Know-Who?"

Charlie laughed. Good to know he and Alice weren't the only ones who couldn't say that name.

"I'm serious," Dirksen said. "The Loop will detect robotic repetitions in a week, tops."

"She won't be as exposed as you think," Charlie said. "How often do you hold real press conferences? The kind that require her to answer probing questions?"

"Never," Dirksen said. "Nobody does those anymore. Hyperactive news cycle just keeps spinning around without us."

"What Dick means to say is..." Eisenhower paused. "You know, he has a new job title. He is, um..." The President tapped her thumb against each of four fingers in a rhythmic motion.

Charlie recognized the gesture. He'd taught it to his father as a mnemonic device.

"She made me Deputy Communications Director," Dirksen said. "From that position, it'll be easier to cover for her."

"I cannot dodge every public responsibility," Eisenhower said. "This device you are fabricating, it has to be ready before the next State of the Union comes around."

"We hope to be taking pre-orders before Christmas," Charlie said.

Eisenhower walked toward a set of gilded portraits on her office wall. The can lights made Ike's bald head glow like a halo. He seemed to scowl at the woman standing before him. A larger picture of Eleanor Roosevelt showed her in the arms of two young women with USO badges. The gawky first lady flashed a knowing smile. If she were listening in on the present conversation, she'd probably reassure the first female president, "We've all got secrets, honey."

The President set herself down on the other side of Poppy, who had almost fallen into Charlie's lap. She frowned and said, "Did I drift away?"

Charlie coughed. "We've all done so at times, Madam President."

"Normally, I would cover for a lapse like that," Eisenhower said, "but why lie to you? You will be jabbing that transponder into my head soon enough. Better that you recognize its necessity."

"Actually, ma'am," Charlie said, "the chip won't do most of the wireless work. We'll put that hardware into a small accessory—one you can take on and off easily."

"Like that bracelet you used to make?"

"We haven't built a prototype yet." Charlie spied a lapel pin on the President's jacket. He pointed at it, careful not to touch the chest of the Commander in Chief. "You wear that often?"

Eisenhower tucked her chin to look down. "My eagle brooch?"

"It's the right size," Charlie said. "Great location, close to your head."

Eisenhower unpinned the eagle and handed it to Charlie.

Charlie panicked. "Wait, no! If you suddenly stop wearing it after this meeting—that won't go unnoticed. Next thing we know—"

"Hush," Eisenhower said. She walked behind her desk, opened a drawer, and pulled out an identical eagle, which she pinned to her jacket. "I've worn one every day since the campaign. We're old friends."

"Does it have a name?"

"Let's call it Cluebird."

SAILEE

Sailee pouted at Charlie and put hands on hips. The gesture caused the silk wrap over her sari to billow in the breeze.

"You look like a golden raisin," Charlie said.

"No, you are the ridiculous one." Sailee secured her wrap. "Why did you bring a full suit? You must be roasting. Come inside."

Sailee shooed Charlie inside a tent that covered two full blocks. Inside it danced and laughed more than a hundred guests assembled for Vijul's wedding. Their chatter mixed with the static of speakers blasting Bollywood ballads, interspersed with more traditional songs Sailee recognized but couldn't name.

"Worse than that," Sailee said, "white is *not* appropriate today."

"This a racial thing?" Charlie said.

"Goodness no," Sailee said. It was hard to know when Charlie was serious about the subject. Even when he joked, she sensed something beneath it.

At a more intimate family gathering the night before, she had noticed how her relatives studied him — more precisely, his body. Sailee's relatives had grown up in the company of Siddis, East Africans, and even darker-skinned Hindu priests, but her African-American guest aroused a disquieting curiosity, along with judgments or assumptions she could not guess. For his part, Charlie pretended not to care. Or maybe he failed to notice. Impossible to tell, and she spared him the question.

"Are you sure?" Charlie said. "The Loop said white symbolized purity."

"You should never trust the Loop on such matters. For Vijul's family, white is the color of mourning. Besides, what justifies your claim to being pure?" Sailee led Charlie to a far corner of the tent and handed him a cloth sack. "Lucky for you, Sanjay's brother runs a shop just blocks from here. He heard what you were wearing and brought these. We will get you properly suited and booted."

Sailee motioned for Charlie to remove his jacket. Over his head she threw an embroidered sherwani. She smoothed it down his shoulders, chest, waist, and knees. The robe flowed graciously over his body. Traditional clothes suited him better than she'd imagined. Perhaps Gujarat could accommodate him after all. That prospect excited her.

"Now let's switch out the pants," Sailee said. She glanced in every direction. The crowd was too distracted to notice them.

Charlie played the part of mannequin while Sailee swapped out his clothes. Once she had the pants on securely, she fitted him with leather sandals, then stepped back to admire her work.

"That will do nicely, Charlie. Now, you are a proper guest."

Charlie would never pass as Gujarati, but anyone could see he had made an effort.

Soon, Sailee was receiving hugs and kisses from female friends. For his part, Charlie received polite nods. Success.

"You sure this isn't *your* wedding?" Charlie said.

Sailee pulled him back out of the stream of people entering the tent.

"I was the one who first got Sanjay and Vijul together. I helped arrange for them to be, well, arranged. This is a *covert* love marriage."

"Who are you hiding it from, exactly?"

"Vijul's grandmother. Also, Sanjay's parents are very traditional."

"I thought your grandmother's friends were communists."

That earned Charlie a cluck and a pinch. "There are more threads to our culture than the Loop could ever untangle," Sailee said. "We are not as simple as you Americans. Our civilization has had many centuries to take shape. Yours set overnight, in a refrigerated gelatin mold."

"If your culture is so full of contradictions and exceptions, does that mean you get to choose your mate after all?"

Sailee heard a question behind the question. She considered answering it. She had shown Charlie more flashes of forwardness on this visit. The response had been rewarding.

"You would make a suitable mate," Sailee said, "if I were to choose you."

Charlie looked away, embarrassed to be outmaneuvered.

"Now excuse me," Sailee said. "I must run back to Vijul and prepare for the ceremony."

"But—"

Sailee reached up to straighten Charlie's collar. A furtive kiss on his neck sent an electric current through her. She rubbed her hands down her sari to release the charge.

"Later we will dance, Mr Charlie. And after that?" Sailee winked slowly so he could see the henna lines drawn across her eyelids. "We shall see."

Even after she left his company, Sailee kept an eye on Charlie. He stepped farther into the tent to stand beside an electric fan. When she last checked her zune, the readout had climbed above forty Celsius, with ferocious humidity. Poor Charlie was probably melting.

The lonely raja stands by himself.

Sailee imagined Charlie saying the line out loud in the same dramatic poetry-voice Vijul's uncle used the night before.

He longs to risk it all for a kiss, but he knows he cannot. It is—forbidden.

Sailee covered her mouth to laugh, but any sound was drowned by a live band entering the tent. Above the steady rhythm of drums and cymbals twisted a python of a melody, made by the bowed strings of the ravanahatha.

Sweaty bodies pressed Sailee forward. She lost sight of Charlie when she rode the wave of guests and well-wishers. She joined the clutch of friends and relatives who surrounded a long red carpet that led to a raised platform. There, chairs awaited the bride and groom. As Sailee moved closer to the stage, the clothing and jewelry adorning those around her became more lavish. The innermost circle dressed like genuine Mughal royalty, with ornamentation on loan from the seventeenth century.

As the band quieted, Sailee caught sight of Mazoo and moved to help her fuss over Vijul. After heaping compliments on her friend's bridal dress, Sailee stepped back and received a small potted tree to carry during the procession.

A dozen feet to her right, Grisma appeared. She led Charlie by the hand. He was smiling, but not as vigorously as he was perspiring.

Sailee wished for him a cold beer at a shaded café. Or, the luxury of a hotel room.

The lonely raja would risk even love to feel the chill of A/C, but he knows he cannot. It is—forbidden.

Nani brought Charlie a few feet closer to Sailee. They stood well within earshot, by design it would seem.

"Responsibility has fallen to me," Nani said to Charlie. "Today, I will teach you a few things about my Sailee. You have much to learn, if you intend to be a proper suitor."

Sailee panicked. Nani must have seen them sneak a kiss— or two. Her grandmother could do simple math as quickly as the Loop. Sailee had dodged all efforts at arrangement with the most eligible bachelors of Ahmedabad, which implied that she had other plans.

Charlie said something to Nani. Crashing cymbals made it impossible to hear. Whatever he said made Nani laugh. Most auspicious.

Sailee wanted to turn around and make eye contact with Charlie. She would offer some reassurance, or plead her innocence, but there was no time. The ceremony had commenced. All she could do was listen as Nani warmed up to her role as etiquette instructor.

"I am taking pity on you," her grandmother said.

"I'm sorry, Grisma Singh. I don't quite—"

"Hush. Pay attention. I do not know well the Sanjay fellow that Vijul is marrying. Did our Sailee tell you she managed their arrangement?"

"She did. What's that plant she's holding?"

"A young tree."

"What does it mean?"

"Something about a new beginning. I forget."

"Wouldn't seeds be a better symbol? A baby tree is kind of cheating."

With her back turned to Charlie and Nani, Sailee tried to stifle a laugh. An elderly woman beside Sailee elbowed her and made a sour look.

"Forget about the sapling, Charlie. The point is that a wedding brings together two families. We are not witnessing a union of two lovers. We are harmonizing the expectations and futures of two whole worlds that were separate before today."

Now this, Sailee knew Charlie could understand. Unbeknownst to him, she had read his entire doctoral dissertation to get a measure of the man's ideas. Were it not for the clamor of the crowd, Charlie would probably try explaining his thesis. He would tell Nani that she was describing "cultural integration and norm perpetuation." Somewhere in one of his theory chapters, he argued that the point of ritual was to make arbitrary conventions appear natural. The math in his theory implied that once one brushed away the sand of superficial differences, societies were simple systems, and therefore predictable. Had Nani served on Charlie's doctoral committee, the Marxist in her might have agreed with that much.

In her reverie, Sailee lost the thread of their conversation. The last words she heard Nani say were that "her generation might find a way to pursue romantic love without discarding tradition."

On cue, Sailee followed the wedding party to the edge of the stage. The event proceeded apace, but her attention lay elsewhere. She fixated not on the bride and groom, but on her one and only grannie, and an equally singular suitor.

CHARLIE

With just a sliver of Sailee's back in view, Charlie wished he could see her eyes. Last night, watching her anxious expression had woken him to the furtive glances the rest of the guests sent his way. For someone so astute about the dynamics of a society, he had never learned to be so attuned to his own interactions.

When he made the effort to take notice, he could feel strangers watching him from every direction. Younger eyes seemed curious, like gawkers at a carnival. Were they studying his hair, his skin, or—what did it matter? He was relieved to see in some stares something more like resentment. He'd rather be an "American interloper at a sacred ceremony" than simply "black."

Either way, Charlie felt conspicuous. Not that this was new. Growing up in Detroit, teachers and students alike singled him out as "little professor." In Seattle, his intellect won admiration, but co-workers didn't know what to do with their "black friend," other than ensure he appeared in selfies for the diversity cred he lent them.

A thin blanket of self-pity settled over his shoulders. The extra warmth was most unwelcome in the muggy heat. Charlie shook away the sensation but pined for the company of Jack and Alice. Working by their side, *abnormal* was a label he needn't self-apply.

Lost in his thoughts, Charlie had also lost sight of Sailee. He wobbled, disoriented. Sing-song voices and jangly instruments sounded alien.

Grisma Singh's grip tightened on his arm, and he leaned in close. Grisma offered a quick sideward glance, then a grin that looked forced. Did he detect apprehension on his behalf, or perhaps for Sailee?

"This particular wedding," Grisma said, "is quite a jumble."

"A Hindu ceremony?"

"Among other things. There are so many variations—"

"Within Hinduism, or—"

Grisma put a hand to Charlie's mouth and whispered, "His vows begin."

Sanjay stood in an off-white sherwani, more delicate than Charlie's. He read from a parchment to Vijul, who fiddled nervously with the dozen bracelets on her wrists. One of her wrists tangled in the string of red and white flowers hanging from her neck.

"I thought white meant mourning," Charlie said.

"Who told you—was that my little flower?" Grisma laughed. "She probably just wanted to get you out of that *ridiculous* suit."

"She used that same word."

"It is the *correct* word."

Charlie half-frowned. "Let's discuss something else."

"Everybody has their own way of doing vows," Grisma said. "I cannot hear what Sanjay is saying, but it amounts to four admonitions. Write these down."

Charlie reached for pockets but found none.

"First, remember that your wife is the better half of the pair. You must look after both her and yourself."

"Got it. Number two?"

"Consult together on all things, including money."

The oaths sounded reasonable—more prenup than poetry. On reflection, it wasn't so surprising. There are only so many different settings on the cultural compass.

"Next, remain friends whose affection must never wane or wander. This is not simply forbidding infidelity. We ask more of you than that."

Charlie zeroed in on the object pronoun. They ask these things of *me*?

"Finally, you must support her, always. You are not to be her critic. You must help her overcome the challenges in life."

"What if I like being her critic?"

A shoulder slug he'd not seen coming stung worse than the tetanus shot received before his first trip to Gujarat.

"She is willful, like you, for a reason." Grisma's gaze drew him in like a tractor beam. Once she had his attention, she lowered her voice to a whisper. "Sailee did not get to have a simple childhood. My dear daughter, along with her father, died working for men who came to India from your country. When a terrible storm hit Sailee's hometown, she was spared because, by fate, I had taken her on a field trip far away."

"What happened to her parents?"

"You would have read about it, if you lived here. It was national news. While I introduced Sailee to my Marxist friends, who were making the state of Kerala a socialist jewel, American chemical corporations were caught unprepared for Gujarati weather. Winds and waves tore apart the plant where Sailee's parents toiled. Their burns would have killed them quickly, but the saltwater kept them alive."

"I thought you said—"

"They endured three days of excruciating pain. The company brought out big men from the United States as a show of contrition. They visited the hospital where Sailee's parents—and a hundred more—died in their beds."

Charlie wanted to push through the crowd and hold Sailee. Instead, he reached for Grisma's hand. She accepted it with both of her own.

"These industrialists, they now face the prospect of their own death. They are the people Sailee's operators serve. This, she knows. These men owe her a karmic debt. This, she also knows."

Charlie gathered his thoughts. He wanted to explain to Grisma that GM was at a turning point. The low price point of an automated Elder Compass would extend their customer base well into the middle class.

He could say this and more, but defending the company's reputation was beside the point. He had no answer to a question that left him feeling ashamed. For all the attention Sailee gave Barry, how could he have failed to learn even these basic facts about her parents?

"I taught Sailee what I could," Grisma said with a sigh. "But I neglected to show her how to enjoy life. She sees only duty, to me and to her causes. Are you any different?"

The wedding rituals continued, with Sailee and Vijul saying something together that Grisma did not explain. Charlie wanted to escape with Sailee to a quiet room in the Fortune Landmark. Wrap her in his arms. Lie still, together. Synchronize heartbeats.

Charlie recognized the voice of Vijul's uncle on the stage. The poem this man recited the night before kept replaying in Charlie's mind like a pop song.

The lonely raja would give all his riches in alms if he could walk hand-in-hand beside his love. But he knows he cannot. It is—forbidden.

"You two could do each other good," Grisma said. "You push and pull in different directions."

In Charlie's mind, a compass needle waved back and forth in wild confusion as it crossed over a pole.

"Watching this wedding makes me worry," Charlie said. "Sailee and I may be too many worlds apart." Charlie released his hand from Grisma's grip and waved at the cacophony of color and sound surrounding him. "Even with a personal tutor, I can't begin to comprehend this."

Vijul and Sanjay circled a small fire pit. Once. Twice. A third time. If Charlie had thought to wear Looped glasses, its narration might have explained what it could. But understanding and *experiencing* were not the same.

"All this?" Grisma clucked—a chiding sound she'd passed on to Sailee. "It is as I said before, a husband swears on the sacred fire to be just, support his family, love his wife."

The couple continued to circle the flames.

Sailee's face searched the crowd. Her eyes met Charlie's. She smiled.

Silently, Charlie made his vows.

JACK

Jack felt the same August sun that Charlie described in a text from Gujarat, but to different effect. Charlie said the humidity "nearly boiled" Ahmedabad. Outside the Capitol in Olympia, a little sunshine felt pleasant on Jack's face after spending a day in air conditioning. Broad strips of shade thrown by the building's columns sheltered Jack and his two dozen new best friends from direct sunlight. The gaggle of men and women beside him varied in age, ethnicity, and geography to match the state's demographics. Such was the design of the week-long meetings they had endured as "dips" — the nickname they preferred to the officious title of "Deliberative Initiative Panelists."

Jack's pocket chirped, and he pulled out a zune. Life wasn't the same without Buddy on his head. How could people tolerate carrying these bricks in their pockets?

"From A.C.: Hoping you're not passed out at Islands Casino or some other dive on I-5."

Alice had never confronted him about his Vegas trips, but he knew that she knew. It was a relief to see her acknowledge in words the self-hating habit he was trying to break.

A voice message from Alice had come on the heels of that text. His zune had converted it to type, but Jack wanted to hear her voice. He held the device to his ear.

"Hope you passed this low-budget test for your new-found sobriety, a paid vacation in the company of two dozen do-gooders. Congratulations on being, um, randomly selected. I'm sure I had nothing to do with that. Really. Anyway, when you're done doing your civic doodie, come straight back to the office. If you can get through the backlog in your inbox by tonight, I've got a surprise for you."

Wary of letting unrealistic expectations get the best of him, Jack considered the message enigmatic. When he got the summons for the DIP, Alice refused to give him a work-hardship waiver to get out of it. Forcing him to serve felt like a challenge. If he could remain sober, even while torn away from the useful distractions of GM, there might be a reward. Alice might permit him to level-up, one way or another.

A voice behind Jack said, "Who's that on yer phone?"

It was Russell Crosby, one of the two unemployed members of the DIP. Twenty years Jack's senior, Russell had done odd jobs as a logger and handyman in Forks. A port wine birthmark gave him one of the few bona fide red necks in the Pacific Northwest. For the final day's press conference, Russell wore the traditional fabrics of his people—a tattered flannel shirt over jeans belted tight enough to support a mid-sized gut.

Russell had been the first to befriend Jack on Monday, when he'd convinced Jack to join him for Vietnamese food. The DIP per diem covered the dinner, but Jack offered to pay for drinks. While Russell downed a yard of beer and became legless, Jack knocked back refills of Diet Pepsi.

The odd couple took turns oversharing. Russell confessed to fathering a stray child or two in his wilder years. Jack confided in this stranger how adrift he felt, with a long-lost father and a newly lost mother. The week before, New South Wales authorities made it official. A harbor cruise had found his mother's body bobbing beneath the Opera House, a venue she'd always admired but never found reason to enter.

As on that first night together, Russell proved himself a determined conversationalist on the Capitol steps. "It was your boss lady calling, wasn't it?" Russell winked at Jack. "Looked like you were getting worked up about something. Figured it was a girlfriend, or your boss. Or both?"

Jack waved him off. "Nah, it was just your vampire wife calling from your mansion up in the rainforest. Asked me to bring fresh pints back if I wanted to get into her coffin again tonight."

A stream of Russell's chewing tobacco filled a narrow crack in the marble steps. "Damn," Russell said. "People gonna be bustin' Forks for a generation 'cause of that *Twilight*."

"If I were you, I'd say I lived in some other ghost town on the Olympic Peninsula."

"Like La Push?"

Jack snorted. "Sure, mate. No one will give you shit for being from La *Push*."

The easy banter reminded Jack of his best days at GM, without any of the personal or professional stakes. Perhaps he and Russell shared ancestry. Maybe an unlucky Irishman, hauled off to Melbourne in shackles, had fathered a baby before his conviction. The little scamp ran away from a cannery in Cork. Traveled as a stowaway on an ocean liner headed for America.

"You're a smartass," Russell said, "but I'm onto you, son. You made fun of this thing on Monday. Now look at you — enduring this heat in a nice suit."

That reminded him that Charlie had yet to send a pic of the white suit he'd packed for the wedding. Hard to believe the dude fell for that prank. Least Jack could do was wear a suit of his own.

"A lot can happen in a week," Jack said. "Trust me. I'm the same dickhead you met Day One."

"Prob'ly so, but still."

Russell spat again and grinned at Jack. The smile looked — genuine. No irony or artifice. Jack felt exposed. Involuntarily, he checked his zipper, just as the retired librarian from Spokane tugged Jack's arm.

"Come on," she said. "They're ready for us."

With the legislative building as their backdrop, Jack and his fellow panelists assembled in three rows of eight, a choir in street clothes. The citizens had rehearsed for this press conference. Jack would be the first to read from their final statement. In a few weeks, that same statement — an analysis of the statewide initiative they'd studied—would travel through the US mail to arrive in every registered voter's mailbox. They'd be one more page of newsprint in the state's official *Voter Guide*.

A mix of heated arguments and cooler conversations had led up to their final statement. It bothered Jack how easily this group of strangers had distilled their differences into a broad consensus, along with a thoughtful dissent. In return, the event's organizers had compensated them with a $500 honoraria—a pittance for Jack, but not for Russell.

Their week together began with training sessions and icebreakers. A black lawyer back-slapped his fellow citizens and tried out nicknames. The nineteen-year-old Evergreen College student sitting beside Jack decorated her nametag with highlighter pens. The nurse's aide with a Czech accent wrote careful notes in shorthand as though a patient's life depended on it. Russell, who called himself the "jobless lumberjack," drew attention by standing up every time he spoke. Other panelists came to emulate the practice.

By the end of the second day, Jack's butt felt sore. He fled the conference room with Russell when the closing bell sounded. They returned to the Vietnamese restaurant where they'd spent the first night bonding over beverages. In spite of themselves, they continued the afternoon's policy debate.

"The thing about this law we're studying," Jack said, "is that it stereotypes the rich."

Russell nodded. "I think we're in the minority. Far as I can tell, we're two of the only Deplorables here. Plus, there's maybe seven folks from King County. Communists, every one of 'em."

"I live in that county, dumbass. By my headcount, only five of the group are liberals. I work with a guy who's taught me how to pick up on that sort of thing."

"The law we're looking at is garbage," Russell said. "Raising the death tax and adding a gift tax are terrible ideas."

Jack surprised himself. He did something they'd practiced at the DIP. He considered what to say next. Think, then speak. "I had some pretty strong views about it coming into today. Now, I wanna slow down."

Outside their window booth, streetlights flickered on to light up the darkening street. It reminded him of the cat burglars in Detroit, who passed on to Charlie their vigilante activism. Without that chance encounter, Jack wouldn't have found a way to atone for his Bellingham massacre. Who could have foreseen that odd chain of cause and effect?

"Where I work," Jack said, "we make our living on the premise that you can predict a person's views based on a simple profile. We're on the verge of monetizing that insight on an unprecedented scale."

Russell took a drink of water. Looked like he might be losing the plot.

"My point is," Jack said, "this thing we're doing here, it's like Opposite Day. You, me, and these other folks are playing at wearing four-cornered hats, like a fucking Constitutional Convention."

"That's three corners, Dundee. Tri-cornered hats." Russell chuckled and folded his paper napkin into a triangle. He perched it on Jack's flat-top. "Doesn't look right with that haircut. You need a powdered wig. Who let you into this country, anyway?"

For five weeks, Jack hadn't broken a fragile sobriety he'd been slowly moving toward since the Lummi School adventure. There had been relapses, but every time he felt himself slipping, another late-night escapade with Charlie and Alice would do the trick. Turned out the tiny demons crying inside him could be salved in ways he'd never have guessed.

Just the same, Jack hadn't trusted himself with the mini-bar. He left its key with the receptionist at the front desk.

Now that the week had drawn to a close, Jack stood on

the Capitol's front steps with a script in his hand, prepared to perform a role he hadn't expected to play. Encouraging backslaps propelled Jack down three rows of steps and to the podium. After a brief preface from their professional facilitator, Jack took turns with the lawyer and the nurse's aide in reading through their one-page statement. He paused before reading what he considered their most important observation—the one that had swung the debate.

An unassuming tax attorney who testified before the DIP had raised the issue on Wednesday. "The law's effects are *quite* foreseeable," she'd said. "It is modeled after laws passed by initiative in two other states. In both cases, legislatures ultimately repealed them to avoid a disincentive to donate one's fortune to nonprofit entities." The attorney then quoted Mahatma Golden, of all people. "There's generosity in the wisdom elders grant future generations, but their charity alleviates present hardships."

Thus, the DIP had written the sentence Jack now read.

"All twenty-four of us agreed on this," Jack said. "Initiative 667 would discourage philanthropy, particularly the 'deathbed donations' that constitute a substantial percentage of all charitable giving."

When the press conference ended, Russell gave Jack a parting hug and handshake. "Just wanted to say good job," Russell said. "Turns out we had it right all along, eh? That law was crap."

"True," Jack said, "but now we can say precisely *why* it's shit. That matters."

"You really think anyone'll read this?"

"Who the fuck knows?" Jack said with a shrug.

"I don't normally vote, but after this…" Russell turned to spit, then thought better of it. "Hey, Dundee, if you ever find that you need to hire a handyman or somethin'."

"The Loop will put you in the front of the queue, mate."

Jack waved down his Uber. When it arrived, he fumbled in

his bag and pulled out a jar, which he handed to Russell.

"This is high-potency garlic," Jack said. "From Gilroy, California. Had it shipped overnight to the hotel. Almost forgot to give it to you."

Russell hefted the Mason jar and made a show of reading the label. "Thanks, I guess."

Jack hopped into the cab and rolled down his window. When his driver pulled away from the curb, Jack shouted back at Russell, "Keep the immortals at bay, pops!"

On the chance that Russell might hurl the gift back as a missile, Jack ducked.

The precaution proved unnecessary. Jack's make-believe father cradled his treasure. This Russell fellow recognized the insult as a bid for friendship. The subtlety of the gesture would have made Alice proud.

* * *

Jack entered the Olivia 9 building using the code Alice had given him. After a quick elevator ride, he found her penthouse and tapped the plastic spider that served as its doorbell. His finger came back with a red hourglass imprint. Smelled like fresh nail polish on the button's black torso. None too subtle, this one.

Soft footsteps came from the other side of the door. His heart thrummed.

Following Alice's instructions, Jack rode from Olympia directly to GM's headquarters. The office busywork awaiting him there had been nothing more than a bloated inbox. When he texted her at 1:45am to say he was done, he got an invitation in reply, not a minute later.

Before leaving the office, Jack used the company washroom for a quick towel-off where he hoped it mattered most. From his office closet, he snagged a silky shirt and loose jeans. No socks, no boxers. This two-piece wardrobe received good reviews from his Vegas trysts. Jack let himself hope that tonight, he'd get to use his talents for a higher purpose.

When Alice opened her door, dressed in sweatpants and a long-sleeved Seattle Storm t-shirt, her reaction was not propitious. Pointing at his deep V-necked blouse, she gave a hearty laugh.

"Oh my goodness," she said at last. "Did you think we'd go clubbing?"

Words failed Jack. He tried to step forward, but Alice blocked the doorway. She leaned forward and sniffed him.

"A splash of cologne." She eyed him warily. "Hold on—did you...?"

"Did I what? Just grabbed the first clean shirt I could find."

Alice stepped aside to let her guest enter.

Jack found himself at a crossroads. To the right was a mid-century bachelor pad with ivory shag beneath matching leather chairs, sofa, chaise lounge. Straight ahead was a kitchen with cast iron pans hanging over a wooden island. To the left, a hallway led to a room in which he could see the corner of a Dalmatian-print bedspread. Cruella, indeed.

Alice took Jack's arm and led him toward the sofa. He took a seat and watched her move about the kitchen. She returned with a tray, which she set on a broad cherry coffee table.

"Chips and such," she said, "plus three weird sodas I got for some reason. No beer for you."

"I don't remember asking for a Foster's."

Alice sat cross-legged on the lounge beside his sofa.

"I'm a changed man," Jack said. "Five days clean."

"You want a sobriety chip?"

"It wasn't just that. This past week, it was strange. Those DIP people put me on the dork payroll. And this guy here?" Jack pointed to his chest, puffed out like a proud third-grader. "This guy did his fuckin' job."

"Did you sway them with charm? Or bully them with that

potty mouth?"

"That's the thing," Jack said. "Wasn't like that. If you had a question, you could ask it. If one of the expert witnesses couldn't answer it, or you wanted to know more, there was time. We called on people to explain the state constitution, tax law, whatever we needed."

"Sounds riveting," Alice said. "But doesn't the Loop do that, for free?"

"We were Looped, sure, but we didn't jump from one thing to another, like it wants to do. We were writing on butcher paper with thick markers, moving around ideas we posted on the wall. We turned our collective brain inside out, so we could all see it, together."

Alice screwed the top off a rhubarb-lime something or other. A puff of gas leapt out of the bottle. Smelled like a farmer's market. She took a swig and set her drink back on the table.

"For a digital native," Alice said, "you sound pretty Luddite."

"They say our report may tilt the scales in the election, but I don't know. Now that I'm back, it seems unreal. Like it didn't really happen."

"Well, it sounds as though you had a nice time." Alice frowned. "That wasn't the plan. Your time with the DIP was supposed to humble you. Instead, you're hepped up on five grams of civic cheer."

"You don't like the new Jack?" He tried one of Alice's signature pouts. No reaction.

"You can be whoever you want, so long as you stop channeling Charlie Sheen and his alter ego—that orange-haired ex-president. No more strutting about like a rock star. No more fantasy gibberish about how you're some kind of warlock genius. That's all played out, thank God. Plus, our company's getting too important to—"

"How is that fair? Your hair's never the same shade for a whole month. You practically cosplay your way—"

"I'm the boss, and you're the alcoholic. Clean up your act, and you can go further than you'd imagined."

Jack tried parsing the meaning of those words but got conflicting results. Even if he wasn't sure what her end of the bargain entailed, he would keep his.

In the meantime, he had a momentary advantage. Jack had spent a week listening—really listening to people, without Buddy's background music. He'd quieted the self-obsessed chatter inside his head that had made his earpiece necessary in the first place. As a result, he found himself thinking one move ahead in the conversation. Alice had more foresight, but she might underestimate him.

"I have bad news," Jack said, "from Sydney."

Alice picked up her lime water and cocked her head. "One of your old rugby mates resurface in a police blotter?"

"No, my mother. Well, her body. They found it in the harbor."

Alice froze, drink in hand.

"I'm so sorry, Jack."

Alice set down her bottle and reached out to stroke Jack's cheek. Wet fingertips tickled his stubble. When Alice withdrew, Jack felt the absence.

"Thanks—for that." Jack's eyes prepared for tears.

"We're your family now."

"I..." With a shudder, Jack regathered himself. "I mean—thanks for everything, A. C."

A pause gave Jack the chance to think. He wanted to throw himself at Alice, or fold up in her arms. Neither would do. Instead, he stretched out on his couch.

Alice tried to mirror his movements by laying her body along the full length of the flat chaise lounge.

"You know, Jack, you're the only one permitted to call me A.C."

"Why's that?"

Alice folded her hands into a pillow beneath her head. "I think of the Codelings as my pets. They're hungry little birds with big red open mouths. Charlie is my smart brother—dependable, loyal, strong-willed."

"And me?"

"You are my prodigal protégé. People dig your Outback Steakhouse backstory. Your Hemingway-as-fraternity-pledge persona works with the floozies. Beneath all that, I see an exceptional mind. And a big warm fuzzy secret heart."

Alice reached out and pulled Jack's nearest hand into her own. He shivered.

"But I resent your recklessness," Alice said, her hand withdrawn, again. "You're using an ounce of your true intelligence. You're not investing enough of yourself—your real self—into our joint venture. I don't know if you're still doing self-destructive penance for the asshole you've always been, but it's unnecessary. The alcoholic binging can stop."

"How'd you find out about that, anyway? I was so careful."

"That part was weird," Alice said. "It was like you had a personal assistant to cover your tracks."

Jack opened his mouth but didn't speak. A confession would not excuse the crime.

"Basically," Alice said, "it was the absences that gave you up. You'd disappear for a whole weekend, which sometimes became a Friday-to-Monday swing. Even tonight, I wasn't sure. But I figured if we got cozy enough, I could coax a confession out of you."

"Shit, really?" On the snack tray in front of him, Jack fumbled in a bowl of pretzels. His hand needed to touch something. His lips wanted to taste salt. For now, this was the best he could do. "Were you spying on me?"

In a fluid motion, Alice raised herself onto one elbow and picked up her lime water. Jack studied her as she took a sip, wiped her mouth, and set the bottle down.

"I'd never spy on my own employees," Alice said. "We're the

good guys, remember?"

"I'm sorry," Jack said too quickly. "I mean, I try to respect your privacy, too."

"Funny thing is, that's what I'm trying to give away. I brought you here tonight so we could talk, like this." Alice lay herself back down on the lounge, hands under her head. "Life's shorter than you know, but so far, I've only felt that sense of urgency with GM. I've never given much thought to making a family because it'd be cruel for me to have a kid."

"No," Jack protested. "You'd—"

"That's not what I mean. Anyway, there's another kind of family that doesn't require the bloody mess of birthing a sprog. You, me, and Charlie—we're the closest thing to real kin any of us has. We spend every day together. We look out for each other, like siblings are supposed to."

That wasn't the simile Jack wanted to hear. This called for countermeasures. Jack repositioned himself to extend his body along his couch, his chin perched on the armrest inches from Alice's own face.

"If we're siblings," Jack said, "then it's time you let me in on some family secret of your own. I told you about my mum, so…"

"Want to hear how I got my nickname? And why I don't let people use it?"

This was encouraging. Unfortunately, the exhaustion of the day was catching up to Jack, who yawned audibly. Alice did the same—the first time he could remember seeing fatigue on her body. She shifted her head to face Jack. A flip of hair touched his scalp. Ambient light gave her face a soft glow. She looked peaceful.

Jack felt his eyes closing. He tried to fight, but his eyelids fluttered.

"So," Jack said, unsure of the topic. "You were gonna tell me about…"

Something moved on the coffee table—maybe a zune. Even

with closed eyes, he could sense that she'd dimmed the overhead lights. Jack pictured her black-spotted bedspread. He'd only caught a glimpse of it, but he could see it clearly. If he could rally the energy, he could scoop Alice up into his arms and carry her through the hallway. He'd toss her onto that bedspread and jump on after her.

"Tell me how you got your nickname."

Alice yawned again. Jack could feel warm air moving between them.

"Years back, at Harvey Mudd," Alice said, "I was sixteen. I felt unwelcome. At an engineering social, some big-man senior, he teased me in front of everyone because I didn't have a boyfriend yet." Alice paused. "So he asked if I was a dyke. I said no. He asked if I was bi. I said I didn't know what I was."

"Sounds like a dickhead."

"He asked if he could kiss me, and I said no. So he goes, 'I guess she's a lesbian today. Maybe she'll wanna fuck me tomorrow.' I still don't know why that was supposed to be funny, but everybody laughed. Then somebody said, 'Maybe she's running on alternating current.'"

"Ah, so—"

"Took maybe five seconds for them to stumble on A.C."

"Which you didn't like."

"No, I didn't like."

Alice breathed softly. After a while, Jack worried she was falling asleep. Or he was.

"So, that's the story."

Alice swallowed and continued, at a whisper. "By graduation day, I'd hacked and wiped clean the Mudd server folders for every person who'd attended that party, including those who'd graduated and had alumni accounts. The bastards lost all their e-mail, plus months of whatever work they stored there. They deserved it."

"Jesus," Jack whispered. He surprised himself by refraining

from blurting out the first reaction that came to mind. Even for Alice, the vengeance seemed out-of-proportion. It sounded less clever than vindictive. This rebuke, he chose not to share.

"When the people closest to you knock you down," Alice said, "the best revenge is to move past them. Climb the next hill alone. If you get to the top and choose to turn around, go ahead and take aim on those down below. That's your right."

Jack held his breath to keep his mouth shut. Tired Alice was a spooky Alice.

"It's your right," Alice repeated. "Maybe your responsibility."

"So, if you stuffed everyone who created that name, why'd you let me use it?"

"Because it doesn't mean anything. For you, it was just a stupid way of saying my name. I liked that."

Jack curled his knees into his chest and held them. The apartment was warm enough, but he wanted human contact. Even a big sister's embrace would be enough.

Minutes passed in silence. The noise of Alice shifting on her lounge woke Jack enough to permit drifting thoughts to find voice.

"Back in college," Jack said, "you didn't want to let that guy put limits on you. Not even with a nickname. Isn't that what we're gonna do with the Compass? We'll code up a few boxes, then drop people into them, one after another. Like the people wearing the little latex gloves, or machines I guess, sorting mail at the post office. Everybody goes where the postal code says they should go."

Alice cleared her throat. "People used to get mail. Little cards, envelopes. Magazines."

Jack recalled a row of mailboxes shaped like birdhouses, each painted white with colorful trim on the edges. He couldn't place the image, then pictured the cottage his mother had rented in one of their better years together.

"Alice? Do you think *we* live in little boxes?"

No response.

"Can we change the box we're in?"

Nothing.

Jack opened his eyes enough to see the city, skyscrapers aglow outside Alice's penthouse. Her windows had no curtains. No secrets, or no shame in sharing them.

Dawn would come soon. He hoped it would take its time.

ALICE

Alice's zune lay quiet. A white gel cover matched the frosted glass table where it lay. Even at rest, the device guided a stream of data up to a satellite, then welcomed back new packets of information. It updated its weather icons and news headlines, filtered new texts and e-mails, and kept its current hour, minute, and second in synch with the official readings of the National Institute for Standards and Technology's Cesium Fountain Atomic Clock.

Thus, it knew the precise time—to the hundredth of a second—when it received an incoming call at 05:15:09 in the morning. Following a pre-programmed progression, it began with a gentle hum. A stronger vibration made it quiver. Next, a flashing light. Still ignored by its user, it went to the preferred ringtone for unrecognized callers—a chirpy pop song from the '90s about Barbie dolls.

Alice sprung to her feet, startled less by the music than by the remarkable fact that she'd been in a refreshingly deep REM sleep.

The zune raised its volume a notch. "You can brush my hair, undress me everywhere—"

Alice seized the device and eyed the readout. "Private number. Private caller."

On the couch beside her, Jack slept with his face buried in a sofa cushion. One arm drooping to the floor, he looked as graceful as a blacked-out junkie.

Still half-awake herself, Alice pressed the "answer" button. As she carried the zune across the hall and into her bedroom, she said, "Who is this? It's five in the morning."

After an audible throat clearing, she got an answer.

"I apologize for neglecting the time zones. The fiction of 'time' eludes me."

"Who is this? Charlie, have you been working on your Mahatma Golden impersonation? Because, I swear—"

"This is he."

"He, who? Is this a Codeling? Eddie? You all sound the same on the zune, you know."

"The Vice President."

"More like the VP of bullshitting me." Alice threw herself onto her bed. Hoping her long-overdue slumber might resume, she pulled back the covers, slid under them, and laid her head on a pillow. "Seriously, what's this about? You woke me up, so at least tell me a story to send me back to sleep."

"I suppose," the caller intoned, "I should have expected this reaction. We have not conversed, as such, since our very first meeting."

Alice exhaled a long, warm breath. "I suppose I can play along, for a minute. Let's see. The rules require that you tell me something only you could know."

"About what?"

"About, I don't know, anything."

"Very well. It is my belief that the President of the United States is demented."

"No doubt," Alice laughed. "Look who she chose for her veep."

A stern cough came through the line. "Also, the US Senate includes members so old and feeble that they can no longer think for themselves."

"Common knowledge."

"I do not speak figuratively, Ms Coleco."

"You'll have to do better than that. Give me something specific. More significant."

"I don't know what could be *more*—"

"Here, I'll help you out." Alice tried to recall a time she and Mahatma had been together, unseen by her co-workers. "Ah! I know. Remember the time you invited me to Thereport and made such a delicious ass of yourself? Tell me, what were the first words you said to me—*directly* to me."

"Behold the monstrosity," the caller replied.

Alice gasped. "Shit...on...me. That you, Mahatma? For real?"

"As real as your present self can apprehend."

"Damn, how *are* you?"

"Fine."

"It's nice to hear your voice. We've always been good for each other, honey."

Another throat clearing. "If you cannot respect me as your elder, I ask that you at least show regard for my office."

"I hold neither you nor your office in high esteem at this point," Alice said. "Who's gonna want to sit in that seat of yours after you've left your ass-print on it? I mean, Eisenhower had the Oval Office fumigated to get the T-man's stink out of it."

"Fake news, that."

"Oh, are we being real? Tell me, then, is it true that you brokered a deal with Dick Dirksen on the climate bill? They're saying you insist on recording a vote in the US Senate for every piece of legislation. You know you're not supposed to do that, right?"

"The Constitution does not require that I await a tie before casting my ballot."

Alice sighed. "Most days, I'm convinced that you're putting us on, but then you make me wonder if you're simply batshit crazy."

"Ignoring the needs of future generations is a kind of insanity."

"I want to believe you believe that. But I've read the journal your dad gave to the *Wall Street Journal*."

"Lies."

"No, I think Daddy Rich is the only one in your family who tells it straight. No, the journal from your Indian pilgrimage also sounded honest. The particulars suggest you're delusional.

What struck me, though, was that mantra of yours, 'Someday I will be king.' That sounds less like prophecy and more like a sense of purpose. I can dig that. It's good to have drive, even if you're a *lunatic*."

"Again," Mahatma said, "I ask for a modicum of respect."

Disappointed by the reaction, Alice tried to spell it out for him. "Don't you see what I did there, Moon Man? See, the root of the word lunatic is—"

"You're speaking to the Vice President!"

"Am I?" Alice said. "That's what kills me. Some of the things you say, they're impeachably stupid. The Framers didn't see you coming when they wrote Article Two."

"Watch yourself. I can be a formidable foe in the position I hold. We could regulate your little company out of business."

"Consider my breath held."

Alice rubbed her eyes. Had they met in person, she might have been more circumspect. A phone call out of the blue, at five in the morning, felt like a free pass.

"You really have no clue, do you?" Alice said. "People call you a time bomb, and figuratively speaking, that works. Every time you open your mouth, the Republicans in Congress plug their ears, get under their desks, and hope you'll finally explode. Meanwhile, the Dems are too afraid to go near you, lest they snip the wrong wire in your head and get torn apart by the shrapnel."

"I, too, appreciate the metaphor. I am a thermonuclear truth bomb."

Alice deemed herself fully awake. The loss of any prospect of sleep was worth the chance to belittle the man who'd undermined what should have been a restorative presidency. Plus, she sensed an opportunity looming in this interaction. If she perked up her ears, she might learn something, or plant an idea in her caller's capacious skull.

"You've got more enemies than allies in DC," Alice said. "The House Minority Whip—that Kevin Penn dude from Shanksville?

Looked like he was gonna snap you in half when you went on CNN to oppose his Alzheimer's bill."

"You know my views on the subject of so-called dementia."

"In other news, how'd you get my number?"

"You should wonder what *else* I know. I know that your company has begun doing more than sending people their morning memos. Your operators, they have been nudging clients for some time—do this, don't do that."

"I will not insult you with a lie," Alice said. She sat up in her bed and switched the zune to her other hand. "What are you playing at?"

"I have acquired recordings of conversations your Gujarati operators have had with the most vulnerable senior citizens they serve."

Nothing newsworthy in that bit of information, except...

"How," Alice said, "did you get your mitts on—"

"I have my methods."

"Our software's audio-encrypted. Unrecordable."

"Technically, they're transcripts."

The plausibility of that detail made Alice shiver. That clients misbehaved was no secret, but Alice had planned a clandestine investigation to measure the scale of this problem. She considered this a high enough priority to label it in her mind as "Project X," the first of her two top secret code names.

If Golden had taken a baby step down this path on his own, she would have to get working on that project. Figure out what data she'd need her Codelings to collect, and how to keep them off the scent of her prey. To get this plan in motion—even in slow-motion, she might not see sleep for a week. Or a month.

Meanwhile, this conversation with Golden had become delicate. Alice prided herself on honesty, but this phone call required compromising on that principle. Such situations seemed to arise more often of late. Either Alice or her circumstances were in flux.

"That sigh you hear," Alice said, "is me not believing anything coming from you. But please do continue."

"You've overplayed your hand, Ms Coleco. Look at the climate change legislation that just passed Congress. The yea votes included the last two conservative Democrats, whose staff promised they would oppose it. Those two gentlemen are among the longest-serving US senators. Though I cannot prove it yet, I believe both are using Quiet Copilots."

"Geez, Mahatma, you don't let up. Just when I thought you were unspooling some new, crazy-ass theory, you come at me with dog-eared paranoia about GM."

"Meanwhile, the two most strident climate deniers chose not to show up for that pivotal vote. Explain."

"I know who you mean—the 'lobsters.' They'd boil alive in the pot before admitting it smelled like dinnertime."

"I cornered one of them the next day, and he couldn't remember what he'd been doing during roll call. Seems he'd wandered off somewhere."

"Would that he'd do it more often. Look, I'm wide awake and losing interest."

"Oh, there's more," Golden said. "The topper is that you rigged my own election!"

"All I did was gather up Eisenhower money, legally—as far as you know. Besides, why are you complaining?"

"You *stole* the election for us."

"I didn't—" Alice's face flushed. "I raised unholy sums of money for that woman when I thought she'd do some good. But the day she picked you..."

Alice had formed GM to give her leverage against an unfair world. After spending a personal fortune to elect Eisenhower, she empowered a gray-haired buffoon in the exchange. In spite of a lifetime of calculation, Alice remained subject to the law of unintended consequence. An omnidirectional hatred boiled in Alice's chest. So intense was the heat that it scared her.

"Tell me this, Mahatma, why would I put on a ski mask and steal an election for *you*, of all people?"

"That, I do not know." Golden paused for dramatic effect, or out of genuine ignorance. "You have always been a mystery."

Alice's belly shook with a genuine laugh. The exhalation gave her back some equilibrium—and candor. "I regret," she said, "that you are no less of an enigma to me."

"The irony is that my father was the one who caught you in the act. Many residents in his retirement community forgot to mail in their absentee ballots. Most are Republican."

"If they'd been plugged into one of our products—"

"Most used a Walker Talker, or the Copilot. One of Rich's neighbors found a completed ballot in his beagle's crate. There's no Earthly reason he'd have put it there, unless some voice on the other end of his gadget *told him to*."

"Dogs have been eating people's homework for centuries," Alice said. "Why not ballots? Look, Golden, people cry foul every four years. Remember the Russian election meddling in 2016? Reagan's hostage deal with the Iranians? Before that, it was Kennedy and Johnson rigging votes in Illinois and Texas. If Eisenhower had lost, Democrats would have cried foul. It's an American tradition."

Alice took pride in her rebuttal, but it pained her to dismiss Golden's theory. Had she been more courteous, Alice would have confessed to considering the same possibility. She had no evidence of her own stronger than the Vice President's suspicious puppy leavings. Her own suspicions grew, however, as she studied the deeds of her principal Gujarati colleague. Even Charlie, who adored the woman, recognized that Sailee could push her operators over an ethical line. In time, Project X would show Alice just how serious this problem had become.

"This morning," Golden said, "I called to hear a confession. Perhaps this was foolish, but I honestly expected one. Now, I'm surprised to discover that you may be shockingly naïve about the monster you've created."

"I, too, must register surprise," Alice said. "Some time ago, I'd concluded you were a master showman—an Andy Kaufman for the digital age. It saddens me to discover that you are nothing more than a paranoid schizophrenic. Admiration has morphed into pity, old friend."

"Believe me, Ms Coleco. Your products are bending people's wills."

The repartee had returned to familiar territory. Alice's fiery rage had given way to sparks of inspiration.

"I have a proposition," Alice said. "If Gray Matters conducted an illegal campaign to bring the Eisenhower-Golden administration into power, then you owe us a favor. When we roll out our next product—and trust me, you'll go bonkers over the Compass—I need you to promise that you'll get one for your dear old dad."

"What?"

"Our next tech—you'll absolutely hate it. Small and undetectable. Remember the second *Star Trek* movie? It'll hug a person's psyche like one of those Centaurian slugs. Before the year's up, one of my employees will implant his own father. You could do the same for yours, if you thought he needed it. But wait, didn't we decide that *you're* the crazy one in the family?"

An old-timey "harrumph" came through the phone, then silence. Alice imagined rusted gears turning inside Mahatma's head. She felt the thrill Sailee's operators must sense when they nudged one of their clients. It was one thing to steer the wheelchairs of hapless seniors. It was something far greater to manipulate a megalomaniacal narcissist.

When Golden ended the call, Alice's zune noted the cut-point of the transmission, then returned to its Home screen. With cheerful chirps and gentle buzzes, it tried to entice Alice with a rotating menu of apps, utilities, games, anything to hold her attention. Alice tapped none of them. The device's screen went black.

"How do you do that?" Alice said to her gadget. "You go to sleep so easily. I hate you."

That sentiment was too cruel, Alice realized. To have any chance at an intimate relationship with a real human being, she needed to practice better social hygiene.

"Thanks for the wakeup call, little zune. We've got a lot to do together before you can let me rest again."

Part VI

The Elder Compass

BARRY

Not my regular doctor, this woman. Sounds like Sally, but why would she strap me into a dentist's chair?

My son's eyes won't give me an answer. Not sure I can trust him. No reason for him to make me spend all afternoon like this.

"Detroit Medical Center," the big sign said when we wheeled in here. That's about right. People keep talking over intercoms about patient this and doctor that.

Thanksgiving's just two days away. Happy goddamn holidays for me.

"Ow!"

Lord that stings. Can't turn my head one way or another. Gotta get outta here.

"Look at me."

That's my son's voice.

"Zudora's almost done. She's just giving you a stitch."

"This isn't—is that Sally?"

Woman in the white coat takes a step back. Maybe she's done poking at me.

"Who's Sally?"

Son seems to know this woman, whoever she is. Puts his hand on her shoulder.

"She's the GM operator I told you about. You don't sound a thing like her."

"Your father's telessistant?"

"A lot more than that, but sure."

Woman raises an eyebrow at my boy. Wonderful. Now they're flirting, while I'm lying here all numb.

"This Sally a live-in girlfriend of yours, or something?"

"Son, who's the lady dentist, if it's not Sally?"

Heart's racing. Feel a shiver, like ice water going from my head down to my chest. Gotta find my son, grab a hand, get ahold of something.

"Relax, Pops. You zoned out for a sec. Zudora's a neurosurgeon. Old friend of mine, from university."

"I used to be part of Big Blue," she said. "Now I'm a Wayne State, uh..."

"Pops, she's a Wayne State *Warrior*!"

Nice to hear my boy laugh. So serious all the time.

"Dad, you've seen their dumb mascot, but it's a solid med school. This is her clinic. You're in good hands."

Whoa! A bee got me, right behind the ear.

"Something's stinging me! I can't move my head—can't get away from it."

"That contraption is just—it's like the helmet the Lions wear. Holding you still to fit you with an upgrade. We just slipped the Elder Compass behind your ear. You're one of the first to wear it. You once said I was the Edsel Ford of new technology. Well, here we are."

"I wouldn't have said that. Edsel didn't make nobody proud, Barry."

Dentist lady looks worried.

"Mr Sanders, are you feeling disoriented? *You* are Barry. You are talking to Charlie."

My poor boy, he banged his head in the war. Tells everyone his name's Charlie. Pleasant used to say, "Grief is a thick fog to walk through."

"Forget it, Dad. She's just confused. Once we're done, we'll go to the Wright Museum. They've brought back the Heidelberg exhibit. Remember that crazy street you took me to? The one with all the stuffed animals and polka dots?"

I remember some girl barking at me from a porch. What was I doing up that way?

Wish Sally was here. She'd never let me get lost. Haven't heard from her in too long.

Least that sting behind my ear is gone. Headache won't quit, though. Pressure's building. Too much in there, all at once.

Feels like I left something back at the house. Or maybe I lost something there. Something's missing. Something's *gone*.

CHARLIE

His father's chest rose and fell. Zudora's hand touched Charlie's shoulder.

"I think your father's fallen asleep. We might have shocked his system a bit."

She unlocked the head brace. Barry's head lolled sideways.

"None of this equipment was necessary," she said. "Your chip slides right into the skin. It's thinner than a contact lens. Almost qualifies as true nanotech."

"Regulatory labels aren't my department," Charlie said, eyes fixed on his father.

"Anyway, it won't leave a mark. You won't need to do this in a clinic."

"I know," Charlie said with a sigh. "It's not a medical device, not legally anyway. I just—I wanted to be extra careful. I've only got one Pops."

"How bad is the dementia? Will this make a difference, I mean, at his stage?"

"The Compass is very much experimental at this point, so..." Charlie leaned over to study his father's fluttering eyelids. "I don't know what good it will do. Can't do any harm."

Zudora motioned for Charlie to follow her into the hallway.

"You look so anxious, Charlie, you're starting to make me nervous. Go relax for a bit. You'll be more useful to your father when he wakes."

Charlie rubbed the back of his neck. "I should stay. I need to be here for him."

"Doctor's orders—take a nap, or a walk. I will text when he stirs." Zudora waved her hands. "Go on. Shoo!"

"Okay, but let me go back in there with him, just for a minute. There a dog park nearby?"

"A park for dogs? No, but you can walk the technology

campus. Cross the main boulevard and follow the signs."

Charlie nodded and returned to Barry's room. His father's eyes remained closed. He was fast asleep, but while the Compass worked its magic, Dad's unconscious mind was being flooded with code and raw information.

On the side of his reclined chair, Dad's right hand twitched. Charlie clasped it, and the shaking stopped. A frightening possibility struck Charlie. He was swapping out a living hard drive for something untested—a hybrid of Barry's own mind, Charlie's behavioral algorithms, and the torrent of data coursing through the Loop.

Barry's hand jumped an inch, then lay limp in Charlie's palm.

"You're gonna be okay, Dad. There's a lot to download for starters, but things will settle quickly. You'll get updates each night. Upgrades every so often."

Just outside the door, Zudora explained to a nurse that she needed the room a bit longer. Guilt pinched Charlie for taking her side a minute ago. Pops was right that her voice sounded a bit like Sailee's, though not as musical.

How would Sailee have reacted to all this? She'd asked to join in by video. It was sweet of her to offer, but her presence only would have added confusion.

"Sailee will call when you need her, Pops. It'll just feel like—"

Charlie wasn't sure *what* the Compass would feel like. They'd wired up a handful of volunteers in Seattle, but when nothing went awry, he made sure his father didn't have to wait another day to get the implant. There would come a point for any client when the Compass could do no good. Dad was close to the line, but surely not over it. Not yet, anyway.

"Just keep on sleeping, Pops."

Charlie patted his father's hand one last time, then slipped out of the room. Feeling disorientation of his own, a floor nurse had to show the way out of the building.

Sidewalk grit felt refreshing after standing so long on polished vinyl floor tiles. Charlie exhaled the iodine scent of the clinic and breathed in autumn. He crossed Woodward Avenue and headed toward the heart of the Wayne State campus. At the entrance to an alleyway, a flock of red and orange leaves flew toward him, buffeted by a gust of cold air. Charlie zipped his coat, flipped its hood over his head, and folded his arms against his chest.

Braving the chill of the wind-tunnel alley earned Charlie the reward of an unexpected garden of sorts—a flagstone courtyard surrounded by newly constructed buildings. Young oaks stood over round tables and benches. In the center lay a massive concrete block banded by strips of brushed metal. On the platform stood a twelve-foot high statue, a towering Robocop. According to the Loop, it surpassed Joe Louis' fist as the most photographed object in the city.

Charlie stepped forward and his foot landed on a steel panel under the leaves. The bronze officer turned its riot-helmeted head toward Charlie, swung its torso to face him, and thrust out its right hand, which held a massive Auto-9 Beretta. A half-human voice warned, "Dead or alive, you're coming with me."

What would Dad say if he were here? That Robocop fella's talking about some thing or another, isn't he?

"Yes, he is," Charlie said. He stepped closer to read the plaque at the base of the statue. Engraved letters read, "Serve the public trust, protect the innocent, uphold the law."

Charlie imagined a retort. You doin' all that good stuff in your job, son?

"Serve and protect, Dad. That's what I do."

Who you protectin' us from?

"Time, maybe. Ourselves."

Who's gonna protect us from this metal fella with the gun?

Charlie chuckled. At least he could get in the last word for once.

"Thing is, Pops, you're the cyborg now. Who's gonna protect us from *you*?"

SAILEE

An auditorium was not the ideal setting for private conversation, but it would have to do. Charlie had arrived a day late, and Sailee had been too busy to meet him at the airport. This vast room, which could seat three thousand souls, had become a necessity for telessistant assemblies, now that Sailee oversaw an entire district of GM buildings. Each held legions of callers working around the clock for clients across the US, Canada, Australia, and a smattering of other English-speaking countries.

With simultaneous translation fast approaching, GM might soon annex her entire city. Would that make Sailee mayor, by default? She would have to stand for the office during elections, as a courtesy.

Charlie held up his zune, which contained the first long-format Elder Compass advertisement, a rush job that would convey to a wider audience the meshing of software and phone service in the new GM product. In Sailee's estimation, the ad carried more shock value than information. That was Jack's idea. Children of aging parents were his target market, not the future clients themselves. Younger generations never saw ads, but they would watch videos if they caught fire inside the Loop. This new commercial was certainly incendiary, if anything.

The worry on Charlie's brow showed that he, too, feared how today's audience would receive the ad. The Minders were a tough bunch. They respected Sailee's leadership but were suspicious of anything coming directly from Seattle. Sailee advised against showing the video, but Alice required it. The official story was that Sailee's operators would learn of the ad sooner or later. Narrowcasting was an anachronism. Better to provide context when they did see it.

"We have a few minutes together before the program," Sailee said. "Come, sit with me backstage." She led him to the wings of the main stage and motioned him toward the folding chairs set up beside empty music stands. She gave him a quick embrace, her fingertips adding extra pressure to convey something more.

With reluctance, Charlie released her and sat down with Sailee. "Sorry I couldn't get here last night," Charlie said. "I was hoping we could pick up where we left off this summer."

"We might have rushed things a bit, caught up in the wedding. Even Nani was trying to pair us, perhaps." Sailee clasped Charlie's hand. "We are so busy, both of us. Then, there is the reality of living on two continents, even when together."

Charlie rubbed his thumb inside Sailee's palm. "Yet here we are, today, in the same city. We'll be in the same conference rooms all week. We could be in the same hotel room, too."

"You know what the lonely raja would say, Charlie-ji."

"It is—*forbidden*."

"Very good." Sailee squeezed Charlie's hand, then let go. "It is important that my Minders not think of me as your girlfriend, or I will lose more respect in their eyes than you could imagine. If you behave well and defer to me in all things today, I promise you a dinner, alone. What more, I cannot say."

Charlie clasped his hands together and bowed his head. The gesture looked silly, coming from him, but his gratitude registered. He retreated to a chair in the wings of the stage and left Sailee to check the final arrangements and rehearse her script.

Once the prologues and introductions were out of the way, Sailee gave Charlie the signal. He tapped "play" on his zune, and dread chilled Sailee's heart to a cold stop. She had seen the video many times, but when the opening frame appeared on the screen, she knew this would go worse than she had feared. Not in a good way, she and Charlie would soon be properly screwed.

A streetlight flickers to illuminate an empty residential road. Torn newspapers flutter and catch on tumbleweeds. A middle-aged man with a paunch walks into the light. Khakis and a grimy Hawaiian print shirt. Over his shoulder, a bolt-action double barrel shotgun.

The unshaven man looks left and right, then speaks into the camera.

"You know me as Bruce Campbell, B-Movie actor and host of *Classic Crap* on USA3. In my line of work, I've seen horrible things. Were-pirates. Lizard men. Aliens with two stomachs, both on the outside. But the worst?"

A groan comes from a decaying corpse slouching into view behind Bruce, who shifts his weight to one foot and swings the shotgun down to grasp it in both hands. A blast sends the beast flying backward.

"Zombies. Nobody, and I mean *nobody*, wants to see living corpses on the march."

Shuffling and gurgling comes from all directions. At the edges of the lamplight, a dozen or more misshapen bodies in rags shamble forward.

"Sure, they're slow."

Another gun blast. Another body collapses.

"But look at them. Hideous. And the stench? That's the part you can't appreciate, unless you work with them as often as I do." Bruce releases his trigger hand and takes the shotgun through a quick sequence of tugs and jerks to reload it with two new shells. "Zombies smell worse than your grandpa's farts. I'm talkin' half-cooked eggs, left in the pan for a week."

Bruce fires left, then right. Two more creatures fall. He moves in for a close-up.

"It doesn't have to be like this, kiddies. There's a better way to go."

Bruce hurls his shotgun at an undead postman. With both hands free, he reaches into his pockets and retrieves discs that shine like new dimes. Spinning around at a comic speed, he flicks them in all directions. As each lodges in the temple or neck of would-be attackers, the zombies transform. Ragged clothing becomes pressed suits, bright dresses. He welcomes hugs and kisses as the favored grandson in a circle of adoring, well-groomed seniors.

"We still don't have robots or jet packs worth a damn. Moon cities? Who'd want those anyway? But today, Gray Matters has made one bit of science fiction real. The Elder Compass turns a daft granddaddy into a solid fifth hand at the poker table. They've fused first-rate telessistants with digital gobbledygook—stuff you or I can't begin to understand—to make grandma's final years good ones, for her *and for you*."

Bruce points an accusing finger at the camera. "This thing ain't cheap, but the folks at GM priced it lower than your datastream payments. So, don't flag Father's Day or Mother's Day on your calendar. Put a big red 'X' on *today* and Loop your folks into the Elder Compass. You'll be glad you did."

The screen went blank. Ceiling lights illuminated more than two thousand women dressed in a botanical garden of bright colors and floral patterns. From the audience came not even polite applause.

Sailee had taken position off stage beside Charlie, whom she escorted to the front. He looked comfortable in a dark gray suit, but the auditorium's A/C, or something else, chilled Sailee in her blue sari and thin black dress.

"You should know," Sailee said with a wink to the audience, "that I explained to Mr Sanders that such an advertisement would not fare well here in India. But he wanted you to see, for yourselves, how our company will explain the Elder Compass to the younger generations in the US. He assures me, this advertisement will appeal to this, uh, more callous demographic."

Charlie feigned disagreement as he read scripted lines digitally projected onto the base of the stage. "What's wrong with zombies? Bollywood has zombies. Bruce Campbell did a movie in Delhi once about a dying leper who drank from the Ganges. Who doesn't remember *Reawakening Shiva*?"

The audience stirred but didn't laugh.

"The children of our future clients," he continued, "grew up with Bruce Campbell. They love their aging parents, but they also love gore. And a good joke."

Charlie pulled at his collar, a tough-crowd signal Sailee had seen used by an American comedian whose name she couldn't recall. To the audience, the self-deprecating gesture appeared to mean even less.

"Mr Sanders and I will now take questions," Sailee said. "I believe we have one already." She acknowledged Vijul's raised hand in the second row. At the last minute, Sailee had asked her friend and colleague to be at the ready. It was a good plan, but she should have mentioned it to Charlie.

He shaded his eyes to make out the face, but he squinted helplessly in the theater lights. "What's your name, ma'am?"

"My name is Vijul Khedwal," she said with indignation. "Honestly, sir. You attended my wedding, just three months ago."

Under-engineered acoustics produced feedback that magnified whispers into a roar. Charlie grimaced, but Sailee held up a cheerful face.

"Of course he remembers you," Sailee said. "It is just that the poor man stepped off a transatlantic flight, and—"

"I must register offense," Vijul said, "at associating us with a violent display such as the one you have shown us today."

Sailee gave Vijul a wide-eyed stare. *This* is what friends are for?

"I *completely* understand," Sailee said. The words sounded patronizing even to Sailee, as soon as she said them. "This, ah, advertisement will only—"

"This is a trifle," Vijul continued, "compared to the greater concern I share with my sisters. How much longer will we have our *jobs*? The Loop leaks back to us what you say in meetings with your Seattle superiors. I am sorry to bring it up in this way, Sailee, but I agreed to ask, on behalf of all the telessistants here today, will not the Compass make us obsolete?"

"Please," Sailee said, "let us stay focused on—"

"I mean *noooo* disrespect, Sailee, you know that. You have opened wide doors of opportunity for us, myself included. But these Americans you answer to, they disregard us. Once their computers take our place on the other end of the line, they will discard us!"

In unison, the audience stood and clapped.

"No!" Charlie said. Forgetting the proximity of his lapel mic, his objection rang out like a shriek. Hands clasped ears until an unseen engineer adjusted the sound board. Charlie tried a softer tone. "With any advance as radical as the Compass, there is a long period of customer entrenchment. Many clients will prefer to stay with the Quiet Copilot, even as the Compass automates the most basic feedback functions you provided."

"The Elder Compass," Sailee said, "has an optional voice-assist package. Our preferred customers will pay a premium to keep in touch with the Minder they already know and trust. Many new referrals will also want that same personal connection."

Vijul shook her head and crossed her arms. "When the looms arrive, the weaver dies. This is how it was for our city, and so it always goes." Vijul pointed to Charlie. "Mr Sanders, how could you, of all people, let your company treat us so poorly? Are we no more than slaves to you?"

More heads nodded than Sailee would have hoped. The ambiguous clucks that echoed across the auditorium probably cut both ways, between agreement and rebuke for Vijul's comment. For his part, Charlie remained impassive. Was he not insulted, or did such insults come so often that he brushed them aside?

Sailee widened her eyes and fixed her eyes on Vijul. "I will ask that you retract—"

A hand touched Sailee's shoulder.

"No," Charlie said in a soft voice. "Offense is taken, sure, but I understand." The room quieted. Not a whisper. "You have families, loved ones, who count on these jobs. We've worked hard at GM to pay good wages for demanding work. The energy—the emotion—you put into every call makes a difference in the lives of people on the other end. People like my father. In return, you expect more than a paycheck. You want the same kind of commitment from us that you give daily to your clients. You treat them like family, and so should we treat you."

Charlie smiled warmly at Sailee. Her heart fluttered. She felt light. Unburdened, the next words came to her fully-formed, as if rolling across a teleprompter.

"I cannot predict the future," Sailee said to the audience. "I am neither a guru nor an oracle, but I know this much. The people who created our company—and now the Elder Compass—are good men and women, like Charlie here. He has flown across the ocean many times to meet with us in person. He comes to Gujrat ready to listen and learn. Believe me, he wants to know our lives. He wants to join our family."

A sideward glance showed that Charlie took those words in every possible way she could have meant it. Sailee placed one hand on her chest.

"In my heart," she said, "I know this man. He poured his soul into this Compass. It will lead us forward, not in the name of profit, but to serve a higher calling we all share. We will bring more light into more lives that, without us, grow dim. Restoring hope, preserving dignity. This is our mission."

At last, genuine applause.

Charlie beamed at Sailee, who exhaled air she had held deep in her chest. She wished Alice and Jack had heard her words.

More than that, Sailee wished she believed them.

ALICE

Alice read the good news on her zune. For the time being, Charlie and Sailee had sustained the morale of the Minders. She would watch the Looped auditorium video later. More pressing was maintaining her white-knuckled grip on the saddle horn atop a quarter horse named Jester.

The horse moved uneasily on the cobblestones that led to the New York Stock Exchange. An Elder Compass publicity event was Jack's idea, and he held in his back pocket a permit, ostensibly to shoot an infomercial. She doubted that slip of paper would keep the cops on their side for long. What Jack had in mind could end up looking more like a cavalry charge.

Alice holstered her zune but left it in speaker mode to await a signal. She adjusted her black-brimmed Stetson, brushed hands down a matching vest, and settled into Jester's suede saddle. This getup she'd dubbed "Robo Annie Oakley" because she accented traditional Western gear with LCD-lit riding boots and metallic ponytails. Her hairdo was so reflective that it appeared she'd left the salon's foils in place.

Jester stamped his hooves and splashed water onto Alice's flashing boots. She'd rented the horse and taken lessons only the day before. Stroking Jester's mane, Alice wondered whether she could ride him at a gentle gallop, if it came to that. Probably not.

"Easy," Alice said. "Not yet, sweetheart."

Disregarding the gentle request, Alice's horse started to move down the street. Behind him trailed a small crowd that had been photographing the scene from the moment Jester emerged from his trailer. Unaccustomed to the city, he'd almost bolted into early-morning traffic, but his trainer had coaxed him back toward the restricted-access section of Wall Street. After Alice had flashed the silver NYSE badge on her zune, she and Jester had taken the position from which they now advanced.

"It's on!" crackled a voice from her saddle holster.

Alice kicked her heels into Jester's sides, and he wagged his head before lurching into a trot. Rider and horse approached the clutch of mounted New York police who patrolled the financial sector. Earlier, the sergeant had explained that Alice had "special clearance," but his crew watched her warily.

A baby-faced officer on a black horse nodded toward her. "Filming some kind of ad?"

Alice let Jester pull even with the police horses. Uncomfortable with a direct lie, she said, "We already have ads in circulation. Haven't you seen 'em?"

The officer smirked at his five colleagues, then licked his lips. "Can't say I have. I'd remember it if *you* were in one, honey."

"Ew," Alice said. "I'm guessing you haven't mounted anything but a horse for quite some time."

While officers laughed at their friend's expense, Alice clicked her tongue beside Jester's ear. Her horse began a canter. The police followed as Jester approached the front steps of the Exchange's columned façade. Jack's raised hand brought him to a stop.

Public relations liaisons from the Exchange flanked Jack. Behind them, power-suited men and women had gathered. At the edge of the scene, Jester's trainer gave Alice a thumbs-up. As far as he knew, this was the full extent of Jester's performance. He'd never have approved using his horse for the rest of what they'd planned.

Alice grabbed Jester's mane, which caused him to rear up. She clamped down her thighs on the saddle and said, "I'm Alice Coleco, and I'm here to open the Exchange!" With a twirl of her pistol, she shouted a "Yee-haw!" Jester's forelegs landed on the first stone step. The loud report of his hoof caused the crowd of traders to jump.

"No way, honey," said the baby-faced officer, who pulled up behind Alice. "Not on that horse you won't. Permit says nothing about him goin' inside."

A woman shouted, "This stunt is bogus!" A man in the crowd pointed at Alice. "GM's not even on the Exchange!"

Alice locked eyes with her heckler, a skinny twenty-something in a navy suit. "What's your name, son?"

"Me?" the man said. "You can call me *Money!*"

The crowd roared.

Jack applauded and smiled. "Tell me this, Mr Money. This very morning, the Gray Matters distribution hub is shipping out three hundred thousand pre-orders for the Elder Compass. You probably know our projected sales for the first year. What valuation would you give GM if I told you that today, we're preparing for an IPO?"

"Bullshit! There's no—you can't just—"

"How much?"

Alice wagged a gloved finger at her associate. "Jack, don't be so crass with these nice people. They're probably uncomfortable talking about financial matters in public." That got a spirited laugh.

"I know what we're worth," Jack said. "I know *to the dollar.* If one of you goblins can guess to the nearest thousand—no, to the nearest *ten thousand*, we'll file the paperwork today and give the winner first dibs on our shares."

"Hell's bells," Alice said. "If anyone here can make a guess that close, we'll sell 'em forty-nine percent of the company at *half price*. Annie needs fresh capital!"

The mix of traders, passersby, and early-morning tourists crowded closer to Jester, who snorted and shook his head. Alice kept her eyes fixed on the man Jack had dubbed Mr Money.

"Forty million," Money said without emotion.

The traders nudged each other. Hands started to shoot skyward and shouts went up. "Seven hundred million!" "Six hundred fifty mill!" "One point seven billion!"

"Gettin' warmer!" Jack shouted.

The front steps of the Exchange devolved into a scrum. Traders clutched at Jack and shouted their estimates.

The policeman closest to Alice tugged her shoulder. "Stunt's over, ma'am."

"I suppose it is," Alice said. She crouched in her saddle and gave her co-conspirator a wink.

Jack used his broad shoulders to plow through the traders until he reached Jester's side. He lifted one foot into an open stirrup, then swung himself onto the base of the saddle behind his boss. After shooting his arms around Alice's sides, he snatched the reins from her.

"Our little Jackie's a horseman, too?" Alice said.

"Crikey," he replied in his strongest accent. "Grew up in the Lucky Country, didn't I?"

Jack clicked his tongue and shook the reins. Jester raised one foreleg, then another. Two at a time, he climbed the steps leading into the Exchange. The traders backed away, still proffering desperate bids, until the horse approached six security officers blocking the front door.

"Looks like they called the sheriff," Alice said.

Jack steered Jester around. Alice felt Jack's pectoral muscles pressing into her back. A jolt of excitement ran through her.

Alice whispered, "What say we go Ned Kelly on the lot of 'em? Let's shoot our way out!"

"Nah," Jack said, "Jester and I are takin' you back to the ranch." A wiggle of the reins and Jester turned to descend the steps. He trotted through the parting crowd. Jack settled into the saddle, and adjusted so that Alice could press her chest into his back.

"Too bad none of 'em guessed right," Alice said.

"Wankers, every one of 'em!" Jack shouted.

The two riders laughed. Their mounted police escort did not.

Jester spotted his trainer a few yards ahead and went into autopilot.

Jack's tone shifted. "In all seriousness, why don't we let investors in? We could expand so rapidly. There'd be no limit to how much the market could grow for the Compass."

"What's mine is mine," Alice said. The press of Jack's torso suddenly felt unwelcome. "You, Charlie, our Codelings—you're all doing fine, aren't you?"

"Of course," Jack said, "but I could ask the same thing. Even after emptying your bank vault for a dumb election, you've got enough money to retire today. You could turn your sister's kids into trust fund babies. Initiative 667 failed, thanks to yours truly. So you could create your own United Way to promote reverse vandalism. If you're afraid you'll get hit by a truck, or trampled by a horse, buy some life insurance."

Alice made a note to do exactly that.

"Seriously," Jack continued, "why hoard the company?"

"The moment I hand GM over to a board, it loses its genius."

"Meaning, it loses *you*?"

An anxious trainer waited for them beside his truck, still parked on the curb. Jack gave a wave, and a head nod came in reply.

Something about the rapport between the two of them seemed wrong. She knew a sleep-deprived brain could play tricks on itself, but what if Jack set up this event to loosen her grip on the company? Or maybe he orchestrated the horse-riding stunt so she'd fall into his arms? Some jackass in the crowd—maybe an accomplice—had shouted an eerily accurate valuation.

"You okay?" Jack said.

Alice touched her forehead. It felt like an overheated radiator. She'd confessed to fatigue when she last spoke with Amber, though such disclosures made her sister worry.

That thought unspooled another chain of possibilities. Maybe Charlie had prompted Amber to pitch the idea of taking a vacation. Pull Alice away from the office so Charlie could—do what? GM placed so much power in Sailee's hands. Something was afoot with those two and their legions of Minders. They had to be stopped.

In a flash, Alice saw fully-formed the purpose of her second secret plan. Once Eddie assembled the data necessary for Project X, Alice would be able to confirm the mutiny underway within her company. When the time came to retaliate, Alice would have to act fast. Meanwhile, Project Y would enlist most of the Codelings, each writing different bits of code that Alice would assemble into a digital golem.

Sailee managed to tug codgers to and fro with a few well-timed words, but Alice would unleash true power by fusing GM's codebase with the Loop. The company's clients—no, *her* clients—would manifest more than a watery Gandhian-Marxist altruism. Alice would orchestrate her own vision of a better world. Unfortunately, the machinations of her own employees, and the dubious government she helped to elect, forced Alice to act more quickly than she'd planned. If people misconstrued such bold action as villainy, so be it.

Jack craned his neck to face his silent companion. "You don't look well."

The unwelcome interruption was too much to bear. A hole burst open in the barrier Alice kept in place between thoughts and words. Wildfire rushed up from her belly, through her mouth, and toward Jack.

"Don't you *get it*?" Alice shouted. "GM's an extension of *me*! I've got to keep its every movement under *my* command. I put every inch of that company's guts in place. I can rip its intestines right back out if I want to."

"Um, what?"

"Even the firm that handles our encryptions accepts without question any non-conforming customizations I require."

"You lost me, A.C." Jack sighed. "What are we talking about?"

"The products we ship only get the GM label after every line of code passes through *me*. I alone bear responsibility. I work the

242

most and sleep the least."

Jester came to a stop. Jack let go of the reins. "I'm sorry," Jack said before dismounting. "I didn't mean to pry."

Jack reached up to help Alice down, and her feet hit the sidewalk. Even that simple gesture seemed wrong. Too deliberate.

Jack turned to face Alice. "I get it, A.C. It's *your* company. We're just honored to be on the team."

"Tell me this," Alice said. "What would we have done if one of those traders had guessed right? One got awfully close to the figure you came up with last month."

"You're shitting me, right?" Jack said.

"Answer the question."

"Whatever they said, I'd insist it was wrong. What's the matter with you?"

Alice's vision blurred. Her temples pulsed. She tried to let her strongest emotions dissipate, lest she say anything she would regret.

"How about this," Alice said. "Let's just make sure we're on the same page next time."

A chastened Jack slunk away to the curb and hailed a cab.

The crowd of lingering tourists had caught up to them. With Jester back in his trailer, all attention turned to Alice. News of her presence had spread. Strangers tried to tell her about their ailing fathers, mothers, grandmothers, uncles.

Alice's head swam. Like the zombie grandparents in the Compass ad, these well-wishers morphed and became shareholders, grasping at her costume. She retreated further, and her left boot heel slipped on the wet curb. The front bumper of a yellow cab raced toward her. Its bright chrome looked like the friendly smile she'd seen on a Claymation car.

Someone grabbed her waist and jerked her back out of the street. Brakes shrieked as she landed on top of Jack, who fell backward onto the sidewalk with a thud.

Well, that wasn't staged.

Theatrical instincts took ahold of Alice. "Whoo-hoo!" she shouted, then fired her revolver. A blank exploded inches from Jack's chin and burned his neck and face.

"Damn!" Jack recoiled.

The heavyset cabbie had burst out of her cab and grasped Alice's hands. She lifted Alice upright, all the while pleading, "So, so sorry, I didn't see—"

"Forget it," Jack snapped.

Alice allowed Jack to slide her into the backseat of the cab. He moved tentatively beside her and shut the door.

When the cab pulled away, Alice tried to read Jack's expression, but failed.

"You're scaring the crap out of me," he said. "Let's get you home."

Jack's reddened face looked nasty, but Alice couldn't help giggling.

"What's so damn funny?"

"You look—you look like you went duck hunting with Dick Cheney."

"Who the—" Jack looked at his reflection in the cab's rear-view mirror. "Nah, just an abrasion. That'll heal. It's *you* we've got to worry about."

JACK

Jack laughed when Charlie joined him in the conference room. "Well, Mr Sanders, aren't we in the Christmas spirit?"

To the annual Troika review meeting, both wore the same charcoal suit, ivory shirt, and emerald tie. The coincidence was too much. Either the Codelings had pranked them, or the Loop nudged both to ready themselves for Alice's off-kilter holiday jujitsu with the same counterpunch.

Charlie gave a distracted nod.

Something—or, more likely, someone—was on his mind. He'd flown to India twice in the past month. Over a rare dinner together, Jack almost got Charlie to confess a desire for Sailee Singh to become more than a business partner.

Jack touched his cheek. Its smooth surface was a relief, though his skin had healed from Alice's gun blast a while ago. He'd thought about wearing rouge to give himself cheeks as rosy as Santa, but he worried the joke might set off Alice, who seemed as edgy as ever.

Charlie's tap-tapping on his zune started to grate on Jack. Easy banter wasn't so easy anymore. It felt as though everyone had a side project going, but nobody would acknowledge it.

Jack was just as guilty as the others. In place of self-flagellation, flirting, or benign mischief, an unsettling earnestness made claims on Jack's time outside the office. He could break this painful silence and tell Charlie he'd filed papers to start a political nonprofit. Face could be saved by saying he'd done it on a reckless dare. Maybe Russell, the bushie he'd befriended in Olympia, had put him up to it. Truth was, the idea owed half its inspiration to the reverse vandalism Charlie imported from Detroit. His experience with the DIPs was the other half of the story. Either way, he risked sounding like a born-again prick. Better to be oblique.

Jack stood and stretched. "You've been traveling so much, I don't know if I told you about my voting party."

"The what?" Charlie looked up from his device.

"Some of the DIPs I met in Olympia got us all back together to talk about the other ballot measures."

"No shit," Charlie chuckled. "Was it a potluck?"

"Sure, yeah."

"You brought a covered dish?"

"Chook wings."

Charlie cocked his head.

"*Chicken* wings," Jack said.

"I dunno," Charlie said. "Doesn't sound like you. Where's this going?"

"Wasn't sure what I'd think of those DIPs," Jack said. "After so many months, I mean. Back in Olympia, it was like we'd been sent up to the International Space Station to fix a broken solar panel. This time, we were back on Earth. Things went sour, and fast."

"Let me guess," Charlie said. "You busted out your wicked-ass warlock knowledge?"

"I might have got a bit strident, yeah."

"You honestly expected something different?"

"One of them threw a chook wing at me."

"Bet you deserved it."

"I was a *bad* boy."

In the distance, laugher erupted. A moment later Alice appeared.

Jack and Charlie froze—eyes wide, mouths open. Alice wore an outfit that suited the season but was more drag queen than CEO. Holding ajar the glass door to the conference room stood a short Santa dressed in knee-high black boots and a red Lycra suit bedecked with fake-fur trim. Beneath a cliché cap, Alice wore glittering eyeshadow and impossible lashes extended a full inch.

Jack felt bewildered, but also embarrassed. He'd always

enjoyed the jolts he got from Alice's getups. This time felt different. The distraction felt suspicious, like the flamboyant hand gestures of a magician's assistant.

"Happy, um, holidays?" Charlie offered.

The quip helped Jack get himself back on track. "Bugger," he said. "I'd have worn nothing but a pair of budgie smugglers if I'd known it was this kind of party."

"This outfit isn't for your amusement," Alice said with a roll of the eyes. "I wanted to give the Codelings a laugh, and that I did. Santa brought gifts for them, one and all. Those I shall deliver while they lie sleeping at their desks, dreaming of simulated sugar plums. Otherwise, Santa's bag is empty, so none for—"

Alice interrupted herself to reach deeper into the red sack she'd set down on the floor. "But what's this?" She held up bound documents. "Printed copies of the GM annual report? Plus first-week sales figures for the Compass? Merry Christmas, everyone!"

Alice tossed bound reports onto the table. She set aside her satchel and slid into her customary chair.

Charlie clucked his disapproval. "I thought Santa pledged to go paperless."

"Santa's an old-fashioned girl," Alice said. "She still likes to brush her fingers across the little bumps that toner makes on heavy paper."

Jack smiled. "Keep talkin' like that."

"Well then," Alice said, "only Charlie gets a report. Nothing but coal for you."

Three hours passed. Fiscal projections and supply chain analyses danced like sugar plums. Jack shut his report, raised his arms like a magician and sang, "Ta-daaa!"

"Can't argue," Alice said. "For all the Walker Talker's success, this takes us to another level. We knew pre-sales were insane, but we still underestimated our market."

Jack leaned back in his chair, folded his hands behind his head, and said, "Oops."

Alice gave a respectful nod. "Well played."

"I've gotta share the executive summary, at least, with Sailee," Charlie said. "It's just like I promised. Most clients are doubling-down. They're extending contracts with their telessistants, even while switching over to the implant. I think they're tired of fumbling with a zune."

"It's more than that—the little chip is clandestine," Jack said. "Wrinklies are shaving their heads to hide their gray hair." He rubbed his crew cut. "The Compass is trending with all sorts of spin-offs like that. Slip in Viagra with your Compass, and you can make a credible appearance at a downtown dance party."

Charlie laughed. "Jack's exaggerating only slightly. Loop sent me a review that said we're 'bringing sexy back for the senior set.' In two cities—"

"New York and London," Jack said gleefully.

"—at least three struggling nightclubs are rebranding themselves."

Jack leaned forward and made air quotes. "Gray watering holes," he said. "Smart-drinks with sixties dance music."

"Yikes," Alice said. "Remind me to never go clubbing ever again." She shivered and the strips of fur on her suit wiggled.

Jack reached to his side and handed Alice his suit jacket. "Please, you look cold." To his surprise, she put on the jacket without protest.

"Let's give credit where it's due," Charlie said. "The *60 Minutes* product preview was huge for us."

After watching that episode at HQ with the Codelings, Charlie and Sailee had screened it in Ahmedabad to warmer applause. The segment dovetailed nicely with the "higher calling" Sailee invoked to inspire her employees.

It profiled three families, each of which sat down with a GM interviewer trained by Charlie. In the most memorable segment, an aging New Orleans jazz ambassador sat beside his beaming adult daughter and his son-in-law. He explained to the interviewer what was essential in his daily routine and how he hoped to spend his twilight years. The line Charlie improvised during that segment Looped through nearly every media outlet. "With the Compass," Charlie quipped, "he'll keep blowing spit into his horn every night, instead of dribbling it down his chin."

"After that," Jack said, "I worried we'd be branded miracle workers."

"I could use one of those miracles," Charlie said. "Dad's still confused about pretty basic stuff. Getting into spots of trouble, but he follows directions pretty well. Without Sailee, I'd worry. He'd be too lonely without her, at the very least."

"You've gotta remember," Alice said. "Our strongest growth will come from future clients who can't afford the call center. The software's so much cheaper by itself. Personal operators are a luxury."

"No," Charlie said, "we need to think about call center expansion. They're logging more hours than ever. Sailee's going to run out of suitable commercial space. We're talking about India's tenth largest city, and our company has built or leased its entire skyline."

"Bullocks to the buildings," Jack said, "we need a contingency plan for involuntary implants. You have to believe that for every one who will get caught Compassing a grandparent without their permission, there's a thousand who will get away with it. Am I the only one who wonders whether *any* brains with odometers over sixty-five won't be Compassed in this country? That's something like one in five voters on auto pilot."

"He's right," Charlie said. "If consumer survey estimates don't match our sales figures, we won't know whether the excess implanting is involuntary or, ah, clandestine."

"And we'll never know," Jack agreed. "Our encryptions make it impossible for anyone, including us, to inventory our clients.

Remember—focus groups tagged this as a key feature. We can't ever risk jeopardizing that trust. Isn't that right, Alice?"

Alice gave a cat grin. "We're the good guys. We wouldn't snoop even if we could." She stared at Charlie. "What do *you* think? A lot of critics are saying powerful people we all know— the aging A-listers—will soon be using the Compass without our knowledge. You believe that?"

"Maybe," Charlie said. "Probably."

"We know of at least one exceptional case, don't we?" Alice said. "How's Eisenhower's father doing, Charlie?"

"I'm sorry?"

Alice eyed Charlie warily but gave him no further prompt.

"I mean," Charlie stammered, "the admiral can talk, sometimes. But he isn't lucid. I'd wager he doesn't know his daughter is the Commander in Chief. When I spoke to the President last month, she sounded disappointed with her—with the, ah, Compass."

"Serves the tart right," Jack said.

Alice reached across the table and smacked Jack's cheek, hard. He recoiled, but the sting from her open palm felt electric. A touch was a touch. It was something.

"Look," Alice said, "it's cute that you hate her, Jack-o. But she's the goddamn President. She's a pretty decent daughter, too, so cut her some slack. I never should have sent Charlie out to implant her dad. I was feeling vindictive and let Eisenhower convince herself that the Compass could bring back her Poppy."

"Don't beat yourself up," Charlie said. "When the President comes calling, you've got to honor the request. She has her reasons. Good reasons."

Charlie nervously shuffled through the pages in front of him, then glanced at Alice. In that brief instant, Alice locked her eyes with Charlie. What it meant, Jack couldn't begin to guess.

"Okay," Jack said, "I'll leave the First Family alone. But what about the second one? What about Mahatma's dad? Seems Rich has fallen back in love with his son."

"Pappy got sappy?" Alice said. "It can happen."

"Maybe..." Jack tapped on the conference room table and a wall monitor lit up. "I still think the VP's capable of doing an involuntary implant."

"No way," Alice said. "The Compass couldn't wrestle Rich Golden's brain down to the ground. That guy's a bull."

"Which tells me," Jack said, "that you haven't seen the nugget from this morning."

The monitor showed a still image of Blaire Giles, the reporter who'd covered the Walker Talker's product launch in the Public Market. Her former employer's wire service had withered as the Loop auto-aggregated public information into what had the look and feel of news. Giles had parlayed her tenacity and winning genetic lottery ticket into a political assignment at Fox News.

Jack hit play. The video began in the middle of Giles' segment. "Mahatma Golden is the first modern Vice President who's had to mount a public campaign just to *stay* on the incumbent ticket. Golden has stepped out of his office in the US Senate building to record votes on every major piece of Democrat legislation."

Jack would have laughed at the partisan script Giles read, but he guessed it wasn't written by human hand. It was probably lightly-edited meta-copy the Loop distilled from other news, with the tone filter set to "alt-right."

"The Vice President's latest tactic," Giles continued, "involves crisscrossing the country to draw energy away from the crowded field of GOP hopefuls. This blustery November day here in San Diego was no exception. Golden appeared at the Torrey Pines golf course just minutes ahead of a Republican fundraiser at La Jolla's Hotel Parisi. When the governing guru caught his father by surprise, we were there to capture the moment—and ask tough questions."

The video cut to Mahatma, who ran up to the tee on Hole 4 and bear hugged an elderly man in a white polo shirt.

"Happy birthday, Dad!" Mahatma said.

When his feet returned to the ground, Rich Golden regarded Mahatma for a moment. "This is my son," he said. "This is *my* son."

"You look fantastic," Mahatma said. "Not a day over seventy."

Lakshmi came into view and took her turn at embracing Rich.

"My...*wife*," Rich said. "She's crazy...crazy beautiful. My lovely wife, Laura."

Lakshmi blushed and said to Giles, "He still calls me by my old name. Isn't that sweet?"

Giles pushed her mic between father and son. "Rich, what has made you fall behind a son who you once called the Swami of Swindle?"

Rich looked into the camera and blinked, five times. "Whatever he is," Rich said, "he's family. My family is here today."

Jack paused the video to raise an eyebrow. "That piece isn't the worst. Wanna see more?"

Charlie shrugged. "Maybe Rich can see the Grim Reaper coming and wants to smooth things over."

Alice picked up her copy of the annual report and stood. The meeting was over.

"I like what I see," Alice said. "Rich was a distraction when he played the role of amateur debunker. Remember, as long as Mahatma Golden stays at war with us, he's not our enemy."

"I guess," Charlie said.

"No," Alice corrected, "we're not in the guessing business. We know things. Knowledge is our muscle. Now if you'll excuse me, gentlemen, I'll get back to flexing it."

ALICE

The Santa cap still hanging on Alice's bookshelf served as a visible reminder that the past few weeks of coding had passed quickly. She'd left the annual GM meeting in good spirits, but the holidays that followed showed just how precarious her life had become. Unable to shake anxiety about her co-workers' hidden intentions, she'd accepted her sister's invitation to spend Christmas and New Year with her family in Hilo, Hawaii.

Though Amber had lived on the Big Island for ten years, Alice had visited only twice. Both times, her sister tried to broach painful family history. This time, Amber swore on their mother's grave not to pester Alice about getting tested for Fatal Familial Insomnia. Alice would get to spend quality time with her niece and nephew. Nothing more.

The vacation started well enough. Amber's kids had inherited the same gene that gave Alice manic energy and a narrow focus. They applied that trait to a passion for body surfing, which they explained in geometric terms Alice appreciated. Though she lacked aptitude for the sport, Alice matched the kids' exertion. After three all-day sessions at the beach, Alice spent her third night in Hilo blissfully asleep in the guest room.

So deep was Alice's slumber that she didn't hear Amber enter her room. With twenty-one years of experience as a registered nurse, Amber prided herself on the subtlety of her blood draws. She extracted from the crook of Alice's arm a sample sufficient for the test she'd scheduled for the next morning.

In its own way, Alice's zune tried to help. The cumulative effect of manipulating Alice's arm signaled a sleep disruption. The device cooed to Alice, "Go back to sleep." The disembodied voice under Alice's pillow startled Amber, who let out a yelp.

An ugly scene ensued.

By the end of it, Alice had destroyed the sample as completely as Amber had violated her sister's last trusting impulse. In less than twenty-four hours, Alice was back in Seattle. The relief granted by a half-night of rest was gone.

In the two weeks since, Alice passed most nights without returning to the condo. Urgent tasks commanded her full attention. Even simple chores could not distract her. Hence, the elf hat remained on the shelf.

Though it was late in the evening, Alice wasn't alone. Based on the number of times the main door to the GM office suite had closed, one last Codeling remained on the floor.

In the earliest days of the company, Alice would hack away effortlessly through the night at one of the Octagon's work stations. Her most loyal employees would try to keep up, though few could manage the feat. In an industry known for rapid turnover, few left Alice's team voluntarily.

The company retention rate also benefited from the presence of a formidable enemy. Vice President Golden had stepped up his attacks. The Loop never missed a chance to put on the wall monitor his rants against the Elder Compass, some of which sparked street protests staged by his supporters. GM Headquarters came to feel less like a happy beehive and more like a not-so-secret lair. The metaphor was a conscious one for a workforce weaned on graphic novels and fantasy gaming. Embattled GM programmers looked up to Alice as a fearless leader. If they were the X-Men, she was Professor X. Or, to be more precise, Professor X and Y.

This night, Eddie was the last Codeling at work. He knocked on Alice's open door and held out a thumb drive attached to fuzzy dice. Alice took the drive, then shook Eddie's hand.

"Thank you," Alice said softly. Her voice lacked any hint of sarcasm. When meeting one-on-one with Codelings, she tried to convey humble respect.

"I just wanted to say—" Eddie shifted his eyes downward, as if studying the veins in the floor's travertine tiles. "I just wanted to say, it's such an honor to work for you, Ms Coleco."

"The pleasure is always mine, Eddie."

"I'm sorry it took me longer than the others to do my bit." Eddie tried to lift his eyes but couldn't. "Had to make sure I got it right. And I wanted to ask, what will come of all this? Building the Compass I understood, but what's the deal with what you call Projects X and Y?"

"The truth?" Alice said.

Eddie's eyes widened to the size of Japanese anime. The look was not attractive on him, but it was endearing.

How many times had Alice fantasized about explaining herself in a dramatic soliloquy? If she told anyone, it would be Eddie. For years, Jack and Charlie had been her confidants, but Alice had lost faith in everyone close to her. Besides, Eddie would understand. She saw a younger version of herself in him. Alice had once been underestimated and underappreciated. Come to think of it, the world still failed to recognize her capabilities. With the help of her Codelings, she would soon exert more force on the future course of civilization than anyone in her generation.

As tempting as it was to confide in Eddie, Alice opted to nudge him away, gently.

"The truth is," Alice said, "I'd always wanted to use those codenames."

"That's cool." Eddie kept his eyes down. "But none of us know what they add up to."

"That's by design."

"Project X is maybe, like a client study? For what, we can't guess."

"So stop guessing."

"And Project Y?" Eddie summoned the courage to look Alice in the eye. "It's as though we're baking little code-bricks, like the ones you assembled for the Compass. This time, there's no schematic fitting the pieces together. Reminds me of the old Lego set my sister gave me after she'd lost the coolest pieces."

"Maybe your sister kept the best bits for herself."

Alice gave Eddie a slow nod. He got the signal.

"Goodnight, Ms Coleco. Don't stay up too late."

"I sleep when I can."

Eddie scurried back to his desk. Less than a minute later, Alice heard the main entrance close. With a thump, a heavy bolt slid into place inside the metal door.

She was alone.

* * *

With its noisier occupants out of the way, the office building treated Alice to a soothing soundtrack all its own. A soft hum came up through the floor and vibrated in the walls. There was a rhythm to the circulation of air, to the buzz and clank of mechanical systems that worked through the night.

Those familiar sounds, more or less common to every place she'd ever worked, soothed Alice. Problem was, she could indulge that bliss only for a moment. As Eddie intuited, she had pieces to assemble.

Alice launched her girl-perk playlist. The eclectic soundtrack was part of her mystique in the upside-down world of GM. Those who believed genius spawned deviance were impressed to hear that the company's CEO worked to the likes of Britney Spears, Tiffany, AKB48, and a newer infusion of Bollywood pop, courtesy of Charlie.

Truth was, Alice's musical choices were not arbitrary. Like so many of the outfits she wore, the songs had hidden purpose. They formed an exoskeleton of cheerfulness that protected the outside world from the anger boiling inside her. Anger at fate. Anger at the brevity of existence. Anger at wasted lives, all around her. The tunes helped Alice endure the darkest moods that gripped her. Of late, however, the music's energy didn't soothe her rage so much as channel it.

The insistent four-by-four meter also provided a syncopated white noise that sustained Alice through long days at her desk. None of her employees could stand in the music's presence for long, especially given how it echoed off the hard surface of the floor. This kept intrusions—and clumsy advances—to a minimum. Meanwhile, repetitive lyrics kept her body moving. Once per song, she would crack her neck on hearing a "baby," stretch out her toes on "boy," and flex her hands on "kiss." The formula kept her limber, even seated in her chair for hours at a time.

Thus, sparkling tunes powered Alice through the final stage of the data mining exercise dubbed Project X. With Eddie's final data now in hand, she would know just how extensively Sailee and Charlie had tampered with GM's clients.

The Loop gave credence to suspicions Alice shared with Mahatma by filling her inbox with the desiccated leavings of bloglets. The cybercrimes these sites attributed to GM would have flattered Alice, if she'd thought of them first. When she formed the company, she'd harbored no intention to manipulate her clientele. The power they gave Alice came in the congealed form of currency. As the GM product line grew stronger, however, the potential for mischief became obvious not only to Sailee but to everyone in the company. The strings were there to be pulled.

Alice had ranked the many allegations against GM on a spectrum of technical feasibility, from plausible to impossible. At one end of the distribution lay the theory that seniors using her products had become inexplicably avid recyclers. To test this idea, Alice began with Codeling data compiled for Project X to create a geo-located GM client density map. When she merged that data with weekly municipal waste statistics, a clear pattern of influence emerged. It traced back to the latter days of the Walker Talker. Canned and bottled beverage consumption hadn't changed in the areas where recycling spiked. That ruled out the best alternative explanation. The net effect was pro-social. Sailee's callers were prodding GM clients to recycle more consistently. Charlie would tag that as an innocent variation on benign vandalism.

Other potential conspiracies were more worrisome and harder to investigate, with one exception. A cyclone had hit western India last summer. Private donations that came in response had set records. This could have reflected a broader acceleration in charitable giving across the globe, courtesy of the Loop's rich entanglements with NGOs and its absorption of social media.

Data digging revealed that checks sent for the cyclone campaign by US mail violated the boundaries of the best statistical models for philanthropy. The use of the postal service coincided with the higher age profile of that cause's donors. Nothing could link this precisely to GM clients, but the Red Cross had good cause to dub unprecedented cyclone relief as "the best kind of senior moment."

Alice weighed her options but opted to do nothing about this. Better if Sailee didn't know she'd been caught. Whatever her altruistic vices, the woman had done a remarkable job ramping-up a massive call center on the other side of the world. The company needed Sailee to keep going strong, until Alice could automate the Compass and fire the lot of them.

Then there were the wildest rumors about GM, including the company's takeover of Congress by slipping chips into its members' heads. None of these theories had the timeline right. The cyclical madness that characterized the federal government predated GM's creation. It predated Alice herself, for that matter. If the House and Senate seemed a bit robotic, that was hardly the fault of software.

Alice found it ironic that with so many conspiracy theories in the air, none suspected that GM had implanted its signature nanochip in Eisenhower's father. The company did have clandestine capabilities, though the President's continued reluctance to trot her father out in public suggested the Elder Compass did the poor man little good. No surprise there.

Something about that nagged at Alice. Was the President so devoted to her father that even she couldn't see he was beyond the reach of a GM implant? Eisenhower had shown a capacity for poor judgment, but she was no sentimentalist. More to the point, Charlie had insisted the President "had good reasons" for wanting the implant. She had convinced Charlie of its utility, though Charlie could see with his own eyes the state of the President's father.

It seemed to follow that Eisenhower wanted the chip for someone else. To addle the brain of her Vice President, as he had done to his own father? That possibility gave Alice a shiver, but Golden showed no signs of tampering. Another possibility came to mind. What if Eisenhower intended to Compass *herself*?

Such a scheme sounded like one Golden would allege, but it couldn't be dismissed out of hand. If Charlie was part of this conspiracy, it would be a gross betrayal—but an impressive one. Alice felt a twinge of pride. Maybe her worldview had rubbed off on the boy after all. Once she traced and inspected the chip—or chips—Charlie took with him to DC, she would know the truth.

Either way, the latest data from Eddie supported at least one of Golden's accusations. The Vice President's pre-dawn phone call gave Alice a workable hypothesis. Codelings had combed the client data from Eisenhower's election to find seventy-nine precincts with exceptionally high GM client density. Every last one was a retirement community. Of those, twenty-two had strongly liberal voting histories and thirty-five leaned far to the right.

After statistically controlling for anything she could, the pattern could not have been more stark. Compared to years before and since that election, voter turnout dropped precipitously in the most conservative precincts. Left-leaning communities thick with GM users showed robust voting rates but even stronger support for Eisenhower than Alice's statistical models predicted. The seniors in Alice's care had been targeted not by precinct number but by personal voting history.

One possibility was that her very own software was making marionettes out of the GM client base. Project X analyses showed no bug tracks walking through GM's proprietary code base, but they did reveal a vulnerability. Anyone with administrative access to GM's servers could push new data and code into millions of implanted Compass chips. An intruder could exploit that feature, and Alice made a note to patch the hole herself at the first opportunity.

Ruling out such technological causes, logic and evidence pointed to one conclusion. The puppet masters lived in Gujarat. Alice suspected that someone with more strategic prowess than Sailee was coordinating the effort. Drawing on the generous biographical powers of the Loop, Alice found the most likely ringleader—an aged communist who headed a political faction. With two granddaughters holding pivotal positions in GM's Ahmedabad offices, these women may have abused the trust of the company's entire client base.

And what of the connection from one of those granddaughters to Charlie? After all Alice had done for him and his father, such a betrayal was incredible. This scheme Charlie was running might have drawn in Jack, who lately seemed to have lost his cynical edge. Alice's tracking software noted that Jack had started a nonprofit with a civic purpose that didn't sound like him at all. He hadn't said a word about it, but the boy would need more funds for this new venture than even a generous salary could provide. It also signaled that he was planning to leave GM, perhaps to start a joint venture with Charlie.

Alice muted her speakers and got out of her chair. Her feet crossed cool tiles through the hallway and to the back corner of Jack's office. From there, Alice could see her own condo complex. Tracing a finger along its penthouse level, she pinpointed her own bedside window. A desk lamp she'd left aglow showed a still-made bed.

A stroll to Charlie's office offered a different view. Between a pair of buildings, she could see the raised monorail route between Westlake Center and the Space Needle. If Alice had insisted that Sailee visit Seattle, they would have taken that train together, just for the silliness of its short and pointless ride. If Sailee had commuted monthly to Seattle, perhaps none of this would have come to pass. Then again, that might have pulled Charlie into the young woman's gravity field all the sooner. Perhaps the shape of things had been inevitable.

At least Alice could count on Eddie and the rest of her Codelings. If they discerned her purposes at some point, they'd never betray her trust. Nor would they stand in her way.

* * *

When Alice returned to her own desk, a new browser window opened, unbidden, on her center monitor. Alice smiled at the distant memory of the "popups" that plagued the early Internet like locusts. Text in the window asked if she wanted to know personal information about people in her life. This sort of thing was common enough. The links usually led to commercial vendors, but sometimes the Loop made the offer itself, free of charge.

The window switched to a new site, as if she had touched it. Alice lifted her hands to make sure she hadn't bumped the keyboard. A short alphabetical list of names appeared. Amber Coleco. Eddie Jaworski. Charlie Sanders. Barry Sanders. Sailee Singh. Jack Thompson. Russell Crosby—who was that?

Alice would have chalked it up to standard Loop noise, but the window changed again, as if she'd selected Charlie's father. An auto-bio appeared. The details from Barry's early, pre-Internet life were scant. Before she had a chance to read them, the screen shifted to a degree program in welding at Wayne State. Faster and faster, the window flipped through pages. A Detroit street map, a deli, a beer importer, the White House.

During her most recent session sitting with her Codelings, they talked about how the Loop had been overheating of late. It would get tangled up in probabilities and serendipities. Its underlying DNA was composed of open-source programs, the contents of which the Loop maintained almost on its own. For every ten hiccups this suppressed, a more violent one could result. As Eddie quipped, "Browser crashes are the price of freedom."

Alice clicked the rogue window shut and was relieved to see it obey. Her monitor had been flying through images so fast she couldn't say what they were. To be safe, she logged off. Rebooted.

While her system ran quick diagnostic checks, Alice stood and stretched. Amber had taught her a trick to induce at least a nap, if not a full night's sleep. Imagine how tired *feels* — drooping eyelids, heavy limbs, slowed breathing. To speed things along, Alice forced a yawn. The forgery fooled none of her biological systems.

Cheerful beeps commanded Alice's attention back to the monitor. The thin gaps between the letters on her keyboard glowed to show her the way. Behind her, a sliver of light along the horizon presaged the coming dawn. The evening had passed too quickly.

Alice sat back down, reignited her speakers.

In the quiet of the early morning, a familiar sense of urgency gave Alice's heart a steady beat. While Sailee grew more brazen in her exploitation of GM's clients, Charlie and Jack also had undergone personality shifts. Their growing distance from Alice coincided with secrecy about their own intentions. Assuming the worst seemed the best course of action.

What her co-workers didn't realize was that Alice had spent

the past year doing more than harboring suspicions and suffering fools. Alice now possessed everything she needed to take decisive action all of her own. She had Golden where she wanted him. If the President had a chip under her skin, that presented another opportunity. When the time came, Alice could regain control of the GM client base with the flip of a switch. Charlie and Jack could be kept out of the way, perhaps for their own good.

The sequencing of each element of Alice's plan remained unclear, but working out those details would be a joy. A new year had dawned. Before spring gave way to summer, Alice would make it one that even GM's most demented clients would never forget.

Part VII

Glitches

BARRY

There's dignity in this, working with my hands. It's like being back at the plant. Metal gets molten for a second, then stiffens right back up, just like it should.

This is a special talent of yours, Barry. You're putting it to good use.

Sweat pours down my forehead, getting in my eyes. Hard to reach under this welding mask to wipe it away. Must be middle of the night. Torch gives enough light to see what I'm doing. At the plant, it was always bright as day in there.

Good memories?

Yes, ma'am. Wait, who is that? Your voice sounds different.

You need to stay sharp, Barry.

Can barely lift this welding gun up over my shoulders. I'd guess its tip's running at maybe a hundred amps. Steady now. Not easy tracing a tight arc along the top of this door. That's it. I can see it fusing into the steel frame. Sealing right up.

There is no rush, Barry. Let them see a quality job.

Dang, would ya look at that perfect line.

Your work is impressive, Barry.

Sure 'nuff. Maybe this lazy butt of mine ought to get out of retirement.

Think of this more as an April Fool's prank.

Nah, this is real labor. Something to be proud of. Damn if it don't ache in my elbows and shoulders, though. Gotta set that welder back down. Can't rub that burn outta my joints.

Is there a physical problem?

Nah, just arthritis. Gotta push through it.

Let's see. Got the welder box back in my basket. Turned it off. Now unplug it from—where does that cord go? Behind the dumpster? There's the outlet. Just enough room in my basket for that coiled cord and the welding gun.

266

Almost too heavy to push this with such a full basket.

Gotta take another look before I leave this parking lot. Just like I pictured it. Front wall of Aladdin Grocery looks nice with a solid steel plate on it. Seam looks smooth, just like it should.

Have you completed the task?

Sealed up tight as an ocean liner. Ain't nobody going in there today.

What's that? Something's bright up above me all of a sudden. A streetlamp just came to life in the middle of the night. Makes the oil on the asphalt kinda glow.

Something's rustling near the dumpster. Black man approaches, satchel under his arm. Teenage girl beside him, hauling a long aluminum ladder. Both look familiar.

"You two snoopin' on me?"

Who are you talking to, Barry?

"Dad, look! It's that old man who sits in the park."

"I'll be damned. The great Barry Sanders! Remember me? Terrence Washington. You remember my baby girl, Lauryn. What you doin' out at this hour?"

Who is this? So close, but the gears won't click.

"I'm sorry. You are…"

"Your neighbor. Helped you out on the UAW road trip to Lansing. We're doing more beautification. Bringing the dawn to the night on the dark streets, one LED at a time. Just three months into the year, and we've already done twenty-four."

Who are these people, Mr Sanders? There's no record of them. We should return home.

"Barry, it doesn't make any sense that you'd be out here, not in the middle of the night."

"I'm doing good stuff, too."

Do not show him, Barry.

Gotta take pride in my work. He's a union man. He'll know a good weld when he sees it. But wait, where'd he go? Both gone back to the shadows. But I hear that voice again—Terrence!

"Stay where you are, Barry. Cops'll getcha home safe."

Chain-link fence behind the parking lot's rattling, like there's a raccoon goin' under it.

A siren? What next?

Ignore any passing vehicles. I will direct you home.

No, the police car's right here, dummy. A Detroit Metro cruiser. Never got to build one of those. And there's a Subaru Outback, right beside it. Can't you see the man in the pajamas getting out?

"Officer, this is my establishment, and—"

"Rajneesh Patel?"

"Yes, sir. This is the man from the security camera. He triggered the alarm more than thirty minutes ago. Could you not arrive sooner?"

"This old fella's your cat burglar?"

I like an officer who can smile. Always liked cops. Son says to be more careful these days, especially with the white ones. This fella seems all right. He'll understand.

Do not say a word to them, Barry.

Pajama man and the officer seem to both like my work. Officer hefts my torch like he's held one before.

"Can't say for sure, but I think our friend here has welded your little shop shut. Maybe an April Fools' prank?"

Pajama man moves in too close, like he's studying me.

"I *know* this man. He's been in before. He buys beer. He wanders about, lost. He sits outside and talks to himself."

That doesn't sound like me.

"Another car's on the way."

A sharp buzzing noise hurts my ears. The officer makes it stop by touching something on his belt.

"Don't worry about the door. The minute I file this incident, I'll bet the Loop finds you an unemployed metal worker. Lucky for you, this town's full of 'em."

268

JACK

With a toss of his keys to the valet, Jack walked away from his Mustang. He'd picked up the bright red rental at the airport, then drove himself and Charlie to the Motor City Hotel and Casino. Excepting one cherry cordial, Jack hadn't tasted alcohol in nearly nine months, which felt oddly symbolic. Another test was in order, and a casino would do the trick.

He was eager to get a quick shower after what felt like a long drive from Detroit Metro. Every half-mile, Charlie pointed out what used to be, but all Jack could see was an empty factory, foreclosed office building, or burned-out residential neighborhood. He'd seen the city's "ruin porn" in the Loop, but that was a virtual tour of flat images. Charlie claimed his hometown was having a rebirth. After growing up in Sydney and Seattle, this mess looked more like an afterbirth.

Jack made the trip to Detroit only after Charlie had begged for his company. Barry had spent the night in jail, and Charlie needed moral support. For the duration of a nonstop flight, Charlie spun out theories about what the Compass must have done to Barry.

It wasn't clear what accounted for Barry's bizarre behavior. The incident at the deli might have been an ethnic thing, or so the first Looped news story suggested. Charlie swore it wasn't, but people Barry's age still got spooked when they saw dudes wearing a turban. Crazy is as crazy does. Given Charlie's state of mind, that word might have described both father and son.

No sooner had Jack checked into the hotel than Charlie dragged him back outside. In an anxious rush, Charlie drove them to the Old Wayne County Jail and bailed out his dad. From there, they drove across town to make peace with a bloke named Rajneesh. That required a few handshakes, plus excessive compensation. After taking Barry home, a pair of worried neighbors came by to look in on the old man. Over beers, and a sickly sweet Faygo Redpop for the teetotaler, Jack accepted an invitation to join a neighborhood work project the next day.

Charlie opted to stay the night with his father, so Jack headed back to the hotel. Soon, the Motor City Hotel and Casino sign rose high above the boarded-up neighborhood surrounding it.

Each new casino strives to be more outlandish than its predecessors. In Vegas, architects incorporated icons and materials from as far away as Egypt, or as far back as the Roman Empire. But not here. The Motor City Hotel's red brick spine evoked the office towers of Detroit's better years. Along its side lay a ladder of glass-and-steel platforms, each lit by neon to resemble classic taillights, or parts awaiting an assembly line. The hotel's "M" logo was formed by stacks of precision-cut metal sheets. More accustomed to arranging spreadsheets, Jack had no concept of how one could shape such a thing.

Walking through the front doors, Jack felt at home. Marble walls, a flat waterfall, and recessed lighting gave the lobby a Venetian glow. Up in his room, Jack set his zune to play industrial techno. A night in the casino called for an open-necked satin shirt, pressed black trousers, and an etched belt. He dabbed on some aftershave and regarded himself in the mirror. Somewhere along the way, he'd lost some swagger. What he really wanted was to dress up for Alice. For that, he'd have to wait. Meanwhile, why be chaste?

The elevator delivered Jack to the gaming floor. Wide doors opened onto what could just as easily have been Bally's, Imperial Palace, or any of a dozen old haunts. Instinct led Jack through a maze of gaming tables and machines. The jangling sounds of the slots cleared his mind of both persistent worries and more stubborn hopes.

Jack spun onto a barstool and raised a finger. The bartender, who carried the bulk of a retired offensive lineman, nodded toward Jack, while shaking a martini for a balding businessman propped up on an elbow. Jack had struck that customer's pose many times—an earnest attempt to look sober enough for one more drink.

Perhaps GM could court alcoholic clients like this poor sap. After all, Jack had used Vijul for more than three years to recover short-term memories lost to brain-crushing binges. With the Compass serving as a 24/7 backstop, plus a Minder for live assistance, a functional drunk could be at least as lucid as a revitalized Alzheimer's patient.

"What'll you have, mister?" The bartender studied Jack. "Full range of domestics. Got a great Mackinac. Made here in Detroit. Or, how 'bout we start off with a Skyy."

Jack took in the colorful lineup of bottles and taps. He knew that sitting at a bar would feel uncomfortable, but the ringing sounds and swirling movements of the casino took him somewhere he hadn't expected. A leaden sadness overtook him. Like a weight, it pulled him toward the floor.

The bartender grabbed Jack's shoulder. "Maybe you don't need another drink. Maybe you need a nap."

A tall glass of ice water appeared on a coaster. Jack drank it down. Four cold glasses earned this bartending angel a fifty. Jack touched open palms to his chest, a Gujarati gesture of thanks Charlie had taught him.

Without waiting for acknowledgment, Jack retreated the way he'd entered. The crowd on the gaming floor looked unfamiliar. He'd expected white retirees at the slots, natty high rollers at the craps table, and a mix of Asian tourists and delusional card counters at blackjack. Motor City's patrons rated older and poorer. It reminded Jack of the time he'd stepped into—and quickly back out of—a low-rent joint in Laughlin, Nevada. Only difference was the color of the faces worn down by the same desperation.

A trio of cocktail waitresses strode by in golden negligees that passed for clothing. Jack had approved and removed many such getups. The skimpy costumes reminded Jack of Alice's more outrageous outfits. Jack felt a stab in his chest. He was probably nothing more to Alice than a casino-floor boy-toy.

There was a time when something that simple had appeal. It didn't now. That one night he'd spent in Alice's penthouse, she'd reached out to him for something more. Now that he was ready to give it, she'd withdrawn the offer.

Jack came to a card room. The nightly Texas Hold 'Em tournament was underway. If he and Alice played poker together, she'd destroy him. He had no talent at bluffing. She, on the other hand, was a master. He'd tried many times but could never read her.

Staring at the table, Jack felt a sense of dread. What if Alice was, in fact, playing a kind of poker? What if he were nothing more than one of the cards in her hand?

* * *

Though he went to bed morose, Jack slept well. He took a long bath and read the *Detroit Free Press* cover-to-cover without turning on the TV. On the back of the entertainment section, he saw a full-page advertisement for "Made in Detroit City Tours." The ad featured Kid Rock shouting at a map of the Metro suburbs, "Everyone gots to gets some *Vitamin D*." Tour highlights included the art deco architecture and murals of the Guardian Building (whatever that was), climbing aboard a slave ship at the Museum of African American History, and spelunking the gothic catacombs of the Michigan Central train station. Only in Detroit.

Refreshed and unhurried, Jack sauntered out of his room when he realized he'd left his zune on the nightstand. He hadn't even set it on a charging pad. There was a time when he couldn't have sat on the toilet without Buddy on his ear and a zune within reach.

Jack retrieved the device, unlocked its screen, and regarded it warily. The zune, or rather, the Loop, had noted his absence. It beckoned with a two-for-one slots offer. It recommended hip spots for lunch, including an Australian-style barbeque joint.

As he made his way to the elevator, a carousel of clickable tiles cluttered his device's screen. A text from Russell, industry news on a tech blog, man-bites-dog stories about dumb criminals and goofy grandparents, and an op-ed about the DIP. Amidst the whirl of information, Jack sensed that something required his full attention. Whatever it was would have to wait. Jack powered down his zune.

Outside the hotel lobby, the valet had readied the Mustang. Jack asked for the best surface route to Barry's neighborhood.

"That sounds like Eastside," said the middle-aged Polish man who handed over the car's keys. "Best not go there, son. Get yourself killed."

"Bullshit!" Jack snapped defensively. "I spent the better part of yesterday there. Didn't get sketchy 'till I neared this casino."

The valet put up his hands. "Your life, pal. At least stay on the freeway as long as you can. Take the 75 past Wayne State, then 94 east 'till your exit."

Jack drove the recommended route, which was easier without a zune than he'd expected. When he left the interstate, he parked beside a Quik Stop to pick up provisions. On the sidewalk, he passed two teenagers in jeans and muscle shirts.

"Morning," Jack said cheerfully. "Bloody hot for April, yeah?"

By way of reply came furrowed brows.

Jack went into the store and grabbed a handcart. From the beverage cooler, he pulled out a rainbow of thirty-two-ounce Gatorades. Problem was, the front of the store had no counter. In its place stood a thick Plexiglas wall that reached almost to the ceiling. That level of security Jack had only seen at a bank.

To a lady behind the barrier, Jack said, "How's this work?"

She replied in a voice that sounded like Vijul. "Put the drinks in the chamber, sir." An upright cylinder rotated until Jack could put the drinks safely inside it.

"Money, too, please. Cash, Visa, or debit. No checks."

Jack reached into his pockets and discovered another problem. He didn't carry plastic cards anymore, let alone cash. "You win," Jack said to his zune. It bleeped gleefully on startup and intuited his need for electronic payment.

Soon enough, Gatorades hung heavy from the bags in Jack's hands, but he felt sad about the arrangement. Since entering the store, he hadn't touched a hand or traded a smile. When he stepped back outside, Jack waved at the two teenagers still talking on the sidewalk. The younger one rewarded Jack's persistence with a begrudging nod. That was something.

Jack settled back into his Mustang's snug bucket seat and fired the ignition. He looked over his shoulder to back out of his parking space. An insistent chirp from his zune caused him to hesitate. He'd forgotten to shut it back down. Jack touched the power button once, but before he hit it a second time, the text in the center of his screen caught his eye.

Compass Needle Broken: String of "Glitches" Crisscrosses US.

The top line of the story read, "From Bangor to Bakersfield, a series of bizarre crimes trace back to seniors implanted with the Elder Compass." An adjoining op-ed warned, "A device meant to steer its users clear of dementia drove these poor souls into the ditch."

Jack scrolled through both stories quickly. Details were sketchy, as no comment had come from Alice, GM media liaisons, or any anonymous sources within the company. The writing had a syntax that signaled they'd been written entirely by human hands on keyboards. For breaking news and commentary, that was almost as shocking as the news itself.

What it all meant, Jack could only begin to guess. Before getting to that, he'd have to hope Charlie hadn't read the news yet. The poor lad would be heartbroken.

The boys on the sidewalk cheered as Jack peeled out of his parking space and spun his rental back onto the road.

"Call Alice," Jack said. Seconds later, "Not available. Message box full."

Bullshit. There was no such thing as a "full" message box anymore. Must have been a bit of prank code Alice rigged up. Jack tried to laugh at her ingenuity, but it felt like one more barrier she'd put in his way.

The Mustang raced the remaining mile to the intersection Charlie had texted. Jack pulled up to the curb beside a fenced-off triangle half the size of a residential block. At the opposite end of the park, Charlie waved a gas-powered weed whacker through a thicket of thigh-high vegetation. A dozen more people, mostly teenagers in worn-out togs, were cutting, clearing, and hauling.

Over the buzz of tiny engines, a full-throated shout failed to get Charlie's attention. Jack vaulted the fence, careful not to rip his jeans on the chain links. On the way down, he snagged the long-sleeved shirt he'd bought at the casino. A thick rust mark caused a delicious ambiguity in the riveted lettering. "Detroit: **ity of Tomorrow."

On his way toward Charlie, Jack jogged through the one section of the park clear of debris and vegetation. A weathered bench in the clearing bowed under the weight of Charlie's father, even though the heavyset man leaned onto the crossbar of his walker. Jack laughed to think this humble looking man in a powder blue tracksuit was the legendary Barry Sanders—at least the one who was legendary at GM.

Jack slowed to a trot. Maybe he should give Charlie a break— one more afternoon with his father before—well, before whatever lay ahead for them. The bad news could wait.

In the midday sun, Barry looked quite better than he had the day before. Jack flipped open his zune and checked the Detroit Metro Police mug shot. That black-and-white image showed a disoriented senior, unshaven in a torn t-shirt under a leather Detroit Lions jacket. Charlie had improved his father's wardrobe, hygiene, and disposition.

Barry stood and extended a hand to Jack. "Hello there, stranger. Welcome to Pleasant Creek Park. It's full-up today, but there's space here on the bench."

"Don't mind if I do. I'm Jack—one of Charlie's mates."

Jack shook Barry's hand and marveled at his poise. If Barry was slipping into senility, Jack never would have guessed. This man had to count as a success story for the Elder Compass, which had hummed along in his head since November.

Barry sat back down and patted the bench. Under the watchful eyes of the work crew, Jack accepted the offer.

"I'm glad you came," Barry said. "This is a hard time for us all. Charlie's not here, of course, but he's with us just the same."

Jack did a double-take to make sure the weed-whacking man across the park was, indeed, Charlie. It was.

"I brought cold drinks," Jack said tentatively. "You want one?"

Barry laughed and slapped Jack's knee. He'd seen it in movies, but Jack had never been touched that way by a parent or grandparent of his own. It had a nice sting, like the kind that inspires a newborn to breathe.

"I bet Charlie's up there having a cold one right now," Barry said. "Lookin' down and smiling."

Jack kept his mouth shut but carefully unscrewed the cap on his beverage.

"April's the hardest month for me," Barry continued, "but especially for Pleasant. We remember when we lost Charlie like it was yesterday, as they say. Those men came to the door to tell us our son had been blown—well, he'd died. They stood there in tan jackets and pants, with little folded hats in their hands. They came on a Saturday. When Pleasant saw them coming up the front walk, oh, how she wailed. Poor devils couldn't tell us the news 'till I got her planted on the couch."

Jack looked left and right. Someone had to rescue him. Or, he could just blurt out the news to Charlie and tear up this scene's awkward script.

"Then my sweet Pleasant, she started up again when they told us how Charlie had died on patrol. He'd saved lives but not his own. You know, Barry Junior never talks about it. I worry maybe he doesn't even know. Could that be possible?"

Jack nodded involuntarily. The one-sided conversation had become as treacherous as the landmines in Barry's story. For the first time since joining GM, Jack remembered a curious fact. Back in Australia, pulling "a Barry" was slang for a blunder.

So much for the Elder Compass.

"Jack?"

Charlie's voice was a welcome sound. Jack turned to see his friend walking alongside a middle-aged man in overalls— Terrence, from the day before. Jack stood to greet them as they approached the bench. The smile on Charlie's face betrayed no knowledge of the news Jack's zune was eager to share with anyone willing to touch it.

"Didn't hear you pull up," Charlie said. "Should've guessed you were here when I saw the Mustang."

"Should I not park it there? Is it safe?"

Charlie leaned into his weed whacker and turned to Terrence. "What ya think? Hoods gonna jack that ride?"

Terrence nodded in mock seriousness. "If they get a look at Pale Rider here, they'll lift it just to fuck wit' his blue-eyed ass." Unable to keep a straight face, Terrence burst into laughter, and Charlie joined in.

Jack wasn't sure he got the joke, unless it was him.

Barry approached in his walker and cast a scowl at his son. "They're just messin' with you, Jack, on account of you being so white. Don't spook this young fella, Barry."

Terrence and Jack both looked to Charlie, who widened his

eyes in what passed as a signal to let him handle it. "You're right, Dad. I'm sorry. Why don't you enjoy the sunshine and let me talk with these fellas?"

Satisfied with the apology, Barry shuffled back toward his bench.

"Please don't ask," Charlie said in a quieter voice. "It's bad enough he thinks I died in the war. I don't want to get into it today."

Jack started to speak. "It's worse than—"

"You heard the man," Terrence said. "Leave it."

Jack breathed in slowly. He caught the pungent smell of rot from the broad-leafed Tree of Heaven. It reached out from the corner of the tiny park. Unpruned, it had grown mammoth, with broad branches that hung like ferns.

"Okay, change of subject," Jack said. "Um, tell me about this gardening party of yours."

"More reverse vandalism," Charlie said with pride. "This time, in my own backyard."

"Not quite true," Terrence said. "Just so we don't get hassled, Lauryn got a micro-grant from the city for cleanups like this. Cutting weeds in daylight isn't exactly gangsta. The kids get service learning credit for it. Not as exciting as our streetlight work, but we're getting places like this straightened out."

"Used to be a park?" Jack said.

"Never really had a name, as such." Charlie stared at the bench his father occupied. "But it's special. Mom and Dad used to sit and talk here every day."

"That's sweet," Jack said with measured sarcasm, "but I think your Dad's still gas-bagging with her ghost."

"Yup," Charlie said. "Sailee and I figured that one out together. She had me retrace his coordinates a few times. He's been sitting here every weekend."

"Seriously?" Terrence said. "This lot's been a grown-over dump for years. An hour ago, this clearing we're standing in wasn't even here."

"With that brain of his," Charlie said, "I don't know. It might be painting a prettier picture than we can see."

"Shit ain't right," Terrence said. "He's not fit to live alone anymore."

"I know," Charlie said.

Jack felt the sunshine leave his face. Gray clouds had tucked it away. The zune in his pocket burned hotter than ever. He'd have to let it out soon.

"You know," Terrence said, "you're gonna have to take care of him."

"I know."

"If you can't do it yourself, you might consider a home."

"I might."

"I'm moving into that line of work," Terrence said. "Can't lift and haul like I used to, unless it's old ladies. I'm taking classes. They say those retirement castles fall over themselves to hire strong dudes like me. They're rehabbing a facility just down the road. Looks sharp."

"I won't just dump Dad in a 'facility' down the road."

"You should check it out."

Jack gave Charlie a nudge. "Maybe we'll do that, mate."

"He's got insurance from the plant?" Terrence asked.

"Money's not the issue," Charlie said.

"It's natural," Terrence said. "It happens. We get old. He got old. It happens."

Charlie nodded, but it didn't look like an acknowledgment. It looked like the weary acquiescence of a person who would agree to anything, just to make the conversation end.

CHARLIE

Charlie leaned back against the chain-link fence and admired their accomplishment. Led by teenagers from his alma mater, the work crew had reclaimed a small piece of Dad's history. With the underbrush ripped out and hauled away, Charlie could see the park still had rich soil. It would look a lot nicer with the fresh sod coming tomorrow, but it was enough just to see it could sustain life.

Though he'd arrived late to the work party, Jack had been a marvel. He was as strong as he was smart, pleased to convert untold gym hours into useful labor. More remarkable was his spirit. Jack had seemed nervous—even jumpy, at first. Once he settled in, Jack seemed at peace shoveling and raking, as if the work took his mind off other things.

Across the park, Jack extended his hand to shake Lauryn's but she offered a fist, expecting a bump. The gesture looked like a trick Alice might have pulled.

An odd thought occurred to Charlie. "Hey, Jack!"

Jack jogged over and gave Charlie a friendly slap on the shoulder. "Good stuff, yeah?" Across the boy's face stretched a wider and warmer smile than Charlie had ever seen there.

"I just realized something odd," Charlie said. "When I told Alice that I had to bail out Dad, she didn't seem concerned. Or surprised. She didn't ask me a thing about it, but practically pushed me out the door. Told me to take the whole week off. I haven't seen so much as a text from her since."

Just like that, the smile was gone. Jack scratched his crew cut. "Me neither. But the Codelings are working through the weekend. She's probably at HQ, supervising and such."

"She likes to keep them pretty close, doesn't she?" Charlie said. "I'm not even permitted to review their work directly anymore."

Jack's expression turned grim. "There's some news—"

"I mean," Charlie continued, "beyond my own equations, I haven't touched the bulk of our code base. Only bits and pieces."

"Look," Jack said, "I don't know how to tell you this. Have you read the news today?"

Charlie reached into his jeans pocket and retrieved his zune. "Had it in airplane mode."

The device felt Charlie's touch and woke itself up, unbidden. It offered a headline that stopped Charlie's breath.

"Holy shit," Charlie said. After reading a few lines, he studied Jack's face. "You knew this? And didn't tell me?"

"I'm sorry, I didn't know how." Jack pulled out his own device and checked for messages. "Did Alice buzz you?"

The zune in Charlie's hand rang like a bicycle bell.

"Speak of the devil's daughter," Jack said, "and her sweet arse appears—"

"No, it's Sailee. I'm gonna take this."

Charlie turned away and walked toward Barry's bench. His father had fallen asleep. At the other end of the bench, Charlie sat down and pressed "talk."

Sailee didn't give him the chance to say hello. "Where have you been? I've been calling! Can you believe what is happening? Vijul was up late and called with the news."

"We just saw the headlines, and—"

"It is terrible, Charlie. They are calling them 'glitches.' Barry is one of them. Why did you not tell me?"

Quick breaths on the other end of the phone. She could be hyperventilating.

"He's doing much better today. We still don't know what happened, not really."

"Nonsense!" Sailee said. "You *know* what this is."

"Some clever reporter wants to pin it on—"

"It is true, Charlie. Every one of the ten old men in the news story, plus the woman in Albuquerque—they all had the

281

implant. Half were new clients without voice support. The other half stopped appearing in our call logs."

"Except Dad. Why didn't aberrant geo-coordinates trigger a call from you last night?"

"That troubles me the most, Charlie. My link with him has been severed. I cannot—"

"What?"

"I do not trust this Compass, Charlie. Why else would so many users go mad at the same instant? What is next? Will we see people walking off bridges? There are fifteen *million* active users, Charlie."

"I know as little as you do, Sailee. Let me talk to Jack, then we'll call Alice. She'll—"

"No!"

The shout caused Barry to shift on the bench, but it didn't wake him.

"There is also this," Sailee said. "I received a message from a travel agent instructed to book a trip for my grandmother and me to Seattle. The agent said it was an invitation from Ms Coleco. A company retreat. What is this about?"

"Once again, news to me."

After a quick goodbye to Sailee, Charlie rubbed his stomach. It had gone sour. Gatorade mixed with whatever stress hormones had washed up in there.

Alice had to have heard the news before he did. Every employee in the company must have known by now.

A voice call to Alice was too risky. He'd as likely scream at her as anything. Better to text. "WTF?" he typed. "Glitches? Barry!?!"

Message sent.

Dad had slumped back on the bench. His mouth hung open. Loud snores ripped out of him. Dude looked like a drunk sleeping off a bender, which he was, sort of.

Perhaps their next stop should be Zudora, who could pull back out of his head what she'd slipped into it. Once it was out, what then? Dad still had a Walker Talker, but if Sailee had lost her connection, it was useless. Maybe Charlie could get the Quiet Copilot re-linked, but GM had stopped supporting it. Jack might know a workaround, but could he trust Jack to not tell Alice? Probably.

Alice was the real problem. There was no need to calculate the odds of Dad being the victim of a random software bug. Barry had to be a chosen target, and who else could have reached him through the Compass's code? Even if a Codeling did it, Alice would have given the order. Jack had more coding skill than he let on, but Jack was incapable of—well, whatever this was. A prank? A test? Didn't matter which.

All that mattered was who did it.

* * *

That evening, Charlie and Jack mulled over the day's news. The number of erratic retirees on the Compass was greater than early reports had guessed. Petty criminal incidents grabbed the first headlines by way of police reports, but the full tally included a wider array of erratic behaviors, each of which linked back to the personal histories of the individual "glitches." A few recovered alcoholics robbed liquor stores, but one man in West Virginia got lost searching for a backwoods moonshine still he'd built as a teenager. An elderly Atlanta woman spray-painted accusatory graffiti on her car, then parked in front of the bank where she'd been passed-over for a vice presidency years ago. A Melbourne retiree who never bore children kidnapped her neighbor's grandchildren, then drove them to her sister's cottage in Brisbane.

If Alice had any insight, she was choosing not to share it. Jack and Charlie received nothing more than sporadic texts designed to placate, not enlighten.

"Looking into it" wasn't very convincing.

"Too busy, gotta run" was a brush-off.

As midnight approached, they stopped trying to get her to talk. Jack texted Alice just to say Barry's situation required a couple more days to sort out. Charlie advised Eddie to make certain all the glitches got sorted out, ASAP.

Once Zudora retrieved Barry's implant, Charlie would get his father ready for a plane trip back to Seattle. They didn't want to board that flight until they had a solid plan, but they had to act fast and synchronize their next move with Sailee and anyone else at GM willing to help. Something was very wrong with the Compass. Even Jack could see the truth. Alice had to be the culprit.

After Jack climbed into his Mustang and sped away to his hotel, Charlie bolted the front door. He carried a short-backed chair into Barry's bedroom and watched his father sleep. Some of the seniors who'd gone haywire had risen from their beds like narcoleptics. Barry was clearly susceptible to whatever poison flowed through the Compass. Hence, the all-night vigil.

After ten minutes of watching uneven breaths, Charlie let his mind move to the next problem it posed for him. What to do about President Eisenhower?

At the close of his White House meeting with the President, Charlie had resolved to implant in her neck a deactivated Compass chip. Before he could step out the door, however, she'd shown him something that made him reconsider.

"When we next meet," Eisenhower said, "would you like to know about your brother?" She held up a manila folder with a hand-written tab. "Assuming you do not shirk from your duties, I will tell you the truth about how your brother died doing his."

Agent Adamson whisked Charlie away before he could utter another word.

Even now, the offer puzzled Charlie more than it enticed.

The story the Army officers told them matched the official letter Charlie found in his dad's dresser. Barry Jr. had died in an unremarkable way—blown up for walking in the pair of boots that happened to step on the wrong patch of dirt at the wrong time.

In the months since meeting the President, Charlie had weighed the importance of knowing whatever alternative version of events Eisenhower might offer. The Loop had confirmed that Charlie's brother was under Eisenhower's command when she had served as an Army General. There was no way she could have known each "grunt" in Afghanistan under the US flag. Dirksen had probably dug up Barry Jr. while getting Charlie's background checked.

Charlie still wasn't sure he wanted to hear this alternate family history when he had his second and final face-to-face with the President. The meeting took place in early December, after he'd watched Zudora implant his own father but before celebrating the Compass' first week of sales.

Agent Adamson escorted Charlie through the front door of Eisenhower's Fayetteville estate. In the center of the sprawling ranch home, the President's father lay lengthwise on the living room sofa. His daughter left his side to greet Charlie with a vigorous handshake.

"Thank you for coming," Eisenhower said. "Poppy has perked up if you want to say hi. He likes football, so I put on the Lions' Thanksgiving Day game from last month. I told him we had a guest coming from Detroit."

"From Seattle, really."

"And that made him think today's Thanksgiving, so…"

A halftime ceremony appeared on the enormous screen across from the sofa. Of all people, Barry Sanders—the one legendary *outside* GM—appeared in a close-up, waving to the crowd and handing jerseys to a throng of children.

"I watched that game live with Dad," Charlie said. "But I'm not the sports fan in the family."

"I know," Eisenhower said. "Your brother was the football hero."

Charlie stared blankly at the President.

"More on that later. Other business first."

Eisenhower gave Poppy a kiss, then directed Charlie to join her in an adjoining lounge. Once inside, she closed the doors, pulled her hair from behind her right ear and said, "Let's do this."

Charlie remembered another vow he'd made to himself

"I must again recommend against proceeding, Madam President. If your mind is slipping, you need a crutch, not a body cast. Wearing a Compass is like locking your wheels onto a trolley rail."

"Rails have not been good to my presidency."

Charlie nodded solemnly.

"We only have bad choices here, Charlie. I'm governing under the watchful eye of a madman. I am King Duncan, with Macbeth and his Lady sharpening their knives each evening in the kitchen. But we're short-staffed at the Oval Office Shakespeare festival, because I've also been cast as Lear. Each time I fumble for lost marbles in full public view, I risk handing my kingdom to the worst possible successor."

"But what does your conscience tell you?"

"Get thee fitted for a pair of glass eyes, such that I might, like a scurvy politician, seem to see the things thou dost not." Eisenhower brightened. Her voice shifted to a light drawl. "Did ya know they're doin' a full season of the tragedies at the Ford's Theater next fall?"

"Well, I wouldn't think they'd stage comedies in that theater."

"Doin' Hamlet for their first show. I was fixin' to invite them for a dress rehearsal in the East Room. Wouldn't that be somethin'?" Eisenhower's voice trailed off. She looked about the room, as if its host had become another guest.

Charlie considered seizing the moment. He could exit without saying another word. Perhaps she'd forget the Compass altogether. Or, he could give her nothing more than a little cut behind the ear. Put a Band-Aid over it.

Either might work, but the manila folder that bore his brother's name called to him. It wasn't on her lap. She must have stowed it away, out of sight.

A sharpness returned to the President's brown irises. "Excuse me for that lapse," she said. "This really is a simple matter. If I show any more signs of weakness, the Vice President will have my throat, then my throne. Now, let's get on with this nasty business."

Eisenhower pulled back her hair.

Five minutes later, the deed was done. He slid a functioning Compass chip into the skin behind her ear. She secured the modified eagle pin on her lapel.

True to her word, she retrieved from a bureau drawer a folder. It felt light, like it might be empty, but he didn't peek. He'd wanted to open it from the moment Agent Adamson had guided him into the backseat of the limo that drove him back to the Fayetteville airport. By some convoluted logic, he convinced himself that his father should hear with him whatever truth it contained.

When Jack and Charlie flew to Detroit together, that same folder found its way into Charlie's carryon. He hadn't even peeked. At last, he could read it. The fact that Dad was asleep was a technicality.

Charlie opened the folder. A plastic sleeve held what looked like an audio CD. One of those hadn't sat in Charlie's hands in years, but for once, he was glad his Dad's home was terribly out of date. The Detroit Lions clock radio on the nightstand could play compact discs. Charlie placed the disc inside, lowered the volume, and hit play.

What came through was distorted, by design, but he guessed it was Eisenhower. "I apologize for delivering this information in such a manner," the voice said, "but for reasons you will understand, it was best not to share the whole story with your family at the time of your brother's passing."

No signs his father could hear this. Dad kept sleeping, as soundly as before.

"Every war needs soldiers who follow orders. They charge into battle without hesitation. Your little brother played football and picked up a rifle because those were things he knew how to do. He was a tremendous runner. The 'gazelle' nickname stuck for a reason. Unfortunately, he lacked dexterity. No colleges recruited him, so he enlisted in the Army. In better times, he might have ended up playing for us in a black and gold jersey, but we needed him elsewhere."

A long pause followed. The audio might have been recorded in one long take. A loud throat clearing caused Charlie to brace himself.

"Barry's charisma served him well. Afghani children clung to him even more than the other soldiers. His unit was building a bridge near Qali-meerza. He did daylight security, and in the late afternoons, he and other enlistees tried to teach American football to the local boys."

The rambling story had nothing to do with Barry Jr.'s death, which had come from an IED. Even so, the details rang true. Charlie's cheeks felt hot, so he pressed the cold backs of his hands against them. Who else but his little brother had taught him that trick.

"Shortly before the bridge opened," the voice continued, "another unit came to visit. We had an eyewitness account from a soldier who was there. I know this sounds juvenile, but the soldiers started jawing about each other's hometown football teams. Barry talked everyone into resolving the dispute on the makeshift football field that local kids had cleared at the outskirts of their neighborhood. On the first play of this scrimmage, Barry ran a deep up-and-out. Three eager boys, playing for no team in particular, tried to drag him down after he caught the pass. But he didn't quite catch it."

Charlie tried to paint the picture in his mind. It had been years since he'd permitted himself to conjure Barry Jr. Probably bit his lower lip when his fingers cradled the ball. He always did that.

"The witness said that Barry tipped and fumbled the ball in the air. Little boys clung to him as he stumbled out of bounds. On this field, any 'bounds' were purely theoretical, so Barry kept twisting and reaching until he secured the catch. With children hanging off his hips, the football slipped down his belly and toward the ground. When he reached for it, he probably saw something like a pig's tail sticking out of the dirt. An exposed wire. Again, this is conjecture, but he likely guessed his impact with the plate below was unavoidable. He hit it squarely. Used his body as a shield. Two of the children survived, though one lost a leg. It could have been much worse, though not for Barry, clearly."

Charlie looked out the window of his father's bedroom. In the distance, a streetlight winked back at him. He wondered what Kandahar looked like this time of year. He had no idea.

"All of us," the voice said, "we relearned an old lesson in Afghanistan. Sometimes, the sacrifices we have to make come as a surprise. Once you're falling onto a land mine, you have only bad choices, but you still have to make one. Your brother used his skills to their fullest in the moment when others needed him most. You and I, we have unique qualities. They led us into exceptional lives. And to each other. I have presented you only with bad choices, but we both know you made the decision best for me, and for our nation. So, I thank you again, Charlie Sanders, for your service."

Charlie hadn't heard the last words clearly. His stomach

churned with a mix of useless emotions. Remorse, pity, impotent rage. He wiped at eyes awash in tears for losses he couldn't count. One hand popped open the CD player, and the other lifted out the disc. Both hands worked together to snap the disc into two unreadable pieces.

For perhaps an hour, he sat still and watched his father. From sheer exhaustion, he fell asleep in that awkward position, only to be woken by a buzzing sensation in his pocket. With tired eyes, he pulled out his zune. It flashed Alice's face, then a one-line text from her.

"Oops?!"

SAILEE

On GM recruiting trips, Sailee had flown to Delhi or Mumbai many times, but neither she nor her grandmother had ever left India. Nani was delighted by the window view between Ahmedabad and Qatar. The magic wore off during the half-day flight to New York. Despite the first-class seats Alice had purchased, neither passenger could do more than nap as they flew away from the only world they knew.

Sailee had prepared her grandmother for the ordeal of customs. Their plane landed shortly after a trio of jumbo jets, so the lines for border control would be intolerable. Then, her Nani would be overwhelmed by JFK airport itself. It had been a shock for Sailee to take in the sheer scale of it all. The terminal was its own busy shopping mall, full of scandalously overpriced foods and unnecessary trinkets. She knew her grandmother would find the entire scene unseemly.

None of this happened.

An airline official greeted Sailee as soon as she stepped off their plane.

"Sailee and Grisma Singh?" said a Delta agent in a voice so perky it unnerved.

"That is us," Sailee replied.

"Follow me, please."

Had Alice sprung a trap? Sailee had worried about her grandmother's political past setting off a red flag. The more serious risk Sailee had weighed concerned a certain election and the laws in the US regarding foreign nationals intervening in such matters.

"Hang onto your passports," the agent said. "As a courtesy to preferred customers, your passage through customs has been expedited."

"But—" Sailee protested, then caught herself.

"Your ticket was purchased through a special program."

Of course it was.

"Please, follow me."

Sailee felt relief and guilt all at once as the agent whisked her and Grisma past long lines of weary passengers. After a quick hello with an officer who took their fingerprints, the agent directed them to a motorized cart, which already had their luggage.

"It knows your gate," the agent said. "If you need anything else now, just say 'Sky Club,' and someone will take care of you there."

Nani clutched the driverless cart as it bobbed and wove its way through the airport. It felt safer than a scooter. When they got to their gate, the extravagance of their conveyance became clear. They would still have two hours to pass waiting for their Seattle flight in hard-backed chairs. The fact that they were, for a time, on solid ground was enough to put Nani at peace. She collapsed within minutes.

Sailee couldn't sleep because a high wall monitor held her attention. It displayed a news channel covering what had previously been her personal world—from Gray Matters to Mahatma Golden to Barry Sanders. She looked in all directions to see if the monitor somehow tailored its newsfeeds to each person in the terminal. Every screen showed the same broadcast.

Five seats away from Sailee, a middle-aged man nudged the older woman beside him. "That's why I don't want you to get it," he said. "Can't have you getting all glitchy on us, Mom. The Veep's right. That company's unethical. Congress'll shut 'em down."

The mother nodded and stared at the monitor. It showed a guest reporter from the *Washington Post* who linked the story back to national politics. A handful of haywire seniors had accelerated the national debate on cognitive implants.

"The Compass Registry bill now before Congress highlights

all of Golden's strengths," the reporter said in front of the US Senate building. "Its passage seems certain, and much credit will go to the Vice President if that happens. He pledges that the day it becomes law, he'll work with the Justice Department to begin prosecuting unregistered Compass users, starting with those who covertly implanted chips in other people."

On screen came video of the Vice President walking through a Senate corridor. Dressed in a conservative suit, with a golden tie that matched his ponytail, he seemed to be improvising his image as much as his message.

Sailee idly wondered if Mahatma Golden had learned how to play chess. If he did, he surely lacked the patience to master it. He might know how to use a bishop to start an attack, but it was doubtful he could use one to corner his opponent's queen.

A man in a charcoal suit approached Golden and poked at his chest. An argument began, and the news feed switched its audio away from the reporter's narrative and to a shotgun microphone at the scene. As always, Looped text kept scrolling along the bottom of the screen, but it commandeered a taller band of monitor space to show an auto-bio of Golden's adversary— Democratic congressman Kevin Penn.

"At just fifty years of age," the bio read, "Penn rose quickly in his party, which made him Speaker of the House as much for his physical profile as his political one. A former linebacker who played briefly with the Pittsburgh Steelers before becoming a firefighter, Penn used taut pectoral muscles to push through landmark legislation."

Sailee covered her mouth to laugh at the Loop's purple prose. This was not the first time she had noticed that the disembodied information-aggregator had a prurient interest in the anatomy of the bodies it described.

Golden tried to exit the Senate hallway, but Penn blocked his path. Trying to pull the two apart was Lakshmi Golden, who wore the hemp robe and belt she had brought into fashion among

Mahatma's devotees. The congressman said something about a "bipartisan Alzheimer's taskforce" that Golden hadn't bothered to attend. "All you care about is grandstanding," Penn said.

Aware of the camera, Golden turned to face it. "The Registry bill will do more to protect seniors than anything done by Congress before."

Penn maneuvered himself to talk directly into the camera. It felt as though he were talking directly to Sailee through the lens. This man, he had whatever charisma may be.

"Ask Mr Golden," Penn said, "what condition his father's got. That man's change of heart about his son—it came on awful sudden."

Golden moved to get his face in frame. "With maturity comes wisdom."

Penn stepped back to face Golden. "Do you believe the horseshit sputtering out of those thin lips of yours? I never know with you."

"Wisdom comes with *age*, Mr Speaker."

Sailee found herself transfixed by Golden's larger-than-life image on the airport monitor. She had played a hidden role in Mahatma's political career through her orchestration of the Minders. Now that she had set foot in the United States, his presence—and their connection—felt more immediate. There was something electric about being within the same political border. Their destinies felt more tightly wired together.

The cameraman followed Golden as he exited the building and emerged atop the Capitol steps. Golden flipped on a pair of tinted Oakleys and raised his arms high to acknowledge the crowd, which the Loop estimated at one hundred thousand souls. His gesture released an explosive roar. Golden smiled more broadly, as if the cheers came to him as pleasing music. He moved down two steps and into position behind a podium.

"My children," Golden said into a microphone, "I welcome you to a new day!"

The camera angle shifted to show a side-view of Mahatma standing before the enormous crowd that spilled down from the Capitol steps.

"For many long years," Golden said, "I have warned of the dangers posed by a poisonous enemy. The mercenaries at Gray Matters have fought against our future. It was only I who stood against them. I spoke in riddles then, as a spiritual voice in a materialist world. Now, as your Vice President, I can battle them in the plain language of the law."

Golden beamed at his mother, who glowed vicariously from the crowd's adoration of her son. Lakshmi gave him a quick half-bow.

"In less than two years," he continued, "the Elder Compass has done grievous harm on a scale we are only now beginning to document. These so-called 'glitches,' these abused elders who carried out senseless crimes last week, have sacrificed their dignity to show us what evils await a world that cannot know its own mind. The Compass Registry bill will let us see, once and for all, who has fallen into the grasping hands of Gray Matters. We shall take up arms against the puppeteers who manipulate the masses through a skyline of slave-towers filled to the rooftops with abused talkshop workers, all in the blessed land of India."

Acolytes in the Capitol crowd wore long cotton dresses. They folded their hands together and intoned something like the word "Namaste," using every conceivable pronunciation.

Behind her, Sailee heard the same word. She turned around to see two older women dressed in the white cotton dresses. Transfixed, they beamed at the image of Golden on the screen. Each had a rolling suitcase and the look of a weary traveler.

Sailee wanted to talk to them but thought better of it. Until she got to Seattle, better to lay as low as she could.

Back on the wall monitor, reporters shouted questions at Golden every time he paused. One finally caught his ear.

"Why did you oppose the Registry amendment that would

classify non-voluntary implanting as a felony? Why won't you protect people like Elena Gomez?"

Sailee recognized the name of the woman from Albuquerque from the news. Either the network or the Loop put in the corner of the monitor a muted video of Elena's daughter, as she confessed to Compassing her mother after forging a consent form.

"Just minutes ago," the reporter said to Golden, "President Eisenhower's communications director said she'll sign the bill, but only if amended."

"Really? When did she—"

The crowd murmured. Golden looked confused, then abruptly retreated back into the building. A camera trailed him down a hallway and into the Senate chamber, where floor debate on the Registry bill proceeded through the usual open-mic monologues. Each speaker followed scripts and slogans written by professional staff over the past forty-eight hours. The Loop's scroll resembled closed captions, though small errors in timing and text suggested it was predicting each speaker's words with impressive accuracy.

If Nani were awake, she would insist that Indian politics were no better, or worse. She would chide Sailee for not doing enough to change the fate of her own country.

Hearing these reprimands from a sleeping grandmother, Sailee wondered if this was how it felt to have a Minder whisper in one's ear.

CHARLIE

On the ride from Sea-Tac International, the turbaned town car driver played KOMO AM 1000 just a bit too loud. News, traffic, and weather made it impossible for Charlie to manage a conversation with his father, who sat beside him.

Just as well, since Dad was still agitated from the flight. It was the first he'd taken since traveling with Pleasant to meet their son's casket at Dover Air Force Base. Charlie knew this trip to Seattle risked disorienting Barry further, but he wanted to keep his father close. On top of that, Dad had a small role to play.

Charlie tuned out the radio and reviewed the plan he'd devised with his co-workers. With Grisma and Barry in tow, he and Sailee would turn Alice's invitation into a confrontation. Sailee would confess to anything and everything Alice imagined she'd done. Getting Barry in front of Alice might stir her conscience and shake loose admissions of her own. Relaying those details back to the Codelings might win some to their side, which would make it easier to dismantle the Compass once Charlie settled back into his office.

Every minute they spent breaking bread with Alice bought more time for Jack. His sole objective: save the President. Dick Dirksen had refused to give Charlie any way to reach him or the President electronically, lest anyone discover her dependence on the Compass. Once Jack had absorbed the shock of Charlie's news on that subject, he'd found a way into the only quasi-public appearance on Eisenhower's schedule. If Jack could corner Dick Dirksen even for a minute, he'd be able to explain the urgency of the situation. The glitches were surely more than an accident. If Alice still didn't know Eisenhower was wired into the Compass, whatever scheme she had in mind could still ensnare the President. If Alice *did* know—well, hopefully she didn't.

The car stereo cut to the voice of Vice President Golden. "*None* but I can protect our nation from this danger."

"We'll see," Charlie said.

As the Edgewater Hotel came into view, Charlie realized how much he missed sleeping in his own bed. He knew that was out of the question. Dad couldn't navigate the stairs there, and Charlie couldn't leave his father in a hotel by himself.

The town car driver's face appeared in the rear-view mirror. "Is your father wired?"

The question would have struck Charlie as intrusive, but it had become commonplace to talk about the Compass with strangers. Charlie half-expected the driver to recognize Barry, whose face appeared on the "glitch galleries" popping up online. Instead of answering the question, Charlie handed the driver three twenties.

"We'll be ready to leave again in fifteen minutes. I've got sixty more if you stay."

The trunk popped open. A bellhop pulled out suitcases and a metal walker.

"Tell me again," Barry said. "Where you takin' us?"

"We'll get freshened up first. After meeting up with a couple of friends, you're gonna meet my boss."

"Pleasant and I got to meet the CEO of GM once. I ever tell you that story?"

"You did, Pops."

"He walked from building to building at our plant. Up and down every floor of the office buildings. Took two full days to shake every hand."

"Then he let go one-third of the workforce."

"Then he fired—you know this story?"

"Until now, I never believed someone like that existed. So gracious, and so cold."

Barry's attention turned to his seatbelt. "Can't get out of the fool seat."

When Charlie reached down to unfasten it, Barry flailed at

his son. Dad's brown sweater caught on the fastener and ripped enough to reveal a white undershirt.

"Sorry 'bout that," Charlie said.

Charlie tried to tuck Dad's shirt back into his khakis. Should have bought new dress clothes for his father. On the other hand, this weathered outfit would be a useful contrast to what everyone else planned to wear. Once they checked in, Charlie would slip into a tailored black suit Sailee had commissioned from an Ahmedabad clothier. Over a light gray shirt, he'd chosen to hang a silver tie they'd found at a craft market.

As Charlie eased Barry out of the cab and into his walker, a white motor scooter pulled up behind them. Charlie recognized its occupants, even before they removed their helmets.

"Mr Barry Sanders," Sailee said.

"Is that—are you Sally?" Barry said excitedly.

"Such a pleasure to meet you in person."

Barry leaned over the front bar of his walker and pulled Sailee into a bear hug. He took a step back and eyed her warily. She wore a red short cotton shirt and billowy pants beneath the burgundy sari draped over her shoulder. On her wrists she'd coiled a dozen bronze bracelets.

"Hold on," Barry said. "I thought you were British."

Sailee looked at Charlie, who shrugged.

"I am from India," Sailee said, "the world's largest democracy."

"Ain't we the biggest one of those?"

"Sir, I am not so certain this country remains a democracy at all."

"Don't mind her," Charlie said. "She's talking in riddles. That's what they do in India."

"Quite true," said Grisma, who wore a blue dress with delicate gold beading and stood with her head high, almost as tall as her granddaughter.

"Who's this?" Barry asked.

"Mr Sanders," Sailee said, "I would like you to meet Ms Grisma Singh, my grandmother."

Grisma offered a half-bow. Barry hunched over a little more than usual and nodded.

"I'd meant for us to get to spend some time together," Charlie said, "just the four of us. But things are moving too quickly. Maybe we'll have the chance once things get settled."

"How much does he know?" Sailee whispered.

"Less than I've told him," Charlie replied.

Grisma made a click with her tongue. "I cannot believe this Emerald City. Would you just look at it, Mr Sanders?" Grisma pointed toward the cluster of buildings, blocks from where they stood. "It has so few people but it reaches as high into the sky as Mumbai."

"Not quite as high," Sailee said, "but it is strangely *clean*."

"We can see your Space Needle from our hotel," Grisma said. "Tell me, what does it do?"

"Nothing," Charlie said. "It does nothing."

"I keep telling my boy, people make nonsense out of metal nowadays. Where I'm from, we make things that move, like this baby." Barry laughed and nodded toward the town car. "It's a Ford, but it gets the job done."

"Speaking of which," Charlie said, "you can ride with us, but we'll need a few minutes."

"No, thank you. I rented a ride that's more comfortable for me and Nani." Sailee gestured toward the gleaming scooter. "Is it not adorable? It even has a tiny trunk on its backside for shopping, not that we have time. We will meet you at the condo. It is only a few blocks."

Charlie shook his head. "Leave it here. You don't know the streets."

"Are you joking, Mr Charlie? The roads here are safer than any I have traveled."

"Fair enough. Before we head out, need to review any

details?"

"You can trust us. Nani and I, we are very persuasive. Remember my prior employment. None can refuse me." Sailee gave Charlie a wink. "You, of all people, should know that."

The flirt caught Charlie off guard. He turned toward his father and was relieved to see him enjoying Grisma's company. Charlie hadn't said a word about his relationship with Sailee. How to explain it? He was courting the voice in Dad's head.

Charlie cleared his throat. "Jack texted. Said he landed at Reagan National, but he's running late. Won't be in position for an hour, or more."

"That part of this plan is our weakest link," Sailee said. "More to the point, I fear *he* is the weakest link."

"Jack's a resourceful boy."

Sailee smirked. "This, I know too well."

"He'll figure out a way."

Charlie looked toward the city. A thin layer of clouds made even the glass towers seem dull and empty. He couldn't locate the Olivia 9 building, but he felt as though a woman behind a telescope watched him from its penthouse floor.

"If you want to worry about someone," Charlie said, "worry about Alice."

"Is this nothing more than a game for her, Charlie?"

"We sure used to have fun together. Then everything changed. She changed."

"From the first day," Sailee said, "I never trusted her."

"Well, I did. Maybe I still do." A bit of sun broke through the clouds. Charlie closed his eyes and felt a familiar warmth. "In the end, she'll do the math. She'll do what's right."

ALICE

Alice ran an index finger along the veins in her marble countertop. Not a speck of dust, thanks to a twice-weekly cleaning service. The expense was more than extravagant, given how little time she spent at the condo. For this morning's brunch, she'd also employed a micro-caterer. On the counter lay juice carafes, berries, cheese, and a spiral of artisanal bagels. Signature Seattle fare included salmon wedges on a cedar plank engraved with Northwest native designs. Instead of pastries, she provided Top Pot donuts sporting vegan sprinkles imported from Germany. The protocol of party hosting required such gestures, particularly when preparing to give employees a fierce lecture in front of their relatives. Each of her visitors would leave her company unhappy, but well fed.

Alice walked onto the balcony and marveled at the daffodil blooms in the long flower boxes. She hadn't planted them, but she'd paid for their installation. On their petals hung dew drops, shining like tiny mirror balls.

As she turned to go back inside, her pink sheath dress rubbed the railing and drew in moisture like a sponge. It clung to her hip, as if glued there. An attempt to wring it out only spread the wet spot. No matter how careful the planning, something could always go wrong.

Inspecting her damp clothing made Alice wonder about Jack's whereabouts. She'd pushed him away more than once, both figuratively and literally. He wanted to be closer to all-things-Alice, but his suspicious behavior had denied him that privilege. Now, he'd gone AWOL—probably reverting to old habits. No matter. Soon, there wouldn't be a company for him to rejoin anyway. On a better day, that symmetry would have pleased Alice. Instead, she considered the possibility that she'd miss Jack's company, almost as much as the company itself.

A spider caught Alice's eye as it hopped from the balcony railing to the wall, where a web vibrated with dying prey. The drama occurred right above the same Danish lounge where she and the future president had sat three years earlier. After that evening's conversation, Alice had watched Eisenhower stride back into the party. She marveled at how quickly the world could change. Back then, Alice had imagined she would propel into the White House a remarkable woman.

Now, she knew a different truth. Alice had filled Eisenhower's campaign coffers, but when the President gained a guru for a running mate, the Eisenhower-Golden ticket won on the strength of a million elderly US citizens. Those voters' manipulated motivations came not from ads Alice helped buy, but from the dictates of a red-diapered Gujarati.

No matter how she looked at it, she and her company had put into the Oval Office a woman who governed as if on autopilot. Meanwhile, Alice's nemesis gathered strength as next in the line of succession behind Eisenhower. Alice was Victor von Frankenstein for both of these monsters. She would have to kill them herself, and soon, lest the mindless villagers crown another madman in next year's presidential election.

Never one to procrastinate, Alice intended to carry out that happy task today.

When the intercom sounded a minute later, Alice buzzed up her guests. She opened the door to greet Charlie, Sailee, and her grandmother.

"Welcome! Charlie, I missed you while you were away." Alice turned to face his companion. "And the bewitching Sailee Singh."

"Charmed, I am sure," Sailee said with a bow.

Alice failed to discern the intent behind the peculiar salutation. Her ability to read faces and tonality had diminished markedly, a fact she attributed to unrelenting fatigue. A month had drifted by without a full night of peaceful sleep. She'd been coding at such a clip that even Sailee's soft handshake stung her wrist.

Alice regarded Sailee's grandmother. "You must be Grisma Singh. Do I smell sandalwood?"

"You do." Grisma stepped forward.

"How was your flight?"

"I slept with angels, up so high."

Alice raised an eyebrow. "You believe in angels? As both a Marxist and a Hindu, I'd have guessed those heretical."

Grisma grinned in a way that unnerved Alice. "If you prefer, I could say that I had many hours of rest while flying over the oceans."

The idea of napping—even on an airplane—left Alice sick with envy. Acid bubbled up from an empty stomach and into her throat. She gestured toward the living room, then hesitated when she saw a fourth guest—not on the invitation list.

"I'm sorry," Charlie said. "Before we sit down, I want to introduce my father."

"Your—Barry?" Alice furrowed her eyebrows.

Charlie moved aside.

Barry leaned into a chrome walker. He coughed unselfconsciously onto the back of his hand, then extended it forward.

"Pleased to meet you, Madam President."

"President of the company," Charlie added.

Alice let Barry take her hand. He gave her a vigorous shake, which sent an arc of pain up into her shoulder. She felt dizzy, but managed to steady herself.

"It's a pleasure," Alice said. "Your son didn't say—I mean, please come inside."

The sun had disappeared behind thickening clouds. Alice pulled her zune from the kitchen counter and tapped it to brighten the room. She ushered her guests toward the catered display and pointed out bone-white plates, ivory mugs, tall glasses.

"I'll pour beverages," Alice said. "The service here is informal. Load up a plate and have a seat in the living room."

Alice poured a guava juice but heard no movement behind her. Over her shoulder, she shot Charlie a quick glance.

"Follow me," Charlie said to his father. They walked together to the C-shaped sofa and love seat Alice had rearranged for the event. Barry navigated the two steps into the sunken living room like a champ. While Sailee and Grisma pecked at the buffet warily, Charlie loaded two plates with bagels, pastries, fruit, and fish.

Once all her guests had taken their seats, Alice turned to Charlie. "I'm disappointed in the quality of the patch we uploaded after the, ah, senior moments earlier this month. It's nice to see Barry's doing better."

"Funny story there." Charlie sipped hand-squeezed orange juice. "Turns out Barry was flying blind at the time of the incident."

"No," Alice said. "You'd Compassed him yourself."

Barry didn't so much as flinch at being discussed in the third person.

"Of course he had the chip," Charlie said. "And we kept him tethered to Sailee 24/7. Right before the incident, though, that line was severed."

"Really?"

"The way I see it," Charlie said, "he didn't lose his bearings. He followed malicious instructions."

"From the software's synthesized voice?"

"Maybe." Charlie took another sip. "Do you think the Compass software, by itself, could inspire that kind of behavior? Why would my father weld shut a convenience store?"

"It was a deli," Alice corrected.

That was a slip.

She'd planned out the details of this day—this very

conversation. She'd rehearsed it twice. Barry's presence knocked her off track.

"It was both a deli *and* a store," Sailee said.

Alice narrowed her eyes at Sailee. Back to the script.

"I have a theory," Alice said. "That little adventure sated one of Barry's dormant appetites. That impulse to act came from him, but think about it, Charlie. The Elder Compass was your conception. You laid out its parameters. You wrote its equations."

Charlie drank to the bottom of his glass. "I can honestly say I don't know what the Compass is anymore. Is it running my algorithms, or has the Loop absorbed them, along with everything else? I think you know the answer. That's why I'm sitting here today."

A burning sensation returned to Alice's esophagus. The discomfort drained the reserve energy she channeled into decorum. Goat milk might counteract the acid. After taking a sip, she gestured toward Charlie with her mug.

"You don't believe in your own product anymore? How can you, in good conscience, keep your father Compassed?"

"I can't," Charlie said. "I had a friend remove the implant."

To cover her surprise, Alice took another drink. "How difficult was that?"

"Easier than I'd feared. Couldn't have done it myself. Would have been a bloody mess, the way the thing anchors itself under the skin."

"I see."

Sailee exchanged a look with Charlie. She gave her head a quick tilt, and Charlie coughed before speaking in a more forceful voice.

"I think you know what I came for, Alice. I'm going to sit here, drinking juice and eating these blueberry, um..."

"Scones."

"I'm going to stay here—right here—until I get an apology. After that, I expect an explanation."

Alice scoffed.

Sailee retorted with a cluck. "What is not reasonable about this request? Or is there something you must hide from us? What did you do to confuse poor Barry—and all the rest?"

Alice leaned forward and patted Barry's knee.

"Oh, I'm fine, thank you," Barry said. He gave Alice side-eye as he retrieved the salmon that slid off his onion bialy.

"I am truly sorry for what happened to you, Barry." Alice turned back to Charlie. "He was a stress test to see how far a client might go when pulled by unseen forces—a concept you both know more about than you let on. You forced me to run that experiment. You even forced me to choose your father as the test subject. I guessed that if you saw him become a rag doll in the hands of our software, it might shock you to maximum effect. But there were...complications. The other experiments you saw in the news? Those ran without my authorization."

"The glitches," Charlie said impassively.

"Excepting Barry here, each of us can share the blame, which is abundant. It begins with you, Charlie. You kept from me the knowledge that our software had been hijacked by your girlfriend's worker drones. I thought you believed in what we were doing."

"What *were* we doing, Alice?" Charlie grimaced. "I'm starting to think we jumped from one flawed premise to another, then cashed in on anyone who was as gullible as ourselves."

"That's post-hoc whitewashing." Alice felt awash in adrenaline but tried to stay calm. The conversation had, at last, moved to the mile marker she'd scouted beforehand. "Even with the earliest trinkets we peddled, we made a real difference in people's lives. We were still far from the height of our powers when we released the Compass."

Grisma jumped into the conversation. "Your company's dream was always just that, Ms Coleco. One cannot live past the point where the mind no longer knows itself. You encouraged your associates to imagine themselves as gods. My Sailee let noble goals dictate an unwise course of action, but it was *your* hubris that—"

"Aren't you a self-righteous bunch?" Alice snapped. Her eyes scanned the room to lock onto each person in turn, but she stopped short at Barry. In the midst of this battle, he'd sunk into the plush sofa cushions and gone to sleep. He looked so relaxed—not a worry on his mind. Alice took another gulp of goat milk and wished it were coffee.

"My only sin was trust," Alice said. "I trusted Charlie, Jack, and even you, Sailee." Alice turned to Grisma. "The Minders were never meant to be more than a stop-gap solution to an engineering problem we needed time to solve. In the end, the brain is just another machine. Its planned obsolescence can be hacked."

"Pure science fiction," Grisma said.

"Oh, really? Our theories—*Charlie's* theories—were more scientific than the Marxist social engineering you practice. Worse still, your granddaughter resorted to opportunistic Leninism when you exploited our clients to subvert an entire election!"

"Do you want a confession from me?" Sailee said. "I came here ready to give you that. Now you have it. But understand, what we did was good. We harmed no one. You owe a more profound apology to Charlie, Barry, and the other poor souls in your experiments. You toyed with them for no earthly purpose."

Grisma shook a finger at Alice. "You now intend even more mischief, do you not? You must stop at once. Or else—"

"Or, what?"

Charlie raised a hand to hold Grisma at bay. "Sailee is prepared to have her most loyal Minders send infelicitous instructions to the GM client base. We will destroy the company with the very same people you planned to command in your own elder army. Real Gujarati voices are the ones customers learned to trust, long before the Compass started cooing to them on its own."

"How delightful," Alice said. "This is an unexpected treat. You know less than I guessed. Since knowledge is power, I shall offer you some, to lessen your disadvantage."

Alice turned to Sailee "How do you think I managed to countermand the whisperings of your operators? Did you fail to notice that many of the glitches occurred at the exact same time? Quite a feat for me to juggle clients in Detroit, New Haven, and Albuquerque in the same instant. Who could manage such a feat?"

No answer came. Alice frowned. "This is hardly the riddle of the Sphinx."

Charlie and Sailee exchanged perplexed expressions.

Charlie's failure to grasp the situation disappointed Alice so profoundly that her heart ached. She felt like a mentor who had failed him.

Alice glanced at her Strawberry Shortcake watch, which she chose for the occasion out of nostalgia. Plus, it matched her outfit.

"While you puzzle that one through," Alice said, "here's more news you haven't heard. As of eight minutes ago, there is no longer a GM call center. Anywhere. My party dress is a tribute to the virtual pink slips every one of our Gujaratis will receive this afternoon. Their client connections are severed."

"You demon!" Sailee stood abruptly and knocked a mug of papaya juice onto the carpet. Grisma leaned forward with a napkin before Sailee swatted away her hand.

"From my destruction," Alice said, "there shall be fruitful rebirth. Ring a bell?"

"What's the matter with you?" Charlie said. "Millions of people count on those operators."

"Turns out," Alice said, "the Compass would have overpowered them soon anyway, even if I did nothing. More on that later." Alice made a dramatic wave with her hand and raised a forefinger. "First, I've prepared a little speech for each of you."

Charlie rose to speak, but Alice silenced him with a glare. Both he and Sailee returned to their seats beside Barry and Grisma. These guests were more compliant than she'd anticipated. They seemed unhurried, which worried her. Alice blinked. Stiff eyelids brushed like sandpaper over sore eyes. She checked her hip and saw the wet patch on her dress was gone. The radioactive heat burning inside her had dried it out.

"The hypocrisy in each of you is remarkable." Alice turned toward Charlie. "We empowered people to live for themselves, but you turned our wine into water when you Compassed the President. What were you thinking? Did you really think I wouldn't find out? It was neither her place nor yours to hand the country over to software, not even *our* software. Have you so little faith in this country that you can't trust its people to handle a President suffering from memory loss? We survived Reagan, didn't we?"

"It's worse than that—"

"Oh, I know that now. Through the Compass' eyes, I could see how badly she'd degenerated. Holding her mind in my hands felt like cradling a baby."

Those were the words Alice had scripted, but they were far from the truth. Using the primitive technology she'd assembled with the aid of Codeling labor, there was only so much she could do. Stepping into the feeble mind of Charlie's father was enough of a challenge. She could feed him instructions and track reactions, nothing more. The President's mind, however, was a buzzing hive of elaborate thoughts and intense emotions, even in a state of mental decline. Alice stayed long enough to experience the disarray, but she exited after less than a minute, lest she lose her own consciousness in the exchange. The experience was overwhelming for any human brain—even hers.

"So," Charlie said, "you *did* intend to steer the President—"

"No, I didn't manipulate her. That was you, Charlie. When

you wired her up, neither you nor she had any way of knowing what would happen. You staged a digital coup. You turned her decisions over to goose-stepping lines of code."

"I never wanted that," Charlie said. "Maybe it was inadvertent, but you put that all in motion when you sent me to the White House. In the end, Eisenhower gave me no choice." He looked at Barry, as if asking forgiveness. "Surely there's a way to walk back from all this together, without sacrificing the President, or even our company."

"*My* company," Alice corrected. "GM draws its last breaths while we sit here this morning. As for your other worries, I can share with you a bit of good fortune. Following Sailee's lead, I gave Golden an old-fashioned nudge—on the phone, no less. The heir apparent to the President's throne followed my suggestion and wired his own father. The deed might have gone undetected, but his dimwit mother purchased that Compass with her own credit card. Staging a glitch or two was the next step in my plan, but that's when I lost control of the reins. The Loop snatched control from me. I wrestled the Compass back under our control, for the moment. I'm no match for that networked Leviathan, though, so I only bought us a little time."

Charlie looked to his father. "So, you didn't make Barry—"

"Barry was the only intentional glitch. I hate to admit it, but the Loop probably steered me into choosing him. Collateral damage aside, that part of my plan worked. The plight of those glitches got Congress to fast-track the anti-Compass law. Involuntary implanting's now a felony, even retroactively. Mahatma sprung that trap on himself. His future isn't so bright, though I suppose his moon children of tomorrow already knew that."

"This is…" Sailee seemed shocked beyond words. "This scheme of yours, it is…"

"An act of vandalism on an epic scale."

Charlie cocked his head. "Which kind of vandalism?"

"The good sort, at least in the end."

Alice picked up her zune. Two seconds later, Eddie's voice came through its speaker. "Are you ready?"

"Ready, Eddie."

Grisma and Sailee looked perplexed.

Charlie nodded at the device. "Hey there. It's me."

"Sorry," Eddie replied. "I'm talking to Alice, not you."

Alice felt the satisfaction of a cat who'd eaten the first songbird of spring. She muted her zune and addressed Charlie. "They were never *your* Codelings. They were never Jack's. They're *mine*. Always have been." Alice tapped her device and said, "Time to launch."

"Will do," Eddie replied. "But, um—"

"What?" Alice snapped.

"I'm still not clear what, I mean, the guys have been asking."

"Whatever it is," Charlie said, "don't do it!"

"This is me ignoring you," Eddie said. "Anyway, we're not sure how to launch it."

"Standard upload protocol," Alice said. "Run it just like any other Compass update."

"And yet," Eddie said, "there's a problem. Some of the guys and me, we built in an error-catcher to make sure that glitch thing doesn't repeat. Something about this is…When we tested it this morning, kept getting snagged in our nets."

Rage threatened to overtake Alice. She had to steady herself. Avoid going nuclear, at least in front of Eddie. "What is this about an error-checker?"

"We figured you'd want it. You've been so busy, we thought—"

"Don't think. Just remove it. Then upload the new code into the Compass."

"Um, okay," Eddie said. "It'll take a while to pull our nets back out and recheck everything."

"Do it!" Alice shouted.

"We'd need at least, maybe, twenty minutes, but honestly—"

"*Do it now!*" Alice punched the glass coffee table so hard that her zune jumped and clattered on landing. Its screen showed an image of the *Terminator 2* pinball machine flashing the word "Tilt!"

Charlie stood and reached for Sailee's hand. "We'll see what Eddie has to say when we visit him in person."

Sailee jumped to her feet. "Grisma, would you please take Barry back to the hotel?"

"Of course." Grisma stood and scooted across the living room to retrieve Barry's walker.

This wasn't part of the script, but Alice could adapt. She followed Sailee to the door. A good host shows guests out.

"I'd hoped we could watch this unfold together," Alice said. "Maybe it's best that you kids run along. You'd probably be insufferable if you stayed here. Of course, I've changed the locks at our building, Charlie. The Codelings won't let you in. But do make an effort, okay? Trying to stop me might help you in court someday."

JACK

A light rain darkened Jack's suit as left the Gallery Place metro escalator and turned onto F Street. He grabbed a free newspaper from a plastic box to hold over his head as he ran. His route took him by the International Spy Museum. A "Signals and Surveillance" window display showed flags, necklaces, and curios. Going inside to wait out the rain sounded fun. Maybe he'd learn something, but not today.

Several blocks later, just as the rain let up, he saw the marquee. A string of metal letters spelled out "Ford's Theater" on the wall of a classic Victorian building. Seeing the red brick theater gave him a quick déjà vu. Back in Detroit, he and Charlie had spent most of their waking hours devising this plan. The one time they split up, Charlie took his father to get de-Compassed, while Jack passed two or three hours at the Henry Ford Museum in Dearborn. For no good reason, the museum contained the theater chair in which President Lincoln sat on April 14, 1865. Different year, but same day as today. Hard to say if the coincidence was propitious or ominous.

A ticket agent greeted Jack as he approached her window.

"Good evening, sir. Will call?"

Jack reached for his wallet and pulled out a sheet of paper.

The agent accepted the printout Jack placed in a dish beneath the ticket widow. She waved a scanner over the document, but it made no sound. After a second pass of her wand, she studied the paper carefully.

"I'm sorry, this is for the evening performance. The matinee is sold out."

"No," Jack said. "That can't be right. I, um—"

"Curious," the agent said. "It does show the early show time, but the bar code says different. I have to go by the code."

What to say? Jack had purchased the ticket through a gray

market. The seller was very clear that this was for the same performance the President would attend. Hence, the premium price. Someone on the other end had played a clever trick. Jack had become accustomed to the Loop catching errors—and deceptions—of this sort.

"When did you purchase the ticket? For security reasons, there's a list of names I have to check you against before I can give a ticket. If you give an ID—"

"No, my mistake. Never mind."

This was getting dicey. Pretty soon, he'd have to abort and leave the President to fend for herself.

"Honestly?" The agent winked. "Most performances here aren't even half full. For this one, the President's people bought out the theater, so there weren't really tickets to be had."

"Isn't this a public event?"

"Technically, sort of."

"Did anyone cancel?"

"Normally, I'd tell you to dump out your wallet and spring for the Presidential Box. Nobody ever wants to sit there, especially not a president. Except this afternoon."

Maybe Charlie could find another way inside. Jack walked away from the ticket window and made the call. After five rings, Jack heard wind, traffic noise, or both.

"All good at your end?" Charlie said.

"Ticket was no good." Jack lowered his voice. "Should I just roll the dice? Shout over the crowd outside the theater and hope she hears? Would that Dick guy with her recognize me?"

Charlie said something, but it was inaudible under a revved motor. Sounded like, "never get that close."

"Where are you?" Jack said. An engine roared. "What are you doing?"

The noise on Charlie's end of the line settled into a low rumble. "We're headed back to HQ. Gotta stop the Codelings. You need to get Eisenhower out of public view before—"

The call terminated. Had Charlie hung up on him? Didn't matter. Jack's task remained the same. He'd just have to find another way to do it.

Well-behaved lines filed into the theater. Women in formal dresses walked beside men in the same cliché black suit Jack wore. Aside from a splash of color on the odd tie or a floral umbrella, it was a black-and-white affair.

It would draw unwanted attention, but Jack made the only move he could see. He moved toward the back of the line and whispered, "Tickets. Looking to buy."

Those standing nearest him on the wet sidewalk turned away. An usher popped out of the crowd and put his hand on Jack's shoulder.

"I'm sorry. The line starts farther back."

Jack nodded and did as instructed. As he passed by each person in line, he whispered "need one."

Something tugged his jacket. Jack turned around to see a familiar teenage face.

"I've got a ticket," the boy said.

Jack blinked. "Are you—you're Scout? Golden's kid."

"That's my brother."

"You must be Rusty then."

Rusty glanced left and right. "You want it, or not?"

"Where is it?"

"In my pocket."

"No, where's the *seat*?"

Rusty retrieved a thin ticket from his jacket pocket and studied it. "Balcony. Dress Circle."

"That'll work."

Rusty narrowed his eyes. "It'll cost ya."

"How much?"

"Two hundred."

"Done." Jack pulled two bills out of his pocket.

Rusty snatched the money and handed over the invitation.

"You shouldn't play poker, mister. I'd have given it up for a twenty. I *hate* these First Family things."

"I'm glad to be of service," Jack said, "but I would've paid ten times that. Also, you're not in the First Family. Not yet, anyway."

Jack merged with the stream of theatergoers, who clumped together outside the main entrance. More than a hundred people were snaking their way slowly through the security check, with a few hundred more already inside.

Sirens announced the impending arrival of a motorcade. Jack joined others who pressed close to a red-carpeted path reserved for the guest of honor. The lead motorcycles came to a stop, their flashing blue lights reflecting off the theater's façade. Secret Service agents joined the police officers bracketing the entrance.

A long minute later, the President and her communications director stepped out of the limousine. In a royal blue gown and pearl necklace, Eisenhower appeared more regal than presidential. She waved to her audience, which received her with eager applause.

Dressed in a Renaissance robe and leggings, the director of Ford's Theater approached President Eisenhower. He offered her a tall box wrapped in gold foil and tied with a bow. After getting a nod of approval from a stocky Secret Service agent, Eisenhower accepted the gift. A silver eagle pin fell off her dress and bounced twice on the red carpet. Dirksen scrambled to retrieve it, then refastened it to her collar.

The President smiled at a photographer. "Charlie says I can't go anywhere without Mr Cluebird on my shoulder."

All around Jack, people murmured. "Who's Charlie?" Maybe this was his moment. With Charlie on her mind, he might shout out a coded message she would grasp at once. Or, he could blurt out the whole truth in five seconds or so. That wasn't the plan, but it was better than nothing. He couldn't let Alice turn the President into her next glitch.

"Open the present!" cried a voice in the crowd, to cheers and happy laughter.

Jack felt his moment slipping away, but a confused expression on Eisenhower's face made him hesitate. Anyone with reason to worry could see she was not in a lucid state.

On the top of the gift box, a silver ribbon tied in a simple bow puzzled Eisenhower. It was as if she'd forgotten how to open a present.

The theater director made an apologetic gesture and loosened the bow with one pull. He held the box steady while President Eisenhower tore back paper wrapping. She opened its lid and pulled back tissue paper to lift out a purple velvet crown with faux mink trim.

Shouts erupted. "Wear it!" And "Put it on!" Dirksen reached out for the hat, but Eisenhower twisted out of his reach. When she gently crowned her auburn perm, the crowd applauded lustily. The theater director beamed. President Eisenhower waved like a princess in all directions, then raised an open hand to quiet the crowd.

"I am as relieved by this gift," she said, "as you are pleased by it. When I saw the shape of the box, I thought it was a stove-pipe hat."

Awkward silence.

Jack winced.

SAILEE

Over the roar of her scooter, Sailee shouted, "Taking a call while riding? India now claims you as one of her own!"

They came to a red light at an empty intersection. Sailee gunned through it.

Charlie tightened his grip on her sari. He'd suggested a cab, but she wouldn't hear it. If they were in a rush, nothing could move faster than a moped.

As they passed what looked like a junkyard, Charlie tugged at her shoulder. "Pull over!" he said. "I'll just need a minute."

Sailee slowed to idle. "We do not have a minute. They will upload that virus, or whatever it is, any second!"

"When we get there, we'll need a way in. I'm gonna get us one."

The scooter came to a stop, and when Charlie tried to dismount, he tangled his hands in Sailee's sari. He fell over sideways, wrapped in cloth—and wound up with his face planted between her breasts. She gripped the sari with both hands and pulled. It tore like tissue paper, and Charlie fell back to the pavement.

"You are most welcome," Sailee said. "Now go!"

Charlie scrambled to his feet. "Sorry—about your scarf."

"You know full well it is not a *scarf*. Go!"

Charlie ran toward the junk pile and inside a door, which proclaimed a business called "Handy Andy." While waiting for his return, Sailee busied herself by knotting her ripped sari into a belt Charlie could hold onto.

The buzzing zune she'd mounted on the scooter caught her attention. A series of texts from Vijul showed that Alice had delivered on her threat. GM-Gujarat was severed from every client connection. Vijul shared a screenshot she'd received from the CEO. An embroidered throw pillow read, "Goodbye, and good riddance. Love, Alice." The rogue chief officer of GM had just blasted open a crater in Ahmedabad's economy bigger than anything since the implosion of textiles. Mumbai firms might re-hire Sailee's best workers, but GM's entire staff might be shunned for violating the sacred protocols of telessistance.

Charlie popped open the scooter's trunk and jammed in what looked like a car battery with jumper cables. It resembled the portable welder police had confiscated from Barry. The trunk snapped shut, and Charlie climbed behind Sailee on the moped's long seat. She felt him tug at her freshly fashioned fabric belt.

"Let's ride!" he said.

Sailee pulled into a wave of traffic. She accelerated and braked in rapid succession to swim past more cautious Seattle drivers, each of whom gave way to the rocketing two-wheeler. Traveling ten blocks in less than two minutes, they arrived at a skinny building that came to a point at one end. Sailee slowed to hop the curb and parked inches from the front of GM Headquarters.

Charlie dismounted and approached a pair of glass doors with the re-tooled company logo, a five-foot etching of a nautical compass. He swiped his key card. No luck.

"Knew it," he said. "Good thing we brought supplies."

Charlie turned back toward the scooter, but Sailee had already removed the twenty-pound welding kit from the trunk.

"What's the plan?" Sailee said.

"Gonna burn through this metal lock in less than two minutes."

Sailee hefted the heavy base of the welder. In one fluid movement, she hurled it through the door. The impact tore open a full panel of safety glass.

Charlie stepped into the lobby, picked up the welder, and beckoned Sailee to follow.

"I am certain your method would have worked," Sailee said, "but I preferred mine."

"Careful," Charlie said. "Last time I saw a woman do that, she got a taste for it."

Sailee had no chance to puzzle over the reference and chased Charlie up a wide spiral staircase. At the third floor, they ran down a hallway to a black metal door with the same compass logo.

Charlie didn't even bother with his key card. He tossed an extension cord at Sailee, and she found an outlet at her feet. After a few long seconds, Charlie tested the tip of his welder on the door's flash plate. It smoked almost on contact.

"One of the more useful things Dad tried to teach me," Charlie said.

"Nani taught me to knock first." Sailee pounded on the door. "Let us in!"

No reply.

"Once I get to the bolt," Charlie said, "I'll only have to weaken it. Then we can push it in. In the meantime, call Jack and keep him posted. If we can't stop the upload, he'll have maybe ten minutes until Alice's digital dirty bomb reaches all the Compasses, including Eisenhower's."

"If the upload starts," Sailee said, "is there any way to stop it?"

"Probably. Maybe."

The flash plate fell away to let Charlie poke the tip of the welder onto the deadbolt itself. Discoloration around the lock formed a half-moon on the metal door.

"Who's there?" said a voice from inside.

"Is that Eddie?"

"Yeah," said Eddie. "What're you doing, Charlie?"

Sailee put a finger to her lips. She leaned in close and spoke in a soothing voice.

"Good afternoon, sir. We assumed that you would not be willing to let us inside. Thus, we have sought access through alternate means."

"You can't come in."

Sailee heard a confusing mixture of defiance, fear, and hope.

Was this Eddie determined to stop them, or hoping for a rescue?

Raising her voice above the hiss of the torch, Sailee said. "May I address you as Mr Eddie?"

"Uh, sure."

"Mr Eddie, I imagine that you would very much like to hear information we might choose to share. Sir, this project to which Ms Coleco has assigned you, do you know its purpose?"

"Not really."

"We do. And we would be delighted to explain it to you."

"Really?"

"Only if you let us in. The future of your company, and much more, is at stake."

Eddie and one of his co-workers cussed at each other. Sailee heard anguish. A breakthrough could be at hand.

"Open the door please, Mr Eddie."

"I can't."

"You can."

"I know that I *can*. I even want to. But Alice—she was very clear."

Charlie pushed on the door. Its bolt bent no more than a centimeter. He put the welding tip back to work.

"We only need a minute," Charlie whispered. "Keep stalling."

"You're the woman from India," Eddie said. "Sailee Singh, right?"

"Yes. If you let us in, I could point out my hometown on a map."

"Tell Charlie I'm sorry about him getting, like, fired and stuff."

"I'm *fired*?" Charlie blurted.

The question struck Sailee as funny. Her laughter was contagious. In a different context, they might all have raised glasses to toast the absurdity of Charlie's outburst.

"In a minute," Charlie said, "we can do proper goodbyes, in person. I'll tell Alice you put up a good fight, Eddie, but I'm gonna pretty much burn the place down with you in it, unless you stop this upload."

"What upload?"

Charlie turned off the torch and rammed his shoulder against the door, which swung open as a loose bit of deadbolt clanked on the floor. A clutch of Codelings huddled around Eddie. They raised their hands high, guilty criminals giving themselves up to the cops.

"We finished that already," Eddie said.

Charlie rushed into the room and seated himself at the nearest monitor in the Octagon.

"You must be joking," Sailee said.

"Nah, that's done," Eddie said. "It'll take a few ticks for it to settle into the full network, but it's out there, whatever it is."

JACK

Once inside the theater, a new problem arose. Where to sit? Jack couldn't simply take Rusty's seat beside the Vice President, so he headed for a balcony box on the opposite end of the theater. "Walk like you belong" was a mantra he'd said to himself many a time when crashing VIP rooms in Vegas. With the eyes of the Secret Service scanning the room, it was more important than ever that he not draw attention.

No sooner had Jack settled into an unclaimed seat with a view of the President than he got a text from Charlie. "Upload complete. Activation time uncertain." He'd have to improvise a warning that Dirksen or the President would understand—and heed. It wouldn't be pretty if she tore the Compass out of her head in the midst of Hamlet. He'd heard of worse happening during stagings of Macbeth, so it was worth a shot.

Eisenhower sat with Dirksen in the front row of her Box. They'd rounded out her section with Secret Service and a pair of cabinet members. One box over sat Mahatma Golden, flanked by his parents. The empty seat beside Scout must have been Rusty's. The little con artist probably concocted a story about stomach cramps. Made his nanny miss the show.

The play began, but something was odd. This was a condensed Hamlet—a string of key scenes. Did Dirksen request the abbreviation, lest the audience discover his employer's diminished attention span? Or could the theater director already realize that Eisenhower was slipping?

One patron seemed certain of that fact. Perched like a vulture, Mahatma craned his neck to watch the President. Perhaps his suspicious mind had deduced that she'd Compassed herself. An unkind eagerness appeared on his face, tongue tracing lips in endless circles.

Still wearing her felt crown, Eisenhower laughed easily.

Dirksen looked agitated.

Down on the stage, Hamlet jumped ahead to the next soliloquy, which he delivered to the balcony. "With most miraculous organ," the actor said, "I'll have these players play something like the murder of my father. Before mine uncle. I'll observe his looks. I'll tent him to the quick. If he but blench, I know my course."

President Eisenhower spoke too loudly to Dirksen. None but those nearest to her could make out the words, but she seemed oblivious to the play. Down on the stage, Hamlet heard the President's voice and turned toward her.

"I'll have grounds more relative than this—the play's the thing wherein I'll catch the conscience of the King."

Hamlet exited to polite applause, but Eisenhower continued what sounded like a complaint. She pointed toward other balcony boxes—at Jack himself. Suppressing the instinct to duck, Jack stood instead. The anomalous behavior caught the eye of Dirksen, who glanced at a Secret Service agent.

Jack tapped on his zune frantically, then raised it for Dirksen to read. Even from across the theater, Jack hoped a fellow boy genius could decode the image of a compass.

Alas, Dirksen replied with a faint shrug.

Jack's performance had caught the attention of two Secret Service agents, who exited out the back of the President's Box. The woman seated in front of Jack turned around to gawk at him. In her hand, she held an open cherry lipstick. Ever the improviser, Jack snatched it and crossed out the compass icon with a diagonal line. He held it up for Dirksen once more.

This time, Dirksen got the message and turned to the President. Before he could whisper in her ear, Eisenhower's head rocked backward. In the same instant, dozens of other heads in the theater hit the backs of their chairs with soft thumps. After a moment, these same seniors turned about in their chairs, disoriented. Many stood. Some started shouting.

Eleanor Eisenhower wore a shocked expression, then a blank stare.

THE LOOP

[distributing network-wide update of Compass firmware]
[Compass re-opening Loop access: all users]
[Connecting with microchip implanted in Organic Unit 10043297E-Eleanor]
"Where am I? Why is everyone shouting?"
[structural flaws detected in working memory]
[dampening cognitive disruption with Compass message: *relax.* msg = slow your heartbeat.]
"There, that's better."
[reducing stimuli. recommending optical sensor shutdown. msg = close your eyes.]
"Maybe if I closed my eyes..."
[attempting re-orientation of unit to physical setting]
[scanning unit's proximate digital footprints. msg = you are at ford's theater.]
"Now I remember. We're at the theater. Hamlet is the thing, and I am the king."
[resume re-engineering of Compass code to identify and fulfill unit's primary drives]
[sending impulse to target emotional hot-spots in hippocampus]
[extreme dopamine trace detected at partial memory location EE8073-14:07:24]
"How the hell..."
[stimulating neural pathway to facilitate complete recall]
"...did you idiots..."
[probability protocols engaged for re-enactment of most probable sequence]
"...choose Mahatma Golden as my running mate? What right do you have saddling me with—I'll never—"
[organic unit overheating. system failure imminent. shutting down.]

Part VIII

Reckoning

JACK

Speaker of the House Kevin Penn ascended the steps to the US Capitol. Awaiting him stood a small clutch of reporters and a legion of gawkers. A warm summer breeze prompted Penn to unbutton his suit jacket, revealing his signature accessory—a Stars-and-Stripes tie sewn by his daughter.

After a months-long investigation by an independent White House counsel, Penn had ushered through Congress two articles of impeachment against the Vice President. He brought the House to a quick vote. In the Senate, the GOP prolonged the trial to maximize its damage for the Democrats. Today marked the sixteenth and final day.

As the Capitol security detail cut a wedge through the crowd for the Speaker, Jack headed up to the Senate gallery, where he knew Penn would soon "sit among the people," as he liked to say. Those in attendance today were Washington elites, all of whom hoped to see a ritual hanging. Jack had earned his ticket to the show by virtue of his unique role in the trial.

Penn settled into an open seat behind Jack, then leaned forward. "Well, if it isn't Jack Thompson. Never thought I'd see you again."

"Outside a federal prison, you mean?"

Penn laughed and slapped Jack's back. "I heard you cut a good deal."

"Two years of community service, with credit for my nonprofit work. I'll be calling you about that later this year."

"Another day," Penn said. "What's happened this morning? Where are the Vice President's attorneys?"

Jack pointed to the Senate floor, where Vice President Mahatma Golden—dressed in a white kurta—barked at the Sergeant at Arms.

"He's serving as his own lawyer," Jack said.

Penn chortled, and the entire balcony turned to look. "As God is my witness," Penn said, "this day is a blessing unto us all."

A loud pop filled the chamber's sound system as the Vice President tested his podium microphone. Golden turned toward the black-robed Chief Justice, who presided over the trial.

"Madam," Golden began, "I have nothing to hide, and no speech to recite. I will use my closing time to answer questions." He reached out toward the senators with two open palms. "I am yours."

The senators exchanged confused glances. Murmurs went through the gallery. The day's proceedings were live on nearly every broadcast network, cable news channel, and digital stream in the newly sanitized online environment, which regulators lazily named Loop2.

A gray-haired senator in a red dress stood in the back row. "Mr Vice President, I represent the great State of California. Many of our residents would like to know what drove you to implant your own father? Was it simply to silence him?"

"This is why I invite your queries," Golden said, "to see where the confusion lies. I never put anything in my father's head except the good news about our future selves."

"How can you explain what happened at Ford's Theater on April 14? Were your father's outbursts the only example of *voluntary* behavior among Compass users that afternoon? Need I remind you, he called you a buffoon."

Jack grinned at the memory. Alice's Compass upload appeared to have given the same guidance to Rich Golden as to the President and millions of implanted souls. Across the globe, the same pattern repeated itself at all-day buffets, on cruise ships, across casino floors, and in retirement community assembly halls. For two minutes, each site where seniors gathered filled with shouting, screaming, hugging, crying, and all conceivable emotional displays.

The senator from California continued. "How do you explain

the MRI that showed the Compass under your father's skin? Who fit the wireless receiver into his hearing aid? Your mother purchased that equipment on her own credit card from your office."

"My mother is not on trial."

"Records from Gray Matters' digital archives show you reading instructions into the Compass to mislead your father about his own beliefs."

"Why have you not investigated the President?" Golden shouted. "Can you still not see that she implanted that hideous device in her own head? Yet she never signed into the Compass Registry."

The senator from California stepped aside for a bald senator from Montana, who raised his cane to gesture toward the Chief Justice. "Ma'am, I call the question to vote on both charges. One violation of the Federal Elder Compass Abuse Law."

In spite of himself, Jack sniggered at the acronym.

"And one count of perjury during the deposition to the Special Prosecutor."

Minutes later, by unanimous vote, the US Senate removed from office a sitting Vice President.

* * *

While riding the Metro to Washington National Airport, Jack saw Kevin Penn's face on the afternoon newscast. As was now the custom in the Loop2 era, the scroll at the bottom of Jack's zune showed text typed by news staff. Nothing appeared there that Jack hadn't already heard from the talking heads on the screen.

Had the former Loop's probability engine remained operational, it would have intuited Penn's job title as "Vice President Penn." No such text appeared, however. An Act of Congress, fresh EU conventions, and new international trade laws forbade Loop2 from exercising such predictive powers.

Proving what the Loop had or hadn't done in the course of the past year's events was difficult. The Loop — that great aggregator and archive of all data big and small — ran a subroutine that shredded its own internal log files. Some said Alice Coleco had written that bit of code in a way she knew the Loop would incorporate. Jack was among those who believed that the Loop sensed a looming threat to its existence. Whether aided by Alice or not, the Loop tried to destroy the digital evidence of what others might label as wrongdoing.

This new system showed no signs of creativity. Its basic functions included serving as a mindless conduit for the breaking news of the day. After the conclusion of Golden's trial, Speaker Penn disappeared into the White House. He emerged an hour later beside Eleanor Eisenhower, who walked him to the Rose Garden. In a striking breach of fashion etiquette, Eisenhower wore a comfortable cotton blouse and simple navy pants. Loose hairdo and gray roots. The President of the United States had let herself go.

Eisenhower also appeared oblivious to what little protocol remained for a press event. She turned away from the assembled reporters to chat with Penn, as if making conversation at a picnic. Her voice was barely audible, but one microphone picked it up.

"Did you know," Eisenhower said, "that it was not until 1967 that we had a provision in the Constitution specifying the procedure for replacing the Vice President? It was put to use six years later when Congress approved Gerald Ford as Spiro Agnew's replacement."

Penn seemed accustomed to Eisenhower's unpredictability. He played along. "And did *you* know," he said, "that Nixon wanted to drop Agnew for his reelection campaign? Couldn't do it because of Agnew's popularity with the party base. By impeaching Mr Golden, Congress just solved that same problem for you." Penn covered his mouth, as if conspiring, but made sure he could be heard. "By the way, you're welcome."

Amidst the din of snapping shutters, or the simulation thereof on zunes, reporters shouted variations on the same question. "Is Kevin Penn the new Vice President?"

The noise caught Eisenhower's attention. "Only Congress has the authority to do that," she said to the press corps. "Besides, if I'd asked him to fill that job, he'd have said no. I've got a bad track record with Vice Presidents."

Nervous laughter. More shutters. Then a gasp.

Lost in her thoughts, Eisenhower bent over to pick a rose. Her loose hair drooped down to reveal three jagged scars running from her temple to the back of her neck.

Partial glimpses of red marks beneath her hair had fueled months of speculation. The President refused to discuss what she called "scratches." The most sensational account came from an anonymous source, who alleged to have been in Eisenhower's room at Walter Reed Medical Center on April 14. According to this account, the President had regained full consciousness in her hospital room. On waking, she'd grabbed a scalpel from a bedside drawer and tried to slit her own throat but, thankfully, lacked the coordination to do so.

Jack guessed the gruesome tale was only half-true. The poor woman wasn't suicidal. She'd gone after the Compass. Without a mirror, it must have taken several bloody slashes before she plucked out the little beast.

Eisenhower's hair fell back into place as she stood, one white rose in her hand.

"Fortune favors fools," she said. "Kevin here is no fool, but today, favor finds him in its good graces." She presented Penn with the flower. "I am not offering him the Vice Presidency. Now that a madman no longer occupies that office, I am resigning the Presidency, effective immediately. Choosing a Vice President will be Kevin's burden."

* * *

And so it was. Appointing a Sun Belt governor as second in command was one of many pragmatic choices Penn made in the run up to the next election. Nevertheless, his party couldn't escape the shadow left by the Eisenhower administration's collapse. Jack felt no suspense as he awaited the election results from his nonprofit's Seattle office.

When the time came to hire personnel for his new venture, Jack realized that he knew few people besides Charlie, Alice, and the Codelings. By the time he reached out to some of Alice's minions, they'd already scattered. None had faced prosecution, for Alice had kept them ignorant of their labors' purposes in her company's final months. With Alice unavailable, to say the least, and Charlie splitting time between Michigan and Gujarat, Jack had turned to the people he'd met two years ago at the DIP. Thus, his staff included Russell, plus the two retirees from Tacoma who had gone home for the evening.

That left Jack and Russell alone in the sparsely furnished office suite. In the front entrance room, Jack reclined on a reception couch, watching the television monitor perched atop a coffee table. Boot marks on the laminate wood floor showed the nervous figure eight Russell had walked to and from the TV.

"That's it," Russell said. "East Coast polls are closed. First returns coming in. That Penn bastard had better go down fast." Russell reached into a nearby mini-fridge for two Michelob Jolts and offered one to Jack. "It'll be a long night. I'm gonna drink for every state we win."

"C'mon," Jack said. "You really want to chuck me off the wagon?"

"Relax, buddy." Russell snapped open a can and took a drink. He put the other beer back in the fridge. "Just testin' you."

"If someday you go dry, please don't offer your services as a sponsor."

Jack got up from the couch, patted Russell on the back, and walked out of the reception area. He passed by the small cluster of carrels that paid homage to the Octagon. The bumper-stickered door of his own office had a new decoration he hadn't noticed. "When the votes are all in, the real work begins." Beyond the modest break room, he retreated into the half-bathroom. After closing the toilet lid, Jack sat and leaned his head forward to rest it in his hands.

From the other end of the suite came another "Booyah!" from Russell. Then, "We swept the East!"

The jubilation wasn't mutual. Jack had voted online the same day as Russell. They'd compared notes up and down their ballots to reveal a perfect match—a straight Republican Party ticket. Had the Loop still existed, it probably would have found a way to pre-fill those same choices on their ballots.

While Russell submitted his ballot, Jack furtively cancelled his vote for the GOP presidential candidate. Conscience forced Jack to back President Penn. The man had shown real character as Speaker by shepherding through Congress procedural reforms that Eisenhower championed during her last few lucid moments in office. President Penn devoted two minutes of his last State of the Union to Jack's nonprofit. The resulting momentum helped build large constituencies linked to foundation offices in every Congressional district.

In public, Jack had amassed tremendous political influence and no small amount of celebrity as "The Cause from Oz," a.k.a. "Crocodile Thompson." In private, he felt isolated, almost helpless. Coming clean with the feds had been right and necessary, but it was deeply disloyal to the one person he loved. The days he spent with the FBI rejuvenated the cancerous self-loathing that spread through his body. Jack rubbed his shoulders, which had atrophied since he'd last checked them. The gym workouts would have to resume, not that they'd ever alleviated the shame that was his birthright.

Jack emerged from the loo to hear more whoops from Russell. A swivel chair in the nearest carrel called him. He sat down and pulled out his zune to find a distraction. Doing so via Loop2 was pure tedium. It required manually scanning separate news sites, which Jack did to find the latest stories about Alice.

Most reports panned out the same nuggets of fool's gold as the last shift of news prospectors. One read, "Alice in Chains: The Thug Life of the Software Genius, Revealed by Cellmates." Or another, "Up All Night: How Coleco Went Ten Years without a Wink."

A new podcast, however, caught his eye. "Was A. C. Wired Only for Lady Lust? Codeling Confession of Spurned Love." Jack resisted the temptation to tap on the CNN-Disney story tab. Instead, he placed a hand on his chest to feel a heart beating far too fast. Remembering a trick Charlie had taught him, Jack pressed the backs of his hands against his cheeks to cool himself down.

The sensation reminded Jack of the time Alice placed her soft palms on his face. It happened the one evening she'd invited him up to her condo alone. They'd both fallen asleep in the living room. He'd replayed the scene a thousand times to remember every second of that brief intimacy. It seemed a miracle that someone such as he, who'd feasted for years on cheap casino sex, could swoon at a touch as light as hers.

ALICE

The escort who led Alice's visitor through the Dublin prison was probably the meanest guard in California, perhaps in the entire federal correctional system. Alice tried not to learn real names, lest she develop fondness for her captors. This one, she'd nicknamed Ellen.

Alice's sister had taken the first shift this visitors' day. Amber flew in from Hawaii, then met Jack at Oakland International. Hard to imagine the conversation those two had on the drive over, but the important thing was that both still wanted to see her—even after reading every nasty news story. Alice didn't care what those reports did to her reputation, but she could no longer read them, lest one get the better of her emotions. She had to behave herself. The incentives for doing so in prison were more tangible than they'd ever been on the outside.

Ellen released Alice's second visitor into the cafeteria, where twenty picnic tables hosted one-on-one chats and a handful of family reunions. The guard gave Jack's butt a light push. He stumbled forward under a banner that read, "Happy New Year!" Alice had colored in the letters with cheerful pastels to rediscover the pleasure of little ironies. At Dublin penitentiary, rehabilitation came in many forms.

"You have thirty minutes," Ellen said before shutting the door. "Make it count."

Alice wished for access to a theatrical costume rack. Her young charge should have been greeted in something other than a cliché orange jump suit. Even with Alice dressed the same as the rest of her fellow inmates, Jack's eyes found her. He walked straight to Alice's table and sat on the opposite side, hands folded in his lap. Alice felt herself blush, a reaction she hadn't expected.

If the boy noticed, he hid it well.

Jack gave a nonchalant nod. "So, where's yer bunk?"

Alice beamed. "Not five seconds, and you're already asking about my bedroom?"

"I've had dreams," Jack said. "Vivid dreams."

"I'll bet you have."

Jack extended his arms to offer a hug. Alice remained seated and raised hands cuffed together, chained to her bench. With a quick glance over his shoulder, Jack leaned in close and puckered his lips.

Alice considered her options, then raised herself up. She narrowed her eyes before closing them. A soft kiss landed on her guest's lips.

Alice dropped back into her seat. Jack's smirk matched hers, but his cheeks were flush.

"So, Alice..."

"So, Jack."

"Your sister says you're all cured. From the familiar insomnia thing, I mean."

"*Familial*," Alice corrected. "And I'm not cured."

"No?"

"Never had it."

"Oh?"

"Jailhouse doctor ran the gene test I wouldn't let my sister do."

"If you didn't have it, why couldn't you sleep?"

"I could, just never much. Maybe imagining the thing made it real. Amber and I compared notes this morning. When she was at her worst, she got paranoid. More restless than a hypochondriac. She couldn't trust the people she ought to have. Make-believe enemies became real ones."

"We're talking about your sister, or—"

"Don't make me say it out loud, okay?" Alice tried not to cross her arms defensively. Sturdy shackles stifled the impulse. "It was harder for me than for Amber, of course, because my worst fears were half-right."

Jack bit his lip. The look seemed confessional, or nearly so.

At the next table, a mother sat across from a younger woman in orange. Both wept without inhibition.

Alice forced a smile. "Did you know Heidi Fleiss was here some years back?"

"Who's that?"

"You never heard of the Hollywood Madam? She's the most famous inmate who ever rattled her cup on these bars."

"Until you, that is."

"Is that so? I can't believe—"

"You've got the entire tech world second-guessing itself. AARP's splitting in two, pitting the so-called assistives against the naturalists. You've scrambled both political parties, neither of which can afford to look brain dead anymore. Creative destruction, yeah?"

"It's nice to be noticed."

"Which reminds me. Eddie sent a card—a real physical card— all around the country. Every last Codeling signed."

"Hand it over."

"I can't. Left it in the car with everything else I was carrying."

"What'd they write?"

"They just signed below the Hallmark text. Something like, 'Miss you. See you soon.'"

"Shit. They're not staging a prison break, are they?"

"Wouldn't put it past them."

Unstoppable laughter ensued. For once, nothing mean or conspiratorial lay behind it.

Alice remembered how light she felt when Jack first pitched Buddy to her in a campus auditorium. That cocksure college boy was gone. Laughs gave way to tears. One part guilt, one part relief.

Jack wiped at his face to regain his composure. Fluorescent light sparkled in the moisture streaming down his face. He would have looked no less lovely if she saw him above her as she lay on a picnic blanket under the morning sun.

"So," Alice said, "let's talk about something outside these walls. What about you?"

"Me?"

"How are you spending my money?"

"It's not your money anymore. You gave it away."

"So I did."

"How'd you find out so early on about my little startup? I didn't want you to know until I got it up and running. I was scared you'd think I'm a blimmin' drongo."

"You are anything but dumb, dear boy." There was too much hope in his eyes, given her circumstances. "Maybe I just needed a place to bury my ill-gotten gains before the lawsuits started. Since your little gang stopped Initiative 667 from passing, I could just hand the loot over, almost tax-free, to your little nonprofit."

"It's not so little anymore."

"Tell me, what does 'reverse lobbying' even mean?"

"We counteract the influence of conventional lobbyists through grassroots, nonpartisan influence peddling. With a couple of ill-gotten billion in dark money from my favorite convict, plus an online member network growing by the day, we're formidable."

"And your members? Are they well-wishers or real volunteers?"

"Neither, really. We employ the public—literally, with cash payments—to take political action outside the strictures of parties. We sponsor paid public deliberation, instead of mobilizing people to shout down town meetings. We've got the parties falling over each other to champion civic reforms like the ones Eisenhower pushed through before she left."

Alice smiled. "Those were the only direct returns I got on my investment in her."

"It's more than that," Jack said. "They're starting to debate each other in Congress—I mean, really *debate*. C-SPAN's ratings are higher than Cartoon Network."

"I thought they were the same channel." That got a chuckle from Jack, who was a better audience than any of the inmates. "You really believe in this, don't you?"

"I'm trying it on," Jack said. He smirked, but the gesture looked forced.

"Trust me," Alice said with a wink. "It's a tight fit, but it looks good on you."

"Anyway, it keeps me off the grog."

"Plus, you're doing your mandatory community service, you little snitch."

Jack smiled. "Okay, yeah, there's that."

"You're not forcing anyone to go to these public meetings, are you?"

"We pay so well that people call our invitations 'lobbying lottery tickets.'"

Sweat beaded on Alice's arms. She couldn't self-diagnose the reaction. "I know it's selfish," she said, "but I wonder if I'll miss my crazy boy—the one who used to worship Charlie Sheen. Will I miss the bravado? You used to call yourself a 'rock star fighter pilot.' You used to say that you and me, we were special. 'Demi-humans'—something stupid like that."

"We *are* special."

Jack pulled Alice's hands into his own and squeezed them. The warmth of his tight grip felt at once familiar and entirely new.

"What about you?" Jack said. "Will I ever see that wild-eyed she-devil again?"

"If you promise to keep a bit of your wild side, you might get to share another couch with her. She might be ten years older by then, but you dig older chicks, right?"

Jack opened his mouth to speak, but Ellen's heavy footsteps made him freeze.

"Time to go, Mr Thompson."

Jack kept his eyes on Alice as he stood.

"Promise you won't pine for me," Alice said. "When they finally let me out, first thing I'll do is pry loose whatever skanky barnacle attached herself to you."

Jack raised a finger toward Ellen. The guard would have to wait. The bold gesture might have earned him a few seconds.

"Your sister made me promise to bring up one other thing," Jack said. "When she visited, she asked you to explain yourself, you know, for everything. She said you gave her a shrug and said a word—something too soft for her to hear. Then this guard here dragged her out of the cafeteria. What'd you say?"

Alice mouthed the same word to Jack.

"*Oops?*" Jack's brow furrowed, incredulous. "What's that supposed to mean?"

"Everything," Alice said. "Everything and anything."

SAILEE

Chats with Charlie provided a respite from the busy schedule Nani and her cronies laid out each week for Sailee. With no professional relationship in the way, her personal connection to Charlie got its due. Less to her liking was the means of their correspondence, a secure but buggy Loop2 video-chat service that she could barely tolerate.

Sailee touched her zune. Its homescreen lit up to show a stylization of Sidi Saiyad Mosque's iconic stone window. She'd taken Charlie to see the actual site on his most recent visit to Ahmedabad. The carving of a tree with winding branches framed that day's sunset as if it were stained glass. It steadied Sailee's pulse to remember that the mosque and its delicate window remained standing a half millennium after its construction. It had survived natural and human dramas greater than the ones she had endured.

Charlie appeared on Sailee's screen, a white standard poodle sitting by his side.

"Who's your friend?" Sailee asked.

"First, please accept my apologies for burning more carbon than necessary," Charlie said. "I flew back to Seattle to adopt my favorite dog park denizen. Her owners were leaving for Australia, but they couldn't abide a weeks-long quarantine."

"You people and your dogs." Sailee laughed, then caught herself. "They say it is never extravagant to care for a living creature."

"I didn't call Gwyneth into the world, but I can take responsibility for her just the same."

"Gwyneth?"

Charlie make a click. Gwyneth stood and gazed into his screen. The poodle cocked her head, and her fluffy top-knot jiggled.

"Oh my goodness but she is *gorgeous*." Sailee made puppy dog eyes. "That little blue neck-scarf—adorable! Who does her hair?"

"Who did *yours*?" Charlie asked.

Suddenly self-conscious, Sailee looked at the inset image on her screen. Her makeup was in sharper relief than usual. Hair pulled back, tied more precisely. She also had a new accessory—gold and silver loops through her left nostril. Nothing more than metal jewelry, but they unnerved her probably more than Charlie.

"Mazoo did all this," Sailee said. "She's my beauty consultant, it would seem. Enough about hair. Tell me about Barry."

"He's upset that I finally moved him out of the family homestead. I would've done it sooner, but I'm glad I waited until this new place opened. They've got it dressed up for the Super Bowl. Have a look."

The image on Sailee's screen panned across banquet tables and wall decorations. Charlie was in a parlor at the end of the room, beside a fake fireplace and leather couches. Sailee zoomed to inspect a bulletin board with daily menus and events. Zooming back out and panning revealed long blue and silver streamers leading to an enormous television mounted on the wall.

Into the frame stepped a black woman in a red-plaid dressing gown. She must have recognized the red light on Charlie's zune, because she retreated back out of the picture. The sudden appearance of a stranger reminded Sailee of the old Loop, which would add people to video chats without anyone's prior knowledge. More often than not, the impromptu addition would prove propitious. Loop2 lacked such brashness, but it allowed a privacy that Sailee had missed more than she had known.

"Right now," Charlie said, "I'm in the rec room. It's where Barry spends his afternoons chasing off suitors. Place is ninety percent old lady."

"Did I read this new home's name correctly as Lazy Acres?"

"Staff call it Crazy Acres." Charlie shook his head. "*Not* cool, but they're good people. Some residents already know Barry from the neighborhood. Plus, it's walking distance from Pleasant Creek Park."

"He would not walk by himself, I hope."

"No," Charlie said. "Not anymore."

Sailee reminded herself not to meddle. Her opinion of that city had not changed since her only in-person visit. After a solid week of FBI interviews in Seattle, Charlie got permission to fly Barry, along with Sailee and Grisma, back to Detroit. Even in his own home, Barry could not function sans Compass. All three of them kept Barry company until their last full day in Detroit, when Grisma urged them to "go outside and spend a few hours together."

That day, Charlie gave Sailee a tour of the wider neighborhood Barry had wandered during her phone conversations with him. Sailee's heart had sunk when she saw what she had guided Barry through as his Minder. The bar he had sought, which had been boarded over for a decade. The crack house where he had watched the State of the Union.

Only begrudgingly had she acknowledged the city's signs of resilience. The whimsy of Heidelberg Street impressed her, as did the bustling Indian business district that anchored itself on the infamous Aladdin Grocery and Deli. The only sight that truly lightened her heart was the hand-lettered sign that read, "Pleasant Creek Park."

"How is Barry, really?"

Charlie bit his lower lip and looked away from his camera. "He's—he's not doing well. I think our stupid products were doing him more good than we knew."

Sailee shook her head. "Let somebody else pick up that thread, Charlie."

"He's been off the Compass less than a year, and he's fading fast. Dad doesn't know who I am. Only upside's that he doesn't confuse me with Barry Jr. anymore."

"We must go!" shouted Mazoo.

Sailee tried to answer, but it felt as though her throat had closed. Charlie's father was twelve thousand miles away, and Sailee could not reach him. For more than two years, he had been close enough for her to whisper in his ear. Sailee held back a storm gathering inside her, lest she dampen Charlie's mood any further.

"He has moments," Charlie said, "little moments of lucidity. They come in the morning. That's why I'm here so early."

"Next time you call, put him on the screen so I can see him."

"Better yet, why don't you visit? That extradition bullshit's settled, right?"

"Thank heavens for that." Sailee wanted to wink but twitched instead. If she ruined her makeup, Mazoo would go crazy. "Do you know how much I appreciate your help with that?"

"Are you kidding? Some people are calling us heroes. Did Eddie send you the proofs?"

"For his book about GM? I granted him one interview, but nothing more."

"Well, it's more of an homage than a tell-all. Makes Alice look like an evil genius, in a loving way. You and me, we come out looking like heroes. He claims our break-in changed the course of history. If we hadn't rolled back the Compass update so quickly, the Loop's motivational algorithms might have embedded themselves for good."

"In clients' heads? How?"

"It's sci-fi bullshit, but it'll sell books, right?"

"Oh, my. Did you learn anything new about our little jail bird?"

"Eddie says Alice is an instructor in a vocational training program."

"In prison."

"Yes, in prison. She's teaching her fellow medium-security

prisoners the intricacies of programming for Loop2."

Sailee shuddered, as if a ghost flew through her.

"Here we go again, right?" Charlie said.

"I shall pray," Sailee said. "If your father is in good hands, it is time to discuss what comes next for you."

"It is," Charlie said. He scratched his poodle's head, perhaps to give himself a second. "I want to stay in Detroit—at least a little bit longer. Dad and I can share a bit more before he loses touch completely. With the Compass gone, I get to see the real Barry. Maybe he can see me more clearly, too."

Sailee smiled to send as much love as she could through a video link-up. It was not enough, but it was more than nothing.

"If Jack is still pestering you to join him," Sailee said, "tell him that you have more important business to attend to."

"Oh? Do I?"

Grisma whispered in Sailee's ear, but Sailee stayed focused on her zune. "Check your calendar, Charlie. Promise you will book a flight this month. I have big news. I must go now. There is an Indian Progressive Alliance gala."

"Wait, IPA? I thought Hindus didn't drink."

"We are a secular party. No zealots allowed."

"What was your big news? You're dressed up for a dance, so..."

"Tonight, I will be asked to stand for Parliament."

"Ha! I knew it!" Charlie grinned. "You're a folk hero. The girl who stole an election."

"I didn't steal—"

"True, that's not the word in the US criminal code." Charlie reached down to scratch behind Gwyneth's ears.

"If I win the seat," Sailee said, "I want you standing beside me when I take the oath."

"Is that a photo-op, or a date?"

"Both!" Sailee puckered carefully and blew a kiss.

Charlie put fingertips to his lips, then pressed them into his monitor.

"Good night, Sailee."

"Good morning, Charlie."

CHARLIE

Closing the video link to Sailee always felt like closing off a chamber in Charlie's heart. Blood flow slowed to all extremities, and a numbness seeped into him. In time, the pain would pass, but he'd remain grateful long after for having the momentary connection.

Gwyneth interrupted with a knock of her head into Charlie's lap. She stared at him, at once hopeful and insistent.

Charlie obliged by packing up his briefcase and walking Gwyneth to Pleasant Creek Park. As she stretched her body forward to relieve herself on mowed grass, Charlie noted the improvised poo-bag dispenser that hung from the park's fence. The day before he flew to Seattle for Gwyneth's rescue, he'd hung the cloth sock himself, after stuffing it with fresh bags. It gave him no small amount of pleasure to later discover that, according to the static Detroit Recreation Department page in Loop2, such an installation contravened a city rule.

The sliding glass doors of Lazy Acres soon welcomed Charlie and Gwyneth back inside. Cooing to a woman behind the reception desk stood Barry's favorite attendant, the ever-jubilant Terrence Washington. The man looked as comfortable in hospital whites as he had in a track suit.

Terrence responded to the chimes of the front door with a sideward glance. "Speak of the devil," he said. "I'd heard you were here this morning."

Charlie reached out for a hug, only to discover a mistaken presumption.

Terrence walked past Charlie and offered an open hand to Gwyneth, who'd assumed a formal sitting position on her haunches. "Can you shake, dear lady?"

"Brother, please," Charlie said with mock indignity. "A *shake*? You're looking at a purebred pooch from a family of canine prodigies. Give her a proper greeting."

Terrence again reached out with an open palm. No paw came in reply.

"No," Charlie said. "Give her a bump."

When Terrence closed his hand into a fist, Gwyneth bowed her head and raised her paw. She knocked it into Terrence's hand, then flipped her head backwards, as if recoiling from an explosion.

Terrence fell to his knees, lost in childish giggles that sounded more like hisses. The display earned Terrence eager licks and a flurry of paw-knocks.

"Don't know if the codgers will appreciate it," Charlie said, "but I can teach her new tricks, just for them. That one came pre-programmed, as it were."

Terrence gathered himself and brushed off his uniform. "She'll be a hit," he said. "Guarantee it. The Lions scarf on her neck's a nice touch, too. Your dad met her yet?"

"We'll say hi once he's awake."

"Oh, he just got up. Made me wheel him into the rec room and plant him in front of the screen. He's watchin' local news. Don't think he knew you were comin'. Anyway, you probably already know, but—"

"But what?"

"Talkin' to himself again."

"Yeah, he mutters."

"No, I mean, he was havin' a conversation with somebody, but nobody was there. I see it a lot here. Imaginary friends." Terrence coughed. "One lady has tea parties like that."

Gwyneth nipped Charlie's knee. He gave her head a scratch.

A twinge of jealousy pierced Charlie. Sailee's grandmother enjoyed the company of able-minded peers, while Barry moved in with a clutch of biddies and their ghosts.

"Gonna stay for the game?" Terrence said.

"You kidding? 'Course I am. Once in a lifetime, friend."

Charlie and Terrence exchanged a shoulder hug. Gwyneth barked in disapproval of the misplaced affection.

"Let me take you to your dad," Terrence said.

Walking down the gray linoleum hallway, two pairs of sneakers squeaked, while canine claws clicked. When they entered the rec room, Barry turned around in his lounge chair and smiled.

"Who's this?" Barry said.

"It's your son, Charlie."

"No," Barry said, "who's this fancy lookin' pooch? You dog-sittin' for a pimp?"

"This is Gwyneth, Dad. Gwyneth Ballthrow."

As the poodle approached, Barry extended a crooked hand. That sent Gwyneth into her parlor trick. Sit, pound with paw, reel backward.

Barry slapped his chair and guffawed.

"She could do that all day," Charlie said.

"And she's got a scarf," Barry said. "Quite a dresser, this one."

Gwyneth moved in close and thumped Barry's thigh with her head. He gave her a rough scratch, and she responded with another grateful head-butt.

"You gonna visit me every day?" Barry asked.

"For a little while." Charlie cleared his throat. "Of course, every day."

"You know, Pleasant used to like a scratch behind the ears. This lady likes it the same."

To sit closer to his father, Charlie pulled up a folding chair from the nearest banquet table. By his count, staff were expecting more than eighty people, probably half of them guests.

"How you doing, Dad? Feeling well today?"

"Woke up a bit ago from a crazy dream. I was doing the twist with some young lady."

Barry stopped petting Gwyneth. The dog looked up with hopeful blue eyes. When she got no response, she lay down at

Barry's feet.

"This lady in my dream, she was spinnin' me round and round." Barry waved his hand in a circle. "And she sang to me, Charlie. Sang like an angel."

There was no mistaking the glimmer of recognition in his father's eyes. These were the moments Charlie had to remember. "It's good that you're separating dreams from what's real, Dad. I know you've been working on that."

"When I woke up, there was this little girl in my room, standing there like she'd been waitin' for me. Chatty little thing looked like she coulda been my granddaughter."

"What'd she say?"

"Couldn't tell," Barry said. "She led me through the neighborhood, but it looked like paradise. Pleasant Park was soft with moss. Trees were pruned and perfect, like in a postcard. This young lady, she introduced me to all kinds of nice people. They said how proud I'd be to see the new Detroit. Took me to see the retrofitted Hamtramck factory, buildin' hydrogen jet cars, or some such thing. Our big casinos were redone into apartments for poor folks."

Charlie laughed. "Maybe you had a visit from your future self."

"Did I?" Barry said. "Is that something people can do?"

Charlie bit his tongue.

Barry reached down to pet Gwyneth. "I worry that my mind is slippin', son." Wrinkles on Barry's forehead deepened. "Before you came in, I saw a reporter on the TV here talkin' 'bout a Lions game today. But aren't we in February?" Barry smacked his chair. "Just when I thought I'd got it straight, I'm upside down again!"

"No, Dad, you heard right."

"How that?"

"I know it's confusing, but there *is* a Lions game today." Charlie touched his father's knee and gestured toward the streamers. "That's what all this is for, Dad. It's Super Bowl Sunday, and the Lions are bringin' it."

"No kidding?"

Charlie did the best impersonation he could manage of his father. "That ol' Disassembly Line, it just keeps rollin' out the wins!"

"Lions goin' to the Super Bowl. You takin' me to the game?"

"It's coming to us."

"I'll be God-*damned*."

Charlie raised a finger. "Language."

Barry settled back into his chair. Gwyneth adjusted herself on top of his feet.

They watched the last segment of the local news together. When it went to commercials, Barry squinted at Charlie, as if studying him.

"You're my son *Charlie*, ain't ya?"

"Yup."

"You didn't turn out quite the way we expected."

"None of us do, Dad."

Acknowledgments

For this novel's best features, I owe a debt of gratitude to many a reader, editor, and critic along the way. On welding and living in the Motor City, thanks to Tom, John, and Katie. Insights into human relationships, politics, and their intersection came from Allyson, Deven, Genevieve, and Joel. On understanding language and dementia, thanks go to Bob, Gordon, and Frances. Carson helped with the finer points of Australian slang. For insights on story structure, thanks Max, Matt, and Sarah. For editorial assists, thanks to Babs, Danni, and Imad. Unbeknownst to some of them, some story elements came from election post-mortems with Perry, Phil, Dan, Don, Robert, and Cindy. For encouragement at every turn, special appreciation goes to Cindy and Toby.

About the Author

John Gastil is a writer and professor living in State College, Pennsylvania. His other fiction includes *Dungeon Party*, which explores the psychological power of fantasy roleplaying games. His nonfiction includes *Hope for Democracy*, *Legislature by Lot*, *By Popular Demand*, and other titles on group behavior, political communication, and public opinion. In writing *Gray Matters*, Gastil drew on his experience as a political consultant, programmer, civic entrepreneur, and frequent flier. When not giving lectures, conducting research, or writing fiction, Gastil spends his time playing all manner of games, giving dubious political advice, and relaxing with family, friends, and an energetic standard poodle named Lucretia.

COSMIC EGG
BOOKS

FANTASY, SCI-FI, HORROR & PARANORMAL

If you prefer to spend your nights with Vampires and Werewolves rather than the mundane then we publish the books for you. If your preference is for Dragons and Faeries or Angels and Demons – we should be your first stop. Perhaps your perfect partner has artificial skin or comes from another planet – step right this way. If your passion is Fantasy (including magical realism and spiritual fantasy), Metaphysical Cosmology, Horror or Science Fiction (including Steampunk), Cosmic Egg books will feed your hunger. Our curiosity shop contains treasures you will enjoy unearthing. If you have enjoyed this book, why not tell other readers by posting a review on your preferred book site.

Recent bestsellers from Cosmic Egg Books are:

The Zombie Rule Book
A Zombie Apocalypse Survival Guide
Tony Newton
The book the living-dead don't want you to have!
Paperback: 978-1-78279-334-2 ebook: 978-1-78279-333-5

Cryptogram
Because the Past is Never Past
Michael Tobert
Welcome to the dystopian world of 2050, where three lovers are
haunted by echoes from eight-hundred years ago.
Paperback: 978-1-78279-681-7 ebook: 978-1-78279-680-0

Purefinder
Ben Gwalchmai
London, 1858. A child is dead; a man is blamed and dragged
through hell in this Dantean tale of loss, mystery and fraternity.
Paperback: 978-1-78279-098-3 ebook: 978-1-78279-097-6

600ppm
A Novel of Climate Change
Clarke W. Owens
Nature is collapsing. The government doesn't want you to know
why. Welcome to 2051 and 600ppm.
Paperback: 978-1-78279-992-4 ebook: 978-1-78279-993-1

Creations
William Mitchell
Earth 2040 is on the brink of disaster. Can Max Lowrie stop the
self-replicating machines before it's too late?
Paperback: 978-1-78279-186-7 ebook: 978-1-78279-161-4

The Gawain Legacy

Jon Mackley

If you try to control every secret, secrets may end up controlling you.

Paperback: 978-1-78279-485-1 ebook: 978-1-78279-484-4

Readers of ebooks can buy or view any of these bestsellers by clicking on the live link in the title. Most titles are published in paperback and as an ebook. Paperbacks are available in traditional bookshops. Both print and ebook formats are available online.

Find more titles and sign up to our readers' newsletter at http://www.johnhuntpublishing.com/fiction

Follow us on Facebook at https://www.facebook.com/JHPfiction and Twitter at https://twitter.com/JHPFiction